SCHISM

SCHISM

A NOVEL

Bill Granger

CROWN PUBLISHERS, INC.

New York

Inquiries should be addressed to Crown Publishers, Inc., One Park Avenue, New
York, New York 10016

Printed in the United States of America

Published simultaneously in Canada by General Publishing Company Limited

Library of Congress Card Catalog Number 81-38478

ISBN: 0-517-544911

10 9 8 7 6 5 4 3 2

For Mal Bellairs,
who gave space and time
and, unexpectedly, friendship

And the nations were angry, and Thy wrath is come, and the time of the dead that they should be judged; and that Thou should give reward to Thy servants. . . . And should destroy them which destroy the earth.

The Revelations of St. John
The Apocalypse

My object all sublime
I shall achieve in time
To let the punishment fit the crime.

W. S. Gilbert

Note

In 1975–76, congressional investigations revealed that the Central
Intelligence Agency had made use of missionaries, medical personnel
and news reporters abroad, recruiting them, for pay or patriotism, into
espionage networks. In 1976, under new guidelines accepted by the
CIA Director, it was stated that the Agency "has no secret paid or
contractual relationship with any American clergyman or missionary. This
practice will be continued as a matter of policy." However, by 1980, the
Director admitted in Senate testimony that he had waived the guideline
three times and argued that there can be "unique circumstances" in which
clergymen and others are the only means available to operate as agents "in
a situation of the highest urgency and national importance."

The late medical doctor Thomas Dooley was posthumously
recognized as an intelligence operative in Laos. He was awarded the
Medal of Freedom by President Eisenhower in 1959, shortly before the
doctor's death from cancer, but the Agency did not acknowledge his
status with them until the late 1970s.

When it was chartered in 1947, the Central Intelligence Agency
resolved never to spy upon American citizens and never to operate
espionage missions on American soil. The Agency has since admitted that
it has frequently broken its charter resolutions.

The intelligence community of the United States consists not only
of the Central Intelligence Agency but also of various other intelligence
groups, including the Defense Intelligence Agency. The National

Security Agency generally acts as the "hardware and software" supplier for the intelligence services.

The Tridentine form of the Mass, largely constructed during the Middle Ages and known popularly as the "old" Mass or the Latin Rite Mass, was radically altered in liturgy following reforms dictated by the Second Vatican Council in 1961–64, held at Rome. Though not expressly forbidden in all its forms, at all times, in all parishes of the Roman Church, the "old" Mass has generally been suppressed by the Church hierarchy.

The Vatican State, the temporal presence of the Roman Church, has long operated intelligence-gathering functions through its worldwide network of embassies and special emissaries.

The Vatican State has followed a consistent policy of accommodation with the Communist-controlled governments of the Eastern European bloc countries, especially since 1975.

These statements are all true.

I
THE
RETURN

1
Bangkok

On the day it began, the Ambassador to Thailand was not even in the capital.

For the second time in six months, the Ambassador had flown back to Washington for consultations with the President on the "declining state of civilization" along the border separating Thailand and Cambodia. He had described it thus in his last message because understatement seemed the only weapon left to him.

Each day there had been new reports of armed skirmishes along the border and, as always, the dreadful daily reports on the stinking masses of refugees in the sprawling camps at the border, whose lives were spent huddling against the unspeakable terror coming from the jungles they had fled. There were no dogs in the region and had not been for a long time; nor birds or monkeys, nor any creature small enough and weak enough to be trapped and killed by those with sufficient strength of body and will among the largely lethargic starving refugees. The people were dying each day like leaves in autumn, slowly and surely tumbling to death as the season moved on. The bellies of the children were taut, bloated by starvation, and the bones of their little arms protruded grossly beneath the dull sheen of their yellow skin. All day, they lay in the shade with their immense eyes staring at nothing, the flies fastening themselves to their lips and nostrils like so many small, living black bumps on the flesh.

And all the while, the black market thrived, in the midst of the wretched camps, with the connivance and consent of the Thai soldiers stationed along the border. Winston cigarettes were for sale next to Bic lighters, the products displayed in rows on blankets thrown down in the sand. There were radios and batteries too, and, most mysteriously, cases upon cases of Aunt Jemima pancake mix that those refugees strong enough to steal, to kill, those who found something still to barter, would buy and mix with cold water and eat without cooking.

"Intolerable," the Ambassador had fumed when he was sent to Thailand. He had not expected this at all when he agreed to take the post in exchange for his key support in the President's last primary campaign. He had expected the posting to be a reward, and so it could have been: Bangkok was still a strange and beautiful city, and the embassy could offer nearly every luxury. There was a glittering life to Bangkok separate from the stench of the refugee camps on the border; there were parties that went from embassy to embassy, night after night.

And yet, because the Ambassador was a man of rare passion, he could not keep himself away from the camps, he could not stop himself from experiencing over and over the pall of hopelessness and death that hung over the camps like fine red dust. He had wired the President from the beginning; he had telephoned the White House too often; he had lobbied privately with his wealthy and powerful friends still in America; he had boldly invited the television networks to come and see what he saw, giving them every courtesy. He enraged the diplomats at the State Department with his unorthodox concern and reportedly made an enemy of the National Security Adviser with his actions; and at every turn, he implored the government in Bangkok to save the children at the very least, to move them away from the camps to the interior of the country, to feed them.

The response to this last line of appeal had puzzled him most and troubled him the greatest because he had come up against the bar of color and caste and national hatred that pervaded the East as surely as it did the West. He was not without skill and would have understood in his own country the subtle nuances of racial animosity yet affinity in rural Mississippi between the redneck and the black, but he could not understand the basic contempt of the Thais toward the Cambodians and their absolute hatred of the Vietnamese who had driven the refugees into the arms of an unwilling host.

"Intolerable." He had said it again and again, and everyone in the embassy agreed with him, everyone in Washington agreed with him, all his old friends agreed with him, the press agreed with him. At every turn, he met a yielding wall of pity for the refugees, for the starving ones, for the children with their bloated bellies and sad, unseeing eyes. No one wanted them to starve—of course not; no one wanted that.

And beyond the border itself was Cambodia, wasted and dead, Carthage of the East salted by war and self-destruction and genocide so that nothing should live there again. The jungles were silent and brooding, returning inexorably day by day to the primeval. Everywhere there was a feeling of death; everywhere the stinking, rotting death, the horror.

But something must be done, the Ambassador had said, and so he was on his way to Washington again. The Ambassador had changed in his three years in Thailand: His face was burned black by the sun yet there was still a quality both pale and fragile in the haunted blue eyes; his hands shook; he drank too much, for the climate and for his age. He had trouble at night sleeping alone in the darkness of his air-conditioned room on the second floor of the embassy. Sometimes at meals he would fall into a sort of reverie, staring across the table at his companions but not seeing them, looking beyond the present to some middle distance of past or future, forming words silently on his lips. The others would be embarrassed at these moments and look away and pretend not to notice, though all conversation would cease until the Ambassador came back to them.

He had stood at the top of the ramp and waved to the two of them from the embassy before boarding the whining 747, and the Assistant Press Officer had returned the wave. Then the APO had said to his companion: "There is a man who cares too much." The remark was intended to be profound and sophisticated because the

APO believed himself to possess these qualities in abundance.

The remark was answered and agreed to by the Visa Secretary who added that there was nothing that could be done and that was the pity of the matter. Both of them were sensible young men of the world and they saw the world for what it really was. The Ambassador was a good man, surely, but he was old, and indignation of an old-fashioned nature had clouded his eyes.

The APO had driven the Visa Secretary back to the embassy and along the way raised the point that perhaps the Ambassador was becoming a nuisance to the President. Certainly, he had made an enemy of the National Security Adviser. The President had his own problems with his domestic program, more complex and more politically serious than the plight of people seen only on the evening news. The APO wondered aloud if the fall from favor of the Ambassador might mean a shakeup in the permanent embassy personnel. The APO longed for a London posting.

On the following morning, October 2, when the Ambassador was still in a restless, drugged sleep in his own home in Fairfax, Virginia, the matter began half a world away from him.

Corporal Rafael Lopez, United States Marine Corps, stood at the outer gate of the embassy in the late morning sunlight and watched the figure hobbling up the street. The man did not walk with a cane but he appeared to need one; he shuffled along, his feet barely raising themselves above the pavement. The shuffle of his lower extremities did not match the rigid posture of his body. He walked with his arms straight down at his sides like a prisoner, his thin shoulders thrown back in a parody of a military man on parade.

Corporal Lopez of Amarillo, Texas, watched the man for a long time because the street at this point afforded a long view and because there was nothing else to watch. The pretty Thai women were gone from the street for the morning, were in their offices or homes or in the markets. Lopez had his own woman, of course; it was the first thing he had acquired after his transfer to Bangkok for embassy duty, and she pleased him as much as she could, but Corporal Lopez wondered at times if she were pretty enough or if he were missing something by not finding another woman.

At the moment, however, it was the man who interested him.

He guessed that he was old, though he might have been young but have gone through some ordeal. His hair was absolutely white, which was not usual in the Orient and yet, because it was thick and unkempt, he might be young. Age was a difficult guessing match in the East.

Lopez began a mental game: The feet were old; the back was straight like a young man's. Perhaps he had been a soldier? Perhaps he was victim of the jungle rot that ate at the flesh of the feet first?

Left, right, left, right. There you go, thought Lopez. Hup, two, three, four. Hup. Yer hup. Swing it along, mister.

But the mental cadence he counted for the old man was too slow and he lost interest in that game. Of course, he had to be a gringo. You couldn't mistake the features, even under the layers of burned skin. He should have seen it at once from the eyes, blue eyes like the Ambassador's, but the old man had been too far away.

Blue eyes. A goddam blue-eyed gringo sonofabitch in black pajamas just like a fucking Cong.

Hup, hup, hup two three four.

Lopez was thirty-one years old and he would acknowledge that he had seen nearly everything in his brief life, including a tour in Nam. Once he had even been busted in rank but he had come back. He had deserved the demotion for trying to kill some bastard in a bar off base instead of waiting until the prick came out into the alley to piss. But Lopez had been younger then and not so patient and he had been caught and done his time, hard time in the Corps, man. Still, the service was not a bad life and, like the swabbies said, you got to see the world.

The old man stopped on the sidewalk ten feet from Lopez, and Lopez felt his body stiffen involuntarily, the way it did when he had been a recruit in North Carolina, when the D.I. would come up to you with his lean, mean face and stare at you, looking for goddam flyspecks on your nose or something. The blue eyes of the old man were watching him. Smart marine, in his smart uniform, rifle at ease: What the fuck are you looking at, old man? You never seen a goddam United States fucking Marine before?

"Is this the American embassy? Please?"

He spoke English. Lopez let his lazy eyes open wide but he didn't move. English but it sounded like a slope talking English, it had that peculiar inflection, an Asian singsong that accented the words evenly and in the wrong places. Lopez stared at the black pajama trousers streaked with ancient red dirt and at the sandals fashioned from old tires. The old man wore a white, loose blouse without a collar. The face was black from the sun and clean-shaven, all bones and hollows.

Lopez thought he could have been a bastard, maybe a mulatto out of a Thai mother with an English or French daddy. He was too old to be of American stock, but the colonials had been in Asia for a long time. The American bastards were still too young.

"Is this the embassy of the United States, please?"

God, he hated the way they talked, the slopes, even his own woman, whining all the time, their little voices like wind chimes. Was this the fucking embassy? What do I look like, a fucking slope? Lopez realized that his curiosity in the old man had turned to annoyance.

"You got it, pardner," Lopez said at last.

"The American ambassador I would like to see, please?" The voice of the old man was still slight, gentle, humble, and its singsong quality had definitely gotten on Lopez's nerves. So that was it: Some bum wants a free ride back home, back to Big Sam. Lost his green, lost his ready, wants a freebie.

"He ain't around, pardner," Lopez said, a slow smile breaking across the brown face like a stain. "He's gone back to the States."

"Then whoever is here, please? In charge, please?" The old man stopped and frowned, as though searching his memory for the right English words.

Lopez gazed at him while he considered. Lopez was there strictly for show; anyone could go inside. Christ, even after Tehran, they still didn't give him bullets for the fucking rifle. But the old man offended him.

"I told you the Ambassador, he's a big man, he ain't around, didn't I? You out of bread, man, is that it? You American?"

The old man seemed to consider this question gravely. After a long pause, he said, "Yes. American. Yes, I am."

"Well, you lost your passport then or what?"

The old man smiled suddenly, a dazzling smile that cracked the darkened face, and Lopez was annoyed by that as well. He wasn't going to be patronized by a goddam gringo fucker looks like a Cong.

"Yes," said the old man. "A long time since, I have lost it."

Suddenly, as sudden as the smile, Lopez wanted to be rid of him, to get the blue eyes off his uniform, to push the old man away. "Go on in then, passports is on the left but you ask at the desk."

"May I enter, please?" the voice came back, rising a note on the scale of the wind chimes.

"It's a free country, man," Lopez said.

Again the old man smiled and again, Lopez felt annoyance. He knew the smile of the Anglos, the mocking smile, he knocked that goddam smile off their faces for them. And then he saw the gentle line of the lips, the open expression formed by the eyes, the white, even teeth. No, this was not the mocking smile. This was something else, like Tío's smile had been when he was a child.

"You got troubles, pardner?"

"A Marine," the old man said, the smile lingering as though relishing a nostalgic moment. "Never to change, the uniform. It has been so long."

Lopez thought the old man spoke like someone who had forgotten a language and was struggling to recall it.

"You go in there, pard, right through there, there's a desk there, you tell them who you are, what you want." He pointed to the door of the embassy, which was embossed with the Great Seal of the United States, portraying a triumphant, angry eagle holding arrows in its claws, its wings spread wide.

The old man bowed in a graceful, Oriental way, and Lopez, his nature made gentle by the smile, saw that he was just skin and bones. Maybe they could fatten him up, maybe he had been a planter in Cam, maybe he had just escaped. The old man shuffled into the compound and to the door and disappeared inside and Lopez turned back to face the street. But it was empty for the moment and there was no one else to watch and so he thought of the old man for a minute longer.

Inside the embassy, the old man shuffled to a desk where a young man with horn-rimmed glasses sat writing in a notebook. When he looked up, the young man had automatically set his face into the universal look of the bored official interrupted by a member of the public. The look hardened perceptibly as he regarded the ragged state of the visitor.

"Something for you?"

9

"I beg your pardon, please?"

"Something? You want something?" He said the words slowly and distinctly, the way a person will speak to a young child or to an idiot.

"Please, I would like to see the Ambassador." The words came slowly and oddly.

"You would? Really?" The official at the desk tried a smile that was not well-meaning. "Who are you?"

"My name is Leo Tunney."

Because it made him happy to do so, the young man wrote the name down in his notebook. There was no reason to do this but it was what he always did first. "And business? Your business with him?"

Leo Tunney gazed at the young man for a moment. "I don't know him. But . . ." He stopped, apparently confused for a moment. "But he will see me. He will want to see me. Yes." He paused again. "Yes, please." The whole of the statement seemed to have tired the old man and he now rested one bony hand on the polished cherrywood desk and smudged the oily finish. The young man instinctively leaned back in his chair, as though the old man might be about to faint and fall across the table. And then he said, "Would you please take your hands off the desk, you're smudging it."

The old man looked up, looked at his hand, and then gazed again at the young official. His eyes seemed sad. He pushed himself erect with the help of the hand on the desk and removed it. "Please," he said. "I'm sorry." The voice was dull and gentle and the official felt a rare sting of regret at his rudeness.

"Now, what can we do for you?"

"I want to see the Ambassador. No, that's not right." The old man uttered three words in a sort of rough Cambodian and then closed his eyes for a moment, pinching the bridge of his nose with his one hand. "No," he said. "The Marine. He said he was not here. I would see the man who is head man, please?"

"I have to know what this is about." Spoken gently this time, as though something vulnerable in the old man had come out to soften the hard shell of the official's everyday voice.

"My name is Leo Tunney," he repeated. "I want to go home. It is time for me to go home."

All rightie, the official thought with satisfaction. He understood this, this was straightforward business. "You lost your passport, is that it?"

The old man stared at him, just as he had stared at the Marine at the gate.

"Passports," concluded the official without further confirmation. Something about the old man unsettled him; he wanted to get rid of him. "Go down to the room at the end of this hall, that's visas and passports, they can help you out down there. You have some proof? Of your citizenship, I mean? Well, they can sort it out in any case, right down there, that's room one fifteen."

Again, a look of immense sadness crossed the blue eyes and then passed. The thin shoulders were straightened again with effort, the body made a slight Oriental gesture of acquiescence and without a word, Leo Tunney proceeded along the waxed corridor, his shuffling feet leaving marks on the shiny tiles.

So, for the first hour of his return, no one could help him.

It was partly a matter of the problem of his speech. At times, his words were nearly incomprehensible, the English becoming tangled in a thicket of awkward syntax. At other times, the speech would emerge clearly but without inflection, as though spoken by a computer. The words were obscure and clear by turns, like the sound of a shortwave radio station picked up half a world away. A woman took down his name and asked him to sit on a bench and wait. He waited and others came up to speak to him, to listen to him. Some made notes and some did not. If it had not been for the accidental intervention of Victor Taubman, the return of Leo Tunney might have been delayed for hours or even days longer.

Unlike the Ambassador, Victor Taubman was a career diplomat in the Department of State. He had gone into State from Harvard in 1946 and for thirty years, he had been in Asia. He was one of the few old China hands not destroyed in the witch-hunt days of McCarthy and the Truman Administration in the early 1950s, days when men who told the truth about the East and what would happen there were called communists.

Victor Taubman was now coming to the end of a long career that had been neither distinguished nor banal; it was absurd, but he was about to play his greatest role—"the man who discovered Leo

Tunney" is the way *Time* magazine would later phrase it.

The accidental intervention came about because the Ambassador was in Washington and because Taubman was in nominal charge of the embassy during the absence and because Taubman was puzzling over a serious problem—the matter of the missing passports.

Nine passports were missing from the safe box and presumably they had been stolen and were now in the dark stream of the black market. The theft meant that someone in the embassy itself had arranged to steal the documents. How had it happened and who had done it? Taubman had devoted the morning to the tedious problem and now he was in the visa and passports section when he noticed the slight, stooped figure sitting on the wooden bench in the foyer.

Who was he? Taubman asked the Visa Secretary, who said he did not know. He had wandered in that morning from the street and no one could quite make out what he wanted or who he was and they just didn't have time at this moment to deal with him.

"An American?" asked Victor Taubman, who was somewhat old-fashioned in his ideas of service to his fellow countrymen abroad.

"I don't really know. I mean, he claims he is but he doesn't talk like an American." Usually, the Visa Secretary was faintly supercilious when talking to Victor Taubman—Taubman was an old hack, he was getting ready to pack it in, Taubman thought everything should run like it did in '49—but the matter of the nine missing passports had struck at his self-confidence this morning. He was willing to answer all of Taubman's questions in a helpful way.

"Did he give you his name?" Taubman bored on.

"Loretta. Loretta took it. Loretta?"

The clerk was a black woman with a wide face and a deep Southern accent that at times comically counterpointed her serious demeanor. The Visa Secretary had often thought that Loretta looked like the face of Aunt Jemima on the empty boxes of pancake mix they found in the refugee camps. "H'yall says he's Lee Turney, h'yall says he wants to see the Ambassador."

"Lee Turney," said Victor Taubman. "Well, someone should take care of him."

"Lee Turrrrrrney," corrected Loretta and she handed him a copy of the name written on one of her cards.

It was the final coincidence of the morning. Though Victor

Taubman was an old Asia hand now, perhaps the name might not have meant anything to him if he had merely heard it; after all, it had been a long time. But the mispronunciation by the clerk had exaggerated the name in his mind as though it were a clue to a puzzle he could not quite understand. And then the sight of the name, written neatly on the piece of paper, made a connection in his memory, jogging awake a long dormant chip of recollection.

Leo Tunney.

Taubman glanced across the rows of desks that separated him from the old man with white hair sitting on the backless bench in the foyer.

Taubman understood in that moment. It was Leo Tunney. But that was impossible. How long had it been? Leo Tunney was dead.

Victor Taubman stood at the low wooden railing separating Leo Tunney from the rest of the office. Taubman looked down at the thin face, gazed at the blue eyes turning toward him. He spoke the name aloud.

The blue eyes seemed to ignite.

"Yes."

The voice struggled on, soft, nearly inaudible: "I am him," he said.

"Leo Tunney," Taubman repeated, as though the name had become an incantation that would recall the past. "But you were dead."

Slowly, a smile crossed the darkness of the face, opening the mouth of white teeth. The eyes were alive now, shining in the darkness of the weathered skin.

"No. As you see." Another pause and then the voice came from a distance: "I thought that too. Sometimes. I suppose I expected they would have to think that, that I was dead. Not dead."

"More than twenty years," Taubman said, scarcely moving his lips. "You must have been—" But he could not speak for a moment. Behind him, the Visa Secretary and the clerks crowded around, not making a sound, witnessing the strange, broken dialogue but not understanding it.

"Father Tunney," Taubman said at last.

"Yes."

"But how could you have lived all this time?"

13

"By the grace of God. Or His curse."

"My God, man," Taubman said, pushing open the little gate on the railing and entering the foyer, reaching down to him and touching the old man to make certain he was not an apparition. He felt a bone in the arm of the old man beneath the white cloth.

"But who is he?" the Visa Secretary asked.

"Father Tunney. Leo Tunney," Victor Taubman said, repeating the name idiotically; they must know that name, the name told everything. But the Visa Secretary stared back at him and Taubman realized that none of them knew, they were too young; twenty years was not the mere past but ancient history to them.

"He came back like a ghost," Taubman said.

And he touched Leo Tunney on the arm again, to make certain the dream was real.

2
MOSCOW

Arctic wind blew all morning; even for Moscow in October, it was extremely cold. The sky was bright and blue in the dry cold; puffs of steam rose from the nostrils and mouths of passersby on the half-empty streets, while smoke curled from chimmeys in the vast housing blocks around the old capital. This was a day to be indoors, to spend luxuriating in the silences of the muted city in the first really cold weather of the season. And that is what Denisov intended to do.

He poured a tall glass of vodka, flavored with lemon peels, and mixed the clear liquor with an equally large measure of apple juice. It was his favorite drink. He sipped it judiciously in the kitchen, to make certain the ingredients were in the correct proportion, and then took the drink to the small living room and put it down on a low bookcase beside the large, worn couch. The bookcase served many functions other than the one it was built for. So did most of the furniture in the crowded apartment. The couch was a bed as well, for instance, and the bookcase was also the repository of Denisov's thin and precious collection of Western recordings.

The moment was delicious, he thought.

He stretched as he sat down, relishing the sheer silence like a connoisseur sitting down to caviar and champagne. Everything was in the expectation of the moment, not in the consumption, and he wanted to prolong the afternoon of rare solitude by contemplating it for a moment.

The luxury of solitude had come to him as his first thought when he awoke that morning in the darkened bedroom and realized the apartment was empty. His wife, his sister, his son and his wife's old mother—who all shared the place—had gone to Gorki for the funeral. Denisov was an important man inside the Committee and it was not impossible for his family to make such a train trip, though they considered it a rare luxury as well. No, he could not accompany them; yes, they should extend his sorrow; yes, they could stay an extra day. He had driven them to the railroad terminal and watched the train steam off with all of them aboard. And when he had returned to the apartment last night, he had suddenly felt so tired that he accomplished a very unusual thing: He slept.

Denisov did not sleep well or often.

Five years before, he had undergone extensive examination at the Lenin Institute where the doctors and experimental scientists were delighted to receive him. They had probed his body and put electrodes on his scalp and given him medications to see what this would do to alter his state of chronic insomnia. After it was all done, they concluded that though Denisov might be doomed to continue in his condition, nevertheless he had learned to function well on one or two hours of sleep a night. He even became the subject of a paper submitted to the *Journal of Soviet Medicine and Technology*. How flattering, he had said to his wife.

Denisov had read the article and had been depressed for days by its conclusions and by the flat, jargon-ridden scientific description of him and his malady (though it did not name him). He did not sleep, the article pointed out, but he was quite healthy for a man in his early forties. Some work along similar lines—sleep research—had been done in the West, the article noted. Dr. Bosboroff had joked with Denisov that "perhaps you should go to the Mayo Clinic." None of this amused Denisov but he accepted the joke, because it was expected of him, as he accepted all things, or seemed to, with a mild countenance and a round face and the eyes of a saint twinkling from behind his rimless glasses. People felt at their ease with Denisov, which was part of his art; he did not threaten; he was as familiar as an old icon.

Dr. Bosboroff had concluded that men did not need as much sleep as they got. That the need for sleep was an animal need, that the animal slept to rest the instincts for survival, to set aside threats from the real world while dealing with the same threats in a satisfactory psychological way in dreams. In a sense then, the doctor had said in his pompous way, Denisov might be a fully evolved man, able to deal with the psychological problems of life by triggering the unconscious mind even while fully awake.

Denisov understood all that was said about his problem but he did not accept the conclusions. Sometimes he yearned for sleep as a lover yearns for the beloved. Let me hold you; let me see your mysteries.

But he had slept last night and awakened refreshed as the cold sunlight poured through the bedroom window. He had relished that moment. Yesterday, it had been the usual morning with the family around, and the din of morning had embraced him; today it was silence; in three days, the din would return.

If they had been here, his wife would now be in the kitchen, banging the pots unnecessarily as though to assure everyone that, yes, she was on the job as usual, as expected—why, God help her if she wasn't, and they had to miss a meal—they didn't have to worry about her. The noise of the pots carried her resentments eloquently.

And his sister would still be holding out in the bathroom as though it were her private dressing room. The door had no lock and she held her foot against it as she prepared her body for another day of flirtations in the offices of the Writers' Union.

Denisov frowned when he thought of Nasha. She was too old for this, she should have been married long ago or at least settled into her spinsterhood; she dressed like a schoolgirl. She embarrassed Denisov, who liked to think of himself as a man of patience and tolerance, even for those in his family. She was certain that she was an intellectual and nearly as certain that she was a writer of worth, though every contribution by her that appeared in the literary magazines attested more to her powers of sexual conquest than to her literary skills. For a time she had insisted that Denisov read her short stories when he preferred the company of a good novel or his television set. The stories were dreadful: All of them were set in the time of the war, which she wrote of in the style of Tolstoi, as though the war against the Fascists were a great, unpainted stretch of canvas that no one had thought to use before Nasha began her great themes. In the hands of people like Nasha, Denisov thought, the style of Tolstoi became a dangerous weapon. And what did she know of the war? She had not even been born until 1944. He remembered it, as a child. There had been darkness in the war, always, and cold, and there was no food.

And his son, Ivan. If they had been here this morning—if his uncle who had been a professor at the Army College of Strategy and Tactics had not so generously decided to die this week and give Denisov two days of peace—then Ivan would be at the door of the bathroom at this point, pounding on it against Nasha's foot. Fighting and pounding, clattering pots and pans; noise that only ceased when he added to it or appeared at the kitchen at last for his morning glass of tea. Fights and shouts, threats and sobs in an apartment generous by Soviet standards but too small for all this emotion. This was the portion of a man's life.

"You must pay your respects to them. He was your uncle; they are important." Anna had been after him the day before but he had ignored her. He had no wish to go anywhere and certainly not to Gorki with its secrets and its air of suppression. Anna was not an unattractive woman, he thought, she had once had a deep and lingering beauty about her eyes that had affected him enormously. She had never been thin but she had been beautiful, ripe and budding, a springtime of a person, full of expectation for the warm lush summer.

Now, in the living room, in the silence of his thoughts, he looked at her as she had been.

Dmitri Denisov smiled to himself and reached for the album he had chosen. It had been brought to him by a courier in the diplomatic mail from London. Denisov had not yet found the silence to listen to it more than once.

It was *The Mikado* by Gilbert and Sullivan. As he held the

17

record sleeve, he spoke the title of the opera and the names of the composer and librettist. Denisov's accented English had once been very good, though he had a tendency to drop malapropisms from time to time. Over the years his great musical passion had become Gilbert and Sullivan's Savoy operas; with his customary patience, he had managed to acquire a nearly complete collection of them through the usual black market available to Moscow's elite.

The record began to spin on the Japanese turntable and the first sonorous strains of *The Mikado* filled the apartment. Denisov watched the record turn as he sipped his drink; then he leaned back on the wide couch and closed his eyes and let the music fill him.

He felt contented. The past eighteen months had not been good to him but the bad time was over now.

> *If you wonder who we are,*
> *We are gentlemen of Japan;*

Denisov thought of the time of his disgrace, of the internal exile to Gorki he had suffered while he was examined by the Auditing section of the KGB. It had all been so unnecessary; he had been betrayed by an American agent named Devereaux. The betrayal had nearly cost Denisov his life when the British sent him back in disgrace to Moscow.

He pictured Devereaux in his mind. They had worked on the opposite sides for a long time, first in Asia, last in England. He would never see him again; but if he did, what would he do?

On a Belfast street, Denisov had killed a man to save Devereaux's life. Devereaux acknowledged this but had not relented; Denisov was the enemy and Devereaux betrayed him. His reception in Moscow was not pleasant. He had failed in that English mission and he had permitted Devereaux to blow his cover.

He thought he would kill Devereaux if he had the chance again.

> *A wand'ring minstrel I,*
> *A thing of shreds and patches,*
> *Of ballads, songs and snatches,*
> *Of dreamy lullaby! . . .*

Then he heard a knock at the door.

Denisov realized he had been dozing when he heard the sharp sound. He frowned and opened his eyes. The knock was repeated; the knock insisted, it had its own rhythm; it had force and sureness to it, as though confident of the correctness of the intrusion it demanded.

The knock of the State.

Denisov reached for his wire-stemmed glasses and carefully fitted them over his ears and nose.

The man in the hallway was named Luriey, an Extra in the Committee; Denisov had seen him before. Beneath an unbuttoned wool overcoat the Extra wore a plain blue, shapeless suit and a white shirt with a dirty collar and a dark tie.

The bulge in the breast of Luriey's suit was doubtless caused by his pistol, Denisov thought. Why did one have to carry a pistol in this city? Especially one so obviously sent by the State?

But he knew: The pistol was power, a sort of benefit paid to men who were nothing but glorified messengers in ill-fitting suits.

Serfs, he thought, not for the first time.

"Dmitri Ilyich Denisov?" The voice was ponderous, as though the name had been memorized. "I am here to summon you."

The Mikado, Denisov thought. Or the Lord High Executioner.

Denisov opened the door wide, feeling the sense of the music behind him; Luriey was invited into the room but he hesitated, even looked shocked, as though Denisov had suggested an immoral act.

"You are summoned."

"To Room Twenty-four," Denisov said. "Come in for a moment."

Luriey held his ground in the gray concrete-and-tile hallway of the building.

"Yes, where else would you take me? I know where I'm to go but you'll have to wait until I dress. It is more comfortable to wait here."

With reluctance clouding the coarse features of his face, Luriey stepped inside and Denisov closed the door behind him. Luriey stumbled after Denisov to the bedroom; he waited at the door for Denisov to dress.

Life is a joke that's just begun!
Three little maids from school!
Three little maids from school,
Three little maids who, all unwary,
Come from a ladies' seminary . . .

Denisov hummed the lyrics as he dressed, slowly, with nonchalance.

"What is this music?"

Denisov was surprised by the voice and question. He looked at Luriey for a moment and said, *"The Mikado.* An opera. An English opera."

Luriey grunted as though he understood everything then, the summons of this man, the place he was to be taken.

Forty minutes later, Denisov led the way as Luriey escorted him down the white-painted inner corridor on the fifth floor of the vast Institute for International Understanding and Control building. It had been erected in 1961 as an annex to the more familiar seven-story main building of the Committee for State Security—the KGB.

It was not untypical of the grandeur of Khrushchev's last years: monumental in scope and a dramatic example of confused ideas of architecture, wasteful and inefficient. The central corridor, for instance, was nearly forty feet in height and the walls, originally the product of the State's gross wealth, had been altered over the years as reality set in: First, the marble began to peel away from the sides of the walls and workmen were always in the building, fixing them. And then, in 1964, the assistant director of the Institute for Forensic Experimentation and Determination was killed by a 600-pound block of marble that crushed him as it separated from the wall. It was then that the Bureau of Buildings and Security decided that the architect had misplanned and the walls could not support the weight of the marble facing, and all the marble was removed at last. Rumor was that the marble slabs had been assigned to various officials inside the Praesidium and Central Committee who used them to floor their luxurious dachas outside the capital.

There were other things wrong with the building as well: The central air-conditioning system produced spectacularly uneven and unexpected results. In summer, the women who worked in the message center routinely wore sweaters and coats on the job, while those in the communications laboratory two floors above had to wear the lightest of shirts even in winter because of overheating.

Fortunately for the people in Room Twenty-four—which was actually a series of connected suites—Gogol was a resourceful man. He had equipped his offices with reliable General Electric air conditioners and space heaters and disconnected the rooms from the main heating and cooling systems. No one questioned Gogol on where he had obtained the supplies; in fact, rarely did anyone ask Gogol any sort of question.

He was the keeper of the dead souls.

Gogol was a code name, of course, but the only one they ever used for him; he did not shed it when he left the building at night; he would be Gogol until retirement or until death. And then, when he died, there would be a report filed that an obscure official with a commonplace name had died and would be buried in the immense cemetery on the hill beyond the Kremlin walls. Gogol would not die; the next man would become Gogol.

"A form of immortality," Denisov had once ventured but Gogol was burdened with no sense of humor and he had not smiled or even recognized Denisov's jest.

Denisov and Luriey pushed against one of the double doors that led into Room Twenty-four. A prosaic nomenclature, Denisov had thought when he first went to the section. But then, all the groups under the umbrella of the vast KGB bore prosaic descriptions, wearing their names like so many anonymous gray suits, each label seemingly descriptive and intricate but laden with flat meanings, ironic and evasive when examined. So Room Twenty-four meant nothing and meant everything, suited to the office as well as to the official name for the section (which was only used in intrabureau records): the Committee for External Observation and Resolution.

Denisov thought of the jest implied in the official name that was never used for the section: "Resolution." How unlike the old Russian language that had grown huge and unwieldy as new words were added to describe precisely a single emotion or action, the word taking in not only the reality of the thing described but its place within the mind of the beholder and the circumstances surrounding it. Now the State had forced irony into the once-precise words.

Nothing was ever resolved by the Committee but it was policy to think it was, to think that an action taken by it, however small, resolved a part of the larger problem facing the State.

No one would be bold enough, of course, to point out that the problems of the State never seemed diminished; that would deny the official optimism applied in the Marxist creed of man's perfectibility.

"Resolution," Denisov said, and it startled Luriey, who glanced at him. The word had become another civil evasion, a polite term given to the uncivil actions that Denisov must perform.

At a metal desk inside the double doors, a large, stone-faced Army officer handed both men section badges. Denisov affixed his badge to the lapel of his dark blue jacket along with the second badge given him when he entered the building: a row of badges like battle ribbons, each granting access to deeper parts of this faceless building. There was so much security.

Like the wooden toy, Denisov thought; a toy he had purchased long ago, when his son was small enough to enjoy it: a large egg-shaped figurine of a peasant girl that opened to reveal another, smaller, egg-shaped figurine, which opened to reveal an even smaller figure, on and on, until the last tiny egg, which was solid and could not be opened. The last figurine always disappointed his son. There must always be more mystery, the child seemed to feel.

Security. The agent code-named Potemkin had once said that in the long run the purpose of security was to find work for the unemployable.

Potemkin. Denisov had not thought of him for months. What an agreeable, intelligent man. They had met at the Language Institute when Denisov was first struggling with French prior to his posting in Southeast Asia. A long time ago.

One afternoon, a lazy summer day of soft breezes from the forests outside the old city, Denisov and Potemkin had shared an afternoon of talk and chess and tea in tall glasses in the Chess Union. Both had just returned from separate postings abroad and both spoke with something like shock of the routine security in the capital. And Potemkin had spoken also of the Barcelona Zoo in Spain: There were three men on the front gate at the zoo. The first gave you a ticket and took your money; the second, a few feet away, examined your ticket to make certain it was genuine; and the third man, in the cubicle at the gate itself, took the ticket and tore it in half and permitted you to enter the grounds. Three men for a simple job, Potemkin said, in a country with a need to employ the unemployable.

They had both understood the parallels with Moscow life in the story but they were wise enough not to articulate them.

They never met again for tea, Denisov thought sadly. There were no friends inside the Committee.

Since Luriey was not permitted beyond the second office, Denisov marched alone—a third badge affixed—through the steel doorway and into a warren of cubicles full of men and a few women who were bent over the papers on their desks.

Beyond was yet another door that led to a hall, which led to three unmarked doors at the end. Which door held the tiger and which the lady?

He smiled to himself as he opened the third door and found himself in still another outer office, a windowless room that guarded the sanctum of Gogol. The last doll to open before finding the one that was solid and with it, the end of mystery.

"Denisov," said the young man sitting behind the desk, frowning as he said the name.

Denisov handed him the security card and placed his thumb under the light. The young man examined the whorls in the thumb, the whorls in the picture of the thumb on the card. Denisov knew him: He was a second cousin to Brezhnev, through his wife's family. Perhaps he, too, was not employable elsewhere—or perhaps he was merely secure, the second man at the gate of the zoo who examined your tickets.

"Enter," the young man said.

Denisov put the card in his pocket and turned the handle of the last door and entered the office of the chief of operations of the Committee for External Observation and Resolution.

Gogol glanced up, nodded to a chair, and returned to the file in the manila folder on his vast, empty desk.

They did not greet each other.

Denisov sat down and noticed that both the space heaters and air conditioners were operating. The room was cool and dry, without windows.

Gogol was thin with almost Oriental features drawn finely on his flat face. Denisov did not understand how a child from the Ukraine—he knew that much about Gogol—looked so much like an Asian Soviet. He was certainly not from Ukrainian stock: He was almost hairless, his eyebrows thinly etched on the ridge of bone that protruded above the deep, brown eyes. He seemed like nothing so much as what he was: a man made for this game, a man for secrets.

The cold room at the end of the dark hall. Final doll in the series; final reality.

"This man," Gogol said, his voice raspy as sandpaper, breaking the silence as though it had not existed and overwhelmed the senses a moment before. He pushed a black-and-white photograph across the expanse of the desk to Denisov who was forced to half rise to take it. He studied the photograph, memorizing the face and background depicted, and then he placed it back on the desk top, carefully out of Gogol's reach.

"Thomas Dooley," Denisov said.

Another man might have registered surprise at Denisov's memory but Gogol merely inclined his head slightly. All his movements were small and economical. "You remember him."

"Quite a long time ago. The first posting I had after the Language Institute, when I came to the section. It was in Laos, when I was liaison and courier to our man in Vientiane. Doctor Thomas Dooley." Denisov paused, more for effect than for anything else. He must not show Gogol how easily memory worked, how much of a trick it was. "He was one of the most famous white men in Laos at the time. That would be . . . 1957, I think."

Gogol said, "A medical doctor." He made a face. "Famous. A man from the United States who became a hero. And not until recently did anyone admit he was an agent for the Central Intelligence Agency."

Denisov waited, his hands folded in his lap. He knew all this but Gogol was building toward something, like a storyteller.

"He made weekly reports," Gogol said, "on movements of the Pathet Lao. It was an unusual situation because he had a great reputation both inside Laos and especially in the United States."

"Mystical," said Denisov.

Gogol frowned.

"Mystical," Denisov repeated.

"He died of cancer in 1959 and the President then, Eisenhower, awarded him a medal. None of this—this that we know of him, about his connection with the CIA—was exposed then."

"And if it had been," Denisov said, "what purpose would it have served?"

Both men lapsed into an uneasy silence; the air conditioner thumped into the cooling mode and they listened to the condenser crackling. Denisov felt his feet becoming warm from the heat of the space heater set up along the baseboard.

Gogol opened the second file on his wide desk and this time he shoved the entire contents across to Denisov. Again, Denisov was obliged to rise awkwardly and retrieve it.

It contained another black-and-white photograph of a young man in the long cassock of a priest. The features were open and smiling in the bright sunlight. The young man was thin, nearly gaunt, and his face was unmarked, like a new chalkboard.

Denisov began to read the attached report printed on yellow paper when Gogol again interrupted, his dry voice scratching out sounds above the hum of the air conditioner.

"Leo Tunney. Also a young man at that time. A priest in the Roman Church who belongs to one of their religious orders called the Order of the Fathers of the Holy Word. He was sent to Laos and Cambodia at the time Docter Dooley was being sent home, to treat his cancer."

Denisov searched his memory. "Sent by his order? This religious order?" he asked.

"Yes. But there was more than that. It was not coincidence that this priest was sent to Laos at the time Doctor Dooley was sent to the United States."

"No?"

More silence. Denisov had played the game very often; he waited and stared placidly at the nervous man across the desk from him.

Gogol said, "No. The order, this Fathers of the Holy Word. We have another file on them, separately. We have all the records." He smiled. "Since 1948, they have used their religious pretexts to act as agents for the Central Intelligence Agency in Asia. They have headquarters now in the United States, in Clearwater, in Florida."

"Where?"

"You will discover that soon enough."

For a moment, Denisov was surprised and let the emotion cross his face. It had been a long time, yet he had known from the moment Luriey summoned him that he was going back into the field again.

And to the United States, a place he had read about, heard about, talked about, probed in a thousand books—and never seen.

"When I was in Laos," he began carefully, "I was not aware of this order. Rather, I was aware of it but not the connection to the CIA."

"No? Perhaps you should have been, especially in your position there."

"Your predecessor, Gogol, never thought to inform his agents of any but a few facts pertaining to the mission. My ignorance might be lamentable now but it is understandable."

Gogol made a dry noise and Denisov glanced down at the file again. He read the yellow sheet slowly, twice, and then closed the folder and placed it back on Gogol's desk.

"Tunney was captured by the Pathet Lao in 1961. What happened after that?"

"Yes," said Gogol.

Denisov waited, hands in his lap.

"In the time since his disappearance, despite our own efforts and despite the efforts by the American espionage agencies, no one could find him. We assumed he had died."

"And he hadn't."

The words came from Denisov flat and certain. Gogol now seemed surprised but Denisov did not explain: The nature of Gogol's statement had dictated the guess.

"You're right, of course, Denisov. Not dead. Discovered five days ago, when he literally walked into the city of Bangkok from the Cambodian jungle border. No papers, no explanation. Still, in fact, a secret. The CIA took him to the United States and he has been in Washington for the past two days, in a hotel room there. They are debriefing him but we can't get the slightest flutter on what has happened and why have they brought him back from the dead, as it were."

"Did they do it?"

"If this wasn't planned, why has it happened?"

"And that is what we want to know, Gogol?"

"Yes."

Again, silence, made more palpable by the humming of the air conditioner.

"But you must have been aware of this," Gogol said at last.

"I wasn't."

"You didn't monitor this news? On your shortwave radio? It has been broadcast on the BBC—"

Denisov opened his hands. "The radio is broken. It has been broken for a month. And it's impossible to find the parts I need for it."

Gogol smiled. "Is that the truth?"

Slowly, annoyance creeped into Denisov's soft, careful voice. "Since you know I have listened to the BBC on shortwave, even that I have the possession of a shortwave radio, you must certainly tell your agents to keep you informed on the condition of my radio. When it is broken, I cannot use it."

Gogol kept smiling. "The Committee for Interior Inquiries in Section Ten supplied us with the information about your radio; we did not request it. You know what they are over there. If they did not justify their allocations, perhaps they would be reorganized out of existence. I do not spy upon my personnel; you have my trust."

"Then I wish you would request that the Committee for Interior Inquiries send around a man to repair my radio so that the next time they have the need to report on my behavior, they will have something of interest to report and something that is accurate."

"I am sorry that the radio doesn't work, Dmitri."

Again, silence.

"You are going to the United States tonight, through the usual northern channel into Stockholm. Your papers will be waiting in Section Four."

"And my nationality?"

"Dieter Jorgensen, from the *Dagblat Svenska.*"

"A Swedish journalist in the United States?"

"Yes. To the United Nations." Gogol paused. "We have to know what the game is that they are playing now. Why has Leo Tunney been away for twenty years and why has the Agency resurrected him now?"

"You are certain this is an operation?"

"No, but it is only logical."

"Logical? It would seem more of an embarrassment to the CIA than to us."

"The political right wing in the United States is attempting to escalate the struggle against us. It might be part of that. We have to know, we have to find out how he stayed alive."

"If he is Leo Tunney."

"Yes. That, too. And what his mission is."

"He was definitely an agent then?"

"We have proofs."

"May I see them?"

"You must accept my statement, Denisov."

"We have our own people in the United States, I don't understand why I—"

"Yes, but there are too many leaks in the network. The FBI has too many spies but they do not know you. And you were in Southeast Asia at that time, perhaps you can understand what the problem has become—"

"The incident in England—"

"Yes. You were not completely at blame there but that is in the past. We have 'burrowed' you long enough. I must know three things, Denisov, about this priest: Why has he come into the light again? What does he know? And is he Leo Tunney?"

"What can he know?" Denisov said.

Gogol pursed his lips. "There are matters beyond you. There are concerns that are not your concern."

"I am not privy to any more information than your predecessor offered in other matters, Gogol. How am I to act?"

"As my camera. As my eyes and my ears."

Denisov suddenly felt tired. "And when that is determined?"

"Observation," Gogol began, as though reciting a prayer. "And then Resolution."

"If he presents a problem."

"The problem exists. He is a mystery. All our mysteries are problems to us because mysteries cannot exist."

"My family is in Gorki—"

"I know. We have notified them to return right after the funeral of your wife's uncle. Now to you. Paymaster has the credentials and the money and the tickets. Denisov." He leaned forward. "Be careful with the money. We are still attempting to make sense of your accounts from the mission in Britain."

"It was a confusing time," he said.

"Yes." The subject of accounts was a sensitive one for Denisov. He had fiddled his expenses, as always, and everyone knew it but they could not grasp the truth in the numbers. "Yes, but you must be accountable."

Denisov rose because he knew the interview was over.

"Dmitri Ilyich," Gogol said.

Denisov waited.

"We must know."

"I understand."

"And your radio."

Denisov looked puzzled.

Gogol permitted the faintest of smiles. "In your absence, Dmitri Ilyich, it will be repaired."

3
Washington, D.C.

The elevator doors closed. Rita Macklin leaned against the wall of the cage as it began its slow ascent to the ninth floor of the National Press Building at Fourteenth and K streets in the governmental heart of the city. It was nearly midnight, she guessed; she never wore a watch, a peculiar foible for one in her profession. Two days, she thought, it had all taken two straight days. She felt the tiredness nearly overwhelm her for a moment, she felt dirty, burned out; she wanted a bath, she wanted to sleep but there was still a little more to be done.

Still, Rita thought, her eyes closed for a moment against the harsh light flooding the small moving cage, still, two days wasn't bad when you considered the odds against winning anything at all.

The doors opened and she hitched up the strap of the Sony tape recorder over her thin shoulder and gripped her purse tightly in the other hand and trudged off. The old corridors were dimly lit at this hour—as they had been at night since President Nixon declared an energy crisis in the winter of 1973—and the lighting gave a sinister, unreal quality to the halls, as though Rita were entering a movie set.

The World Information Syndicate offices were near the end of the corridor. And Kaiser was still there.

Rita carefully opened the door with her key and then stood for a moment in the corridor, listening, waiting to be certain it was Kaiser inside and not some goddam spook from the FBI or the CIA going through the files. Kaiser called this caution her professional paranoia, it went with the territory of the job: Think the unthinkable and then guess a little bit more.

"Kaiser? Is that you, Kaiser?"

"No, but is that you?"

Rita let the door shut behind her and she moved into the shadows of the outer office. Kaiser was alone in the second room of the suite, a single lamp illuminating him at the double desk, the green filing cabinets arrayed on one wall behind him.

Kaiser was a heavy, bald man with black, bushy eyebrows and a gross belly that pushed hard against the edge of the desk as he sat. He was always there, it seemed to her, always at the same desk, all day and sometimes, like now, all night. Across from the double desks that were butted into each other to form one monstrous, littered surface was a battered leather couch, of the kind that once was found in nearly every pressroom in the country. On some nights, Kaiser made it his bed. When Rita Macklin had come to work for him nearly three years ago—she was the best reporter on the *Green Bay Press-Gazette,* she said, and she showered him with her clippings—she had guessed that Kaiser was an old man. He wasn't really. Nearly fifty now, but he looked as though he had lived two lives in those fifty years. His hands trembled with the palsy of too many strong drinks—but Kaiser was never in a bar, never upstairs in the National Press Club, never seen at lunch with a source or a publisher. His teeth were yellow with nicotine and neglect, his breath was foul, his stomach rumbled at odd moments, his thick glasses were mended with Scotch tape; he was a huge, shambling wreck of a man whose outward appearance nevertheless carried an aura of massive dignity and vitality.

Rita Macklin sat down on the couch across from him and sighed as she sank back into the leather. She slipped off her shoes and reached down without looking to rub one stockinged foot.

"Women who wear shoes like that deserve to have their feet hurt. A good reporter takes care of his feet first of all. The legs go first."

"Who am I talking to? Mr. Health Nut? Mind your own business."

"A little honest commentary, a small morsel of advice. Abuse is my lot."

"Your feet would hurt too if you ever walked more than twenty feet a day."

Kaiser lit another cigarette. "Did it work out?"

"Yes."

"That surprises me. But then, you are always a surprise, Rita."

"Why? Didn't you think I'd get the guy?"

"No. It was a wild-goose chase to start with." He paused thoughtfully and removed his glasses, squinted, rubbed his brow. He yawned then, a noisy, wide yawn, and shoved the glasses back on the bridge of his red, drink-distended nose. "The odds, little Rita, were against you. But you're very good, I think I've told you that once or twice—"

"Yeah. It beats giving me a raise—"

"You make enough, you live, you eat and sleep, you buy bad shoes, what more does a woman want? But you're hungry, Rita, and I won't be able to keep you much longer—"

"I like it here."

"Seymour Hersh liked Pacific Press Syndicate but that didn't stop him from going to the *New York Times*. I don't think that's for you, though, Rita, you're not the type, it turned out Sy isn't the type

31

either. But there's no doubt that you're going, on and up, to bigger and better things. Perhaps the *New York Daily News,* that would be it, I think."

"That's not it," she said, suddenly annoyed. She stopped rubbing her foot. "Let's cut the shit anyway."

"Little Rita," Kaiser said with fondness rumbling in his voice. "As you put it. Let's cut the shit. Now, how did you get to our reverend gentleman?"

She smiled. Kaiser was her audience, her father-confessor, her only colleague trustworthy enough to confide in. Kaiser would understand; Kaiser would appreciate. The trouble with being an investigative reporter rather than a regular newsman was that, to be any good at the game, you had to keep your mouth shut. So Kaiser had explained long ago as he began her course of instruction in the Washington game. You had to get used to being lonely, he said, out of the mainstream of the rat-pack journalism that is the most fun of all—the press conferences, the gangbangs in the halls of Congress, the bragging and swearing in the bars after the story was delivered. No, Kaiser said as he explained Rita's game, you are entering a cloistered order; you have to keep secrets growing until their time; you labor in a hidden garden and work in the darkness, hoping for a day when the work will all pay off.

Kaiser was her escape valve, she knew. Kaiser replaced all the fun of the other reporting life.

"The CIA had him buttoned up in room twenty-one forty-three at the Watergate Hotel. Appropriate, huh?"

"A very nice hotel."

"How would you know?"

"I think I was there when it opened. On a freebie, of course. Yes. And then later, when our greatest President and greatest crook had his little problem. But, go ahead."

"They had to let him out sometime, so I waited. He couldn't stand being in the room all the time. It was just a matter of waiting. He took a walk."

"With company, of course."

"Of course. There were two of them. You know the kind: They have little buttons in their ears, they hear voices all the time."

Kaiser smiled. "Our modern-day Joans." He rubbed his ink-stained hands together. "And little Rita got their photographs. 'Take yer pitcher, mistah?' "

"Sure I did. I'm getting better with a camera all the time. When I started here, I didn't know I was going to have to be all things to all men."

"Not all men. Me, Rita, just me. A well-rounded girl. You're certain to attract a good man."

"You know the sidewalk behind the hotel that leads down past those bushes? That little woodsy setting? That's where I got them." She pulled a yellow cylinder out of her pocket and put it on the desk.

"Delightful, delightful." Kaiser's voice soothed like fine sandpaper on soft wood. The room was blue with cigarette smoke; he lit another unfiltered Camel.

"Leo Tunney," she said. "He looks like a ghost."

"One picture is worth . . . ah, worth something I would guess at the moment. Not day after tomorrow but right now."

"And him. I got him too."

Kaiser blew the smoke out of his lungs with a violent cough. When he had finished hacking, he managed a smile.

"Surprise you?" Rita asked.

"You are a constant surprise."

"I walked right up to him."

"Marvelous. Dangerous and nervy, you are a dangerous woman, Rita. Just when one thinks, when one says, 'Oh my goodness, this is an attractive little piece of cake, doesn't she have nice legs, I like her face, a really pretty face, deep with some intelligence to it, like a cat's face,' just then you think, well, I'd guess she wasn't half dumb after all, you surprise. Constantly. Insistently. Did you get him in the garden behind the hotel?"

"No. I didn't want the Button Ears to jump me with no one around. I wanted someplace halfway public where they couldn't get away with too much muscle."

"And the camera? What did you do with the camera?"

"I dropped it in the bushes before I made my duck. I took out the film. I didn't pick it up because I was afraid they might get me if I stopped for it. I had to get out of there."

"From the beginning, Rita."

"They came back into the hotel, from the back entrance. I

walked up to him. I had the Sony on but it took Button Ears a moment to figure out what was going on, they weren't expecting me. I asked him the only thing I could think of."

"And that was?"

"Where had he been for twenty-one years?"

"Marvelous. Neil Armstrong, who labored long and hard to find the right words to say as he stepped on our beloved, American moon, could not have done better. The direct approach. It never fails."

"It fails all the time but this time I guess I threw them off just enough. The whole thing happened so fast I wasn't even sure he had heard me. He looked at me—Father Tunney, I mean—well, Kaiser, I could write a sidebar on just that, on the look on that man's face."

"Was there lust in his heart?"

"Cut the shit," Rita said.

"Your favorite expression, it suits you. As you say. Go on."

"What a beautiful face, Kaiser. He looked like a baby, you know what I mean? Just like a baby, a new baby, all open—"

"He drooled?" Kaiser asked, grinning viciously.

"You'd laugh at a funeral."

"Funerals are laughing matters, Rita. I delight in the misfortune of others; I'm paid to do so. Please, Rita, I'm just trying to bring you down gently. You're overwrought."

"He said, 'I was lost. In the jungle.' Just like that, I got it on the tape. I said, 'You didn't know how to get out?' He just stared for a moment, I could see the Button Ears were starting to make a move, he said, 'I was there, inside. I saw the wars, all of them. All the horror.' "

"Marvelous," rumbled Kaiser. "That's really very good." He nodded his head, grinning, the cigarette smoldering in one sausage fist.

"And then one of the Button Ears made a grab and pushed me. He tried to grab the Sony. I smacked him."

"Good girl."

"The second one hit me. Here." She touched her blouse, indicating her left breast. She had examined herself afterward, in a gas station washroom. She had a bruise where she had been struck.

"And how did you get away?"

"The priest. He said, well, he told them to stop it, that he hadn't come back for this. Something like that. He put out his hand to stop the second one—the sadistic sonofabitch who hit me here, here in the chest—I guess he got thrown off balance—"

"The priest?"

"The priest, yes, he got thrown off balance, he fell down, down on one knee, and a crowd started to gather. The other Button Ear pulled back, he leaned down to help the old man up—you should have seen him, Kaiser, this frail old man—"

"I will see him, Rita, in your words, in your photographs."

"I made my duck then. I wasn't going to get any more by hanging around and for all I knew, they'd have me arrested. But I got out, I told you I had to leave the camera—"

"You must retrieve it. I'll retrieve it—"

"—so here I am. I don't know how long this is good for, but it's all mine, Kaiser."

"Are you sure? Excellent, excellent. No one around when this transpired?"

"Mine, I said. No one. I think the *Washington Post* had sent someone over to the Watergate earlier, I don't know if they knew anything or if they were just checking out all the places, but he didn't get anything. Everyone is still camped out at Agency headquarters in Langley."

"And now the real work begins," Kaiser said. "And the problem."

"What problem?"

"What do we do with it?"

"What do you mean? We write it."

"It's nine minutes to midnight, Rita. This is hardly the moment to start selling this to the papers."

"Hold it."

"Hold nothing, Rita. The first rule of successful and profitable journalism: Hold nothing. If you have the story today, use it today. If you wait until tomorrow, someone else will inevitably have the same story."

"What are you going to do then?"

"It depends, ludicrously enough, on your abilities as a photographer. The photographs must turn out."

"Television? Are you going to give this to television?"

"Bucks, Rita. Big television-sized bucks."

"But what about the story? I still have a story to write—"

"Ah, pride of authorship, the complete reporter. Yes. There'll be a story but that comes in the afternoon. You'll be famous, Rita, a celebrity of the moment."

"Fuck famous," she said. Her face had flushed in that moment and her green eyes gleamed. She realized she was angry and that she was tired and it might end up in tears. But she wouldn't allow that to happen. She had light red hair—almost too light to be called auburn—but it seemed to become more red as she felt the anger rising in her. At times, her fine-featured face looked delicate, but now it looked tough and determined.

"Rita," Kaiser warned. He waved his cigarette in front of her. "This is a business, Rita. I can call Stu at home, Stu with NBC, he'll be getting up anyway for the 'Today' show in a couple of hours, he can get the ball rolling, we'll receive full credit and we'll still have plenty left over to sell to the newspapers in the morning. But you know and I know that I can't sell to the papers right now."

"Then hold it, I told you—"

Kaiser lit another cigarette while the first still smoldered in a tiny ashtray on the desk. "What makes you think Father Tunney is still in the Watergate Hotel at this moment? Where do you suppose they will take him tonight, now that you've spotted him?"

"I don't know."

Kaiser closed his eyes for a moment; when he opened them, he did not see Rita. "Three programs," he said aloud, but to himself. "Three beautiful networks. What can I squeeze them for? My God, Rita, get to the closet and get those pictures developed." His fist banged the desk. "Did they follow you? Do they lurk without?"

"Are you kidding?"

"Anything is possible at the Creep Intelligence Agency. Oh, that those photographs turned out. Please God, let Rita's pictures turn out and I promise I won't play with myself on the Rock Creek bus anymore."

"You're disgusting."

"Look, honey," Kaiser said. "There's maybe ten grand in this thing. We can hustle television, hustle the syndicates. Tomorrow the world—the *Omaha World* and the *Chicago Tribune* and the *New*

York Post or the *News* and . . . Rita, I told you I would make you a famous reporter and so you shall be. And then you'll leave me, leave the nest, I can feel it in my sad old bones, you'll thank me and leave poor old Kaiser all alone, going away to Knight-Ridder or—"

"Anything to stop this." She smiled. "I'll do the pictures. Is there any coffee?"

"If you have a clean cup, we have dirty coffee. I made it an hour ago."

"I'm glad you're getting exercise."

He reached for the phone and dialed the area code of Long Island.

Rita went to the Mr. Coffee machine on top of a filing cabinet, and opened the top drawer and removed her cup, a child's milk mug that said "Rita." It was the first thing she had purchased the first day on the job. The glass coffeepot had long since been broken and replaced, for reasons of obscure economy, with an aluminum saucepan. She poured the dark liquid in her cup and stirred in a little nondairy creamer. The mixture tasted as bad as it looked; flecks of powder floated on the surface of the coffee.

Rita Macklin stared at the cup as she wrote the story in her head. She saw the words coming together, first in the lead, then in the second paragraph. She was never afraid of writing; she never had a "block"; the words were always there, always waiting for her, if she had done the work. It was like planting a garden, watering the black soil, waiting for the first burst of green shoots pushing through the clods of earth.

She went to the closet they used to develop film in emergencies.

She was so lost in her own thoughts—in recording her impressions of the past two days, turning the random flashes of light into orderly rows of words—that she did not even listen as Kaiser began to pitch the sleepy man from NBC.

4
Vatican City

The tour operators in Rome were on strike again. There had been a bombing the afternoon before in Milan, at the Galleria near the great cathedral, and two people had been killed. The bombing was blamed on the Fascists this time and they claimed credit for it; so the unions, which were mostly Communist, chose to protest the act of terror with a strike. The trains of the national railway would not run this morning but service would resume in most places by mid-afternoon; the truck drivers would strike in the afternoon but work in the morning; and the tour bus operators decided to strike all day. In this way, the city and the country were merely inconvenienced; it was the traditional Italian labor action.

So the great square in front of St. Peter's Church was relatively empty on this sunny, warm October afternoon. The independent city-state of the Roman Catholic Church was located on Vatican Hill in Rome and though it was close to the center of the ancient city—just across the lazy Tiber, a brisk walk down from the turrets of Castel Sant'Angelo—most tourists felt intimidated by the enclave and claimed they were unable to visit the Vatican unless they were escorted there by tour bus.

All of which suited the two priests who walked together in the colonnade encompassing the square. They spoke together as they walked, their heads low, their arms behind their backs.

Franco Cardinal Ludovico was the older man but it would have been difficult to tell that by his bearing and appearance. Both wore plain black cassocks in the manner of Italian priests because Ludovico eschewed the signs of rank—the crimson robes, for instance—that would have differentiated them. Ludovico was fifty-six years old but his face was unlined, his hair thick and black, and his build was still as slender as it had been when he first became a priest thirty-five years before, in the northern port city of Genoa.

His lips barely moved as he spoke. The breeze under the cool columns stirred their cassocks and made them flutter; pigeons above the square wheeled in the air suddenly, all rustling wings and feathers, making circles against the flat Italian sky.

The second man was nearly twenty years younger, a little taller and a bit heavier than Ludovico. Father Martin Foley was dark Irish—his hair was thick and black with just a hint of gray at the sideburns, and his face bore a gravity of manner and the deep lines of experience. He was born in the Republic of Ireland but when he was six, his parents moved to Liverpool to find work. He was educated there and by dint of competitive examinations that were just beginning to open good schools to the lower classes, he got into Cambridge. His parents, his priest, his relatives, were amazed by his progress in this alien and hated society of the English, but they were even more astonished when he decided to become a priest. Though Liverpool was the most Catholic and most Irish city in England, it was still in England; his father thought Martin had "thrown up his chance" to make his mark there by becoming a priest, though he did not speak against it. The two men—father and son—eventually reconciled because the old man saw that his son would "make his mark" just as boldly in the Church as he would have done in Britain, for he was sent to Rome very early—and he remained there. He had been in the ancient city for ten years and was a Roman in taste and temperament, finding the ways of the capital city as familiar as those of the English society his family had adopted. Most of his success had been due to Cardinal Ludovico.

Ludovico had taken Martin Foley under his protection early and advanced him through the intricate Vatican bureaucracy with advice, with generous aid, with access to Ludovico's own formidable alliances and networks. He had been a second father to Martin Foley at a time when Martin felt estranged from his natural father. Now their relationship was on a more businesslike footing but still the old affection lingered. Ludovico, an instinctive man able to make startling deductions on the basis of scanty evidence, had seen in this somewhat serious, somewhat plodding young man qualities of intelligence that might have taken a lesser mentor years to discover.

"You see, Martin, you are brilliant," Ludovico had once said in his elegant, purring English. "But you hide this spark so well under the layers of your pedestrian nature that it requires a person equally brilliant to see the kinship with your intellect."

"But I don't have your Excellency's brilliance."

"Oh, you do, Martin. You are like a thousand little lamps darting flames at the darkness. If you would only concentrate all these flames into one light, the world would see it too, as I do."

But Foley remained something of a plodder and Ludovico had finally, reluctantly, concluded some time ago that Martin would always be a key operative in the network but never succeed him to head the operation.

The two men were speaking of the operation now, in the open square that Ludovico preferred. Too many walls in the Vatican listen, he had once said. "Our Church is full of mysteries, Martin, but it has no secrets."

And secrets were most important to both men.

Franco Cardinal Ludovico was Director-General of the Congregation for the Protection of the Faith.

It was a dull name for an extraordinary organization with a budget in the millions of lire and a century-old mission to serve as the eyes and ears of the Pope in matters temporal, as opposed to matters spiritual.

The Congregation for the Protection of the Faith had been established by Pope Leo XIII, who saw the restless upheavals of the industrial age—and the no-longer-docile working classes—as both an opportunity and a threat to the Church. Openly, the Pope wrote of his concerns in the classic encyclical *Rerum Novarum*. Privately, he founded the Congregation and charged its first director: "I do not wish to know the words of ambassadors or kings; they cannot speak the truth. I wish to know the simple truth, the hard truth, the truth that is naked in the world." So the network of "holy spies" began.

In the era of the young Mussolini, strutting for the first time across the stage of the world, the Congregation brilliantly gathered a ring of evidence and information that forced the Fascist dictator into a compromise that led to the Lateran Treaty of 1929, granting Vatican City the status of an independent state. The power of the Congregation was great then and it grew, especially after World War II. Now the Congregation for the Protection of the Faith was rarely spoken of—in the Church or out of it—which suited Cardinal Ludovico very well.

Only once had a pope seriously threatened the existence of the

Congregation. In 1961, John XXIII met in secret with the man who was then Director-General. The peasant Pope with the wide, beaming face and the shrewd eyes had gone over the budget requests for the coming year and concluded, in his gentle voice, that "secrecy is very costly, isn't it? Would this money be better spent on the poor?"

The Director-General made the mistake of offering the wrong reply. He had not yet taken the measure of the man: "The poor have no secrets."

For a moment, the Pope was silent and then he said, still gently but with an implied warning in the turn of the words, "That is too cynical, Cardinal. Even for you."

The Director-General had realized his mistake at once. "I beg your pardon, Holiness. I did not wish to offend you."

"You have offended yourself."

"Our Lord said to us we would have the poor with us always. Let us hope that the Church will be able always to serve them well, even in these times."

"Do you doubt then, Cardinal, that the Church of Christ will last until the end of the world?"

The Director-General bowed his head in defeat. "No, Holiness. But the Church might again have to hide for half a millennium as the world plunges down into ignorance and darkness. Even in a new Dark Age—and I fear it is very close—we would have the poor with us. But how can we serve them best when we must ensure our own survival? Our Lord said to us the Church would last until the consummation of the world. But He did not say that it would be triumphant in every age of the world."

So, shrewd and insistent in his arguments, the Director-General saved the life of the Congregation, though he could not forestall cuts in the budget. Fortunately, the reign of John was brief and the next Pope—Paul VI—had been a diplomat in the Vatican and was a thorough bureaucrat in his time and understood well the needs of the Congregation—and its uses. The budgets grew fat under the reign of Montini (who was Paul VI) and Montini was pleased with the clear, wise, direct intelligence reports from the new Director-General, Ludovico. Ludovico received his red hat within three years of taking over the Congregation.

Some in the Vatican said he was the second most powerful man in the Church; it was a mark of Ludovico's power that he knew those who said such things.

"Do you understand the delicacy of this, Martin?" Ludovico now said as they walked at the edge of the square.

"Yes, even I understand that," Martin Foley said. His voice was low, with still a slight lilt in the accent reminding Ludovico of his Irish birth. There was a trace of bitterness in the reply; the bantering of their first years had been hardened somewhat by a feeling in Martin that Ludovico had already made a final judgment about him.

"Now, Martin," Ludovico said gently, in his light, amused tone. "You must understand the delicacy of it or I would not have told you about it at all; but I was speaking of the delicacy of what must be done."

"Leo Tunney is an embarrassment, you said."

"Not yet but there is every indication he will be. There are two problems here, Martin. We must know what he does. What did he see or do or feel in . . . in the wilderness, as it were? And why has the CIA kept him closeted for six days? Not a flutter from them. This is all rather ominous, Martin, and I think our prodigal missionary should be advised at the earliest opportunity to make his report to his Church. First. And last."

"Will he obey an interdict?"

Ludovico shrugged as he strode on. "We must assume he will. The problem comes with the CIA. How do we get to him?"

"That's ridiculous," said Martin Foley. "They can't keep him prisoner."

"Of course they can. They have. But that is doubtless temporary. What I cannot understand is how and why he came out of the jungle now. Why not ten years ago? Or twenty?"

"Is this a plot then? Of the Americans?"

Ludovico smiled. "I thought so at first. Now I have second and third thoughts. The idea twists and twists upon itself. If the CIA engineered his return, what would the reason be?"

"Leverage," the priest said.

Ludovico murmured approval. "Good."

"I presume the Americans can be as interested in our good graces as the Soviets."

Ludovico laughed aloud. "Precisely. It would all be so logical, except for the first part of the plan. To engineer any plot, to set it up, they would have had to have Leo Tunney in the first place. Did they hide him for twenty-one years?"

"No, but perhaps they found him and decided to use him—"

"That's not very logical, I think."

"Nothing in the return of Father Tunney seems logical."

"Yes, Martin. Exactly."

"He was an agent for the CIA, then?"

"Agent is not the word. Too strong. The Holy Word Fathers had a certain . . . shall I say, confusion of missions in the 1950s. They certainly weren't the only order affected but they were the worst affected. The CIA was using priests and nuns and other religions and lay people connected to our hospital and relief efforts throughout Asia, as part-time listening posts, couriers, watchers. They were Americans, it's true, but their loyalties to their vows, to their mission, became confused with their sense of patriotism. In the Holy Word Fathers, however, we have more than patriotism. Or perhaps I should say, less." Cardinal Ludovico paused and stared across the nearly empty square at the Egyptian obelisk at the center of it. "Most generous bequests came into the motherhouse of the order and that's when I decided to investigate all this nonsense. They were living like royalty in Florida, the father-general had a yacht he kept at a private pier at Clearwater Beach, they were generating scandal every day. And there was a matter involving a young woman . . . well, that's ancient history now." Ludovico started to walk again, this time across the square. Foley followed. "We cleaned our own house then, Martin; there was very nearly talk of disbanding the Order."

"And Tunney was involved?"

"I don't know. I don't think so. He went to Asia in 1958 via the Philippines and then to Korea. He had been ordained in 1955. The question could be, why did he choose to join the Holy Word Fathers but that's . . . well, what did he know of them? That they were being funded largely through laundered money from the CIA in the last years? He wanted to be a missionary priest. They advertised in American youth magazines in those days—join the Holy Word Fathers and see the world while you're saving souls."

Martin Foley laughed aloud.

"Yes, Martin. Yes. He was very young. Perhaps he was naïve about the Order. Perhaps it didn't matter. But when he was in Asia, finally in Laos, he certainly did his part for the Americans. Yes. You might have called him a patriot. Nothing too demanding: a report on troop movements, a report on famine in a village. Information and information. I don't blame the CIA. Perhaps even the priests are not to blame. We all fought the same enemy in those days—'godless communism.' So they thought."

The last words carried an odd bitterness in them, foreign to Ludovico's usual speech. Foley stared at him. Ludovico paused again, in the middle of the square, and raised his eyes to the great roof of the church where stood the heroic statues of Christ and the Apostles.

"Inside," Martin Foley said. "In the jungle. During all those years and wars. He must have seen it all, seen the Americans. And he didn't come out."

"Until now."

"What do I do when I make contact?"

Almost with reluctance, as though he had been disturbed at prayer, Ludovico took his gaze away from the church and stared at Foley. "You are an emissary of the Pontiff. Not a papal delegate, mind, just an emissary for this matter. Very low-key, all of it, but not unofficial. Leo Tunney is not to think that there is a decision involved in this, that he can say yes or no."

"Will I work through Ramirez?"

"You can't avoid him, I'm afraid, but keep your distance." For fourteen years, Ramirez had been the Congregation's man at the United Nations, sending back charming and witty and nearly useless reports on the prattle of diplomats at cocktail parties. Ramirez was also de facto chief of American intelligence operations for the Congregation. Twelve years before, Ludovico had made a move against him, to shake him out of the Congregation, but the Spaniard had revealed his own base of power in the Vatican bureaucracy and Ludovico had decided that, in the long run, it was easier to leave Ramirez where he was. "Out of harm's way," as Ludovico had explained it somewhat lamely at the time.

"Besides," Cardinal Ludovico now said aloud, "our colleague in New York is not much interested in matters that would take him beyond the Hudson River. He has become a New Yorker over the years."

"Not unlike our Romans," said Foley.

"No, Martin. In New York, it is chauvinism to be interested only in your city and its matters. Here in Rome, it is a cosmopolitan insularity."

Foley smiled at that.

"Martin." Again, the older man began to stride across the square, to the steps of the church. "This is the best time of year. The season is so melancholy and yet so clear, as though we can at least see all the trees, the colors of nature, the cycle of things as they really are. Don't you think so?"

Foley had never heard him speak this way. He didn't know what to say.

"And what if Tunney has something?"

"Yes." Ludovico did not look at him as they walked. "Yes, a secret."

"What could he have known?"

"I don't know."

"Has he told the Americans?"

"We can only ask him."

Ludovico thought then that it was not fair of him, that there were layers of matters beyond Martin Foley that would make it easier for him to operate but that could not be revealed to him. Things were hidden from every eye except his own. Things were written down in files that would be closed for a thousand years; and yet, despite the secrecy of the files, they would be kept always. The Church had a passion for files, dossiers, histories; everything was kept, wrapped and silent, in tombs and catacombs.

Waiting for the last day, Ludovico thought with a melancholy that had become part of his nature in the past few years.

Tunney had been part of a secret for a long time. He should have been dead, Ludovico thought. In fact, once, Ludovico was certain he was dead. And now he had come back to life and created a delicate imbalance. He must be dealt with, before silence came again and he was put back into the forgotten files, waiting for history.

"He has a secret," Ludovico said. "Enough to worry a nation like the United States."

45

Or a church, thought Martin Foley. But he did not speak again as the two men continued up the steps of the church, through the vast doors, into the silent, brooding and grand interior. They would pray.

5
Bethesda, Maryland

Dawn broke through the black sky without warmth or drama. Gray light covered the buildings and flooded the deserted streets of northwest Washington.

Rita Macklin felt cold at the wheel of the ancient gray Chevrolet and she flicked the heater switch. The mechanism whirred into noisy, reluctant life and after a moment, heat rose from the vents.

Too damned cold, she thought, but in a moment, she felt too warm and she turned the heater off. She was just tired, she decided.

She crossed the District line on Wisconsin Avenue and when she reached Old Georgetown Road, turned left and followed the winding highway to the apartment complex she lived in near the old naval hospital. She parked in her assigned stall under the apartment building and took the elevator to her one-bedroom apartment on the sixth floor. The sun was just above the line of trees in back of the building when she turned the double lock on her door.

Because she was tired, she was not cautious.

She pushed the door open.

Something was wrong. She felt it first, then saw it.

Instinctively, she backed out the door, pulling it shut behind her.

And then she felt the pressure against her back and she was being forced suddenly, violently, into the apartment, slammed against the far wall. She opened her mouth to cry out when one of them put his hand over her face.

She hadn't seen him. The hand smothered her. She bit down

and tasted his flesh while she dug an elbow in his ribs.

"Fucking cunt."

The second one clipped her then, very hard, across her delicate face, with a closed fist. There wasn't any contest.

She went down to her knees, felt sick for a moment, as though she knew she would throw up. And then the feeling passed, replaced by a wrenching rage. She grabbed for a leg, there were legs all around her, but they moved too fast. One of them kicked her hard, in the side, and this time she was sick. The pain was white as she vomited on the carpet.

No, no, goddam it, she thought.

But she saw the stain of her vomit on the rug.

Goddam them. She pushed herself against the floor, trying to get up.

And then one of them grabbed her from behind and threw her down on the couch.

The room was torn up. Every drawer had been opened. Every book was pulled out of the elaborate bookcase she had constructed from plans in a newspaper.

Every goddam book, she thought. She wanted to cry but the feeling merged back into the tearing rage inside her.

Now the first of them sat down on the coffee table in front of her. He stared at her with a flat face, with flat eyes that might have been blind. It was the one who had clipped her in the face and then kicked her.

He stared at her for a moment.

She wiped her hand across her mouth. Goddam them, she thought again.

"Get out of here."

The one with the flat face said, "Not yet. Not just yet."

"You bastards, you dirty bastards."

"Not just yet," he said again, as though she had interrupted him. After another long moment, he dropped his gaze and reached into his pocket.

The man in gray sitting on the coffee table held up a card at eye level in front of Rita. Rita, terrified, was holding her sides now, her arms folded in front of her.

The card bore a color photograph of the man and the outline of the Great Seal of the United States and other words. The name of the card was Smith. Other words said: National Security Agency.

"Get out of here," she said slowly, in a voice choked with anger.

"She bit my hand, the fucking cunt."

"Shut up, George."

"I could get an infection."

"Shut up, George," the man said calmly, as though he had said the same words often in the past. He wore a gray suit with a white-on-white shirt and a collar pin and a striped tie that might have meant he was a Yale man.

"This is against the law, in case you didn't know that."

"Is it?"

"Morons."

"Please look at this."

Another piece of paper held at eye level. She turned away. Then he struck her once sharply across the face, stinging her eyes with tears.

"Please look at this," he said with the same flat voice.

Rita stared through her tears. It was a search warrant but she had never seen one before. It bore the signature of a federal district judge but she could not make out the name.

"What is this?" asked the gray man. "I can't hear you."

"A search warrant."

"That's right, Miss Macklin. For these premises. In the course of our legal search of these premises, you attempted to stop us from performing our legal duties and you injured a special agent. You were forcibly restrained when no other method was available to restore order."

"I thought the CIA wasn't supposed to spy on civilians anymore."

"This is a case of national security and I have already identified myself as a field operative of the National Security Agency."

"Go fuck yourself."

"Do you want me to hit her?" It was the second agent, the one in the brown suit named George.

"I don't want you to do anything, George. Just shut up, please."

"Maybe I could restrain her again," said George.

"Shut up, George."

"I want to talk to a lawyer."

"Miss Macklin, please shut up, too." He stared at her until he was satisfied that she had decided not to speak. "We want the photograph."

"What photograph?"

He struck her then, as he had before, hard across her cheek. Again, her eyes were stung with tears. She hadn't seen his hand move at all.

"The photograph that you took of a man outside the Watergate Hotel last night."

"I don't know what you're talking about."

"This is tedious, Miss Macklin. We want the photograph."

"I don't know what you're talking about."

"We've been working on this all night."

"Poor baby."

"We want the film of the photograph you took."

"Of Father Tunney, right?"

She smiled. Her eyes were still wet, she felt the sting of his slap across her cheek, her ribs hurt, but in that moment, she felt much better.

"Are you aware of Section C, paragraph forty-nine of the United States Code, volume seven, number one seven eight four?"

"No, but I have a feeling you're going to tell me about it."

The gray man went on, seemingly unperturbed. "It deals with acts of sabotage against governmental security procedures, Miss Macklin. I won't go into details but the penalties upon conviction include ten years in prison and a fine up to a quarter of a million dollars."

"I don't have that much."

"This isn't a game."

"I'm serious. I don't even have a savings account."

"Do you want to give me the film? And the tape recording?"

"Are you aware of the part of the U.S. Code that quotes the First Amendment?" she said.

"Where's the photograph?"

"What time is it?"

The gray man appeared startled. "Why?"

"Because if it's seven o'clock, you can see the photographs for yourself on Channel Four. On the 'Today' show on NBC."

The gray man stared sadly at her, as though she had disappointed him.

"And the sounds," said Rita Macklin, tears stopped, voice rising. "Sounds of a poor defenseless girl reporter getting beat up by two Button Ears in the Watergate when she tried to talk to Father Tunney whom they were holding against his will."

"That's not true."

"Turn on the TV and see what's on."

"How did you know we were at the Watergate?"

"How did you know I took photos?"

"You left your camera."

"Bright boys." She stared at them for a moment. She felt very frightened because of their calmness, because of the chaos they had made in the apartment with such care. "Really bright," she continued, her voice even. "I hope Uncle Sam pays you enough; you know so much about me and you don't even know I'm a reporter." She said "reporter" as though she hoped the word would frighten them.

"Of course we do." The voice remained dull and calm.

"Then you shouldn't have done this."

"We went to World Information Syndicate on M Street, only we couldn't find you there." Just a trace of embarrassment entered the voice now. The one who said his name was Smith let his fingers tap his knee as though the fingers had a secret nervous life separate from the controlled body.

"M Street," Rita said. "You went to M Street." Slowly, she began to smile, wiping the tears harshly from her cheeks. "We moved from there a year ago. My government can't even use an up-to-date phone book."

The two men looked at each other. One said, "I didn't look in the phone book." The other said nothing.

Rita spoke with light sarcasm. "The White House phone number isn't in the phone book either but I know what it is. You guys amaze me. Just when I think you're smart, you're stupid."

She let herself laugh as the gray man stared sadly at her.

George, sucking his palm, went to the black-and-white television set in the corner of the battered living room and turned it on. In a moment, the image of Tom Brokaw was on the screen. He turned the sound up just as the first picture of a startled Leo Tunney between two government agents appeared on camera.

George said, "She took a picture of Harry."

"You really ought to be proud of yourself, Miss Macklin," the gray man said. "You people are all alike. You'd sell the country down the river for a story. You really ought to be proud of yourself. You people will do anything for money, won't you?"

"Like beat up women? No, I leave that to my government."

"Christ, the A.D. is going to hit the fan," said George.

They heard a scratchy rendition of Leo Tunney's singsong voice on the set.

"You think you're pretty smart, don't you?"

"A lot smarter than you or I'd have to be on government welfare too." She felt good again and in control; they had really scared her; in those first moments, she thought they were going to kill her. Maybe they would have if it hadn't been too late to stop the photographs from getting out. Kaiser was right, after all; never hold on to a story.

The gray man said, "We're running a scanner on your income tax returns now. You better hope you're clean."

"I'm not a congressman. I'm too poor to cheat."

"We are going to look into you, Miss Macklin. We're going to go through your files from day one. Do you understand what I'm telling you? Who do you think you're playing a game with? We are the government."

"Booga, booga," Rita Macklin said.

The gray man got up from his perch on the coffee table and turned. "Come on, George."

"Aren't you going to put the books back?"

"I wouldn't say anything more. About this, about anything."

"Fuck you."

"I wouldn't," said the gray man. "This was a legal entry, a legal warrant. If you want to embarrass us further—your government further—then we just might have to do some things."

"Beat me up again?"

"Indictments, for one thing. We would have to go to court with something. You might beat it, you might not, but we could tie you up for a couple of years. Lawyers, we could fix it up. You wouldn't work anywhere for a while. You know we could do it, don't you, Rita?"

He said it evenly, in a hissing tone, and she felt the words and shivered. Yes. They could do it; they could do anything.

The gray man stared at her for a moment longer and then joined George at the door. The two left without another word. The door clicked reassuringly behind them. She got up, half ran to the door, and pulled the bolt shut. But she didn't feel safe; maybe she would never feel safe in the apartment again. She leaned against the door and shivered.

Bastards.

6
New York City

The doors of the unmarked police car opened simultaneously, front and back, and three burly men got out with guns drawn and approached the Saab sedan. The police car had forced the Saab to the curb in front of the St. Moritz hotel a moment before and already a sidewalk crowd was gathering to watch the little drama. A thrilling sense of impending violence rippled through the bystanders, as though they were waiting for the worst with eagerness. The third policeman, who wore a brown leather jacket, stopped at the opened door on the passenger side of the police car and kept his pistol half-pointed at the Saab. He used the car door as a shield.

In a moment the doors of the Saab were flung open. The driver was a kid, skinny and dazed. The two in the back seat who emerged were about the same age. The man was fat and had long greasy hair, and the girl wore a miniskirt that was as unfashionable as it was skimpy. It clung to her thin shanks like wet paper. Her arms were thin as though she had been ill a long time.

The three young people stood frozen while two cops searched the car and the third cop stood behind the open door with his pistol in hand. It was a ballet without music but all the participants understood their steps.

The audience at the metal tables of the St. Moritz sidewalk café watched the show as though they were critics.

Suddenly, a young man with long brown hair, a black beard flecked with gray, wearing a faded Army fatigue jacket, stumbled to the front of the walk and spoke: "Man, why can't you pigs leave these people alone, I mean? You are the worse, the worse—"

"Beat it, Jack," the cop behind the door hissed.

"You think this street is so fucking great? You think this city is worth saving? You think I did two years in Nam for this shit? Do you?"

None of the characters in the drama looked at him. The thin girl with glazed eyes—large, brown eyes that did not see—shivered and folded her arms.

"Nothing," said the first cop, emerging from the Saab. The second cop shook his head as well. They went back to the unmarked police car and climbed inside without a word. The kids climbed in the Saab. Only the veteran was left, holding his arms outstretched. He was still crying: "Why do you let this happen to us, for Christ's sake?"

He spoke to no one. The sidewalk crowds moved on.

"Nice to be home again," said Devereaux, placing the glass of vodka back on the tablecloth.

"Sarcasm," Hanley said, as though required to classify the remark.

They had been silent during the brief tableau. Now talk exploded around them at the other tables like wine poured from a bottle. "The guy with the beard has the right idea," Devereaux said. His face was impassive, his gray eyes unrevealing, his voice low and cold and comfortless. "Perhaps all we can do is cry."

Hanley had chosen the meeting place. As usual, it was bizarre and public. Hanley preferred a public place away from microphones and intentional eavesdroppers.

Hanley was a bit of a paranoid on the subject of security, which was not unusual, given his profession.

Devereaux felt tiredness like pain, like an open wound. He had expected leave when he got home—not another assignment. The flight back from Tehran had been a little dangerous and very complicated. First, there was the matter of becoming a Swiss businessman flying from Tehran to Zurich via Ankara. And then that identity was literally burned away in a small fire in a washbowl in the Zurich airport men's room at midnight. The second identity took him as far as London where he spent a long, dull morning in the monotonous confines of Heathrow, listening to the flat voice of a woman announcing flight departures to every city he had ever been to. Some of the names stirred painful memories, some merely hurt with the warmth of nostalgia. The third identity he assumed, his real one, Devereaux, took the Pan Am flight to New York. He rested in first class and tried to sleep; the plane was an hour late, bucking headwinds over the North Atlantic. He had been traveling for a little more than twenty-four hours when Hanley's message greeted him at Kennedy Airport.

Hanley was the Second Man in R Section, a title made powerful by all that it did not say about his job, just as R Section itself, a complex cog in the sprawling intelligence establishment of the United States, was powerful in its peculiar, obscure way.

R Section was established in 1961 following the Bay of Pigs fiasco. President Kennedy had depended on the single accuracy of Allen Dulles and the CIA for the success of the invasion of Cuba, a plan hatched in the last Eisenhower year. The CIA had guessed wrong. R Section partially answered the question Kennedy had posed then: Who will spy on the spies? Who will gauge the accuracy of their information? Who will find their moles, their double agents? Who will be a check on their covert operations? Written into the budget of the Department of Agriculture, R Section became a field reporting service established to determine mundane matters like crop yields in the Warsaw Pact countries and grain expectations within the Soviet Union.

It performed these functions—and others that were never named. Hanley called the KGB the "Opposition." He never called the CIA the "competition" but that was what it was. R Section and the other agencies under the umbrella of the intelligence establishment—including the National Security Agency, the Defense Intelligence Agency, the Senate Permanent Subcommittee on Intelligence Operations (which had its own espionage staff)—were all competing with each other for federal favors and moneys. There was no charter for R Section to mount the operation just launched in Tehran, but nonetheless it was part of Devereaux's job.

"It's been a long time," said Hanley. He frowned. "I had no idea the drinks were so expensive here."

Devereaux wrested a smile from his cold face. Hanley was notorious to the agents in the field. For twenty years, he had routinely eaten lunch in a small bar and grill down Fourteenth Street from the Department of Agriculture building in Washington where R Section kept its headquarters. The bar was like a hundred other cheap places clinging to life at the fringes of official Washington. Lunch was always the same for Hanley: a cheeseburger without onion and a dry martini, straight up. Hanley lived alone and had not bought a new suit for six years. He seemed the kind of man who carried a small change purse, though he did not.

"Yes," Devereaux agreed. "An expensive drink on an expensive expense account. It makes the drink more enjoyable."

Hanley made a face and sipped his rye. He always drank rye in New York because he had decided ideas about the city, gleaned from a childhood of watching movies about it at the neighborhood movie house in Red Cloud, Nebraska, where he was raised. New York was fixed in his memory at a time just before the Second World War. He was a dull man, in appearance and speech, and he had never traveled outside the triangle of Nebraska, Washington, D.C., and Boston. He lived a vicarious life through the lives of the agents he directed in the elaborate network of R Section.

Devereaux closed his eyes for just a moment, as though sleep could be snatched in seconds. The vodka was not working for him; he knew nothing would work anymore to flog the tired body back to life. When he was like this, at the point of full exhaustion, he could only find a safe place, take a pill and sleep around the clock.

"There is some urgency to this," Hanley said then, because Devereaux's appearance finally betrayed his exhaustion.

"So you said."

"A priest named Leo Tunney. A Catholic priest."

Devereaux waited, staring at Hanley, his mind a blank slate, waiting to be filled in.

"This developed in the past week but we didn't know what to do. And then you came out of Tehran ahead of time."

"I'm tired," Devereaux said. "I need a rest, starting with a good sleep."

"You drink too much. It takes your energy."

"Can we forget the health message?"

"Tunney. Do you remember the name at all? You're the man for this." Hanley raised the glass of rye.

"There are still others in the section."

"Tunney. You remember the name, don't you?"

A reluctant flicker of recognition crossed Devereaux's winter-hard face.

"Eight days ago," Hanley continued. "He came out of the jungle in Thailand, literally walked into the embassy. Eight days."

"There was a Leo Tunney in Asia," Devereaux said. "Before my time. Around 1960, I think." For a moment, he saw it clearly—the blood-red Asian sun across the paddies, men squatting in their pajamas, talking and smoking like farmers at rest the world over. He had never gone back to Asia after 1967, after he filed his famous memo on the coming Tet offensive that everyone in the bureaucracy ignored; because they were all embarrassed by it, they found it convenient never to return Devereaux to the East. It was like exile for Devereaux because he had considered Asia his home, the only home he had ever wanted to know; instead, for more than fourteen years, they had cast him adrift in this hostile Western sea, a cold world he had been born in but which he had never wanted to be part of. Now, as he remembered the name of the missionary priest, he was warm again, in Asia again.

"A missionary in Laos at first," Devereaux said slowly, like a man describing a dream. "The Pathet Lao overran the village he was in, and he was either killed or captured. No one ever saw him again."

"And?"

"He had been a stringer for the Agency. Very low level stuff."

"Yes. The Langley Firm used him." Hanley was into all the

jargon of the Washington intelligence establishment; it made him feel he was part of the field, part of the wider operation, and not just a clerk who ate his lunch every day in the same place and lived alone and wore neat, old suits. Thus, "Langley Firm" for the CIA.

"Out now? Tunney came out?"

"Yes. Extraordinary, isn't it?"

"Where is he?"

"Langley is playing a game with him," Hanley said in his dry, flat Nebraska voice. "They have him in a box." "Box" was more slang, for "deep custody." "Two days ago, a reporter found him in the Watergate Hotel with two of their field men."

"Why do they have him? He can't be working for them."

"They moved him after the story came out but they can't keep him buttoned up much longer. The news people are hounding them." Hanley, who detested reporters himself, seemed pleased however by the thought of discomfort in the senior branch of the espionage service.

"And what am I supposed to do?"

"Devereaux, you can see the question as plainly as we can. Why did he come out? How? What does he know? And why did Langley keep him under wraps for more than a week?"

"Was there a peep when he came out? In Bangkok?"

"A UPI stringer. Talking to one of the men in the embassy, the acting ambassador at the time. Taubman."

"Victor Taubman. Still in service." Devereaux spoke the name softly because the memory was tinged again with nostalgia for other days in Asia.

"Taubman told the stringer; there was a wire story, an inquiry for more from the *New York Times* to their Japanese bureau . . . but then nothing. We suspected Langley had him in a box, the reporter at the Watergate confirmed it. But why on earth?"

"He has something they want to know."

"Yes."

"Yet that wouldn't be logical either. If he had something good, Langley wouldn't have drawn attention to itself by keeping him in a box. And if it was something against them, they would have erased him."

"Then what is it?"

Devereaux stared at Hanley, waiting for the computer of brain, memory, senses, to tell him. "He hasn't told them yet. They don't know what he wants to tell them."

"Told them what?"

"And we don't know. They know one thing and they aren't sure about the priest. Does he know their secret as well? Does he suspect it? Did he come out to tell the world? The Firm is still dealing in Southeast Asia."

"They're in Bangkok."

"He came out *to* Bangkok. But before that, he was inside. Somewhere in Cambodia. Laos. Vietnam. China."

"I can't follow that."

"If this man is really Leo Tunney who disappeared over twenty years ago, he came out now because he had to," Devereaux said. "All the years of the wars, our war, their wars, he stayed. Now he comes out; it must mean he has something to tell us. But for eight days, he hasn't told the CIA."

"Yes, it could be as you say." But Hanley seemed to doubt it. He bit his lip. Devereaux signaled to the waitress for another vodka.

At that moment, a woman came down the sidewalk past the bearded man who still stood weeping, his arms extended. She was dressed conservatively in a brown coat and a green dress and carried a small oil portrait against her bosom. She came to the table where they sat and showed the portrait to Devereaux.

It was a naked woman reclining on a couch in a lascivious pose, her legs open. The portrait bore the face of the woman who now held the painting for Devereaux.

"I'm an artist," she said, without smiling, without any expression. "Do you want to buy this? I'll sell it to you."

Hanley drew back from the table; he felt afraid; he was not a man for the unplanned moment.

"No, take it away," Devereaux said. His voice was gentle, full of a dirgelike sadness, as though he saw through the portrait, the woman, the moment and was cast into some bleak time that he could not speak of. His stony face was broken, was made not so hard, by the sound of his voice in that moment.

Hanley stared at him. The woman snatched up the portrait and started to walk away. Hanley tried to see the bleak moment in

Devereaux's eyes but they did not reflect any meaning. Devereaux did not show emotion, did not reveal himself.

What did he see now, Hanley thought.

Devereaux continued to stare for a moment, oblivious to the waitress placing a drink before him, oblivious to the street scene, to Hanley, to this moment.

In Tehran, one of the women who was part of the underground had hidden him for three days.

Two weeks later, he had watched them stone her to death in the courtyard outside the old embassy building.

They had buried her up to her neck and the mullah had read prayers and then the words of sentence were pronounced. All the while, she had cried and her eyes had been wide with horror and pleading. She would have done anything to end this moment; she would have betrayed them all. They began to stone her.

Some of the stones were large but most of them were small, like baseballs. She screamed when the first one struck her face and gashed it and then she kept screaming until finally, mercifully, she was not conscious anymore. But not dead. They kept stoning her until she was dead.

And he had watched it all, lying in the shadow of the ledge of the roof across the wide plaza. If he had had a machine gun then, he thought, he would have killed them all.

"Devereaux," Hanley said.

Devereaux stared at him and finally saw him. New York made sounds around him. He had returned to the present moment but his memory was now a moment older, scarred one more time with the laceration of watching the woman die in Tehran; with the laceration of a woman selling a portrait of her nakedness; of a bearded man crying on the sidewalk.

"What do you want to do?"

"The Agency has him in Maryland. We know that much. They're talking about moving him."

"I wish we had moles who worked as effectively inside the KGB."

Hanley said, like a disapproving schoolteacher, "We think they're going to dump him. The news people are giving them too much heat. We think they're going to move him to Florida. That's where the motherhouse is. The Fathers of the Holy Word. At Clearwater, Florida. Soon."

"Who's in the box operation?"

"Rice. Do you know Rice?"

"I know of him. I've never crossed paths with him."

"That's what the computer said. Another reason to use you. We want you to go down. There's some delicacy in this."

"I have no reputation for delicacy."

"There might be a trick here by Langley. Our side has been sending out feelers to the Opposition. To make an arrangement for a new partial SALT pact, defuse the Indian Ocean and the South China Sea."

"Politics."

"The Firm is not pleased."

"By SALT?"

"It's not that formal a proposal yet. The President wants it. I think détente does not please Langley at all."

"They're right."

"It's not for us to take political sides, Devereaux. The Section has no political position."

"Bullshit." He sipped the vodka. "It was a political creation from the first day."

"There is a game here," Hanley said. "Tunney launched the game but perhaps it is out of control."

"Like a member of the Mafia who decides to go to the FBI?"

"Something like that."

"You're dreaming, Hanley. They would have wasted him in Bangkok."

"Crudely put but not necessarily true. Taubman found him, let the world know he was alive."

"People die."

"I still think—"

"What can a man like Tunney possibly know?"

"Why have they kept him for more than a week?"

"I don't know."

"Why did they risk a lot of embarrassment to send two agents to search a reporter's apartment and when they were confronted, to actually beat her up?"

"Perhaps she hurt their feelings?"

"Sarcasm, Devereaux. It won't play." He stared at the agent, at the crosshatched lines on his rugged face, at the gray eyes that held Hanley in a pitiless gaze. They did not like each other, master and agent, the head of the network and this man who was but a small web in the network. But they had been effective together.

"The Agency fumbles from time to time," Devereaux said. "They protect secrets that aren't secrets; they mount foolish operations that aren't necessary. . . ."

"Why are you fighting me on this?" Hanley asked.

"Because you're offering too many suppositions based on your own prejudices," Devereaux said. "Tunney. What about him? He might just be an accident, like a volcano."

"Volcanoes are the end result of movements in the earth."

"Do you think the Chinese kept him all this time, is that it, Hanley? Some sort of Manchurian Candidate, set to blow us up at a given moment?"

Hanley said, "That's unlikely."

"Everything you've said is unlikely because the central base of your suppositions is the unlikeliest matter of all—that Leo Tunney came back from the dead."

For a moment, both men stared at each other without speaking.

Devereaux thought again how cold it was although it was really warm for New York in October. Why was he cold? His feet felt numb beneath the table. Perhaps it was only the tiredness that had taken over his body now, the memories that had come back to him in his exhaustion like a recurring fever, wounding him until he wanted to put them to sleep inside himself.

"Here." Hanley removed an envelope from his suit pocket and put it on the table. "Instructions."

"Beginning tomorrow."

"Beginning now, I'm afraid."

"I'll leave tomorrow." He would not tell Hanley why, that he could scarcely stay awake, that an overwhelming sense of despair and dread was visiting him in these last moments of exhaustion. He needed a hotel room, a bed, darkness, sleep.

Devereaux started to pick up his glass of vodka, then put it down. He felt nothing now; no taste or sensation from outside his body could penetrate the veil of gloomy tiredness. He took the envelope and pushed himself out of his chair. The single suitcase of canvas and leather, crushed and old, was next to the chair. He picked it up without a word.

Hanley began to speak again but Devereaux, staggering like a drunkard, had started off. He wanted to impress the mission upon him, but instead said nothing as the waitress approached with the bill. He watched Devereaux turn the corner, lost in the crowd of strangers passing back and forth, disappearing like a shadow at evening when everything became a shadow.

7
Langley, Virginia

The matter had been complicated from the beginning and the Assistant Director had accepted that; it was all part of the job and, if the truth were known, part of his private relish for the game he thought the job really was. People like Rice, now sitting across the desk from him, looking unhappily out the single window of the large room, would never have understood this quality in the A.D., who appeared to be a dull bureaucrat of few words and fewer opinions. The A.D. had risen in the Central Intelligence Agency because he knew when to keep his mouth shut and how to shift the blame for failure or garner the praise for success—and because he knew enough never to let them know he actually loved the complexities of it all, the conspiracies within conspiracies, the secrets.

Sunday in Langley, a faceless Washington suburb that broke the rolling countryside with too many official buildings. The fame of the town—some said, infamy—came from its status as home of the CIA, which occupied an immense, modernistic, low building that seemed to be supported on spider legs. It looked like a big motel.

It was not unusual for the A.D. to be in his big corner office on

Sunday; he often came down after church because Sunday seemed the proper day for spies. The corridors were empty, the offices locked, but the message rooms were manned and the cables still came in, word by painful word, from all the watchers and counters and full agents all around the world. Came to him, alone, on Sunday, in the big corner office. He would have been down on Sunday in any case, even if the Tunney matter had not taken a new, ominous turn.

The problem presented by the reappearance of Father Leo Tunney in Bangkok nine days before was in danger of exploding out of control. The problem was no longer an intellectual exercise, no longer amusing and harmless like the Sunday crossword puzzle. The problem grew by the moment, a hopeless cancer in the terminal stage of illness.

Again, for emphasis, the A.D. let his carefully manicured hand fall on the front page of the Sunday *Washington Post* lying open on his teakwood desk. Rice watched the gesture and knew it was meant to be an indictment of the way he had handled the matter.

"The first mistake was three days ago," the A.D. said. "How did you let this . . . this reporter find him? And in the Watergate?"

"We've used the hotel before. It's a good, anonymous place, there's—"

"And when she did find you, you let the damage go on and on. And Maurice—" The A.D. interrupted himself with silence. He couldn't start talking about Maurice because it would make him angry. "This should not have been so damned difficult."

It was not all Rice's fault but someone would have to take the blame. In twenty-four years with the Agency, the A.D. had never done so.

"If Maurice was going to take her out, it should have been right away or not at all. You should have known that."

Rice ran his hand through his thick brown hair. He was not a tall man but he had large shoulders and a square, earnest face that was beguiling in its simplicity of expression. He listened as though he had never before heard what he was hearing; it was one of his most useful tricks of appearance. "Maurice. I think a lot of blame here accrues to Maurice making the wrong decision in the field." He felt the burden the A.D. was shifting to him; he was already beginning the process of shifting it to the absent Maurice. Maurice had decided to go to Rita Macklin's apartment; Maurice had searched and stupidly not discovered that Macklin had gone to her office; Maurice had been caught in the act of burglary and Maurice had made the decision to bluff it out with his false National Security Agency card and the standard "search warrant" always carried on burglaries.

"What are we going to do to control the damage now?" the A.D. asked.

"We've had Tunney buttoned up in Bethesda Naval since the Watergate incident. He's under fairly heavy medication." He paused. "His condition could get worse."

Both men understood the suggestion. The A.D. placed the tips of his fingers together to make a tent and stared again at the story on page one, which pieced together the reappearance of Leo Tunney with the business of Rita Macklin and continued with an analysis of the use of clergy and church organizations by the CIA in past years. Damage, the A.D. thought. And it was spreading.

"No. I don't think so. If Tunney is permanently controlled now, there would be too many obvious connectors. And there are leaks that can't be contained, like Taubman in Bangkok. He can't recant. It's just too late for a simple solution; maybe there never was time in the first place."

"Not in Bethesda," Rice persisted. "We could give him a carrier."

The A.D. closed his eyes and leaned back in the big leather chair and contemplated it. The "carrier" Rice referred to was an assortment of capsules, bacterial or viral agents in pill or liquid form, or infections transmitted intravenously or absorbed through the skin. The carriers could result in a sudden, unexplained illness a week from now or a cancer six months from now—or a heart attack tomorrow.

"I don't think so. Not now. It's an option but not now. We intercepted a cable last night from the Vatican to their man at the United Nations. They've sent an emissary to see our patient. Too many, Rice; too damned many people are interested in this."

And still, that was not all. The A.D. could not tell Rice that he had received a visitor in his home last night, who strongly implied that further inquiry by the press into the matter of Leo Tunney might bring grave damage to a certain long-standing arrangement between a banking conglomerate in New York City and the Agency. But what would be more damaging than Leo Tunney's sudden death while in Agency custody?

"If we had only controlled him when he came out," Rice said.

"How? We weren't aware of . . . of any problems. Not at first. And our man in Bangkok didn't box him until that meddler Taubman had already had him for twenty-four hours. Sending uncoded—*damn* him—uncoded messages about his great find straight back to Ambassador Do-Good and his other friends. They think the reappearance of Tunney is the best thing to have happened since Catholic relief set up a food chain for those refugee camps. 'Leo Tunney will help focus the problem on the refugees,' the Ambassador told Taubman. They think it's all a game, a little publicity stunt. There wasn't any way to handle Tunney in Bangkok, not as long as people like Taubman made it known that we had him in a box. A box with a thousand holes in it."

"So what do we do?"

"Open the box." The A.D. paused. "Put him up for adoption. Wait for this thing to cool down. And then reexamine the problem." The A.D. said this in a flat, dull voice without any edge of menace.

"Ship him back to Florida?"

"Tonight, if possible. Then back off. Just a discreet distance. I want you to handle it yourself."

"You know," Rice said, trying once more. "He does have some real problems besides the ones we could give him. He's suffering from exhaustion, malnutrition, some jet-lag fever, a cold, there's a kidney problem of some sort. And he has a skin infection on his feet; he could deteriorate on his own."

"No one dies of athlete's foot," the A.D. said.

"He's weak."

"Make certain he lasts until we have him signed and sealed in Florida. What was the name of the man in charge down there?"

"McGillicuddy. He hasn't made a fuss, he understands our problem. He did some work for us in Morocco twelve years ago."

"Fine. McGillicuddy could be our link to monitor the patient. Have him take Tunney off our hands and with some discretion. The farther we take him from Washington the better I'll like it. There are too many reporters in this city."

"But what if he starts talking down there. To reporters, to the priests . . ."

"He has shown no inclination to say anything thus far, Rice," the A.D. said dryly.

"Perhaps he doesn't like us," Rice said.

The A.D. frowned. Rice had no sense of conversational savoir faire; the A.D.'s comment had not called for a joke.

"Damage, Rice. Damage has been done. It can't be undone but it can be mitigated. Getting him away from here is the first step. In the next few days we simply watch and determine how much more damage he has in him."

Rice stared at the A.D. while he spoke and then nodded in agreement and looked out the window. It was too dirty, too complicated, too many things had already gone wrong. He wished again he was away from here, home again in McLean, sitting on the patio in the soft autumn light, watching the Redskins game on the tube. "There's more damage, isn't there? That can be done?"

"Yes," the A.D. admitted. "Much more."

"Can I get into the picture?"

"No," the A.D. said. "Not now." After all, secrets compelled other secrets and a shared confidence now, even with Rice, would be a betrayal.

8
Clearwater, Florida

He only remembered parts of it, as though the landscape of his memory had been covered with a thick fog that made shapes indistinct but which lifted from time to time to show places and people in different frames of time.

They had come for him at nearly five in the afternoon. He was sure of that, he had seen the watch one of them wore. He had opened his eyes and they were around the bed—the one with the gray suit, called Maurice, and the one called Rice, and the one called George—they had lifted him from the bed effortlessly, onto the gurney cart. Then orderlies had covered him with sheets and the two agents had strapped him down on the cart. He saw a clock again in the corridor as they wheeled him away. Yes, it had been just five o'clock.

Then fog. Just a vague memory of the ride in the ambulance. Darkness, lights, sirens. The straps cutting into his thin arms. He was thirsty.

Next was the plane itself. It was very loud inside, he could hear the engines whining, it might have been a cargo plane. There had been bumpy weather just after takeoff and then the plane settled into smooth flight. He slept; the fog descended on his dreams.

He awoke as the plane landed. He was thirsty still and said so but they ignored him. Tunney was certain he had spoken aloud to them; he was sure he had heard his own voice. But perhaps that too had been a dream.

Sleep, fog, dreams: He was in the jungle just outside of Pnon again, with the woman and the child. The dream always came back to him this way.

In the morning, the company of Marines had come through the village, burning the huts. Some of them had used cigarette lighters to start fires at the corners of the thatched roofs.

Voices that were so familiar. He nearly called out to them; almost, nearly, but hesitation overwhelmed him as it always did.

He had taken the woman and the child into the jungle instead, as the flames from the burning huts raced through the village.

A child was in the road, sprawled in death, his belly already exposed to flies.

They hid, they did not speak; they huddled together. Shots, single shots and then bursts of bullets. The whoomp of a flamethrower coming to life. And screams.

The dead child in the road. A merciful death in light of what followed.

He saw Van Lo run from the village, the flesh of his arm

turning white and then black, the skin melting as the flames made him a torch. Beyond screams. What did it feel like to be so hurt?

Tunney, huddling, holding them to him. She was so close to him, she was weeping, he knew, keeping the tears from falling, a dry weeping that wrenched his heart. He had told her they would not harm her. Everything was a lie in the end, of course.

Van Lo danced in the flames. One of the Marines thought to shoot him then. His body burned to a tight, black core.

Fog, sleep, dreams again. He awoke and he was in another car, it was deep night and the streets were wet with a recent rain. Palm trees like broken umbrellas stood sentry along the streets.

"I'm thirsty," he told them again. Yes, he was sure of it this time, he had definitely heard his own voice; this wasn't a trick of memory. But they didn't answer him. And Maurice, the man in the gray suit. He was gone.

He closed his eyes and thought he was going to sleep.

Another time and place: Now they were in a hut, away from the village, or perhaps before the horror came. The woman slept next to him; he touched her face. She was only a child though her own baby slept in another part of the hut, on the grass matting. Child, child, he had thought, giving the word two chances to describe both of them.

In the darkness, next to him, in the festering heat of night, he could smell her next to him, he felt her flesh next to his flesh, felt the small, yielding softness of her body.

He was unstrapped from the gurney and lifted onto a bed. . . . Screams. He had been screaming all day and night in the tiger cage, screaming into madness. They knew he was mad then and it amused them. His hair had turned white. When they let him go, he was bent over, crippled by the weeks in the tiger cage.

Cool sheets. He opened his eyes. Water. One of them gave him a glass of water and he reached for it, felt the cool glass in his hands. Rice was there. And others. But this was not a hospital, he thought. Outside the windows, he could see rows of palm trees illuminated by street lamps; a city with wet streets. It was raining again. He thought he heard the distant growl of automobiles. Was he awake? But no, refreshed by the water, he could not fight off the sleep.

Later he realized that it was only a trick of his mind, that the fog of memory was merely lifting and he was watching the tableau played out again. Bombs from airplanes coming in low over the village.

This was a different place, in the mountains. It was very cold. The woman was sick, the child they had saved was dead. A fever only, not the war.

He had scrambled at the sandy earth to bury the child; he had said prayers that were only words to him. No, they told him, do not do this.

They had taken the body of the boy from him, placed it on leaves and grass, and they had burned it.

May his soul and all the souls of the faithful departed through the mercy of God rest in peace. Amen.

They sang their songs against his prayers.

The woman was too sick to pray, to sing, to cry. To see her son turned to ash and float away in clouds of smoke rising from the clearing. They had been kind to them, strangers in their midst. The village headman was a Viet Cong, but that was only politics. The bombs fell all day.

She had been so sad, grown from a child to a woman by her grief. Her baby, her baby, she crooned to herself, turning her face to the wall of the hut.

No, it will be all right, he had said. But her sadness was killing her.

Only the second child brought her back to life. Only the second child gave her a new sense of hope.

A beautiful child.

Tunney's child.

9
New York City

When Devereaux awoke, it was nearly noon, and despite his instructions to the desk and the Do Not Disturb sign on the door, he had been awakened twice by maids who wanted to clean the room. He had told them to go away both times but the subsequent sleep had been that much less restful for his feverish mind and his exhausted body.

Still, there was nothing more to do; he had to get out of the hotel and down to Washington. During the last hour of sleep, he had dreamed of Rita Macklin.

Hanley had given Devereaux a photograph of the reporter from the article on her "adventures with FBI agents" in the *New York Times*. She had guessed correctly that the man named Smith was not really "Smith" and that he had produced phony identification; but she had affiliated the burglars with the wrong federal agency.

He had studied the photograph briefly before falling into bed. He had dreamed of other times at first—one dream piled on another, faster and faster—and then the dreams had died as a deep blackness descended over the vision of his mind. He had been an agent with R Section for fifteen years, since they recruited him out of Columbia University where he had taught Asian politics and history. He had been moved by some sense of idealism then, by both a vague patriotism that had been stirred in him by President Kennedy and a belief that problems begat solutions, that by working at difficulties one solved them.

He had a heavy load of dreams to drag around with him now, from capital to capital, from room to room in anonymous hotels. He had killed twelve men in those fifteen years, each killing (except the first) done without anger, without remorse. Killings that needed to be done for the sake of the mission.

He had to dream those faces of dead men; and dream the other deaths he saw; and dream the agents from the Opposition he had faced in his time; and dream the innocent ones, always the innocent ones, caught in the deadly game without understanding it or escaping it.

Along the way, patriotism had not served him well, nor had any vague sense of idealism or faith in final solutions. Only a stubborn sense of his own survival had pulled him through because he never asked the final question of himself.

For a moment after he awoke, Devereaux lay in the tangle of sheets, listening to the sounds of the city beyond his window. In these rooms, so uniform and clean and bare in their modernity, he always awoke wondering where he was for a moment and then wondering at what stage of the game he was.

Rita Macklin. She had a thin, attractive face, wide green eyes and prominent cheekbones; a generous mouth that was not smiling in the photograph.

Hanley had wanted him to run to Florida ahead of Tunney's release. It was typical of Hanley to throw him headlong into a problem without any idea of how Devereaux was supposed to get out.

He could have argued with Hanley but it would have been pointless. The bureaucrat would have bristled, become stubborn, cited regulations, cited his authority. It would have blown up if he had tried to explain it to Hanley. But Devereaux would do it his own way, nonetheless.

He pushed his feet off the bed and sat for a moment, staring bleakly at the floor and his feet and at the prospect of the day to come, and then he got up and went into the bathroom and turned on the shower.

Twelve minutes later, he was out of the room, his bag in hand.

Two hours after that, he got off the shuttle at National Airport in Washington, D.C. Hanley, he thought with satisfaction, would not have approved.

He stopped at a bank of telephone booths in the waiting room and removed a small code box from his baggage. He eschewed gadgets but when the National Security Agency had come up with this gimmick a year ago—after five years of research, arm-twisting and coordination—he had acknowledged its usefulness. He dialed an 800 number and waited as the relays were completed. Finally, a voice identified herself as an operator; in fact, the voice was made by a machine. He spoke three words and four digits. Another relay was tripped. Then he held the code box up to the receiver and pressed the button. The box emitted a high-pitched whine that triggered still another relay and this time, a real human voice.

Devereaux wanted two telephone numbers. He gave the names to the woman and she gave him the numbers. They were not listed in any telephone book.

Devereaux broke the connection and replaced the black box in his bag.

He dialed Rita Macklin's home telephone number and waited while her phone rang fourteen times. Then he hung up and dialed the second number.

"W.I.S., Kaiser," came the male voice.

"Rita Macklin."

"Who is it?"

"You don't get a name," Devereaux said.

"She isn't here."

"When's she gonna be here?"

"She's out of town for a day or two."

"Okay, I'll call back."

"You leave your name, I can get a message to her."

"I don't even know you." Devereaux hung up. Out of town. It was worth the risk.

He arrived in Bethesda in a rented car in late afternoon and drove past the apartment complex on Old Georgetown Road twice. On the second pass, halfway up the street from the apartments, he saw the Agency car, with two men in it.

He pulled down a side street, parked the car and got out. He crossed the street, went down to a second crossing, and then, abruptly, started across a small open lot that led to a stand of trees. He descended the slight knoll to the concrete parking lot of the apartment building. He went in and punched an elevator button after reading her apartment number on the mailbox: R. Macklin.

The halls were empty; Devereaux thought the Agency had been too frightened by its last encounter with Rita Macklin to have a man in the building itself.

He found the door of her apartment and entered it within seconds. The apartment was empty and still in disarray. Some of the books remained stacked on the floor, not yet replaced on the shelves.

In the little kitchen, reached by pushing through swinging doors trimmed with painted flowers, a jar of peanut butter sat on the table. There was always a jar of peanut butter on the table in the apartments of single people, Devereaux thought. He had gotten into Arthur Bremer's apartment in Milwaukee the night Bremer shot George Wallace. He got there before the FBI, before the police, and among the few scattered, confused furnishings, he remembered seeing a peanut butter jar on the kitchen table.

Milk in the refrigerator; a can of coffee. A jar of instant coffee, nearly empty. White bread. Ginseng tea in a jar.

Devereaux always searched the kitchen first. It was the last place touched by professional burglars, the first place searched by those who wanted information about the person who lived there.

He found what he was looking for beneath the vegetable crisper at the bottom of the refrigerator. He pulled the drawer out and saw a black notebook.

It was a diary with entries beginning on the day Leo Tunney emerged from the jungles of Cambodia and walked into the United States Embassy at Bangkok. It also contained carefully clipped stories from the *New York Times* and the *Washington Post* on the emergence of the priest, as well as Rita's own notes, in a neat, schoolgirl hand.

Had they found it, the pros from the Agency? But no. She wouldn't have left it here if they had.

He took the journal into the living room and sat down.

Her notes filled fourteen pages. All about Tunney, all about the use of religious orders for spying purposes in Asia in the 1950s and 1960s.

Devereaux smiled. Notes about Tunney, and she was now "out of town" for a few days. In Florida, no doubt.

He put the black notebook back in the refrigerator, under the crisper tray.

He went into her bedroom and looked at her belongings. There was a string of pearls—fake. And a locket of Victorian design containing a picture of an older man and woman. On the wall was a sampler in a picture frame. The sampler was quite old, he thought. It said: God So Loved The World.

Her dresser contained clothing, sweet-smelling from soap she had placed in each drawer.

An old-fashioned girl, Devereaux thought, going through her things, trying to draw a psychological frame of her in his mind. She was in Florida, he was certain; she was close to Tunney.

From the first, sitting with Hanley at the sidewalk café, he had decided that Rita Macklin was the key to the complex puzzle of Father Tunney. Why had she been so dogged in her pursuit of the case from the first? How had she known that Tunney was at the Watergate? It hadn't been asked, hadn't been explained.

He found photographs on the dresser.

Mother and father in drab, proud dress, dark clothing, standing in front of a frame house. The photograph was produced by a small shop in Eau Claire, Wisconsin.

Another photograph of a young man in a school football uniform. St. Martin High School.

And a photograph of Rita Macklin with the older man and woman—her parents—along with the same young man, but now wearing a sports jacket. Her brother? Yes, probably.

She had been about sixteen then, he guessed. Her body was thin; she was probably too tall for her age. And her face was extraordinary—bold and shy at once, the eyes open and unafraid, the cheekbones high and prominent, and yet some quality of softness to the features that suggested fragility.

He spent two hours in the apartment and when he emerged at last, the light had faded into a dull twilight of gray and black. He climbed along the ridge of trees to the side street, found his car and pulled back into the traffic buzzing homeward along Old Georgetown Road. The Old Man—Admiral Galloway, the wily old bureaucrat who had guided R Section for a turbulent decade—lived in a posher section along the same meandering highway.

It was time now, he thought.

He could go to Florida and find Tunney.

And wait to use Rita Macklin to make some sense of Tunney's reappearance.

10
Clearwater

Leo Tunney had not touched the meat offered him; in fact, he had quietly shoved away the heavy white china plate as soon as he thought it polite to do so. The meat appeared gross to him, red and oozing with blood and juice and colored by wine sauce, the beef tinged brown at the edges, barely warm at the pink center. Tunney felt ill and ashamed but he could not explain these feelings to the other priest eating at the opposite end of the table. The table was too large; it muted conversation and permitted Leo Tunney to suffer in silence. Finally, the door to the kitchen swung open and the rectory housekeeper approached the table. She removed the plate without a word. She means well, Tunney thought to himself; they all mean well.

At last he asked her for a portion of rice and she stared at him oddly, one hand on her hip, then shrugged and returned to the kitchen. A few minutes later, she produced a bowl of flaky, dry white material that resembled rice but did not taste like it. It was as though it had been boiled over and over until all its taste had been drained. At the same time, she brought a white serving bowl of broth made from the congealed grease of the roast. Tunney tasted the broth, which was too salty, and dug the long, elegant fork into the rice. He drank glass after glass of water during the meal; he had been so thirsty, all the time, during the four days he had been in this place.

Four days he had dreamed and slept and dreamed while his thin body fought the infections inside him with fevers and sudden chills and bone-shaking tremors in the middle of the night. Once, when he awoke in the afternoon on the second day of his fevers, he was certain he was going to die. The certainty had calmed him; many times in the twenty lost years in the jungles of Southeast Asia, he had been presented with the face of death and he thought he had found a way to accept it, with an Oriental bow, with a graceful acknowledgment of inevitability. He mistook his calm certainty of death that afternoon for acceptance until he realized that it was only a frozen fear, a suppressed and barely moving panic inside him, waiting for an end to pain and memories.

He had not died.

This morning he had felt well enough to get out of his sickbed. His first steps had been uncertain, and he had felt dizzy from the effort. He had asked Father McGillicuddy for a cassock and collar. McGillicuddy had scoured the closets for a cassock that would fit his thin frame and finally found an old-fashioned black garment with buttons from collar to toe. Somehow, the cassock seemed to embarrass McGillicuddy.

"There's changes, you know, in the Church," McGillicuddy had said. "During the time you were gone." But Leo Tunney, though ill and thin and disoriented by the events of the last three weeks, was not a fool: He knew there had been changes, but the point none of them had understood—Rice, the men from the Agency, the Ambassador or the embassy staff, and now this fat, self-assured man—was that Tunney had changed as well, in different ways, and that he now needed a touchstone like this black garment to return to an idea of himself that he had lost in Asia.

Leo Tunney thought of this as he stared at the bowl of instant rice in front of him. He did not remember this dining room or the entire rectory building; it had been built as an addition to the original motherhouse of the Order in 1958, the year Leo Tunney had gone to Asia.

"Are you all right, Father?"

McGillicuddy was finished eating and he leaned solicitously over his place setting at the other end of the long table.

"Yes. I'm all right."

"Well, first solid meal and all in the rectory. We'll soon have you fattened up again." McGillicuddy spoke with assurance; he was a fat man himself with a fat man's gestures. He waved a cigar as he spoke, conducting his orchestra of words. The cigar was wrapped in brown leaf and tapered elegantly; he had not lit it yet but waved it as though he were reminding himself and his guest that he would soon be enjoying it. A similiar cigar had been offered to Tunney but the frail missionary had declined.

Cyrus McGillicuddy had a face as pink and clean and cherubic as that of a freshly bathed child. His voice was a pipe organ of tones, always on the verge of a shout or of laughter. In fact, the only part of his appearance that betrayed the image of the jolly cleric was the eyes: cold, baleful, calculating, watching every reaction to his words and gestures, gauging the mood he was creating moment by moment.

"I am sorry. I wanted to eat more." Leo Tunney paused; his voice was still a bit odd to the Western ear, singsong in inflection. "I thought I did. My apologies."

"There's no need to apologize, Father," McGillicuddy boomed suddenly. "Not after everything you've been through, I can imagine how it puts you off your feed. Don't give it a thought. To tell you the truth . . ." He waved the unlit cigar again, dismissing the sentence. "I really like rice as well but that's Mrs. Jones again, all over. I give her a generous budget to manage the kitchen but I swear she buys food of the most wretched kind—convenience foods, fast foods—the other night she served bread stuffing that she had made in a pan on the stove. Served it with ham. Ham and stuffing? My God, I told her, it was an abomination. Now, before Mrs. Jones came to us, we had a real cook. Mrs. Andretti was here for so long—do you remember her from your time before you . . . went to Laos? A grand cook, God rest her soul, she died two years ago, just fell asleep one night and didn't wake up. A good death." In memoriam, McGillicuddy let his cigar lead a silent funeral dirge. "But what a cook," he said then, returning to it. "She was from Boston, you know she knew how to cook. She cooked like an angel, an angel. Mrs. Jones, on the other hand, well, I'm afraid we're all not doing as well as we once did. She's a native of Florida, Father, from the panhandle. Well, there is absolutely no cuisine from this state, nothing at all. And I can tell you, I like most things about the South, Father, I'm a man easily satisfied, I can tell you. But, well, when it comes to cooking, real cooking, well, when these people try to go beyond fried chicken, they're just as lost as children."

At that moment, the object of Father McGillicuddy's scorn entered the room with fresh plates containing wedges of apple pie topped with ice cream.

Mrs. Jones was not young; her thin face was etched with hard lines that suggested she was either a widow or a woman who had never married—not from choice. She put the dishes down before the two men as though she had heard everything Father McGillicuddy had said, and returned to the kitchen through the swinging door without a word.

Leo Tunney stared at the apparition of fruit and ice cream melting into piecrust, at the sauce swimming around the edges of the concoction. He felt sick again. His face was white, his lips were dry. He reached for a glass of water.

"Well," McGillicuddy boomed, slapping the unlit cigar down on the white damask tablecloth. "I must accept surrender when it comes to her skills at desserts." He picked up a clean fork, inspected the prongs for a moment, and then stabbed at the piecrust. "She can make desserts with the best of them, I give credit where credit is due, and I can tell you you should taste her pecan pie, there's nothing like it. It's probably been years since you've had anything like this, eh?"

Leo Tunney did not listen to the words but to the voice rising and falling and interrupting itself with slurps as McGillicuddy shoveled the pie into his mouth. That afternoon, McGillicuddy had insisted that Leo Tunney needed a "little fresh air" and taken him for a drive in his large brown Cadillac. Leo Tunney had permitted everything to be done to him. The cold leather of the interior made him feel an echo of the chills that had alternated with the fevers of the last few days. The air conditioner hummed from the dashboard vents and Father McGillicuddy only turned it down when he noticed Tunney shivering in his cassock, his thin arms folded across his chest. All afternoon, Tunney had endured McGillicuddy's tourist-guide monologue as the car traveled across Clearwater and over the causeway to the island of Clearwater Beach, then down Sand Key to the tip of Treasure Island. Leo Tunney had listened to the voice and not the words and stared out the tinted windows of the automobile at the unfamiliar landscape: palm trees over stucco buildings in endless rows, old men and women shambling along the sidewalks of Clearwater Beach in shorts and loose shirts and wraparound sunglasses. He had not spoken at all.

At two o'clock, McGillicuddy had insisted they stop at a seafood restaurant on Gulf View Boulevard on the beach. Tunney had not felt hungry but when the fish was brought to the table, he had been surprised by a return of his appetite. He had begun to eat the fish with some relish when he noticed that McGillicuddy was staring at him. Then he realized he had been separating the flakes of grouper with his fingers.

"I'm sorry to embarrass you," Leo Tunney had said with the ghost of a smile on his white face. He had looked around but no one was staring at him.

"Nothing, nothing at all, Father, don't give it a second thought," the fat priest had replied. But it was clear that Tunney was expected to pick up a fork.

Why had he found it so difficult to reacquaint himself with the Western tool after those years away? Even when the Agency had confined him to his room, sending meals up, Rice had noticed his difficulty. Yes, of them all, Rice had understood from the beginning. About many things. They had procured chopsticks for him after the first day in the hotel and even ordered his food from the Chinese restaurant down the street.

The brief excursion in the sun, at the restaurant, driving down the rows of motels and hotels and shopping plazas, had exhausted Tunney. He had slept in the late afternoon, after promising to dine with McGillicuddy in the rectory.

"Don't you care for the pie, Father?"

"No. Again, I'm afraid I . . . well, let me apologize. I am not accustomed to so much food."

"But you've hardly eaten, man. We won't get you fat this way." McGillicuddy smiled, holding a piece of fruit and melting ice cream on his fork.

"Once, for a time, from full moon to full moon, I think, we lived on bark and leaves. That was after . . ." Tunney paused, he could not remember the time, perhaps there had been too many times. Perhaps he was still dreaming of it and it had not happened.

"Leaves? God, I know what you must have gone through out there. I was in Morocco myself before I was given charge of the Order, Father. I was in Morocco for many years, in fact. I can tell you a few stories myself."

"Yes."

"Oh, yes, I can. I sometimes think I would like to go back there, to see it. . . . Well, we must serve where we must serve."

"The motherhouse is so empty," Tunney said.

79

"Yes, I'm afraid we have all fallen on bad times. These are bad days for the Church, my friend, bad days. The devil tries us." McGillicuddy shoved the last of the pie into his mouth. "Old Father Clement is with us, of course, but he prefers to sleep in the old student wing. What a queer old man he has become. And Father Malachy is subbing for the pastor at St. Mary's over in Bradenton, the pastor broke his leg, jogging, can you imagine it? And Father Cletus. Well, I've given permission to Clete to live on the beach awhile, I think he's got a lively prospect lined up, for a benefaction, and you know you've got to spend money to make money."

Tunney stared at the cloth of the table, not hearing, his consciousness flooded again with dreams of the past.

"Father? Are you all right?"

Tunney looked up. "Yes. I'm all right." He pushed the dish of pie and ice cream away. "I would like a glass of beer. If you have it? Do you have beer?"

The last thing he thought Tunney would ask for. McGillicuddy brought the beer himself.

It was tasteless, yet another tasteless cousin of the milk and the rice and the other food he had eaten here, but it warmed him. The beer they had made in the mountains was different, harsh and strong and smelling like bread. This was not as good but it was good enough.

The Agency had been interested in what he had done that winter in the mountains and he had not told them. He had told them only the things he wanted them to hear. He had wanted Rice to assume he was an idiot and to leave him alone; he did not want to deal anymore with their secrets or with thoughts of war. He wanted to speak only of himself, to himself, to understand at last—

"That's put color in your cheeks," McGillicuddy said, finishing his dessert and reaching for the cigar. "Now, Father, I don't want to rush you, you take all the time you need, but there was a fellow here today from the *St. Petersburg Times,* the word is out that you're down here and let me tell you, you are something of a celebrity."

Tunney stared at him in silence.

McGillicuddy waved the cigar after lighting it, creating a wispy brown cloud in front of him. "I sure would like to set something up, sometime. Something dignified, that would let the people around here know we're still here. You can't imagine the controversy we've had in this region about religion. This outfit calls itself the Church of Scientology, they came down here and set themselves up in Clearwater to practically take the town over, there was a lot of scandal about it and you know who pays, it's the legitimate churches that pay for it. Talk about taking over the city, that's what they said in the papers, making this a church-state. . . ."

Tunney listened but did not hear more than sounds. This had happened in the days before, during the Agency interrogation when he was still in confinement. He had suddenly departed from the present, the words had become as garbled and meaningless as the background sounds in the jungle.

"Another reporter came by yesterday but I shooed her off. You remember Rita Macklin, the woman who took your picture up in the Watergate?"

McGillicuddy's tone of voice had changed and Tunney looked up. The fat face was still cherubic, pink and clean, smiling. But something had appeared in the priest's eyes, and his voice reflected it.

I must be careful now, Leo Tunney thought.

"Said she wanted to do something really good, really in depth, not just a smash-and-grab—you should hear the phrases they use—she said they wanted to do something really good with you. So I called up this editor of hers and you know what he said?"

Tunney waited. He remembered the woman surprising them, remembered her small, delicate face with fine features reminiscent of a figurine in a temple of Buddha, full of color and come to life.

"Well, I'll tell you. His name is Kaiser. Yes, he runs a small syndicate up there. I talked to him. I checked up on him. This girl is acting on her own, she's not even part of that agency anymore. What do you think?"

The words seemed gibberish again, his attention faded. And then Tunney remembered what he wanted to ask.

"Father. I would like paper, please."

"The papers? We get the *Times* delivered and in the morning—"

"The newspapers? No. I would like to write. I would like—well, Father, let me make this confidential. I would like to write down some things, matters."

"What you were doing in the jungle," McGillicuddy said. The cigar had stopped waving. The face, still smiling, was set and intent, the eyes shrewd.

"Perhaps. But not that. I would like—"

Cyrus McGillicuddy saw the body at the other end of the table becoming smaller, seeming to shrink into the white cloth, retreating from the brink of confidence-giving. He moved the cigar in his hand again. "No, I understand completely. I have just the thing for you. We have journal books in the office; let me get you one. A nice blank book in red leather. And pens. Would you prefer a fountain pen or a ballpoint? We have felt tips now, didn't have felt tips when you . . . when you left the States. A lot of things have changed."

"Yes, if you would be kind enough—"

"I understand, I understand. We can go to the office after we've finished dinner; I'd like to show you our little church as well—"

"I would like to . . . offer Mass, if I—"

"Yes, yes, I thought you would. We have the facility. Father Clement is on loan in the mornings to St. Martin's up in New Port Richey, you know how it is, we just don't have the priests to go around, but if you'd like to offer Mass in the chapel, well, I think when you see it it'll knock your eye out. And Father? If you want to confess, I would—"

Tunney shook his head. Too quickly. The eyes of the Father Superior caught the lie in the quickness of the rejection. "No, I have taken care of that. Before. But—"

"Yes, I understand, Leo—can I call you that?"

Leo. The name was so unfamiliar to him; it had not been used for twenty years and the generation in the jungle had erased it from his memory. They had called him Li. Half a lifetime. Leo. White rice without taste, forks, and pale beer.

"The woman? They struck her?"

For a moment, McGillicuddy seemed confused. "Oh, you mean—yes, this Macklin woman. She followed up on it, she is persistent. She got you the release from the Agency, if you ask me. They were embarrassed to hold you any longer. A spunky girl. Got on TV, in the papers, did you see it?"

"I didn't know. I asked, but they wouldn't tell me."

"I understand," McGillicuddy said. "It must be terribly confusing."

"All of it," Tunney agreed, weakening for a moment, allowing himself to be soothed by Cyrus McGillicuddy's voice.

"So much has happened in those years, since you left here. We've had a war since then, I can't believe it as soon as I say it—"

"I believe it. I saw it."

"And you didn't come out."

Silence. There was nothing to say to him, nothing to explain.

After a while, McGillicuddy took him to the darkened office and found a journal book, bound as promised, with numbered pages. The priest handed him three pens.

"We keep the chapel locked at night, you can't be too careful," McGillicuddy said, leading him across an open portico to the little church. The day had been soft, the heat lush like the heat of the jungle. And now, at night, the heat lingered with just a trace of water on the breeze blowing up from the Caribbean.

McGillicuddy turned on a small group of lights at the door that illuminated the altar in the middle of the room. "This was built in 1963, after Vatican Two, we followed all the dictates."

"I don't understand," said Leo Tunney, not for the first time.

"No. You will though. There's a lot to learn."

Without a word, Tunney shuffled slowly up the aisle to the altar railing and knelt down on his thin knees, sinking into the vinyl kneeling cushion. He blessed himself. With some reluctance, Father McGillicuddy followed and stood behind him.

The chapel was stark. The marble altar was plain except for the small golden tabernacle in the center flanked by two elaborate candlesticks. The front of the altar was decorated in ceramic tiles that formed the image of a lamb, a cross and a fish.

McGillicuddy stared at the altar and at the golden crucifix hanging by a golden chain above it. All had been built in the glory days of the Order when the halls were filled with young men fresh from their seminaries, awaiting instructions and assignments to the missions of the Order that were marked in red on a map of the world in the central refectory hall. There was an exciting international air to the place then; good days and good years, McGillicuddy thought as he stared at the altar. And then decline, the investigation by the Congregation for the Protection of the Faith, the cutoff of funds from the Agency, the general falloff in numbers of clergy entering the service of the Church.

Tunney's eyes were closed, his hands clasped.

McGillicuddy looked down at the frail old man. A journal with a red leather cover. And pens.

He thought again of Rita Macklin at the door yesterday.

McGillicuddy turned at last, leaving Tunney alone in the half-darkness of the church. He walked quickly to the door, dipped his hand in the holy water font, and made the Sign of the Cross as he left the church. He crossed the open portico to the main hall of the rectory.

Mrs. Jones met him at the door.

His face flushed with annoyance; he had a thought that he wanted to pursue and Mrs. Jones was a perpetual distraction with her flat southern accent and pinched widow's face and dry manner.

"What is it?"

"A fella," she said. "Says he come down from Rome."

"Rome? Rome what, Mrs. Jones? Georgia?"

"Rome." Mrs. Jones was a Baptist and her assumption of the housekeeper post had been accompanied by suspicion on both sides.

Yes, McGillicuddy thought. Perhaps he had been expecting this as well. The Agency, even Rome. But perhaps he could outsmart them all, even that old priest praying in the chapel.

When he opened the door of the middle parlor where Mrs. Jones had shown the visitor, McGillicuddy was not surprised by his youth or by his lack of clerical garb.

The young man turned from the window that opened on a garden beyond the walls of the rectory. He was tall and lean and muscular, with a flat expression on his face.

"I'm the Father Superior," began McGillicuddy, extending his hand.

The young man only stood and stared at him for a moment and McGillicuddy let the hand fall to his side.

"Yes," the young man said. "I know. I've come to see Leo Tunney."

"Well, who might you be?" McGillicuddy said with a note of

joviality that was all the more false for its faint tinge of annoyance.

"Martin Foley."

"And you're from Rome?"

"Yes."

"Well, I'm being protective just now of our Father Tunney, he's not been well, he's—"

"This is not a request."

"It isn't? It isn't?" He knew his voice was rising but he couldn't seem to help it. "And just who the hell are you then?"

"From the Congregation, McGillicuddy. I think you're aware of us."

And the priest stood perfectly still then, the anger fading from his face with the draining color. "Yes," he said at last, the voice suddenly old. "Yes. He's in the chapel now, praying."

"We'll wait for him then," Martin Foley said, smiling thinly.

"Yes," McGillicuddy agreed. His voice was limp. "Yes. I suppose I should have expected someone . . . someone from—"

"From Rome? But that was inevitable, wasn't it?"

"But what does the Congregation—"

"In time, Father. Everything will be revealed."

But the old priest knew that revelation was the last thing on Foley's mind.

11
Sand Key

Dawn came but there was still no real morning light, only the thin line of red color in the east defining the blackness of the rest of the sky. A smell of rain came on the wind blowing steadily from the Gulf side of the island.

Rita Macklin pounded along down Gulf View Boulevard, the main road of the island that formed Clearwater Beach. Her yellow running shoes pushed her relentlessly forward through the gauntlet of sleeping, shuttered hotels along the beach and past a solitary car near the causeway. When she reached the bridge at the south end of Clearwater Beach island, she decided to keep on, despite the threat of rain in the air. Her head still was not clear, she still did not know what to do. The two days she had been in Florida had been wasted.

As she ran, her red hair fell free on her shoulders and her long arms fell into an easy rhythm across her belly. She wore white tennis shorts and an old blue sweatshirt from the University of Wisconsin. A line of sweat glistened on her pale forehead and her cheeks were flushed. Her green eyes were as clear and bright as a deep pool found in sunlight, in a woods.

Two days ago.

She had driven south all that night after the confrontation with Kaiser. It had been so unexpected and so angry that it lingered in her like a poison that would not be flushed away.

There really had been no point in driving all night but rage had demanded it; she had pushed herself because she felt the need to punish herself after the angry words with Kaiser, to push beyond physical and mental limits. The argument had made her feel guilty and angry by turns; first it was Kaiser's fault and then it was hers. It was a quarrel she had never thought she would have with the middle-aged man who had been her boss for nearly three years and had been more than that: a friend, unexpectedly, and a confidant, finally, and someone she had come to care for every much. All of it had been blown away with the angry words of that afternoon.

She had needed money and cashed a large check on her small account at the grocery on the corner and then went home, put together a few clothes in an old bag, threw the bag in the back seat of the car, and just took off, south on Interstate 81 through the gently rolling valley of the Shenandoah. All night she had driven, through the Tennessee mountains, down and down the map toward Florida. In the mountains, the rage and guilt had been replaced by a numbing fear as she drove through rain and fog, the blackness of the mountains looming against the blackness of the moonless sky. For long hours, she had driven in silence, a silence more profound for the steady humming of the tires on the pavements and the whoosh of a passing semitrailer, its rig of lights winking like the lights of a ship.

She played back the quarrel in her mind and then, for long periods, thought of nothing at all; and then, just as the silence seemed to keep her company, she would need the sound of voices again to wake her to the rest of the world. Turning on the car radio, she punched buttons back and forth, the red needle of the dial flying across the numbers, searching a thousand miles of country for night sounds. Country music came clearly from a powerful station in Chicago; another turn of the dial and a rat-a-tat diet of news and non-news came from another clear channel station in New York. At last, in the hills of eastern Tennessee, she settled on a mail-order preacher coming from somewhere in east Texas, the voice cracker-rough, selling God and crucifixes that glowed in the dark and dashboard-mounted Jesuses "for those long nights on the road for you truckers when you want to be thinking on Him who rides along in the seat next to you."

Gospel music, hymns, a cowboy's lament and the sound of urban disco and then, as the car followed the elegant serpentine highway around the sleeping city of Chattanooga at the Georgia-Tennessee line, a small radio station bravely puffed out the final movement of Beethoven's Ninth Symphony.

Tiredness seeped into her back muscles, burning across her shoulders. She sat up straight, slumped down, leaned against the door, rested her arm across the back of the front seat; she took off her shoes and then her socks, pushing the accelerator barefoot to keep her awake. In all the dark, empty night's drive, she was never afraid except at dawn, in north Georgia, when a truck driver at a gas station suggested they share his cab for a while. Then she thought of it as it really was: Her quarrel with Kaiser had cut her adrift from the world of Washington journalism toward which she had directed her whole life. She was just someone on the road in Georgia now, pursuing an idea.

But she had to follow Tunney.

Kaiser could not understand that and as the quarrel began and built, she could not explain it to him.

"Little Rita," he had said. "This is a story for the *Times,* for reporters who have the leisure of weeks and months to beat an assignment to death. We're a wire service, my dear; the old in-and-out." And he had grinned in what he thought was a lascivious way but she had been too enmeshed in the quarrel by that time to let him deflect her.

"I have to go," she said.

"Personal? Is that it, Rita? Is this a personal mission of yours? Well, I can't afford it—"

"You owe me vacation—"

"Not now. I can't afford your absence in any case."

"Well." And there it had been. "That's too goddam bad."

She had to go and Kaiser should have understood it, should have understood that her stubbornness rested on the rock of a matter that went back very far. Leo Tunney. When she had read the first dispatch from UPI from Thailand, the name had drawn her. It had to do with Tommy, it had to do with her own past and sense of childhood; it had to do with Tommy's letters to her. It had to do with her brother Tommy's death.

But how could she explain that to Kaiser?

Finally, there was nothing more to say. He had turned his back on her in the narrow, dirty office on the ninth floor of the National Press Building. He had been so angry, so unreasonable that she could not speak to him further. There was nothing to do but leave; nothing to do but continue the pursuit of Tunney and of the strands of her own past.

And of Tommy's letters.

Rita thought of the confrontation now as she jogged steadily across the steel bridge in Clearwater Beach. The bridge soared steeply over the ship's channel cut into the shallow waters of the Gulf; the channel gave harbor access to the shark hunters and fishing boats and pleasure craft moored there, near the causeway. She felt the rain begin, a slow and misting rain like an afterthought; she did not turn back. The rain felt cool on her skin and it refreshed her. At the far end of the bridge, the tollkeeper in his booth stared at her but she ignored him and ran on, down the main highway of Sand Key, the next island in the little chain.

The road glistened with its mix of oil and rain. There were no cars, no sounds; all the low houses were dark. She tried to think of Tommy again. She had conjured up his image in memory dozens of times since she learned that Leo Tunney had come out of the Cambodia jungle two weeks before. Always, oddly, the image was not of

Tommy himself because she could scarcely remember him anymore as he had been, flesh and blood, full of voice, touch, laughter; it was always a black-and-white Tommy in a photograph, kept on the night table next to her bed. That was all right too, she thought; both Tommys were the same man, both were real.

And then she thought of what she would do.

She made a slow, jogging half-circle in the roadway and started back down the highway that ran the length of this overdeveloped semiresidential island in the Gulf. Ahead of her—she found it hard to believe she had run so far—were the twinkling lights of the bridge and the tollbooth.

Morning was making headway in the east. All around her, the low buildings, the hotels, the cars parked in the driveways, were taking on a dingy gray cast, becoming more distinct in the gloomy light. The red eastern sky was turning gray as well as the clouds from the Gulf moved east and overwhelmed the sun. The rain came down harder.

"How'ya doin', honey?" the tollkeeper asked as she jogged past the booth, but she did not wave back. She had been on her own for seven years and she was city-wary; she was twenty-eight years old, she had learned all the rules of a woman alone on a public street: Never wave back, never respond, never become angry, never become involved, never go too near, never seem more than a passing object. When she ran in Washington, she thought of herself as invisible, jogging along the winding streets in Bethesda, unseen by all. In a way, by thinking of herself as invisible, she became invisible.

At the bottom of the bridge, back on Clearwater Beach, she saw the car again and saw now that it was waiting for her. There was nothing she could do.

She pushed herself forward, a little faster, and a pain started in her side and filled the right side of her rib cage. She ran too fast but the pain kept up with her.

No headlights. The windshield wipers whumped, whumped slowly across the streaky glass. She could not see the driver clearly.

Rita turned into the main road, lined with high-rise hotels along the beach and low-rise hotels across the street.

The gray car growled into life and slowly began to trail her.

She was aware of it, she could even see it behind her, but she would not turn and look at it. Maybe it was just a kid, getting his kicks following a running woman; maybe it was nothing that she feared.

Her feet slapped steadily along the wet pavement. A mile to her hotel, a cheap place snug in the main shopping district of the Beach, down from the old fishing pier that jutted into the water.

At the last hotel, she veered sharply and started to run along the beach. At least the car could not follow her on the sand.

She half turned as she reached the waterline and saw the car, wipers moving slowly back and forth, sitting sadly at the far end of the parking lot. Florida plates, she thought. Rental car.

Professional paranoia, Kaiser would say.

Goddam Kaiser. He couldn't understand it. About her. About why she had to talk to Tunney. About Tommy as he had been, a real person, not just a photograph and a memory cut into her like a brand.

Gray, gloomy clouds held down the sky. Already, at dawn, a couple of old men with metal detectors were on the white beach, moving the detectors back and forth across the sand, looking for forgotten change or watches or rings. The gulls on the beach, with their malevolent, calm eyes, watched her pass. Above, on the breeze, they careened around her in slow dives and circles, making no sounds, watching her and the old men and the sand and the sleeping hotels at the edge of the water.

The pain in her side eased as it always did and she ran under the pilings of the fishing pier. Under the steel platform, on the beach, in a green duck sleeping bag, a boy and girl cuddled for warmth against the morning chill. She slowed down as she crossed the sand toward her hotel and was walking, catching her breath, when she reached the door. She stood for a moment on the beach and looked down the narrow street that ran perpendicular to the expanse of sand. The gray car turned into the block and waited at the end of the street, near the empty cabstand. Rita's eyes narrowed. She repeated to herself the numbers and letters on the orange-and-white Florida plates.

No sounds. The wipers on the gray car continued to work slowly back and forth. She could see the outline of the driver but not his features.

Her chin hardened and she realized she was angry again, the way she had been angry at last in her own apartment in Bethesda, after the government agents had left. *Wait, Rita; do nothing.*

Slowly, with a winking turn signal, the car backed into the main road and then swung around and started down the street, disappearing behind the bulk of the new Holiday Inn.

Rita stared at the empty street and felt cold; it was probably the rain next to her skin, she thought. The blue college sweatshirt clung heavily to her slender body. She realized slowly that she was soaked.

A man in a gray car, watching her.

Because of Tunney? Or just some moron, a kid, a punk, a lonely man with bad thoughts following a girl running alone down a morning beach?

Kaiser. If only she could tell Kaiser all this she would not feel so alone. But that was all past now and there was only Leo Tunney to make sense of her movements, to make the quarrel with Kaiser at least have some purpose.

She would get to him somehow. She couldn't let him remain silent.

He had to tell her the truth; that was all that mattered.

II
MIRACLES

12
Martin Foley

It was not what anyone expected, certainly not Martin Foley.

Six of them were waiting when Father McGillicuddy unlocked the doors of the little church just after seven in the morning. Usually, he said the daily Mass for the straggle of faithful who attended each morning; there were never more than three or four. Six people was an unusually large number and everything that followed was also unusual.

He had laid out the clothing of the Mass for Father Tunney. Alb, white, and chasuble, red: the color of blood and of martyrs in the elaborate symbolism of the Church. The old priest threw the alb over his thin shoulders and pulled it down, unmindful of how ludicrously large it was on his frame. He was praying to himself as he dressed, his eyes open yet turned inward.

McGillicuddy had watched him from the door of the sacristy. He did not want to be with Martin Foley just now; he had risen early and said prayers and eaten a quick breakfast in the yellow kitchen. He wanted to stay away from Foley for as long as he could, especially after the cold, methodical interview with him last night.

Leo Tunney mumbled Latin words. He pulled the white rope

tight around his waist. It was the cincture, the reminder to priests of the rope that bound Christ on his last struggle to Golgotha.

Like the alb, the red chasuble was too large and hung in elegant folds.

"I'm sorry about this, we have smaller garments but they're in mothballs, I'm afraid, I told you that most of the other fellows are on loan to the parishes and . . ." He let his voice trail; it was all so hopeless. When Tunney had arrived at the motherhouse he had seen it as a good sign, that better days were coming to the Order. But now Martin Foley from Rome had been most emphatic about keeping the presence of Tunney a loose secret. No publicity, no interviews with the local press, no holy freak show. Holy freak show. McGillicuddy felt mortified by the words of warning from the younger man; as though he, McGillicuddy, could be capable of transforming the suffering of this man into profit. It was just that the Order . . . for the good of the Order . . . that Father Tunney's life could be an example to—

"Nothing," Martin Foley had said, like a judge. "Not a word."

"I'm ready now, Father," Leo Tunney said gently. "Sometimes, in the jungle, when I thought of this moment, it was almost too much to bear."

"But you offered Mass in the—"

"No. Not for a long time, Father." The blue eyes looked with infinite sadness at the fat priest. "I remembered all the prayers, I said them to myself. I offered the Mass but no one was there. And then, for a long time, I was not worthy."

"None of us is worthy, Father."

"No. But few of us know it, know it so deeply that we are ashamed of our sins."

"Father." McGillicuddy felt moved in that moment and the feeling was uncomfortable to him. He was a man of the world in his way and it was so obvious that Tunney had left that world long ago. He was like a child with a face of suffering, gaunt and gray, his blue eyes piercing McGillicuddy like lasers.

"I'm sorry," Tunney apologized again, half-bowing in that Oriental manner of artificial grace.

McGillicuddy nodded, started to speak, and thought of nothing to say. He left the sacristy and entered the church, kneeling heavily in the second pew on the right.

So it began, as none of them expected it.

Tunney entered the sanctuary and went to the altar and placed the chalice on the white cloth and came down the steps and stood facing the altar.

The old woman who always came to Mass began it; they could hear her tears after the first few words. They were happy tears and the sobs were not so loud but they could all hear them and they understood why she wept.

Mrs. Guidotti, Father McGillicuddy thought. A retired widow and the gossip of the neighborhood.

She would tell everyone what had happened in the chapel with the new priest, an old man with white hair and blue eyes.

Father Tunney blessed himself at the foot of the altar and then said:

"In Nomine Patris, et Filii, et Spiritus Sancti. Amen. Introibo ad altare Dei. Ad Deum qui laetificat juventutem meam. Judica me, Deus, et discerne causam meam de gente non sancta: ab homine iniquo, et doloso erue me. Quia tu es, Deus, fortitudo mea: quare me repulisti, et quare tristis incedo, dum affligit me inimicus?"

In the back of the church, Father Martin Foley stood, his mouth open, a frown slowly clouding his face. Outside, the gloomy morning rain continued to fall, no longer soft but hard as winter.

McGillicuddy turned, saw Foley, and he could not help smiling when he heard the sobs from the old woman. The Tridentine Mass. The forbidden Latin Mass. None of them had thought of it but it was all that Tunney knew. He had been gone so long that he did not know everything had changed, that the Latin Mass was banned. . . .

A man in a green twill work shirt and green trousers picked up the words after the first few minutes. He was a middle-aged landscape gardener with a sun-blackened face who lived alone with his aged mother. He remembered the words and his voice joined the priest's:

"Confiteor Deo omnipotenti, beatae Mariae semper Virgini, beato Michaeli archangelo, beato Joanni Baptistae, sanctis apostolis Petro et Paulo . . ."

McGillicuddy found himself saying the words of the Confiteor aloud as well. He knew this would not please Martin Foley.

The old priest had been in the jungle for twenty-one years. All the reforms of Vatican II, all the changes in liturgy in the Roman

97

Church over the two decades had washed over the world without touching him. And the intense nostalgia for the old Mass had moved an elderly woman to tears and a middle-aged gardener to the recitation of prayers buried in his subconscious for twenty years.

Leo Tunney again made the Sign of the Cross, asking for pardon and absolution in words of a dead language. Slowly, with medieval grace, the old Mass proceeded at the stark, modern altar and Tunney spoke the words like a man in a trance, caught in the past, unseeing in the present.

At the moment of Communion, the congregation rose and came forward, kneeling at the rail in the old-fashioned way, holding their mouths open and their tongues extended.

McGillicuddy had thought himself incapable of being so moved. With the others, he rose and joined the congregation at the railing; he knelt and waited, with eyes closed, for the Communion wafer.

Only Foley still held back, standing in the rear of the chapel, a frown creasing his broad features. He was incapable of action.

Leo Tunney, his eyes shining with tears and his thin hands trembling, came down the three steps from the altar and went to the old woman at the railing. He picked the wafer out of the chalice, held it and said, *"Corpus Domini nostri Jesu Christi custodiat animam tuam in vitam aeternam. Amen."*

He placed the wafer on her tongue and went to the next and the next, saying the holy words, placing a wafer on each tongue.

McGillicuddy, receiving the host, felt as though he were still a child, still that little boy from Boston he had been so long ago, when the air was perfumed with incense and the expectation of great things about to happen. A child lost in the mysteries of the Faith, his eyes closed to the world, open to thoughts of God, heaven, hell and death, love and sacrifice, crucifixion and resurrection.

McGillicuddy felt awed, as though it were miracle enough that he could touch—briefly—the soul of himself as he had been, fifty years before.

When he turned from the Communion railing, he saw that Foley was gone from the door.

Slowly, the Mass proceeded like a dream to McGillicuddy and to the rest of them. After the Last Gospel and the admonition to leave, when the Mass was ended, after Tunney had disappeared through the door to the sacristy, the congregation lingered, unwilling to break the spell.

McGillicuddy went through the second door to the sacristy and found Leo Tunney standing at the chest of drawers, leaning on it, his face pale beneath the patina of sunburn.

"Father? What's wrong?"

"I am tired," Leo Tunney said slowly. "I was so . . . moved. Because of them."

"They haven't heard a Mass such as that for a long time."

Tunney looked up, puzzled.

McGillicuddy, still moved, came to the white-haired priest who already looked smaller in the voluminous folds of the chasuble and alb. "Dear Father," he began, touching his hand.

Tunney stared at him.

"You wouldn't understand now. Everything that has happened, all the changes. . . . Father Foley will want to speak to you, no doubt."

Still Tunney stared because McGillicuddy was smiling. "I'm sorry, I shouldn't say it. No, it won't do at all. But it was glorious, just glorious. To hear and speak those words again—"

"What? What are you saying, Father?"

"—like a miracle, in a small way. Yes, precisely, in fact, because that is what it was."

Mrs. Jones stood in the kitchen door and watched the old priest eat. She was beginning to understand him. He had been sick is all, she had told her neighbor, Mrs. Custis. In the jungle or some such but sick and his stomach needed gentling, is all, she had said. So she made two soft eggs this morning and corn bread and he seemed able to eat it all. She'd watch over his diet in the future. All of a sudden, she had told Mrs. Custis, the house was filling up again and now there was this young fellow from Rome, in Italy, and he spoke with a real accent. These Catholics were always coming and going, all of it pretty mysterious if you asked her. Mrs. Custis said that she knew a Catholic once and they had ten kids; nice kids but ten kids is a lot of kids, even for Catholics.

"Everything all right, then?"

Leo Tunney looked up as though she were an apparition and

then his face seemed to remember something—his eyes stared away, he worked his lips—he nodded to her and tried a smile. "Yes, this is fine. This is fine, Mrs. . . ."

"Mrs. Jones," she said.

"Mrs. Jones. Yes, thank you for your trouble."

"Wasn't no trouble to do for you, that's what I'm paid to do, you just speak up and holler when there's something you want. You were sick, is that it?"

"Yes. Sick. For a time. And so many things have changed—"

"You come from some jungle I heard Father McGillicuddy say?"

"Yes. Thailand."

"Thailand." She rested her hands on her apron. "Mrs. Custis lives over the way, that's my neighbor lady, she has a boy was in Thailand or one of those places, I think. About ten years ago, it was in the war?" She had the habit of making statements sound like questions by ending them with a rising tone. "That boy come home full of hell and fire, if you will excuse me saying that, Reverend. Hell and fire and couldn't settle him down at all, it was a shame."

"I'm sorry," he said as though she had told him of a death.

"Terrible shame."

" A waste," he said. "All to no point."

"Well, I suppose he had to go when he had to go, you couldn't have told him anything anyway. His daddy was in Korea, seems that there's always something."

"Yes," said Tunney, who placed his fork at the side of his plate. The yellow stains on the plate were all that was left of the eggs, along with the yellow crumbs of the corn bread.

"I was saying to Mrs. Custis just yesterday, I was saying to her—"

Martin Foley entered the kitchen.

Mrs. Jones darted a quick, suspicious glance at him. A handsome young man, she had told Mrs. Custis, but there was a cast to him. Cast to his eye? asked Mrs. Custis. No, a cast to him, as though something just weren't quite right, about his color or the way he looked at you. A cast to him.

"Father Tunney? If you're quite finished then?"

"Yes. Yes, I'm finished." He said it like a man called to an unpleasant task. He looked down at the empty plate and then at Mrs.

Jones who still stood in the doorway, frowning slightly at the intrusion. "That was very good."

"No meat," she said. "You don't want no meat yet until we get that stomach put back together, if you'll excuse me saying so. Meat is for a healthy man. Get you some broth I make special for my church, just the thing for you."

"Good," he said, smiling in the way of a stranger who intrudes too much. "Good. Thank you." He rose and looked at Foley who was the same height but fifty pounds heavier. "When you're ready, Father Foley."

Foley led the white-haired priest to the middle reception room, the room where he had waited for Father McGillicuddy on his arrival from Rome.

Tunney sat down in a straight chair with a velvet cushion; Foley sat behind a small desk and stared across at Tunney.

"You said you were too tired last night to talk. How do you feel this morning?"

"Better. Or the same, really, but I have energy in the morning."

"Good. I wanted to ask you . . ."

"Yes?"

"Well, we can come back to it. How aware are you of the changes that have occurred since you . . . disappeared?" He was choosing words carefully, the training in diplomacy combining with his natural caution to create an even greater hesitancy.

"Not at all," said Tunney. "No, that's not so. I knew about the war. Obviously. I knew about the death of President Kennedy. Vaguely, I was aware of matters. Protests here and such. But it was always difficult to know what was true and what was propaganda."

"Ah, true, true," Foley said, making a cathedral of his fingers, looking at them as though they were the most interesting thing in the world. "And you were aware of the Church? Of changes here in the Church?"

"Changes? What changes?"

"At Mass this morning."

Tunney stared at him, his eyes faintly quizzical.

"Well, we can come back to that in time." Foley paused again, staring at his hands. If he began by insisting on the strictures against performing the old Mass, perhaps it would unhinge the old man. He

101

had to proceed carefully; the correct forms of ritual could wait, along with the letter of canon law.

The two priests sat apart in the oak-paneled room, replete with glass and pecan cases full of books, each waiting for the other to speak. On a buffet of maplewood, a Sessions mantel clock ticked loudly; outside, the faint hum of the city brushed lightly against the windows. The sun had returned but the streets were still damp from the morning rain.

"Leo Tunney," the young man began.

Tunney did not acknowledge the voice. He waited because he knew what it was to be interrogated. He knew the tricks of the inquisitor. Rice, from the Agency, had been his friend and Maurice had acted the role of his enemy. And before them, so long ago, there had been Van Thieu who broke his fingers, one each morning, for ten days. Ten broken fingers that took half a year to heal, the hands swollen with pain, the agony preventing sleep or thought or any sanctuary until the pain could not be endured and the body slipped from consciousness. Then, in the tiger cages they had used, he was crammed and left alone, living in his own filth and excrement, bent nearly double by the boxlike cages until the fire in the muscles of his back and buttocks and legs burned night and day, until he longed for the inquisitors' visits and for the tricks of the questions as relief from the pain and despair of the cages. That was when he had finally broken, the salve of tears flooding over his wounds, begging for their kindness and forgiveness, crawling to Van Thieu across the broken ground, his legs hanging uselessly from the trunk of his tortured body. That was when he had gone mad, the final mercy of God.

"For ten days, Father," Foley continued slowly, "the agents of the Central Intelligence Agency kept you in confinement."

Tunney thought of the cages still and his body began to bend and shrivel as he sat in the chair across from the young priest.

"They obviously sought to learn many things from you."

"I suppose . . ." Tunney hesitated, saw his healed and gnarled hands beginning to tremble in his lap. He must control himself now, he thought. He must not remember. "I suppose they did. I don't know what they wanted."

"You must have told them—"

"I told them everything."

Foley looked up from the tent of his fingers, stared across at the old priest.

"And what is everything?"

"Nothing. Nothing at all. They wanted to know something beyond what I told them. I don't know what it is. But they didn't seem satisfied with me."

"Then why did they let you go?" The tent of fingers began to move again, tapping one against the other. "Why did they let you come here?"

Tunney stared at him, through him. They both felt the silence of the room envelop them. "I don't know."

"What did they want to know?"

"I don't know."

Foley let his fingers drop. He wore a sports shirt today, a silken Italian weave, and dark trousers. His face, like Tunney's, was dark with sun but Tunney looked vaguely pale despite the tan. "Father? Last night I told you that I was an emissary from the Vatican, from the Congregation for the Protection of the Faith. You didn't answer me then. Are you aware of who we are?" Foley could not eradicate the faintly pompous tone in the last words.

Tunney kept silent. The clock on the shelf struck ten unexpectedly, ringing the notes sharply one after another, and then the silence resumed.

"Father Tunney?"

"Spies," he said.

Foley stared at him.

"Spies for the Pope. Am I right?"

"We are sent to gather intelligence for the Pontiff, if that's what you mean."

Tunney smiled. "Spies. Intelligence agents. Field men. Extra men. Second men. The whole sorry nomenclature. Section chiefs. Network masters. Runners and couriers. Box men and station masters, station chiefs and station keepers. All those words."

Foley could not keep astonishment from his face.

"Yes. I know. I'm not an idiot, Father Foley. I knew all those terms, all those names. I knew what I was. I thought I knew what I was." The last was said softly, as though it were not intended to be heard.

"What are you?"

"A man. Like you. Perhaps a greater sinner."

"What happened?"

"When? What do you want to know?"

Tunney smiled, a slow, sad smile, like a child's smile when the hurt has passed.

They listened to the clock ticking, to the hum of the city beyond the window.

"Everything," Tunney said at last. "There is so much to know, so many who want to know it. What is everything?"

"This is not a game. You were an American spy."

"In Asia? In Laos, do you mean? Of course I was. I knew what I was." The words came harshly now though the voice was still weak. "I know what I am now."

"What did they want you to tell them?"

"Everything. Just as you want everything."

"What did you tell them?"

"Nothing. In the end, it was nothing."

Martin Foley stared at him. He had thought it would be easy after meeting Tunney the night before. The priest was old and weak and a little addled. His movements were shaky, he seemed near collapse. Was that from the CIA interrogation? Or just his general condition? Had the CIA been able to break him down the first day or the second? What had they learned that the Vatican should know about? Ludovico had given him secret instructions at the last moment, revealed the urgency of all that had to do with Father Leo Tunney. When he had met Leo Tunney last night, Foley was sure it was too late, that Tunney had already collapsed and told everything to the Americans.

He saw now how tough the old priest had become. He had an Oriental fragility that was only a paper mask over iron.

"You must tell us everything."

"I want to be left alone. To pray and be solitary. To say Mass and pray and not speak." The words were bleak.

"You must tell us. We are the Church."

"You are spies, Father Foley, no less or more than other spies."

"Father Tunney, are you still a servant of God?"

"An appeal to faith," Father Tunney said, perfectly still, the voice masking steel. "Yes. I would still be a servant of God if He would let me."

"You are a priest."

"Yes. That too. As well. And I have been other things."

"Why would the Americans want to keep you under observation?"

"Because I had belonged to them as well. Servant of God, servant of man." Tunney rose slowly, his body seeming to bend under the slight weight of his thin flesh. He walked across the rich patterned carpet to the broad window and looked out at the empty side street, at the palm trees, at the little stucco homes in a row. "Do you know the dying words of Cardinal Wolsey? From Shakespeare? Servant of the King and Cardinal of the Church and abandoned by both at the end." Tunney turned from the window: " 'Had I but served my God with half the zeal I served my King, he would not in mine age have left me naked to mine enemies.' "

Foley let his voice fall flat in the silence. "That is poetry, Father. This is reality we are dealing with. You are a sick man and you have decided, for your own reasons, to return to the world. I am speaking not for myself but for the Pope, Father Tunney. I command you—I do not use such words lightly—I command you to submit yourself to that authority to whom you made your vows. I command you to observe a strict vow of silence; not to speak of these matters to any other authority. I have already spoken to Father McGillicuddy about this. And I command you to make a detailed report to me as the representative of the Papacy, to tell me everything. Everything. Everything you told the Americans and everything you did not tell them. From the moment in 1961 when you . . . disappeared."

"I did not disappear," Leo Tunney said quietly. "I made no choice; I did not go into the wilderness like the prophets. It was quite mundane. You know the political realities in Laos then. I was in Qua Lai village near the border with North Vietnam, and we were overrun. It was a Sunday morning and I was preparing to offer Mass. I was in my hut when they came. Twelve of them, Pathet Lao. They went from hut to hut, they shot two men and a woman. I suspect they knew those three were part of the government neutralization force. I had used one of them—Loc Dong—to take messages south for me. For my network chief. A man named Carruthers who, in turn, reported to another man named Samuels in Vientiane. Well, that's nothing now."

He paused, staring out of the room, through the oak-paneled walls at the past. "After they killed Loc Dong—they shot him, he was a traitor in their eyes—they came to me. Their intelligence was remarkably good and I wondered who it was in the village who knew about Loc Dong and me and about the reports to Carruthers. . . . They tied me up and took me with them. There was a place in the jungle, about twenty kilometers from the village. We were there by late afternoon. For three days they didn't talk to me or feed me. I thought they meant to starve me. You see, they did that as well."

The voice was so calm that Foley felt disoriented, as though the voice and words had broken apart from each other, so that he was hearing through the bleak, weak sounds of the voice a strong, un-emotional narrative of ancient history.

"One of the prisoners was Di Phou Lo, they starved him to death while I was there. Never harmed him, never spoke to him. I think he was to serve as a living reminder to the rest of us what they could do to us." He paused again and wet his lips with his tongue. "I was very frightened." He looked with empty eyes at himself as he had been. "I was naïve then. You see, I feared death instead of pain. I have seen such deaths since, hundreds of them, the starving: their eyes growing dim day by day, the voices feeble, bellies bloated, bones protruding from beneath the skin. Such deaths do not frighten me anymore. There are more terrible ways of dying. When you starve, the spirit goes out of you in a subtle way; at first, there is only hunger, which can be endured. Then, after a time, there is nothing but a dull perception of the world around you that becomes duller each day. There is much sleep, rehearsals for death."

"Father. Please, Father—"

Leo Tunney saw that his hands had begun to tremble again. "On the fourth day, when they called for me and talked to me, I lied to them. I am a patriot, you understand? Or was? But they were patriots as well." The trembling was much worse. "When I lied to them, they did what they did."

"Father—"

"Is this what you want to know, Father Foley? It is all the

truth. As you wanted it." No, the tremors had spread, he could not control his body anymore, he was bending again, the fire was in his back, his legs were numb, beyond pain, the tiger cages and the filth and the cries of pain. . . .

"Father." Foley's voice was sharp, alarmed. "Father! Are you all right?"

Tunney glanced up and looked around wildly. But the walls were receding, the cages were opened.

"Yes. I'm all right. I'm all right."

"Father, I don't wish to cause you pain—"

Tunney began to smile. "No. No, you do not cause me pain. I have only memories of pain."

"Matters of state intrude, sent me here. I would like to return as soon as possible to Rome, to leave you—"

"Yes. I understand—"

"—great shifts in the political world—"

"—and my poor little secrets . . ."

The two men realized they were talking past each other and that the words were carrying meanings unknown to the other. Again, they waited in silence for the other to speak.

It was Tunney, the voice softer than it had been; the trembling of his hands had diminished. "I asked Father McGillicuddy for a journal book." Weariness crept into the pale face. "I began my journal last night. After I spoke to you. I realize I will not have any peace at all. . . ." He stared at the younger man. "In a little while, you must wait for me, it will all be there, in that book, and then you can leave me alone with my pains. It will be everything you want."

"Is that why you came back?"

"What? To tell you? To put it down for you?" A smile of infinite pity spread across his face. "No, Father; matters of state do not concern me anymore. Or of Church. I only have God left to satisfy, if there is God, if He can be satisfied."

"Why did you come back then?"

"Because—" He paused. "Secrets, perhaps." The smile was not for Foley, it was turned in toward Tunney's own thoughts. "Perhaps God would not let me rest until I returned. I don't want anything from Him except an end to the pain. I am in pain all the time."

"We can call the doctor again, perhaps—"

Tunney laughed then. "Not that pain. That is merely suffering. My pain is new every moment, as thought it has never happened before to any person, as though God devised it for me alone of all the men who have ever lived."

"Father Tunney." But Foley paused. What was he going to say, what could he command? Do not be mad? Do not feel pain?

Cardinal Ludovico had told him everything: "Tunney may have a secret." And told him nothing at all. Why would Cardinal Ludovico be so worried by this one old man?

What had been held back, even from him?

13
Devereaux

The tiki bar behind the hotel on the beach side was designed like a grass hut, open on all sides, with a dozen stools set in place around it. Few sat at the bar, though; most of the customers were at little iron tables scattered over the immense concrete patio that led to the swimming pool. No one was in the pool and the clear, green water shimmered undisturbed. Waitresses teetered between the bar and the tables, serving drinks, their high heels clattering on the bare cement. Besides Devereaux, only two others—both men— sat at the bar itself.

The blood-red sun was still forty minutes above the horizon. The sky over the gulf was streaked with clouds against the expanse of blue, layer upon layer of blue colors that gave the sky depth. The afternoon had been warm, languorous, and it seemed that the sun had been holding the same place in the sky for hours. At one iron table, an old man, glistening with a deep tan on his oiled body, reached across his lounge chair to pick up a blue robe and offer it to a pale, nervous young woman who seemed embarassed by her white swimming suit. She accepted the robe and shrugged it on and the old man laughed then at her modesty.

Devereaux watched them from the shadows of the thatched roof over the bar.

He had been waiting for an hour.

Three swizzle sticks were lined up precisely next to his current drink. Yesterday, he had waited as well, until darkness closed the bar and he knew she would not come.

Six days before, he had followed Rita Macklin and Leo Tunney to Clearwater. For six days, he had waited and watched and studied the problem, prying at the mousehole of a solution like a cat with infinite patience.

Hanley in Washington would not have understood. Hanley would have expected action; Hanley would have expected Devereaux to be bored by waiting. Hanley did not understand the agent in the field because he had never been in the field and because Devereaux had taken part in so many covert operations in the past that required violent action, Hanley thought he knew his man.

He would never understand. Devereaux was the same man watching and waiting that he was when he planned and executed an operation. Devereaux weighed each movement and ploy against the consequences of failure or success. His only touchstone in the field was survival. In everything he did, he moved for his own survival because he had decided at some point that only a fool throws away his life for any cause.

The game was always patience, waiting, setting a trap in a deep wood and baiting a lair and waiting and waiting, collecting a jumble of impressions, sorting them slowly in the computer of the brain, storing them finally in the compartments of memory.

The steel band began to play again after a short break. The black musicians were on a small stage on the other side of the patio; the stage was under a grass roof, nearly a replica of the bar where Devereaux sat. They started their music without an introduction. In a moment, the music changed the mood of the dying afternoon as the steady, erotic beat and the strange echoes from the drums hinted at dark moments past and yet to come. It was the last set of the day and it was always different from those that went before, wilder and faster; the people sitting at the wrought-iron furniture seemed removed from the music, as though the players were playing for themselves alone, on an empty stretch of Jamaican beach in the back country, instead of surrounded by tourist motels off the Florida mainland.

Devereaux closed his eyes for a moment, feeling the music move into him. He was perfectly still.

He had observed Rita Macklin at all times of her day. He had watched her jog along the beach in the mornings and one morning had observed the gray car that seemed to follow her. She had gone to the motherhouse of Tunney's Order four times in the past three days. He might have intercepted her casually at any of a dozen places—after he decided he would have to use her—but he had finally chosen this place, at this time, listening to this strange music.

The music. He had never heard it before yet it was so much a part of his past from the first moment he heard it that it was as though he had known it all his life. If he had admitted it, perhaps he was only delaying the moment of meeting Rita and setting the game in motion in order to be alone a while longer, listen to the music and watch the sun setting in the blood-tinged sea. To remember Asia again because that is what the music turned his thoughts to: Only Asia had stirred him in his life; and the music, however distant from that place, drew him back to his own youth.

In Asia, Devereaux had allowed a pleasant veneer of idealism and duty to cover what later emerged as his native cynicism. He had wanted to believe then that service to the Section meant more than it did; he had gone to Asia on assignment to find the truth, however naïvely he would put it in later years. He had found it. He had peeled back layers of lies from the reports he stole from filthy offices and from the words of insolent, corrupt bureaucrats in Saigon and Hue and the other places; he had sifted through the natural lies of the villagers and found little grams of truth hidden by thieves who worked the streets of Phnom Penh and Hue; he had taken the truth at last from the farmers who squatted on their thin haunches in the cold, sunken rice paddies, who gave up the truth without a struggle. In the end, he had found too much of the truth and it was too horrible not to change him, finally and irrevocably.

Devereaux stared at his drink. Perhaps patriotism had moved him at last to give in to the insistent little recruiter for the Section. Perhaps that or just a vague, restless idealism that did not seem to be satisfied with the dull, safe life of a professor of Asian studies at Columbia University.

So one day a small man in a brown suit with a bow tie fastened to his white shirt stopped him on the steps of the library and engaged him in a fantastic conversation. The little man hinted at a world of spies.

Devereaux had listened and been persuaded because he was ready to be persuaded then; because he wanted then to believe all the words the man in the dull brown suit told him. He put aside his lectures on Asian culture and the ethics of the East to find out how little he had really known of that world. This is the real world, the little man had told him, this is knowledge you won't get out of a book or a report.

Knowledge came with a price.

Devereaux picked up his drink and finished it and signaled for another.

The little man knew all about him. In the Section, the little man said, they had discussed him and they had decided that Devereaux could be a useful man. Devereaux had listened quietly while the little man recited all that he knew about him.

"You have no parents—"

"Of course I do. Everyone is born," Devereaux had said. And the little man laughed like a merry teapot singing on the stove. Devereaux so amused him.

The little man who never gave him a real name told him about himself, Devereaux's self, about a childhood on the streets of Chicago's South Side, about gangs and troubles with the law, and about near murder committed once. Devereaux did not correct him or add that he had killed first at the age of thirteen when there was no other way to resolve the problem at hand. The little man did not know everything.

And yet. Despite it all, perhaps because of Great Aunt Malvina who took him in at last, perhaps because it was only his fate, Devereaux improbably entered an academic world.

"Do you see the pattern, a wonderful pattern?" the little man bubbled. "Violence, gangs, loyalties and lies. And then you reverse all this and achieve academic distinction, assume a mantle of intelligence. . . ." The little man stopped, he was starting to laugh again. Devereaux so amused him.

And in the end, Devereaux sealed off another part of his life and plunged into the world of shadows and embraced a new world of lies and ordinary deceits and little murders. Was the new world less a fantasy than the academic world he left behind or the long-ago world of a kid on the slum streets of Chicago? What had he expected to find besides agents and double agents, moles and networks, controls and operations both covert and overt?

All that had happened a long time ago and Devereaux wondered why he thought about it now. But it was the music. And the lingering afternoon. And the vodka that he drank to conceal memory and dull conscience and which whimsically betrayed him now.

If he had once had a fragile faith in his new life of secrets, it was broken in Vietnam.

In everything he saw of the war—in all the secrets he extracted from friends and foes—he saw a betrayal of intelligence. It was a war fought against logic, against reasonable self-interest, against the facts, against the truth of things as they really were. He had found a nugget of truth buried at the core of lies and he had told them the truth; told them in Saigon first where the Section reports were funneled through the vast CIA apparatus, and then told them the truth in Washington. But they chose not to believe it because to believe Devereaux would have broken their faith in a war they would not win.

Devereaux had been taken out of Asia at last, after the final Tet offensive that he had so ruthlessly predicted in one of his last reports (which had been ruthlessly suppressed by the National Security Adviser) a year before it happened. They did not know what to do with him but they knew they would never send him back to Asia; so he had been cast adrift in the cold sea of the West, a hollow man in exile stripped even of the faith he needed to fool himself into making his life a comfortable lie.

Even his code name within R Section seemed to suit his chill, bare existence: "November." He was the November Man in Section nomenclature.

"November" suited his looks as well; perhaps that was why an anonymous ciphers clerk in the Section had linked him with the code name. Devereaux's hair was black and gray, as it had been since college days. He was in his early forties and, despite the heavy intake of alcohol, still fit. His face was perpetually pale and drawn and crosshatched with worry lines. His eyes were large and remote and calm, gray as the Arctic sea, cold and unyielding.

November.

The music rose to a frenzy, spreading across the patio like a potion, infecting all who heard it.

The pale woman in her white bathing suit and robe let the old man touch her and kiss her and she seemed to shiver at his touch. The drummers made spastic gestures like puppets twitched to life by gods. The drums made echoes of thunder. The sun was very far away and fading too quickly and the sky was filled with red, strange light across the clouds.

At the moment it seemed unbearable in its frenzy, the music ceased without warning. There was a moment of sheer silence while the players stood, transfixed, their black skins gleaming with sweat and passion.

Then applause began, scattered and broken at first.

No, Devereaux thought, pulled back out of his reverie. Not that. There should be silence or wailing but nothing as polite as applause. The music had been too wild and pure for mere applause.

He put his drink down; he had to leave.

He got off the stool, pushed change into the trough and turned just as Rita Macklin appeared and sat down at the next stool.

Three times in six days he had followed her to this bar; and it was here he finally approached her. He had made contacts like this hundreds of times as an agent. Yet now he didn't know what to do or say.

"They shouldn't applaud," Devereaux said.

She looked at him quickly and then ordered a gin and tonic. "Yes," Rita said. "I was listening to it as I came down the beach. And then they spoiled it by clapping."

Did she understand? For a moment, Devereaux did not speak. But this was the moment of contact, he had to make a move. At last, he let a smile appear and said, "Rita Macklin."

She held her drink. Her face was flushed with the sun or the warmth of the day, her red hair reddened further by the reflected rays of the last of the sun. Her large green eyes were deep and yet not clear, like flawed emeralds.

"I don't know you," she said.

"I'm sorry. You look like Rita Macklin." Devereaux paused and then resumed the line he had prepared. "I thought it was you, I wasn't sure—"

"Who are you?"

"Devereaux. You were—wait, I understand now." He sat down, still smiling, adjusting the smile mechanically by watching the reaction on her face. "You came here because of Father Tunney."

For a moment, she looked afraid and then annoyed.

Hanley would not have approved of this contact; Hanley was the most careful of controls. Hanley saw risks where none existed; he had never foreseen the real difficulties of details.

"Who are you?" she repeated.

"Just a fan." But she did not react to his smile now and he let it die, like a bulb going out. He took his glass and finished the dregs of vodka and placed it sharply on the bar. The woman behind the bar turned at the sound, glanced at him, and reached for the glass.

"I'm sorry," Devereaux said. Rita had turned away from him.

"I'm a reporter," he said. "With Central Press Association."

"Never heard of them."

He tried his smile again. "Well, I never heard of World Information Syndicate until I saw you on the 'Today' show." He took the fresh glass. "Nice piece of work you did at Watergate. Where would Washington reporters be without a Watergate? I was curious about you, I asked around. Our paths never had crossed in D.C. and it's not that big a town. Not for reporters."

"You work in Washington?"

"Home office. I work all over. Central Press is on the thirteenth floor of the National Press Building."

"Is that a fact?" Her voice was level, a little bored, a little challenging.

It would be difficult now. Most of the time, lies were quite simple and were simply accepted; Devereaux had always used lies like burglar tools, prying at secrets. Now he would begin to lie to Rita Macklin, to use her and find her secrets. But she was a reporter, she was used to lies and saw through them; the difficulty would be in making the lie so easy to accept that she would not want to see through it.

"How did you know about me? And Tunney? Are you down here on the same story?"

"I knew about you from television. I knew about Tunney from

the *St. Petersburg Times,* they had a long piece about Tunney returning to the motherhouse or whatever they call it of his Order. In Clearwater. So I saw you just now and I thought of your story in Washington and Tunney being here. Simple connection."

"You're with Central Press?"

"I'll show you my press card if you'll show me yours."

She smiled at that. "And you're not on a story?"

"No. Not at the moment." He flicked back his smile. "Reporters are so suspicious. I work for Lou Gotti, you might know him. He's the general editor back in D.C."

In case you want to check on me, he thought. He knew she would want to; and he knew her suspicions would be lessened when he offered her such an easy way to check on him. For a little while; for long enough.

"Are you going to tell me you're on vacation?" Rita said.

"Vacation," Devereaux nodded. "First one in two years. I was in Tehran at the start of the hostage crisis and then we all had to get out after a while. You remember. I went down to Tel Aviv and then roamed around a bit, Egypt, Saudi Arabia. . . . I got into Afghanistan with the rebels and when I came out, I was just getting sick of it. I wanted to come in from the cold, get a little shot of America, white bread and all."

He smiled again, a smile tinged with melancholy. He thought not of the lie he was constructing but of the truth left in it, of the loneliness that was out there in the field. "They owe me reams of time so I thought I'd just come down here." No, that part had to be fine-tuned, he thought; it was too pat. "When I was a kid, my folks came down here a couple of times in the winter. A little sun. A little white bread."

"And a little nostalgia," she said, finishing the thought.

He was surprised by her words and by the empathy they seemed to express.

"Sure. Nostalgia. You can't go home again but maybe you can go to the places you saw when you were a kid. To see if they're as big as they were then, if they still have magic."

"Do they?"

Winter on the snow-packed streets of Chicago had always been cold, always gray, always mean, always violent. There had been no parents, no idylls in the Florida sun. And yet, in this moment, Devereaux could believe his own lie.

"No. The beach is built up. But I like this bar; that's an improvement."

"I didn't know the 'Today' show would make me famous."

"For a little while at least." He tasted his drink and put it down. She stirred the ice cubes against the sides of her glass, staring at the wedge of lime floating around and around at the top of the glass. The steel band had begun to play again. The sun was nearly touching the horizon and all the windows in the hotel reflected the redness. The light was indistinct, caught between afternoon and the sudden darkness that descends on the Florida coast.

"You're the first person who recognized me from the TV show." She glanced up sharply when she said it, as though the words had sprung from an unconscious feeling and had bypassed her mind. It *was* a little odd, wasn't it?

Devereaux gave her a quick, shy smile that briefly lightened the icy burden of his cold face. "No, probably not. Just the first to say anything to you. I think most people would just stare, just think to themselves that you reminded them of someone."

"A star is born."

They smiled at each other, disarming any hostile thoughts. The conversation was working, though they perceived it from different perspectives. Was she buying his little lies?

And later, if she called or when she called, she would discover that there really was a Central Press Association in the building on Fourteenth Street in Washington. And she would discover that for the most part, it was a legitimate news-gathering syndicate, one of the hundreds in the capital, feeding a diet of political news to a string of daily papers in the Southwest and in southern California. Central Press was funded out of a double-blind trust set up at a bank in San Diego by the National Security Agency's "Provisions" section. "Provisions" was the hardware store for the various intelligence agencies that came under the umbrella of the NSA, including the CIA, R Section, the Defense Intelligence Agency and the ultra-secret Mole Group. In 1964, NSA had set up Central Press out of the bones of a faltering news organization called Southwest Central News; it was the cover for various agents in both R Section and the CIA.

Rita Macklin called for a second gin and tonic and smiled again at the man next to her. After a moment of silence, they resumed talking; it was a soft, friendly conversation that had nothing to do with anything.

The echoes of the steel drums ebbed in a last song full of melancholy and farewell. The sun dipped into the sea and darkness spread around them.

"You're right about Tunney. I've been here six days trying to get to him. It's as hard as anything I've ever done."

"Unless you compare it to interviewing the Ayatollah Khomeini." He grinned. "That was after the embassy seizure and my editor thought it was the easiest thing in the world, to talk to that madman."

"Editors are always like that."

"Yours?"

She stared at her drink. "I'm a free woman at the moment." She took a sip. "We had a disagreement about this story. So I split."

There was nothing to say.

She put the drink down. "Typical tourist-hotel drink. It's hard to taste the gin for the ice."

"Persevere." He raised his glass. "Cheers."

"Cheers." Her response was listless. "Nearly a week down here and I still haven't got to first base." For a moment, she felt weakened by an easy self-pity. She decided to shrug it off. "To hell with it. What did you do in the Middle East? Besides Iran, I mean?"

"Whatever came up. Israel is always a story, even the politics of it. And the Sinai transfer. And once I got down to Ethiopia to see if there were really Cubans there."

"And?"

"Sí."

She laughed aloud. Her laugh was natural, low and rather whimsical, as though it always came unexpectedly to her but was made welcome in any case.

"It sounds like fun," she said. "God, that's what I want to do in my next life. Foreign correspondent. I even have a trench coat."

"Some of it was fun. But you know what it really is—most of it is just airports and waiting around."

Devereaux appraised Rita, sitting comfortably beside him now. She wore earrings and a light blue sweater with a plain round collar. Her only makeup was lipstick; her whole casual manner carried a certain brash elegance that pleased him. He felt warmed suddenly to be in her company.

She said, "I never thought I'd have the patience to be a reporter. I hate to wait. I hate lines and standing around. Maybe I should have gotten into a different end of it."

"Like television?"

"I'd have to be too beautiful for that. I couldn't stand it."

"Everyone on TV isn't beautiful."

"I don't think they're ready for a female Walter Cronkite, and even he's retired. I mean, if you're a woman, you can't allow yourself the luxury of wrinkles or growing old or having gray hair."

He didn't speak.

She smiled at him, sipped more of her drink, and put it down on the bar. She crossed her legs. She wore no stockings beneath the tan skirt. One sandal dangled from her toes as she swung it back and forth.

"What's the Tunney story going to be?"

She just looked at him for a moment. "I don't know. That's the surprise. But there has to be something there."

"Why?"

"Because the CIA put him in a box for a week. And because when things got too hot for them in Washington, they shoved him down here and now the priests have put him in a bigger box. But it's still a box."

Devereaux was startled but he made no gesture. He waited a moment for his voice to find a calm range. "A box?"

"That's CIA slang. For when they put you in isolation—that's what they call it in the official reports, 'isolation.' But when they talk about it, they call it a box."

"You know CIA people?"

"Some. Not enough. I get information from them, and there's the Freedom of Information Act reports I get out."

"Well, what do you think they want from him?"

"Who?"

"Tunney."

Darkness had gathered while they spoke. The sun was gone, the steel band players had moved inside, those on the patio were starting to drift into the hotel to dress for dinner. It was still warm and humid and the opaqueness of the night made the heat thick and uncomfortable. The swarthy old man stood up and beckoned the young woman in the white bathing suit and robe. She rose and was much taller than he, but she seemed fragile next to him, as though she were a child.

"I don't know. But it's worth it to me. And if I don't find out, I go back to Green Bay and try to get my old job back on the *Press-Gazette.*"

"You really burned your bridges with your boss?"

"Kaiser? Yes. That's his name. Yes." She seemed suddenly full of regret. "Yes. I think we got rid of each other." She smiled as though she didn't mean the smile.

"You liked him."

It was not a question. Rita stared at him, annoyed.

"Yeah."

The woman behind the bar began to close up, banging down the awnings and locking them.

"Yeah." She stared down at her hand tracing a circle in the wetness on the bar top. "You either like someone you work with or you hate him."

"Why did you fight?"

"He didn't want me to go after this story."

"Why was it important? I mean, to do it?"

"My reasons. It's a good story."

"Yes."

"But there are other reasons. I guess I'm a little crazy on the subject."

He waited for her. The silence between them seemed to press on her. Rita had to explain herself.

"My father," she began.

He stared at her, his cold gray eyes not moving from her face that was turned half away from him. Her profile was fine-boned,

119

stubborn from chin to nose. Only her eyes were soft, wondering, as though still believing in miracles that the rest of her face had learned to scoff at.

"My father was in the State Department. A long time ago, in the forties. You remember about the witch-hunt? McCarthy?"

"Communists in the State Department."

"There were communists but he didn't know it," she said. Her voice had become cold, flat in its precise clipping of the words.

"I don't have to tell you everything," she said. "But they forced him out. I mean, he wasn't a communist but there were . . . well." She paused. "He didn't let himself become bitter. He always said . . ." She looked at him; could she tell him?

"He always said that this was the greatest country in the world. Do you think that's funny?"

Devereaux saw the test offered by a woman who had allowed herself to be temporarily defenseless. He avoided it without a sound, with only a slow shake of his head. As she had intended him to do.

"He was that way. All his life. He said McCarthy was a mistake. He even went back to Wisconsin to live, the state McCarthy came from."

"What would this have to do with Tunney?"

"My father," she said, not speaking to him, not looking at him. "And my brother. Both of them. I couldn't . . ." Again, she came to the edge of words and there was only unmarked forest ahead. She seemed confused for a second and then turned back. Devereaux knew she would not be able to say any more.

"It's just your story," he prodded gently.

"Yes. That's part of it. It's my story. It's there and it's mine and I've got to know about him, why he came out." She said it in a dogged tone, like a child explaining ownership of a prized toy to an adult who cannot be expected to understand.

Devereaux smiled at her again.

This time, it was not for effect. Something in her manner was honest and direct, like a handshake between partners. It was a quality he rarely came into contact with anymore.

"I hope it's worth it," he said. "Let me buy you a drink."

"Bar's closed," said the woman unfolding the wooden awnings and letting them drop with a bang against the bar top. "Bar inside the hotel."

"Florida charm," Devereaux said.

Rita laughed. "I've got to be going."

"Let me buy you dinner."

She glanced up at him sharply.

He smiled. "From one reporter to another."

"No." She put down her glass, unfolded her legs and stood up. "No, I don't think so."

"Not here. There's a good seafood place called Fisherman's Wharf down at the end of the key, near the bridge. Really fine, a group of Albanians from Chicago run it."

"How do you know that?"

"I ate there. I talked to them."

"The natural reporter. I never talk to anyone unless I'm on a story."

"That's the way women are trained. Nice girls don't talk to strangers."

She smiled. "Like you? I talked to you."

"I talked to you first. Come on, Rita. What do you say?"

"What kind of a line is that?" she asked.

"Terrible. Terrible line." For a moment, they stood and looked at each other. "I've been out of work, too, Rita. And I've had stories that just lie there and don't bark."

"Come on, now you're appealing to self-pity."

"Mine. Or yours?"

"Do you feel sorry for yourself?"

"All the time. Like now, when I make a perfectly honest and straightforward offer of dinner and the woman turns me down."

"Maybe I have something else to do?"

They were suddenly shy with each other. They stood apart in silence a moment longer. "I have other people's money to spend," Devereaux said at last.

"That's romantic."

"To a reporter it is. Some expense money I didn't turn in yet. Dinner on the company is always better."

It was as though she had decided something about him in that moment. "Are you alone? I mean, down here?"

"Alone. Sure. Is that all right?"

For a moment more, she gazed directly at him, her face impassive. And then she shrugged. "Why the hell not?"

121

He left change on the bar. He took her arm and they walked down the ramp to the sidewalk in front of the hotel entrance and then on to Gulf View Boulevard. Traffic streaked past them quietly on the narrow thoroughfare. "We can walk," he said, and then they did not speak at all as they walked the half-mile to the restaurant set at the water's edge near the iron bridge to Sand Key. They took a table near the windows in the semicircular wood-paneled room. The place was almost empty at this hour. Evening closed in the Gulf waters. A few night shark-hunter boats were moving slowly down the channel under the bridge into the blackness of the open sea, their running lights winking in the gloom as they passed.

When the waitress brought white bread, Rita smiled. "Here's what you came back for. White bread in America."

The fish was red snapper prepared in the Greek-Albanian style. They shared a bottle of sparkling German wine and ate slowly, savoring the meal and the small talk that they made in the soft lights of the room.

She told him a little of her life story and he listened, absorbed it all, only broke in now and then for little probes of questions:

"How did you meet Kaiser?"

"Kaiser? I just met him when I went to work there. I was bombarding everyone with applications. On my vacation, when I was still at the *Press-Gazette,* I came out to D.C. I had a friend at AP. I interviewed at the *Post* and the *Star* but they didn't have any use for someone as inexperienced as I was—"

"But Kaiser did."

"Yes." She sounded the note of regret again. "He said I was bright." She blushed quickly, modestly, and stared at her plate. "I worked cheap. He said that too. And I did."

"You hated fighting with him."

She looked up. It was so unexpected of him to say that. For a moment, she studied the winter face, the harsh lines cutting through the dry, pale skin like scars of old roads. Was she attracted to his unconventional good looks? Or was it just the quality of vulnerability that seemed to hide beneath the hard, rough layers?

"What about you?" she said at last. "This is a two-way street. Where did you come from?"

"Chicago," he began. That was true. Very little of the rest was true until he reached the part about going to Columbia University twenty years before to teach Asian studies.

"And you went to Asia?" Her voice quickened.

"Of course. I was so sure I knew so much about it that I had to go to have my facts confirmed."

"And were they?"

"No. Not at all." He spoke quietly, staring at the last of the wine in his glass. "I knew nothing." He looked up and smiled quickly. "Then I went to Central Press. I wanted to go back to Asia. I had contacts in the business in New York. They sent me back to Asia, to Vietnam to cover the war."

She made a little fist then and held it tight against the white tablecloth. "Stupid war," she said.

"As opposed to intelligent wars?"

"Don't get me wrong. I'm not a pacifist."

He sighed then. "Neither am I." No, that was the last thing I would be, he thought. For a moment, he had been distracted by her, by her charm and her quiet voice and the sincerity of her words. He must remember it was only a game and he was merely constructing a simple deception for her.

And yet.

He felt warmed in her company, had liked her from the moment he met her in the music of the dying afternoon. The music had broken his reserve of cynicism, thawed the coldness that had frozen a world of regret, feeling, desire. The music had wounded him. And now he saw that her eyes waited honestly for the trap he would put out for her. He had to stay in control of himself. He had to remember that she was only a device in a complex game.

"I give out catchlines," she said. "Maybe I should have gone into television. 'Stupid war.' What does it mean?"

"It means we didn't win," Devereaux said.

"Yes. I suppose. And that's why World War II was not stupid."

"A good war," he said with a bitter edge.

"My father was a patriot. He was in that war. And my brother—"

"Your brother?"

She glanced away. There was a secret there after all, Devereaux thought suddenly. Something was hidden and she had almost shown it to him.

"What about your brother?"

"Nothing about him. War. We were talking about wars."

"Good wars and stupid ones," Devereaux said.

"Pour me some wine."

He gave her the last of it. She drank it slowly, the color filling her cheeks, her green eyes turning smoky and velvet.

"To good wars," she said, mocking herself, saluting with the wine.

"The good wars are the ones we survive," he said quietly.

"Is that cynical? Or only true?" she said.

"Both." He stared into the night beyond the windows. He saw memories he could not describe. His words became detached from his thoughts, running alongside them, obliquely defining them. "The man who makes the summing up is the only winner because he's the survivor. The hero dies in battle and when he's gone, he's gone, blown away, obliterated. All the monuments and graves and memorials don't mean anything next to that."

"No," she said, firmly, just as quietly. "That can't be true. We can always remember."

"Who? Your father?"

The words were calculated to cut quickly, like the first slash of a razor.

She was wounded; he saw and did not feel pity, only curiosity. He had led her to this moment; would she reveal her own secrets now?

"Yes. And others. We all remember someone. And it makes us act now the way we do."

"Survival," he said. "That's all that counts."

"For what reason? For what?"

"Ah." His smile became cold now, it came from the cold place within him. November. "That is the puzzle I've never solved. I know that survival is winning but I don't know why. Maybe its just that the survivors make the rules of the game after the game and decide who won and who lost."

"But what if you didn't play? What if you didn't want to play? What . . ." But she did not continue.

He felt unsure of himself now. He was lost. The brother was the boy in the photograph he had seen in her apartment. The father was the old man. Names to be checked out in the NSA computer. Names and memories. Or demons that pushed her now.

Rita sat for a moment staring at something in her path of memory. Now she chose to look away.

"After this? What do you do after this?"

"After my vacation? I don't know. I wanted to spend some time in Washington, get back to my roots." He smiled quickly again. "You must see how desperate I am for a little American living to think of Washington as a place to have roots."

"Where do you live?"

"I own a little house in Virginia. On a mountain. Do you know where Front Royal is?"

"At Skyline Drive you mean? In the Shenandoah Valley. I was there last summer—"

"I have a house there. Up the mountain." He thought of it now. "You should come see it someday." But as soon as he said it, he knew that was a lie too; that after he had used her and she discovered it, he would never be able to see her again.

She drank the last of the wine. "Yes. That would be nice. But why come down here? It must be lovely in the mountains in the fall. All the color in the leaves—"

"I was cold." The words were flat and he realized they were true, more truth than he intended to speak. "I was cold in Washington. I came down for sun."

But it wasn't that coldness that drove him.

"Are you going to stay here long?" She blushed; it was too naked a question.

"I don't know. I have time coming, I have my money and when that runs out, I have the little green card you should not leave home without." He smiled. "I suppose I might have gone back if I hadn't met you today. No. Don't say anything."

He touched her hand.

She looked frightened.

"Friends, Rita," he said. "I was just saying that as a friend. I can be friends without being lovers. No line involved. Or at least I don't think so." He let her hand go and sank back in the wooden chair. "I wanted to talk to someone. Share a meal. I guess I came back for more than white bread."

"It was a good dinner. Thank you."

"Brandy," he said. The waitress came and they ordered it. In a moment, she brought them two glasses filled with amber liquid that tasted like smoke.

"I might get drunk," Rita said.

"There are worse things."

"But I can't. I have to be a good girl. Got to go to Mass in the morning."

"To see Leo Tunney," Devereaux said.

She smiled as though looking for a bond. "Are you a Catholic?"

"You say it like a Catholic."

"Yes. I suppose I do."

"I was a Catholic. When I was a boy. Or you're always a Catholic, isn't that it? Even if you choose not to be?" His smile was not pleasant; his face had become cold again.

"Yes. Catch 22 situation. I'm sorry, I didn't mean to be nosy." She said it quickly, as though she had said the apology a thousand times before, after a thousand awkward questions. She touched his hand on the tablecloth. "I suppose I was including you. In my little story. I need company too." His hand was large and broad, the fingers flat and not very long. Her own was as delicate and strong as a piano player's, quick and certain in gesture.

She told him a little about trying to reach Tunney at the motherhouse. And about realizing that Foley had been sent from the Vatican.

"I wanted to know if you were a Catholic because of the Mass. Tunney was in the jungle twenty years, he missed all the reforms in the Mass. He says the Latin Mass. There's a man at the house from the Vatican. You'd think he'd step on Tunney, tell him to get his act together."

Devereaux did not speak but he thought of her last words. Yes. Why didn't the man from Rome make him toe the line? Because he didn't want to force him?

Because he was waiting for something from Tunney?

"I got a note to Tunney twice in the chapel. He knows I'm here but he's so distracted. . . . He looks lost, a little harassed. I don't know what I'm going to do but I'm going to keep after him."

"Maybe you should be after the man from Rome," Devereaux said slowly.

"Why? I mean, he'd just shut me off—"

"Force him to shut you off, to lie to you—"

"Why?"

"To find out he tells lies."

She stared at him.

"That's a funny thing to say."

"You think Tunney has some secret? Maybe this man from Rome thinks he has some secret too."

"Involving what?"

"Yes. What?"

They both were silent now, each furiously combing through their thoughts.

"The CIA. And the Vatican? What could interest them both?"

"In Asia," Devereaux said.

"I never made the connection."

"Perhaps none exists."

"Are you sure you aren't here on this story?"

He laughed then. "No. Not at all. I can't help probing conspiracies. They're like the Sunday *Times* crossword puzzle."

"I'm glad then. It's only a game to you," she said.

"Yes." A game.

"This has been very nice," she said with intentional softness. "Sometimes it's easier to talk to strangers than friends."

"Kaiser was your friend," he said, probing again at her secrets.

"A friend."

"This was nice." He relieved the pressure. "Can we meet tomorrow? I know I'm pressing." He glanced down at the coffee cup and fingered the handle. "For long periods, I go without company at all. In the mountains, my place there. I like it that way, like the stillness in the woods." All of which was true; there was just enough of the truth in the lie to make it work.

"And then, sometimes," he continued, "I have to talk. I want your company."

Her green eyes shone darkly. "Yes," she said at last, as though she had decided something. He touched her hand and he felt the warmth of it yielding to him.

There was nothing more to say. Complexities beyond words

were at work. He had constructed a logical lie and laid a trap for her so that he could use her to probe Tunney. But in the end, she could reject it all.

Trust me, he thought.

"Yes," she said. "Tomorrow. That would be nice. I'd like that but you don't have to buy me dinner. We could meet."

"All right," he said.

"We can tell each other lies tomorrow," she said.

He was startled but his face registered no emotion. Did she see the lies? Or did she ignore them because of some stronger feeling in her?

Devereaux, not for the first time, felt uncertain with her. He had set the game and drawn the rules but now he felt as trapped in the rules as he wanted her to be.

They left the restaurant together and walked along Gulf View to the open beachfront. They walked on the hard sand by the waterline, feeling the salty wind at their back. They were wrapped in the silence, held together by it. Words would have broken them apart.

When they parted, they did not touch or kiss.

Before he finally fell asleep, after midnight, after more vodka and memories, he remembered her face as it had been in the soft light of the restaurant, staring at him across the table, and smiling as though she understood games and rules and lies behind them.

Perhaps she did.

14
Lu Ann Carter

She was still a young woman but it was not apparent at first because of her hideous deformities: She might have been of great age or no age at all. She walked painfully along the sidewalk, aided by two aluminum canes strapped to her arms. She pushed her body forward in lurching steps that seemed to throw her off balance with each effort. She was an instant object of pity. Some turned away rather than look at her.

It was very hot for nine o'clock in the morning.

People had come to the chapel all morning, from the moment Cyrus McGillicuddy opened the doors at 7 A.M. McGillicuddy was pleased and he stood on the front steps, nodding and smiling at the throng passing through the chapel doors. The bishop had been a problem, of course; but for the moment, the bishop was Martin Foley's problem. McGillicuddy had decided to defer to the man from Rome when the bishop called up.

What was going on down there, McGillicuddy? So the bishop had asked in his usual peremptory way. McGillicuddy said there was nothing going on and then said, oh—you mean that, and then said the bishop might want to speak to the Vatican representative who had come to stay at the motherhouse. The bishop had said, somewhat flabbergasted, that he was not aware of any Vatican representative in *his* diocese and . . .

McGillicuddy gave the phone to Martin Foley and left the room. Later, Foley had recounted the conversation in diplomatic words. The matter in the motherhouse of the Order of the Holy Word Fathers was one of extreme delicacy.

But, the bishop had insisted, he had heard that the old Mass was being said again, the ritual of the Tridentine Mass of the Middle Ages. An exception was being made, for the moment, Foley said.

Foley had decided at last to forbid Tunney to say the Mass. Much to his surprise, Tunney had shown an Oriental stubbornness on the matter. Tunney did not oppose Foley but he bent away from his orders. It was upsetting him, he told Foley; he was having trouble completing the journal. Foley understood the blackmail and accepted it. Again and again, he had felt himself caught in the middle of a situation beyond his grasp; the orders from Cardinal Ludovico were general and vague, yet the matter was important. That much had been made clear to him. It was important to have Tunney's information. And Tunney had implied that the information might not be forthcoming if he were interfered with. And so Foley found himself placating the bishop and Tunney and warning McGillicuddy not to make a public fuss about Tunney saying the Latin Mass.

Of course not, McGillicuddy agreed. He denied ever talking to reporters and he did not understand why the *Clearwater Sun* had sent a reporter to the chapel.

So, in an uneasy way, forces counterbalanced each other inside the rectory. In the mornings, Tunney said his Mass; in the afternoons, he wrote—for hours until exhaustion claimed him—in the red leather journal, filling page after page in his cramped hand.

And no one could see the journal until it was finished.

All of which was satisfactory for the time being from McGillicuddy's point of view. People at Mass meant money at Mass; the publicity was not hurting him either.

This morning, the stream of people going up the three steps into the chapel divided around the slow-moving young woman lurching forward on her aluminum canes, her head bent and her brown hair tied back severely. She had a transparent chalk-white complexion. Her spine curved oddly in two places and made her shoulders seem somehow detached from it. Shoulders and arms were one segment of the body, spine and lower back another, useless legs a third.

McGillicuddy watched her and was struck with pity. He made way for her and led her inside the church to a front pew.

"Y'all Father Tunney I read 'bout?" Her voice was low and scratching and ugly, a voice out of the swamps of Florida's backlands.

"No, no, ma'am," McGillicuddy said, helping her settle in the narrow pew. Her canes clattered against the hardwood. She leaned against the back of the pew ahead of her, half resting her behind against the seat, her legs propped on the rubber kneeler on the floor. "Father Tunney'll offer Mass in a little while."

"I ain't Catlik," she said. The voice moved slowly like water disturbed in a rain-forest pool. "Heard about him, read about him in that paper and come to see this. This service I ain't never seen before. I ain't Catlik. God knows, I pray all day but I ain't Catlik."

She suddenly fastened one very strong hand on his arm and looked into his face. He stared at her and could see the veins working beneath the translucent whiteness of her forehead. Her eyes were black and muddy and her eyebrows had been plucked and painted, as though all the deformity of the body was to be mitigated by a little cosmetics on her face.

"Baptist," she said. "I been washed in the Blood of the Lamb and born again when I was seventeen."

"Yes." He half turned, started to move away from her, but the strong hand held his arm.

"All right then I come down to see him?"

"Yes. Certainly." He tugged away from her. "All faiths are welcome to worship with—"

"Father Tunney's holy man," she said, holding on to him. "Holy in the Lord. He be blessed." The voice was dead and deep and McGillicuddy pulled hard against her touch, panicked for a moment by her words.

She released his arm suddenly and slumped back in the pew, pushing her soft, deformed body against the hard wooden surfaces.

McGillicuddy turned and hurried back down the aisle to the rear of the church. At the far door, he saw Foley standing beneath the plaque of the Ninth Station of the Cross. As always since his arrival in the motherhouse, Foley wore a sports shirt, which annoyed McGillicuddy; everything about Foley annoyed him.

Tunney appeared at the door of the sanctuary, dressed in the robes for Mass, holding the covered chalice in his hand. The Mass began.

The middle-aged man who had been at early Mass the first morning was serving the Mass with the priest. He wore a black cassock and white surplice and his hands were folded in front of him. He had chosen to serve because he knew the old Latin prayers from when he was an altar boy. None of the regular altar boys at the chapel knew the old words.

"*Gloria in excelsis Deo.*

"*Et in terra pax hominibus bonae voluntatis.*

"*Laudamus te. Benedicumus te. Adoramus te. Glorificamus te. Gratias agimus tibi propter. . . .*"

Leo Tunney pronounced the words of the Gloria slowly and precisely in his slight, whispery voice. As the Mass proceeded, the voice would grow stronger. McGillicuddy had noticed that.

Because it was Sunday morning, a sermon was usual in the middle of the Mass. Tunney had insisted he would deliver it and McGillicuddy, worried about the old man's frailty, had reluctantly agreed.

Now Tunney broke from the prayers of the Mass and turned to the congregation. He stepped down the three steps of the altar and moved to a lectern used as a pulpit. He rested his bony hands on the wood for a moment, his face pale and his head trembling slightly.

He blessed them with the Sign of the Cross and began.

"My dear friends in Christ," he said, his blue eyes searching from face to face as though he were looking for someone he knew.

McGillicuddy had opened the windows of the church so that the overflow congregation gathered on the lawn outside could listen to the Mass.

Sweat formed a line across Tunney's temples. He brushed once at his short white hair and then let his hand fall again on the wooden lectern.

"I would like to speak to you of forgiveness."

Silence settled on the crowd.

"None of us, least of all me, is worthy of God's mercy or His forgiveness. None of us, least of all me, is deserving of a first chance, let alone a second chance. None of us—"

He paused, looked up at the ceiling and then stared at the back door of the church where Foley stood and waited.

"God who made us," he began again. "God has loved us in the act of creation. Creation is love. And we are not worthy of His love and—"

He thought of Phuong for a moment and the face faded and he thought of the child.

Tears welled in his blue eyes.

In the front pew, a woman began to weep and her neighbors stared at her. She took a handkerchief from her purse and wiped her eyes.

"I'm sorry," Tunney began again. "It is so difficult to say the simplest things. I wanted to speak to you of the absolute mercy of God but I cannot do it. I am not worthy to speak to you of it. I must tell you that: I am not worthy—"

For the third time, he paused. He stared out at them in the pews and was overwhelmed by a feeling of fear and intense pity for them. None of them understood, really, but they wanted to understand. They came and knelt and prayed and asked for just a moment of peace. Let me understand.

"Pray for me," he said finally. He raised his hand over them. "In the Name of the Father, and of the Son, and of the Holy Ghost."

For a moment, he stood and looked at the congregation and then turned back to the altar. He began the prayers of the Mass again.

At that moment, Tunney heard the voice. It came muddy and unyielding from behind him. He stopped and turned.

The crippled woman had pushed herself up in the pew, leaning forward on the back of the bench in front of her, her legs propped against the kneeler. She had spoken but the words were unintelligible. Everyone suddenly turned to look at her.

McGillicuddy felt sick: A crazy woman enmeshed in her own strange life of pain and prayers, she was going to make a scene and Foley would use it as an excuse to stop Tunney. No more Latin Masses, no more caving in to Tunney. No more people in the chapel—

"Father!" The voice, turgid and opaque, calling from the swamplands. "Fer God's sake. Help me, Father!"

A man in the next pew thought the plea was a commonplace call for help, that the crippled woman had become stuck somehow. He half rose to assist her but she did not look at him. Her black eyes stared at the priest in his robes at the altar. Her eyes began to flow with tears.

Leo Tunney turned slowly and stared at her.

"Father!" The voice was half shriek of pain, half prayer. She sobbed once.

Tunney put down the chalice he was holding and came down the steps to the communion railing. The woman propped her body with one hand and held the other outstretched in the universal gesture of pleading.

"Bless me! Bless me, you holy man!"

Tunney paused, frozen by the voice, by the shaking sight of the pleading woman. Tears fell down her pale cheeks.

"Bless me!"

"I cannot. I can do nothing—"

She cried again and said words no one could understand, words that growled up inside her and seemed detached from her.

Slowly, as though in a trance, Tunney raised his hand and began to make the Sign of the Cross.

Suddenly, the crippled woman fell to her knees and then sideways to the floor, violently, as though struck by a car. Her canes clattered around her falling body, there was a loud report as she banged against the pew, like a rifle shot on a foggy morning.

Tunney stood transfixed and then bent forward to help her.

She cried out again, again making a sound that was like a word but without any meaning.

The woman in the first pew who had wept during the sermon now cried again.

"My God, my God!" a man screamed, rising suddenly in his pew in the middle of the church.

Excitement rippled across the congregation and a kind of frenzy filled the close, hot chapel.

The crippled woman stirred at Tunney's touch and pushed her canes away from her. She cried, "Holy, holy!" and then reached for the side of the pew and pushed her body up against her matchstick legs encased hideously in dense stockings.

Slowly, inch by inch, she rose.

And stood.

And straightened her body, aligning her shoulders and arms with her spine. She was weeping like a child now and made no other sound.

Tunney, who still held her, stood amazed. His eyes were wide and frightened.

"Blessed be God!" the crippled woman shouted and she threw her arms out, stumbling away from the pew, standing alone in the aisle, turning and turning, showing herself to the people in the pews. "Blessed be God!"

She repeated the words again and there was an explosion of sound like water bursting through a dam. Shouts and prayers mingled in a single frenzied cry that boomed through the church. The woman screamed and held her arms up to the ceiling. And then she shouted the word that changed the plans of all who had come to uncover the secrets of Leo Tunney:

"Miracle!"

15
Kaiser

"Me," Rita said on the telephone.

"What is it?"

"I have something for you."

"You don't work here anymore."

"You have the heart of a turnip."

"No. Soul. I have the soul of a turnip."

"Tunney said Mass today."

"Quite a usual thing among Catholic priests. And it was Sunday as well."

"Kaiser, are you going to listen to me?"

"It's your dime."

"I can call someone else."

"Yes."

"Kaiser, at Mass this morning. He's saying the old Mass and—"

"I didn't know there were fashions in religious celebrations."

"Kaiser."

He waited, wreathed by smoke; a cigarette burned in one ham fist, another smoldered in an ashtray. Outside the window of his office, a huge orange anticrime streetlamp smothered the darkness.

"Kaiser. A woman was cured. He touched a woman this morning in church, she had a deformed spine. She straightened. Just like that. In front of a hundred people in the church. The local radio station is going crazy, a reporter is down from the *Miami Herald*—"

"I don't believe in miracles."

"That's irrelevant."

Another pause. "Yes, Rita, I suppose it is. The phenomenon is the story here. UPI already has quite a long takeout on it. Why did you take so long to call?"

"Kaiser. You bastard, you knew about it."

He chuckled. "Rita. Your refreshing naïveté is the quality that helps you be a good investigative reporter. Believe everything, everyone, at least once. I am charmed, again, by your innocence."

"Cut the shit, Kaiser."

"As you say. Little Rita."

"I tried to reach you at home."

"I was in New York yesterday. My granddaughter was baptized."

Another pause. "I didn't know you had a kid."

"Yes. A son. It seems unbelievable, doesn't it, and now a second grandchild." His voice carried a momentary sense of awe, as though the incongruity between his appearance and parenthood had never occurred to him before.

"I didn't call about that. I have a story. I was there. What are we going to do about it?"

"You left me, not the other way around."

"I told you there was a story here."

"You didn't predict a miracle. Your word—'miracle.' I never saw one before. Was it inspiring? Did it make you believe in Jesus Christ?"

"Tunney seemed as confused as anyone else."

"Yes. Our poor dear sainted prodigal."

"I have a story."

"Yes. And I have a news service. What a fortunate coincidence."

"I'm staying here, Kaiser. I talked to this old priest, McGillicuddy. Tunney's keeping a journal—"

"What?"

"A journal. The Vatican has sent a man here, a priest and—"

"What did you say?"

"The Vatican—"

"A journal? He's keeping a journal? Leo Tunney?" The harsh, tobacco-choked voice had changed in the last moment. Now it was tense, wary.

"Yes."

"Who knows this?"

"What do you mean?"

"Who knows this?"

"About the journal or the miracle?"

"Forget the miracle a moment, little Rita." The voice had become softer with an intimacy that suppressed the interest behind the words. "Who knows about the journal?"

136

"Me. And thee."

"This is a secret, isn't it, Rita?"

"Not if McGillicuddy can help it."

"You mean he knows too. Who is he?"

"The head man down here."

"What about this other fellow . . . the Vatican man?"

"Young guy named Martin Foley. Irish Irish. He's a cold-looking guy."

"Why on earth would the Vatican take an interest in this old man?"

"Before we keep talking, Kaiser, we have to figure out where we stand."

"Ah, the bottom line. Cutting the crap, eh, Rita?"

"I won't work for you anymore."

"No? Why this call?"

"Maybe I just wanted to stick it to you."

"Did you? Revenge, Rita? I don't think so."

"I'll free-lance this for you. This story. And if there's anything else, maybe I'll free-lance it for you too. But I want money up front. You owe me for my last week of salary and two weeks' vacation."

"The check is in the mail."

"The famous lie," she said.

Kaiser chuckled. "I can have six hundred dollars in your hands by tomorrow night if I get what I want tonight."

"That would be decent, I suppose."

"I am a generous man."

"I'll call back in an hour."

"Please."

She paused again. "Kaiser. Did you ever hear of a reporter named Devereaux?"

"No."

"I was wondering. What about Central Press Association?"

"Yes. They're somewhere in the building. Mostly serves papers of the "right" persuasion. Oklahoma, I think, and Arkansas, Arizona, New Mexico, some papers in Texas. Why?"

"I met a reporter here."

"From them? On this story?"

"No. Not on this story. On vacation."

"Is that a fact?"

"What does that mean? The way you just said that?"

"It is a neutral statement, Rita. Do you think he's a reporter on vacation who happens to be in Clearwater Beach at this moment?"

"Not when you say it that way."

"But I am a cynical man, Rita, born for this cynical age. You are, I believe I have said, naïve in your human dealings."

"I'm not naïve."

"Perhaps you would prefer 'open' as an adjective. You are honest and open. You detect the devious motives of others at great emotional price. You are a believer, Rita, and I am not. Is this man a believer as well?"

"No. No. I don't think so." Her voice was slow, unsure, soft.

"Rita? In an hour?"

"Yes."

They hung up.

Kaiser sat at his desk, staring at the telephone, staring at the smoldering remains of the cigarette in his sausage fingers. He ran his hand through his thick, greasy hair. "Rita," he said softly, with gentleness. "You *are* a reporter." His voice sounded sad.

He picked up the receiver and dialed a number with the area code of New York City.

"Yes?" The voice was soft, cultured, with the trace of a New England accent.

"Me," he said.

The man in New York City waited. The line buzzed.

"Is the line clear?" Kaiser asked.

"Quite clear. I'm in the study. We have people coming over tonight."

"Rita just called."

"I thought she didn't work for you anymore."

"True. But she just called from Florida."

"Yes," the voice said, no judgment in the tone.

"She has one story. I'm buying it."

"You're a newsman. Does it concern me?"

"No. But she mentioned the other man we spoke of. He has been keeping a journal. And there's a man from Rome watching him at the house."

"Extraordinary," the voice said.

"Well, I wanted to tell you."

"Yes," the voice responded, now in a tone of weariness. "This has been annoying from the beginning."

"I have a business to run—"

"I'm aware of that. I don't interfere with you. But in this one matter, I wish there had been more . . . well . . . discretion on all sides."

"Rita is a reporter," Kaiser said dully, as though she were beyond the pale.

"Yes. That covers a multitude of sins." The voice made an imitation of a laugh, a dry chuckle that made Kaiser feel very old and very tired.

"What is it that you want to know?"

"Ah. That's the problem. I can't take you into my confidence without telling you what the secret is. And if I tell you what the secret is, it isn't a secret anymore." Another chuckle.

Each waited for a moment for the other to speak and then they started to speak at the same time. Kaiser deferred.

"—let the matter proceed. We will see how much farther it will go, before I have to become involved. I would prefer not to be involved at all."

"Yes," Kaiser said.

"Keep me informed."

"Yes."

They broke the connection.

Kaiser stood up and pushed his belly around the desk to the decayed coffee maker. He poured a sludgy cup and tasted it. He went to the window and looked down at the deserted street. Night in a lonely city.

"Little Rita," he said with fondness. His heart ached for her in that moment and for himself.

He was surprised that there were tears in his eyes.

16
Devereaux

Rita Macklin had left him a message at the front desk of his hotel, breaking that evening's date for dinner. The story came first, the one that had exploded that morning in the chapel of the mother-house.

The "miracle" had changed the situation in any case, Devereaux thought. He knew Hanley would now want him to make contact.

At five o'clock, Devereaux telephoned the number in Washington from a telephone booth off the lobby of his hotel. The number connected him with the security desk of the Department of Agriculture building, which was usual on weekends. When he reached the senior duty officer in the old, massive building near the Ellipse, he spoke four words that would have seemed innocuous to anyone eavesdropping on the conversation. The duty officer did not respond. Devereaux hung up and took a long walk down the island to the causeway that connected the beach with downtown Clearwater.

The causeway was nearly two miles long and on both sides of it, the shallow waters of the Gulf inlets stretched away from the sandy, rough shoreline. Palms lined either side of the four-lane divided highway. Devereaux had walked the causeway several times in his week-long stay on the island. Despite the constant surge of traffic on the roadway, the causeway seemed detached from the drumbeat of tourism. He could smell the sea and watch the pelicans and gulls whirl in the clear, lazy sky about fishing boats chugging back and forth from safe harbors to the deep.

What could he report to Hanley?

There was nothing to say beyond the reports already on television, which would be fully covered in the morning papers. An incident had occurred in a Catholic chapel during a worship service. A woman named Lu Ann Carter claimed to be the recipient of a "miracle."

But what is the real truth of the matter, Hanley would demand.

He didn't know. The agent in the field knew so little in the end.

Not for the first time during the past year, he thought of Hastings, who had been the station man for the Section in Scotland. Hastings had run a ramshackle network of spies—real and imaginary and all drawing salaries—out of his stinking little rooms in a dreary house in Edinburgh. All day long, Hastings had clipped items of interest from the *Daily Telegraph* and *Irish Times* and embellished them with his own considerable imagination, then passed them back as reports to Hanley in Washington. Devereaux had been sent to find out what Hastings really knew about a new IRA plot. Hastings had died because he had gotten in the way of another espionage agency.

Devereaux thought of Denisov.

Denisov had been sent by the KGB with incomplete instructions to obstruct Devereaux's investigation of Hastings' network in Ireland and Scotland.

In the end, Devereaux had just managed to survive by betraying Denisov to the British authorities. They had expelled the Soviet back to Russia.

Thoughts of Hastings and Denisov vanished. It was time. The dreary present had to be served.

Devereaux dialed directly a different number in Washington from the one he had dialed one hour before.

This time, he heard Hanley's voice clearly on the phone.

"There have been developments," Devereaux began in a quiet voice.

The line was secured by a double scrambler box at Hanley's end. Devereaux could see his control officer alone in the chill of his bare office, his hands resting on the empty desk top. Hanley rarely took notes. Hanley rarely left memos. In this business, he said, only those things that are not secrets are written down.

Devereaux recounted the incident in the chapel that morning; and the gray car; and his information about the man from the Vatican now residing in the motherhouse.

"A priest?"

"Yes. Most probably." He hesitated, turning away from the

phone booth, unconsciously surveying the field around him for any face, car, shadow that did not seem usual, that might be watching him. It was the spy's game, to segment the field of vision in a glance and then let the mind examine each piece for an element that did not belong there.

"What is their intelligence apparatus?" Devereaux said.

"Why? Do you suspect—"

"I suspect everything."

"The Congregation for the Protection of the Faith. Would the man from Rome be one of them?" Hanley asked.

"I don't know. Perhaps there's a way of finding out. The Rome station man."

"January," Hanley said. "He can make inquiries. . . . And the Agency?" Hanley continued after a moment. "Are they still on the field?"

"Rice," Devereaux said. "He's getting a suntan. We played a game at the beginning of the week. He pretended I wasn't here and I pretended he wasn't here."

"Does he have any connection with the gray car you saw? Following that reporter?"

"No. It's not their usual procedure in any case. And I don't think they want to get burned twice by Rita Macklin. Not on the same case."

"But where does the gray car come from? Is this a third element?"

"Or a fourth? Or fifth? If the Vatican has sent an agent here and we're here and the CIA is here—" Devereaux paused and smiled. "A surfeit of spies."

"Yes. And now this damned business with this woman in the chapel. It was all over the evening news programs—"

"Miracles aren't 'damned business,' " Devereaux said.

"Miracle?" Hanley made his imitation of a laugh. "Miracles don't happen. That's what's wrong with it all. Someone set it up."

"Who?" Devereaux said. "If it was rigged, who rigged it? The Agency doesn't gain by more publicity directed at the priest. I guess they were waiting around down here for the matter to cool down, to have another go at Tunney. And the Vatican hasn't announced its presence here. So who gained with this show this morning?"

"I don't know," Hanley said. "You're supposed to find out."

"Perhaps it was a miracle after all." Devereaux knew it would annoy Hanley.

"Dammit. Nothing makes sense, not from the minute this man came out of Thailand."

"No," Devereaux said. "Not even our involvement in it. Why are we concerned?"

Yes. It was the same question that had dogged him from the moment Hanley put him on the assignment in New York. Why was R Section delving into a matter involving a fellow intelligence agency?

"We have to be concerned is all," Hanley said in the vague way of a man dismissing an irrelevant question.

Devereaux waited and let the silence hum on the phone lines. Dusk had come quickly and night was dark and purple over the Gulf.

"Talks with the Soviets, we don't want a hitch," Hanley said. But it was not the truth and the voice of the Control could not carry it.

"Or just our usual interagency jostling for position."

"It's more complex than that."

"What is?"

Silence again.

"Devereaux?"

He waited.

"This is a matter of delicacy. Tunney was their man in Asia. When he came out, they wanted him in a box. And then they had to let him go and they are not satisfied. He has something they want."

"And we want it first."

"Yes."

Devereaux let his breath explode softly against the green mouthpiece of the plastic phone. He was standing in the open yet he felt constrained, as though he had been placed in a small cell without windows, pitched in total darkness. He closed his eyes.

"Why do we have to know?"

"There are matters here. Delicate matters," Hanley said vaguely. "Agency to agency."

Devereaux thought of Hastings concocting his reports from the clippings of English and Irish papers. Until the day he really found something important, something that he did not make up, and was killed for it. He thought of Denisov, the Soviet KGB man, floundering as blindly as he had floundered in the trap of Hastings' knowledge. It was happening again. There was nothing new to say about this matter of an old priest from Asia yet vast forces seemed to be grinding slowly toward each other, groping and clumsy, sending blind agents against each other, and no one knew why: They only knew they had to play this game, at this time, in this place.

The matter with Hastings and the Irish had been over for a long time but he could not help thinking about it now. He felt as trapped, as alone, as he had felt then. He felt that his survival now was not certain.

"What if Tunney has no secret, has nothing to say?" Devereaux said at last.

"Ah." A long pause. "Then it will not have been worth it, will it?"

There was nothing more to say. They hung up at the same time. For a moment, Devereaux stared at the night waters, listening to the birds cry against the darkness.

It will not have been worth it.

But it was always this way in the field: not understanding in whole or part, working to bend to the question at hand, never seeking beyond it. Never to know too much. Or end up with too little. The world of spies was an infinite series of watertight compartments and the agent went from one to another only after locking the last compartment behind him.

Don't think of Hastings or what happened to Denisov. That compartment was closed long before.

He felt immensely tired as he began to walk slowly back down the causeway to the island. The hotels along the beach were gleaming and the boats in the harbor bobbed darkly in the water.

Unconsciously, as he turned his thoughts back to the present, he watched the scene around him and segmented the field of vision. Trees. Boats. A jogger flashing along the trail. Posts. Cars.

Car.

A gray car.

The car moved past him in the stream of traffic moving toward the island. He watched it as he ambled slowly. The car turned at the far end into the Howard Johnson's parking area, then crossed to the other roadway and slid into the parking lot near the harbor.

He quickened his pace and tried to keep his eye on the car.

The streetlamps above the palms on the causeway were too dim. Had someone left the car?

He began to jog toward the parking lot.

When he reached the lot, he walked directly to the car. He had no need for pretense. The same car had followed Rita Macklin. The same car was now following him.

Empty.

He opened the side door. A rental car. In the glove compartment, a tourist map of the Florida west coast.

Nothing in the ashtray.

Clean, empty.

No rental agreement. He opened the rear door and felt beneath the seats for bits of garbage. Nothing. The car might have been new except for the 3,149 miles on the odometer.

And the faint smell of soap, mingled with a smell of sweat, proof of the presence of someone. Someone had watched him; someone had followed him, followed Rita Macklin. A fourth element or a fifth?

He closed the door and looked around the parking lot, segmenting again. A woman standing next to the restaurant, waiting for someone, holding her hands in front of her and grasping the handles of a straw purse.

Two old men on a bench near a shipping-supplies store.

Two teenagers roller-skating down the sidewalk.

A shadow of a man near the docks. He walked quickly across the lot to the place where the pleasure boats were moored. Empty. Bobbing in the water.

No man; no more shadows. But there had been someone there watching him.

Who had followed him?

At that moment, a man in a white suit suddenly came behind him, bumped against him. Devereaux froze, then turned, his hands outstretched.

"Beg your pardon, wasn't watching." The smell of whiskey on his breath, smell of aftershave, a man with brown eyes and gray hair. In a white suit.

Devereaux let his hands fall. A moment ago, he would have killed him.

The tension drained out of him. His hands began to tremble.

"Sorry, friend," the boozy man said, stumbling on.

Devereaux stood still.

A delicate matter, Hanley had said. Agency to agency. A little game played to get the secrets.

Devereaux's hotel was the first in line on the south end of the beach. He entered the bright lobby and pushed through a crowd of elderly tourists being sorted out by room numbers at the front desk. It was a noisy hotel and the steel band players were now entertaining in the inner bar and lounge. He did not feel the music tonight; he wanted to be alone in his room, to sit and stare out the window of his balcony, to drink a bottle of vodka alone and not think about old deaths, old friends, or old enemies.

He took the elevator to the ninth floor.

He had pushed a wisp of his graying hair in the jamb of his door, imperceptible below the door handle, when he left.

He turned the key in the door and saw the hair was still there.

He opened the door and was framed for a moment against the light from the empty hallway.

He knew the room was not empty.

He had not expected this; he stood motionless for a moment. He did not have a weapon except for the weapon of assassination contained in the strands of wire in a copper bracelet on his wrist. The garroting weapon would be useless now.

The room was dark but he saw the shape in the shadows, the shape of a man.

He felt he could not move.

"No. Do not use the light. Be so good to come in and be quiet."

The voice came from a grave of memory. Heavy, childlike, serious with a trace of sadness at the edge. The voice of a man he had betrayed.

Devereaux pushed the light button on the wall. He had to see.

The other man held a pistol in his large, hairy hand. He had the gentle, kind face of an icon.

"Be good to turn off the light," the other man said. "I see you well enough in the darkness. And there may be watchers."

Devereaux pushed the light switch again and the room plunged into half-darkness. He let the door close behind him. "I didn't expect this," he said.

In the shimmer of moonlight in the room, Devereaux saw the gun barrel move slowly up, fixing itself on a line with Devereaux's chest.

"No," Denisov said at last. "Neither did I."

17
Denisov

For some minutes they sat in the dark without speaking.

Gradually, Devereaux's eyes became accustomed to the thin moonlight that gave an uncertain illumination to the room. A hotel room, his home for fifteen years, each room a mirror of the next he would occupy: bed, nightstand, white telephone, the inevitable motel room art hung above the bed; mirror and dresser and desk done in phony teakwood, the desk filled with a clutch of postcards and never-used stationery bearing the hotel's name. Devereaux let his gray eyes catalog the elements of the room, the elements of his life, while he waited for Denisov, for the split-second sound of the whump of the silencer, the last sound he would ever hear. This was the way a spy would die, he thought calmly: in a hotel room, in a bizarre place a thousand miles from any roots or real memories, working at a dirty little game that no one understood. He was amazed at his calm.

The room itself might not have been occupied, it showed so few signs of its tenant. Devereaux had lived in a thousand such rooms and he had learned not to make his mark on them, just as he did not make his mark on the lives and scenes he moved through; when the house-keeper cleaned in the mornings, it was as though a ghost had occupied the place, leaving a faint impression on the sheets, dampness clinging coolly to the walls of the bathroom, and that was all. Devereaux's life was contained in a single small, battered suitcase resting in the closet. It carried all his clothes and identities and all his other needs, including the inevitable small pharmacopoeia shared by professional world travelers—pills to wake up, pills to go to sleep, pills to give an illusion of security on cold nights in far places when illusions were all that was left.

Did Denisov consider these things as well?

They had been on the same duty in Asia, mirrors of each other. Denisov was cultural attaché with the Soviet embassy in Cambodia; Devereaux posed then as a Central Press Association bureau chief working out of Saigon and Phnom Penh. They made their moves and countermoves, nudging pawns forward into little acts of death, the pieces circling each other with the slow patience of wrestlers. And then, at endgame, nothing was resolved.

Each had known, after a time, that the other existed. Once, in the famous old bar on the roof in Hong Kong where all the correspondents gathered, they had recognized each other and realized they were both away from their game on leave. Denisov had purchased a drink at one end of the bar and sent it to Devereaux at the other end; but Devereaux had not tasted it. He had left the place and not seen Denisov again until the next game.

Three games in all in fifteen years. The last had been played out in England and Ireland. Denisov, for reasons of state, had even saved Devereaux's life. He had claimed to be Devereaux's friend.

Devereaux had returned the lie with another: Trust me. In their mutual wariness, in their professional paranoia that made all shadows good and usual, all light evil and frightening, they had begun to understand each other. Which did not make them friends, even if they had wished it; it made them, if anything, dangerous enemies.

Devereaux had paid Denisov shabbily for the favor of his life. He had arranged to deliver him to the British who had expelled him to the Soviet Union. For two years, Denisov had been in exile, out of action, at home in Moscow, disgraced by his failure and by his exposure.

A man with a gun. Sitting in the darkness.

Devereaux thought of his own death now and examined the thought with curiosity.

"So you were the man in the gray car," Devereaux said at last. Denisov was silent.

"Why did you come here?"

"Perhaps I was not in the gray car. Perhaps, I say, because you use that word to say nothing, to mean nothing. Denisov does not lie to you."

"Why have they let you out of the Soviet Union?"

He said it to provoke the Russian but he heard no sound, no sharp intake of breath, no indication in the half-darkness that Devereaux's betrayal two years before had hurt him.

"You are to provoke me? I do not grudge."

"Carry a grudge."

Silence. "Yes. As you say. You see how badly is become my English since it has been? In England, two years ago, I spoke well."

"And then they called you back to Moscow," Devereaux said.

"You betray me."

"Yes."

"And I do not grudge. I am not your enemy now. I am come to you."

"My enemy has a gun in a dark room."

"Do you think I am come to kill you?" The Russian voice struggled gravely against the rusty usage; he had once spoken the intricate language with barely an accent.

"Yes. You have a gun."

"I save you your life in Ireland."

Devereaux waited.

"Did I do this?"

"Yes. And you tried to take it in Cambodia."

Denisov made a face and spoke softly. "Another time, Devereaux. We must change to this time. The gun is to make you listen to me because you are too quick to the act, Devereaux."

"You have my attention."

Another face, as though Devereaux would not understand him. "No jokes. I come to you from my country, to expose myself to you."

"The second miracle of the day."

"We cannot trust the CIA. You know they are here and that this is against your law. They must not operate in this country, is it so?"

"And you must not operate in this country."

"Devereaux." The Russian stared sadly at the gray, hard-faced American standing in the half-darkness at the door. "After so many bad starts, America and my country speak now. In Denmark. We speak of peace, of a new treaty."

"That's politics."

"Yes. And the CIA is in politics again. This priest is their agent."

"Is he?"

More silence, heavy and ticking like an unseen clock.

"This is not a game against us, you and me, your country and my country," Denisov said, struggling ponderously with the language. "The priest Tunney was an agent for the CIA in Laos. That is true. The priest is an agent now but not to watch, not for intelligence. *Agent provocateur.*" The French came easily. Both men knew French and had spoken it when they had played against each other in another game in Southeast Asia long before. "You must trust me."

"Trust me," Devereaux repeated. His voice was cold, without tone or resonance.

"You are here because you do not trust the CIA. We can give you proofs. We have proofs of this man Tunney, he is an agent, he is still working for the CIA, that he is in their plot to destroy the treaty of peace between us." Sweat broke in a line on the heavy forehead.

"What proof?"

"Papers. Many proofs. Photographs. I can give you proofs."

"Let me see them."

Slowly, Denisov put down the gun on the dresser. Devereaux did not move from the door. It was as though he were watching Denisov move in slow motion.

Denisov reached into his coat and took out a paper-wrapped parcel. He placed the package on the long plastic "teakwood' dresser and slid it soundlessly to the other end. The package fell with a soft thump on the thick carpet.

"You see," Denisov said. He did not move toward the gun again.

Devereaux picked up the parcel and opened it, removing the string carefully as though he intended to save it. He unfolded the brown butcher paper.

The first item was a photocopy of a routine teletype transmission between the office of the Assistant Director of the Central Intelligence Agency and the payroll department. The message indicated that Leo Tunney was resumed on salary "immediately." The internal message was open, uncoded. It was dated ten days ago.

The second piece of paper was also a photocopy, but this time of a coded transmission. The code was translated at the bottom of the paper, first in Russian and then, painfully on what appeared to be a manual typewriter, in English:

CONTINUE CAMBODIAN PROBE.

EXPECT FRESH EVIDENCE SOON.

RETURN OF M8SLASH44 WILL HELP OPERATION ABORT.

HAWKSHIELD.

The third piece of evidence was a photograph of Leo Tunney, a shy and smiling Tunney, in the embassy grounds at Bangkok. Devereaux knew the embassy and he knew the second man in the photograph who was also smiling. Victor Taubman.

"What is Abort?" Devereaux said.

"A CIA operation against the treaty for Salt Three in Denmark."

"Do I take your word for that?"

Denisov stared at the package in Devereaux's hands. "The last piece."

Two pages, crudely phrased, outlining Abort.

"From your section on Disinformation," Devereaux said with distaste, glancing over the sheets. Besides operating normal propaganda sections, the sprawling bureaucracy of the Committee for State Security—the KGB—also operated a clever section devoted to inventing whole new "truths" for dissemination in Western media.

The American intelligence community referred to these "truths" as "disinformation."

"Four pieces of proof."

"Four pieces of paper," Devereaux said.

"Information," Denisov said patiently. "You know it is like this, in bits and pieces. Leo Tunney is their agent, but now an agent to fabricate lies against us, to turn your public and your Administration against the peace treaty."

It was true, of course; real information—the stuff gleaned after sifting through mountains of lies, thousands and thousands of pieces of unrelated information—was usually just as fragmentary as these four sheets.

"Why would I reveal myself to you, Devereaux?"

"A bluff."

"You are obliged to give this to your Section."

"I have no obligation to you."

"Devereaux, Tunney is not what he seems."

For the first time, Devereaux smiled, a hard smile without mirth. "Don't you believe in miracles, Denisov?"

"This is not for a joke," Denisov said. "The Agency is to deceive you, to deceive us, to destroy our détente again. But we are not deceived. Do you think I would give you this—to give you the work of a mole inside the CIA—as a ruse? The Agency has gone too far. They cannot put the sheep over our eyes."

"Wool," Devereaux corrected absently. He looked at the papers again. Photocopies, bits of information. Or disinformation. Part of it might be true, part of it a lie. All of it might be true, all of it lies.

He put the papers down.

"Tunney will use the television to denounce us, to invent a lie about us."

"A lie?"

"This is an Agency operation," Denisov said.

What lie?

Devereaux suddenly made a series of connections: the Section's interest, Hanley's insistence on using him because of his Asian experience, the odd behavior of the CIA throughout. But what about this incident at Mass in the church? And what about the presence now not only of the Vatican but of the Soviets?

Four factors. Five factors. And there was the matter of the gray car as well.

"The Agency does not want the truth," Denisov said. "The Agency does not want friendship between our countries."

"And they kept this old priest on ice for twenty years to use him at the right moment."

Denisov said, "Who knows what they have done?"

"You've read too many Russian novels."

"Conspiracies exist, my friend. Even if you must make a joke of them."

Devereaux stared at the other man in the half-light. He had known him for eighteen years as an enemy. It was nearly as good as knowing him as a friend. They had sparred against each other across half a world. Was that what Denisov had risked in this contact? That somehow Devereaux would think again and again about this package of "evidence" and use it to extricate himself from this assignment?

But what if it were all true?

They both knew that the CIA had been involved in a complex double operation in Ireland, directed against both British intelligence and R Section. That was another day, as Denisov would say.

"There are Soviet conspiracies as well," Devereaux said finally.

"Yes. But I have come to you. I have shown myself to you."

"Because you had to. If this is the truth. Or if it is a lie."

"I am not a martyr."

But you have the face of a Russian saint, Devereaux thought. The face of a man without guile. My mirror image and yet you distort me. We are both liars, both spies, we would betray each other. Devereaux felt as though he stood on the edge of a trap.

"I betrayed you," Devereaux said.

"Yes." He said it too quickly and they both realized it. It wasn't something they had forgotten.

"There was some problem. For a time." Denisov let the words stand alone but they collapsed in the silence. When he continued, the voice was soft, without self-pity. "I was sent to Gorki for a time. For an examination."

The neutral voice of the intelligence agent, reciting all he knew. Or most of it.

"I know. We have our watchers as well."

"Did you care, Devereaux?" For one moment, the neutral voice broke. There was a bitterness to it that brushed against Devereaux's conscience.

"No. I was interested."

"Interested. A word that does not mean anything. As you say 'perhaps.' Without commitment to anything."

"Why did they send you out again?"

"Because they trusted me. Because a contact had to be made. Because you were the other man."

"And if you fail now? To convince me?"

"You must believe what I say to you."

"No," Devereaux said, the voice hard as ice. "I must not." And yet it was so beguiling, so near the truth. The little "proofs" in the brown parcel. He could smell the beast in the trap, hear the breathing of the beast. The beast was very near to him. It was in this room.

"They need to make contact. They sent me to you."

"And if I choose not to give the proof to my Section?"

"Other ways will be found to expose them," Denisov said. "There are newspapers, there is television."

"The media have been used before."

"Yes. For the truth."

"For disinformation."

"I cannot argue, Devereaux. These are the proofs. Why has your Section sent you to this man if they trusted him? If they trusted the CIA in this matter?"

Yes. The question he had asked Hanley and Hanley chose not to answer. Denisov now sets a trap; Denisov does not set a trap. Choose or do not choose.

It would be easier to give them the proof and let them play out their games without him.

He thought of Rita Macklin then. He could walk away from this, he would not have to use her, he would not have to betray her.

"And if I did not give them the proof?"

"That would be a problem."

"Yes," Devereaux said.

Denisov picked up the pistol again. "Do you see, my friend?"

Devereaux stared at the black gun in the moonlit room.

Yes. He saw.

18
Martin Foley

Another morning of rain. It fell in sheets outside the windows of the rectory; black clouds held council in the dead calm of the storm above the sprawling white city. The streets were shining wet and traffic edged slowly along Route 19, the congested old artery linking the bloated resort cities of the west coast of central Florida.

Tuesday morning, two days since the "incident" in the chapel.

Martin Foley opened his eyes just before dawn. He listened to the rain and thought himself a child again in Liverpool, sleeping on a free morning, listening to the rain in the darkness. Gray light searched the room until he opened his eyes. The gray light reflected his mood.

The "incident." Father McGillicuddy had called it a "miracle" but Foley had angrily cut him down. "This is an incident, an unfortunate incident," Foley had said. And he had been stern in his admonition to McGillicuddy: no more public Masses for Tunney and no interviews.

The world press had noted the miracle and dragged up Leo Tunney's alleged connection with the Central Intelligence Agency.

Cardinal Ludovico, who was in Prague, had wired a sarcastic and scathing cable to Martin Foley. He wanted results from Tunney, not miracles. He wanted the truth.

But Tunney, stubbornly, continued to scribble in his red journal. "The truth takes a little time," Tunney said. And Foley, caught between the new press of public attention and McGillicuddy's exploitation of it and Ludovico's admonitions, had felt trapped. So Monday had passed and now it was Tuesday morning.

He said his prayers in the darkness of his bedroom and then turned on the television set on the dresser. The screen pictured a young woman with chalk-white skin and dark, damp hair clinging to her high forehead. Lu Ann Carter talking about miracles.

The Bishop of the diocese had not been pleased but Foley had pulled rank on him. Foley was from the Vatican; Foley was the agent of the Pope. The Bishop had retreated and washed his hands of the "miracle" or "incident" that had occurred at Clearwater.

Foley shoved the "off" button savagely and ran his hands through his thick hair. A mess. On Monday, a thousand people had been waiting outside the little chapel to see Tunney. It had rained that day as well and they had waited in the rain, without complaint, waited on their crutches and in their bandages and leaning on their aluminum walkers, waited huddled under blankets and in wheelchairs. Old men and old women waited and children with broken bodies, ushered in their wheelchairs by anxious, suffering parents; men in gray work jackets and cloth caps waited as well as the simple tourists in colorful shirts and shorts festooned with Polaroid cameras and buttons claiming they had been visitors to Disney World or Busch Gardens.

Foley stood at the window now and watched the rain. Maybe they would not come out today.

It had been a circus yesterday. He had forbidden Tunney to say Mass in public but when the old priest had seen the immense Monday morning crowds in the side streets outside the chapel, he had gone out to greet them.

He had told them he could not offer Mass for them. He had stood alone in the rain, his face fragile and ethereal, and they had crowded around him and shoved umbrellas over his head so that he would not get wet. They had groaned in their expectations and their common misery; they had surged around him and cried out to him to cure them; they had held up their rosaries and old missals containing the words of the Latin Mass; they had shouted for him to touch them.

And, at last, Leo Tunney had begun to pray:

"Our father who art in heaven, hallowed be Thy name; Thy kingdom come; Thy will be done on earth as it is in heaven. . . ."

He had prayed and then begun the decades of the rosary that someone had thrust into his bony hands. They had knelt in the street, in the rain, and answered his chants. At the outskirts of the crowd, policemen from Pinellas County and Clearwater had attempted to shove the crowds out of the thoroughfare but they could not bring themselves to push these old, crippled, broken bodies. Finally, the police had merely blocked the streets with their squad cars, the roof lights circling red and blue, making the scene even more eerie and unreal in the pale morning light.

McGillicuddy had watched from a window. Foley had fumed at him but there was nothing he could do.

"Touch me, touch me," some of the Monday morning crowd had cried. And Tunney had raised his hands and made the Sign of the Cross over them.

All day they had come but Foley kept Tunney inside after the morning incident. Television camera crews came and a man who said he was from the *New York Times* and three reporters from *People* magazine and a correspondent from the *National Enquirer.* All were turned away, including the surprised man from the *Times* who kept explaining to McGillicuddy that he was from New York and could not be treated this way.

But the woman who claimed a miracle—this Lu Ann Carter was available for interviews. She said she was from near Homosassa Springs, Florida. She said she had suffered from scoliosis, curvature of the spine, for ten years, a gradual and wasting disease. Twenty-nine, she said she was. Her cousin, who owned a small chicken farm, screened the reporters who wanted to talk to her. He accepted money from some of them.

Lu Ann Carter was not articulate, which seemed to make her more sincere.

But was it a miracle?

She was straightened, she said.

Would she become a Catholic?

No, but God put holy men in all religions.

Her face was produced on Monday on a thousand Associated Press photo transmission machines in a thousand newspaper offices. On Monday night, the story of her miracle at the hands of the "prodigal priest" (as NBC called him) was an item on the network news programs. It was an item of hope: Yes, there was a war in the Middle East, and yes, the nation still was sinking into a torpor of economic disaster, and yes, the talks with the Soviets in Denmark were not going well, and yes, there were still horror stories coming from the starving people in Thailand housed in the refugee camps along the Cambodian border. But this single story of a "miracle" was good news and it lightened the heavy load of bad news that day.

Was it a hoax? Why was a priest working for the CIA? The media played it out in public.

Foley stood now at the window and watched the rain as he had watched it as a child in Liverpool. Endless rainy days making the River Mersey gray and heavy . . .

He felt so trapped, by Tunney, by this "incident," by his assignment to get information from a mad old priest, information he was not even sure existed. He felt at the center of events he was not a part of.

On Monday night, he had confronted Tunney in the kitchen of the rectory. "Do you think you're a bloody saint, is that it? A miracle worker?"

Tunney had only stared wordlessly at Martin Foley.

"We need that journal and yet you make a mockery—"

"No."

The voice had been firm and quiet.

"No? What is 'no'?"

"I am not a saint. Or a miracle worker. I am not even a good man."

"Don't lay that rhetoric on me again. This is false humility, this—"

Tunney slowly nodded.

"Yes. of course. You're right, Father Foley."

He bowed his head. In the next room, Mrs. Jones was listening at the door. Later she told her neighbor, Mrs. Custis, that she had known all along there was something "special" about Father Tunney, that he was one of God's special people. She had known it from the first.

"Yes," Leo Tunney had said. "I am willful. That is why I went outside this morning when you forbade me to say Mass. All those people had come." Suddenly, his eyes opened very wide, seeing things far from the room in which he stood. "In the village, you see . . . When the people—when we—when we had nothing at all, when hope was gone along with the food, when the dead were piled around us and we had become too weak even to bury them . . ." Again, he paused, fell into a brief reverie. When he spoke again, his voice was altered, agitated. "I gave them nothing then. I had nothing for them. Nothing at all. All the gifts, all the powers I thought I had

. . . And this morning, in the rain, when they came to the chapel and I could not even give them the Mass, I saw all their suffering, as it had been before in the villages. I could bless them now, I felt, inside me, that I could give them prayers to say and they would believe me. As they had not believed me in the villages. I gave them words, Father. I had to give them words, it was my second chance—"

Suddenly, the old priest sobbed, his eyes filled with tears. He rose from the chair quickly and went to his knees in front of the younger man. "Father, forgive me. Forgive my arrogance and pride."

So Foley had been shamed to silence. Tunney had returned to his journal and worked on it late into the night. The crowds surged around the complex of buildings that were the motherhouse of the Order.

Foley saw that they were still there this morning in the rain-swept streets.

Miracles.

Foley dressed in the gray light of Tuesday morning, then opened the door of his room and went down the hall to Tunney's chamber.

The door was tightly closed.

He knocked once, hesitatingly.

There was no answer.

It was just after six in the morning. Foley went down the carpeted hallway and opened the inner door of the chapel. The old man was there.

Tunney stood at the altar, his hands at his sides, staring at the sanctuary.

Quietly, Foley closed the door and returned down the main hall to the side corridor that led to the little bedrooms.

He pushed open the door to Tunney's room and closed it.

Carefully, quickly, in the manner of a man skilled in intelligence work, he began to go through the drawers in the chest at the side of the room. He examined each article in the room, opening and closing, returning each to the exact place he had taken it from. There would be no trace of his presence.

Where was the journal?

Shaving kit.

A shirt of flowered design that McGillicuddy had pressed on the old man.

A new breviary of daily prayers.

A rosary. The rosary that someone had given him in the rain on Monday morning.

For a moment, Foley paused and frowned: The old man went to chapel to pray without the tools of prayer. Without a book or a rosary.

The old man stood at the altar and prayed, not on his knees.

Or was he praying at all?

Minutes passed. Sweat broke out across Foley's broad forehead. His blue eyes darted back and forth as he examined all the drawers and then the night table and then the desk.

Nothing at all.

He looked between the mattress and spring, then opened the closet. But it was empty.

The journal was not in the room.

It was hidden.

Against whom?

Not for the first time, Martin Foley felt lost, felt himself grasping at loose sand on a cliffside, sliding slowly down the shallow cliff, down to the ledge of an unspeakable chasm.

He stood in the middle of the room and looked around and could see no hiding place. Quietly, he left the room, closing the door carefully.

In the dim hall, there was a massive bureau of Spanish oak, a crucifix upon it, and a small silver plate of the sort once used for calling cards. On the wall above the bureau was a very bad reproduction of da Vinci's *Last Supper* in an expensive frame.

Hidden against Martin Foley, hidden against the Church.

Foley felt frustration choking him again. He had to get out of this-house for a while, away from the priest, away from his peculiar madness, away from the trappings of this . . . this circus.

On the sidewalks and street, a large crowd waited again. There were television cameras as well, and reporters standing around in trench coats.

Foley moved away from them, down the sidewalk to the first intersection, then left down a broad avenue of white stucco houses.

Rome seemed so far away and yet, if the journal were completed in a few days, he could be back there by the weekend, sitting in his favorite trattoria in the old quarter, listening to the lies of the owner who bragged of his direct descent from the family of the Caesars—

The gray car had turned at the corner. It followed him discreetly down the street.

The city seemed so empty to him. No one walked, the streets were never full of people. And now, at lonely dawn, in the rain, he felt the emptiness more and felt his sense of isolation from this strange American culture. Block after block of stucco houses, each as large as a villa. So much wealth, he thought, so much emptiness.

The rain began to soothe him and he walked at a slower pace.

The gray car stopped a hundred feet behind him and a man in a dark jacket emerged from the driver's side. A second man slid from the passenger seat behind the wheel of the car.

Foley let the thoughts of Tunney and the journal and the secret—if there was a secret, whatever the secret was—recede from his mind.

He thought of the soft days in Ireland when he visited his uncle's home in Wicklow.

He thought of the melancholy over the green, lush fields on those days of endless, gentle misting rain.

But he was not a child.

He was lost in this strange country, trying to extract the secret of a journal, a secret he could not even be told by Ludovico.

Foley crossed the wide street and stood now on the shoreline of the city, a half-mile from the entrance of the causeway to the island of Clearwater Beach. Boats in the shallow waters of the harbor moved slowly back and forth. There was little traffic on the causeway and he started down the street toward it, in the shadow of the sleeping downtown buildings.

Why had Tunney hidden the journal?

"Pardon." The voice was rumbling, soft.

Foley turned, felt the nudge, pushed away. The stranger smiled at him for a moment. The face of a saint behind wire-rimmed glasses, the eyes huge and mild. The stranger smiled as he hurried on in the rain. He carried an umbrella. He had poked Foley with the tip.

There was no reason to have the umbrella facing forward, Foley thought. There was no wind, the rain was falling straight down.

He felt the coolness of the drops on his uncovered heart. A soft day is what the old Irish countrymen would call it as they took to the soggy green fields in their tweed caps, faded black suit jackets, and high rubber wading boots worn against the muds of spring. Soft as he had known the days of his childhood.

His vision played tricks on him for a moment and he stopped and looked across the causeway at the towering hotels on the beach; or, perhaps, it was not a beach but Liverpool again and he was a child down by the docks, playing in the shadows of the Lever towers.

But that was madness.

He wasn't a child, he was . . .

He was Martin Foley, yes, that was it.

An umbrella point like a pinprick. He knew that from somewhere. Was it a trick?

He started to walk across the causeway. Here, the rain felt colder as it dropped on his head.

He felt the drops. And then he felt each drop. Each drop, drop, drop, each one heavier than the last.

He held up his hand against the drops. The drops of rain were crushing him. Each fell like a hammer blow. His head exploded as each drop struck him, savagely, again and again, each drop like a stone. They were stoning him and each drop was a rock. He bled.

He wiped rain from his forehead and saw that it was blood. He was soaked in blood. He was dying with the blood forming across his eyes; he could not see.

Dying.

Jesus Christ, succor me in my last moment.

He was a boy visiting Aunt Mary, outside the cot, outside in the green fields, he smelled smoke and dung, the peat fire. . . .

Mother Mary, Aunt Mary, Mother of God from Dun Laoghaire.

He was running. Yes, he was definitely running. A ridiculous thing to do in the rain. The rain fell too quickly, too harshly, but if he ran faster and faster, the rain would fall behind him, he would be out of it. There, he was running between the drops of rain. All he had to do was run back and forth between the drops of rain. . . .

And then he saw him.

Jesus Christ, standing on the sidewalk across the roadway, on the other side of the Memorial Causeway. This causeway was a memorial to Him, the Lamb of God.

Christ beckoned him.

Jesus Christ. Full of grace and beauty.

He began to run. . . .

It was quite a traffic problem, Officer Montgomery Duvall said later, much later, in his unofficial report at the Pinellas County sheriff's office. First of all, he explained, the pickup truck that hit the priest skidded in the wet rain and damn near slid right off the causeway itself and that would have been a helluva mess. But the worst was when the other traffic stopped to help, and the priest, he got up just like that, ran right across the roadway, bleeding from when the pickup hit him, and they said you should of seen it. Ran right into the water. Waded right out until he drowned.

The found the body by late afternoon because the waters were calm and not very deep.

Because the death could have been listed as a suicide, and because suicide was the single unforgivable sin in Catholic belief, Father McGillicuddy used all his persuasion to get a detailed autopsy.

Which was the reason, in turn, that a bright young medical examiner discovered the massive amount of LSD in the blood of the victim.

A rumor came out of the morgue that the priest had been on dope and that even the old one in the motherhouse, the one who worked miracles, was part of a new dope cult. The edgy citizens of Pinellas, who had been witness to the protracted struggle between local politicians and the bizarre cult of the Church of Scientology, were quite ready to believe anything.

After three weeks, the body of Martin Foley was returned to Liverpool for a final funeral and, at last, burial.

But by then, the secret he had wanted to learn—because of which he had died—was finally known.

19
Denisov

"What I can do for you?" The accent was thick, suspicious. Denisov had difficulty understanding him for a moment until the man repeated himself.

"My name is Jorgensen," Denisov said.

"Yeah?"

"I am with the *Dagblat Svenska*."

"What the hell is that?"

"The largest newspaper. In Sweden."

"In Sweden? You Swedish?"

Denisov nodded. The room was at the end of a hall in a motel on Gulf-to-Bay Boulevard in the city of Clearwater. Outside, traffic surged back and forth restlessly along the miles of franchise food shops and restaurants and motels with small swimming pools on the roadside.

He had had difficulty finding the place at all.

"I would like to speak to this woman," Denisov said, smiling. "I am too interested in what has happened in the church."

"You are?" The lean face of the middle-aged man appeared to have a permanent five o'clock shadow etched around the chin. He wore a white shirt open at the neck. His face and arms were deeply sunburned, as though he worked outside.

"Well, I tell you Mr. Anderson—"

"Jorgensen," Denisov said. The mistake annoyed him.

"Little ole Lu Ann is pretty tired right now and she's set up to see this fella from the *National Enquirer* later tonight. So I don't think I can help you out."

"Please," Denisov said.

"Well, look. I'll put it pretty straight to you and I hope you appreciate that. Lu Ann's only got so many minutes in the day, God knows, and so I'm sort of managing her time for her."

"Who are you, please?"

"My name is Willis," the man said. "I'm her cousin, if it's business of yours."

"Please," said Denisov. "I would like to see this woman."

"I'm sure you would—"

"Who is it, Willis?" The voice was small and cracker-rough. It came from the bathroom.

"Fella from Sweden he says," Willis said, holding the door in one hand and calling over his shoulder.

"What's he want?"

"What's he want? Wants you, honey, is what he wants."

"Tell him to go 'way, I got a headache now, Willis."

"You heard the lady."

"Please. I have come too great a distance."

"I appreciate that, I surely do," Willis said in the manner of a person who did not appreciate it at all. "Look here, let me put it right out to you, I don't believe we got to be pussyfooting around. You got money on you? American money, not that ole Swedish money or whatever."

Denisov was startled. When he had read of the incident in the church, he was puzzled, first by the reaction of the American media and then by the woman herself. He had studied her on the television screen and he still did not understand what her part was in the puzzle of Leo Tunney. He finally decided she was an American agent, for the Section or for the CIA. He had decided to be absolutely certain before killing her.

"I do not understand."

"Man, you understand. Look, money talks and bullshit walks and that's the way of the world. If I'm going to manage ole Lu Ann, we are going to have to keep this on a civilized basis, you dig?"

Denisov blinked at him. He understood some of the words but they did not seem to be in a sensible order.

"How much you got?"

"What is it you want?" Denisov said slowly, so that the other man would slow down his words as well.

"Money. Green. What the hell you think I'm talking about?" His laugh was like a bark. "Lu Ann is an innocent chile and I don't want you to get the wrong idea but I gotta protect her."

Denisov understood at last. He opened his pocketbook.

"What the hell kind of money is that?"

"Traveler's check," Denisov said. Issued by the KGB, acquired from the Gordny printing complex in Byelorussia, where a steady stream of the checks was forged in a variety of currencies.

"I don't want no goddam traveler check, I want Uncle's paper."

"I do not understand."

Willis started to close the door.

Gently, with strength, Denisov pushed against it. The door opened as though Willis were not there. He was pushed back against the bureau behind the door.

"Hey, now, you can't push a American like that."

"Please to sit down," said Denisov slowly, gravely. He closed the door behind him.

"What's going on out there, can't ah take a pee without all that fuss?"

"Nothing, Lu Ann, honey," said Willis.

"Please to come out here," said Denisov.

"What's that? Is that fella here?"

She emerged from the bathroom dressed in an Oriental bathrobe with dragons and kimono-clad women printed on it. She was thin and her face was as chalk white as it had appeared on the television screen that morning.

Denisov looked around him. On the dresser were the remains of a Kentucky Fried Chicken bucket dinner. Congealed gravy had stained the plastic top of the dresser.

There were articles of clothing on the floor, male and female pieces, mixed together.

Both beds in the room were rumpled and the bedclothes were bunched at the foot of them.

The television set was on with the sound turned down. A cartoon about a mouse was playing on the screen.

Denisov felt in his pocket for the familiar pistol. A very small pistol of French make.

"I am Jorgensen," he said and repeated the name of the paper. "I would talk to you about what happened."

"He come busting his way in here honey, I—"

"Be quiet," said Denisov, the voice as ponderous as the march of a bear.

Willis took a swing at him then.

Denisov took the blow and shook it off. He turned his mild eyes to the other man who stood for a moment undecided. Denisov said, "Be quiet." He said it as an adult speaks to a child.

"Willis." The voice of the thin woman was hard. The words cracked like sounds of a whip. "Sit down like he said. This man ain't messing around."

"No," said Denisov. "You understand. This is not too long. I must know about this in the church."

For the first time, Lu Ann trembled.

Denisov noticed the fear in her eyes. Why was she afraid? he thought. Does she know who I am?

"It was everything like I said," Lu Ann Carter said. "Just like it. I'm just a girl from the swamps, ain't got nothing, ain't never gonna have nothing."

"Yes," said Denisov. He stood perfectly still. Willis sat on the edge of the bed and stared at him.

"I was a cripple and Willis'd testify on his mother's grave to that. Folks coming in here trying to say I'm some fake or something, smart-aleck reporters from the North and all, well, I am what you see—"

"Who are you?" Denisov said.

She took a step back. She crossed her arms across her chest. She never let her dark eyes leave his mild face.

"Lu Ann Carter. Just Lu Ann Carter."

"That miracle was real, I swear to God it was," said Willis. "I don't want you to get riled, I—"

"Be quiet," said Denisov.

He stared at her and she trembled again as though she understood his thoughts.

What would Gogol instruct him in this instance? But it was too bizarre. It was beyond any scenario, he thought.

"Lu Ann Carter," he repeated.

He felt the pistol in his pocket. He decided.

He reached for the handle of the door and opened it. He closed the door behind him without a word.

"Oh my God," Lu Ann Carter said when he was gone.

"Honey, honey, you're shaking all over." Willis took her in his arms. "Honey, honey," he crooned. "He ain't gonna hurt you none. I didn't know who he was—"

"Oh, shut up, Willis," Lu Ann said.

He realized she was crying.

"Ain't nothing to cry about," he said, holding her trembling form next to him.

But she knew there was.

20
Rita Macklin

"I would like to see you," Devereaux said. He stood at the pay telephone in the lobby of his hotel; habit impelled him to avoid a room telephone. Every contact came from an anonymous place.

"What time is it?"

"Seven."

"Seven? In the morning? God, I feel like I'm drugged, I'm so tired. But I should be up." Rita's voice sounded pleasant and husky; Devereaux imagined her in bed, half-asleep, carelessly entwined in sheets the way a child sleeps. The image pleased him.

"I got the coroner's report for you. On Father Foley's death."

"Really?" She paused. "Really? How did you do that?"

"An old reporter's trick," he lied. "From days I worked in Chicago before I got polite."

"All the rumors are he was drugged—"

"Yes. That's true."

"LSD."

"Yes."

"It was a suicide—"

"No. At least, they don't think so now. They're a little confused. Let's not talk on the phone," Devereaux said. "Could we meet?"

"Ah." She was smiling and her voice reflected it. "You want to ply me with breakfast, is that it?"

"Of course." He grinned and she might have been pleased to know it.

"Smooth talker."

"It's a part of my careful line. I feed you again and again until you're so fat you have to give in to me, there's no one else."

"You like fat women."

"No. But I like you and I'm willing to sacrifice the aesthetics of the situation in order to have you."

"All right. Meet me here. On the beach, in ten minutes."

Like his hotel, her place faced the Gulf on the north end of the public beach. It was a low, ugly place full of Canadians and Germans on a budget and the room rates were a quarter of what Devereaux paid in his high-rise hotel. But then, he told her, he was writing it all off on expenses.

The sun was up and the day was clear and fine and the slight breeze from the Gulf was warm. He walked along the beach to her hotel a mile away.

In a little while, the beach tractor would be rumbling along the white sands, sifting and cleaning the beach of impurities left behind by the previous day's sunbathers. Then the tractor would pull along a cartload of colorful sun umbrellas to be set up on the length of the beach as far as the fishing pier; these would be rented out by the day to the bathers. Devereaux remembered that once he had been assigned to Nice in the south of France, along the Côte d'Azur. That white beach full of sharp rocks had been a monument to class and caste distinctions. Parts of it were sandwiched off into exclusive clubs and only the rich could afford to sunbathe in comfort on air mattresses and deck chairs set up on the beach. But then, the French were such snobs about the privileges of the wealthy; this beach, Devereaux thought, cleaner and more comfortable, had a rough, jovial equality about it that seemed to make the idea of sunbathing so much easier.

Since that first planned meeting at the tiki bar, Devereaux had met Rita Macklin twice.

They had hit it off. If she had any lingering suspicions about him, they had been put away for the moment. She seemed more open to him.

Trust me. Believe me.

Devereaux had not known about the existence of a journal until his second meeting with Rita. That would have been worth the risk of contact, he would explain to Hanley. There was a journal and Tunney was putting it together under the supervision of the man from Rome.

And then the Vatican agent died.

Was killed.

So there *had* to be a secret from Leo Tunney worth having, after all; at least, worth a death and worth this gathering of spies in the middle of Florida.

And Rita Macklin was his unknowing agent.

She would get the story.

And Devereaux would take it from her. At endgame. It was all so clear to him. The only puzzle now was who killed Martin Foley? He was not concerned with justice or with murderers; he was a killer himself. He just could not understand the purpose of killing Foley. Rice could not have been behind it. But someone else in the Agency?

Or was it Denisov?

Devereaux had not told Hanley about the "proofs" that Denisov had given him. No agent in the field ever gives *everything* to Control, not at first. He refrained from mentioning the papers to Hanley as well as Denisov's presence here in Florida. Aces to be played at a later date.

Devereaux crossed the beach under the concrete pilings of the fishing pier which stretched into the shallow Gulf waters. Leaning against two pilings were a pair of young drifters with thin, sallow faces; they sat on the dry sand and stared at him as sullenly as sea gulls.

"Hey, man," one began.

The other picked up the ritual greeting. "Hey, man."

Devereaux barely glanced at them as he passed.

"Hey, man, you got some money?"

"Sure. A lot."

They watched him, their faces stupid, and they did not reply because they did not know what to say. In a moment, Devereaux was beyond them.

Minutes later, he saw Rita emerge from the beach door of her hotel. She looks so fresh, he thought, with something like regret.

In the endgame, she was merely to be used and discarded.

Her bright face broke into a smile as he approached her across the thicker sand away from the shoreline. She waved at him and he waved back, once, gravely, and thought again of how unsuited he was for this, unprepared in emotion, in the well of feeling she had uncovered in him, unprepared for the honing anew of sensitivities in his nature he had long ago blunted down in order to survive.

They were like two galaxies passing through each other, stars and planets millions of miles apart, passing in and out of each other's lives without colliding. She would never understand his world, but he had once been part of hers.

He had killed men in order to survive and to complete missions. He knew from the first meeting he could never explain that to her, or justify it. Killing had stained him and the thought of killing and of being killed had marked him; his dreams had become dreams of blood and death, of fears like poisons seeping into him moment by moment, paralyzing emotions; his nightmares did not flee in the morning. He dragged around the memory of dead men like chains.

She, unconsciously, with a smile and the empathy of her words, had broken through all these layers of death in life and had silenced his bad dreams without even realizing they existed. She had touched him.

"You look tired," she said with easy concern.

She did not. Her soft red hair blew away from her lively face, from the green, sparkling pools of her eyes, in the gentle wind.

"Hello."

Then she kissed him.

She had not kissed him before. He had not moved to touch her, not for the sake of the mission—what had he not done for missions in the past?—nor for the sake of the inevitable betrayal that he saw coming, but because the fragility of their relationship had become too exquisite, like a small glass animal in an old woman's collection, a beautiful thing that caught the light in a dark room but was never touched, only caressed with the eyes.

But her kiss broke nothing, Devereaux realized. It was as soft as morning light.

He held her for a moment, his arm around her thin waist, staring down into her face. "Why did you do that?"

She kissed him again, lightly. "Because you are so grave and formal. 'Hello.' A gentleman of the old school, a man for the ladies."

"Thank you," he said gravely. "The old school."

She laughed and they held each other a moment longer than they had planned. And when they turned to walk away from the beach to the little row of shops and restaurants on the commercial strip, they were arm in arm.

They had found a little place that served breakfast without a jukebox or radio blaring. "I hate music in the morning," she had said. The breakfast was not very good but they liked the silence and staring at each other.

She ate eggs and bacon, potatoes and two orders of toast.

Once, she smiled at him as she raised the fork to her lips. "Just a farm girl."

He sipped coffee and stared at the remains of a poached egg on his plate. He did not want to eat this morning; he never ate for pleasure, not since he was a child. He ate for fuel and for social reasons.

"You're just healthy," he said. "All that butter you ate as a girl in Wisconsin."

"I must have clogged arteries by now."

"Don't worry about it."

"And you're a coffee-and-cigarettes type. Very Bogart."

"I don't smoke."

"The only thing lacking in the image, you're going to have to consider it." She smiled again and touched his hand with affection. "But that's not what I mean." The gesture of affection so uncalculated, warmed him. He did not know what to say with her; he had not bantered with a woman for a long time.

"Foley," he said, because he did not know what else to say. "Died of LSD."

"So the rumors were right. This town is positively jittery on the subject of bizarre religious experiments."

"Coming on the heels of that 'incident,' " Devereaux said. "The miracle."

"The miracle," she repeated. "I don't believe this is happening except I'm beginning to believe everything. Nothing is as bizarre as the truth." She stopped eating and stared at him. "When those black children were murdered in Atlanta. And a bunch of thugs called the Guardian Angels came down from New York to teach the kids of Atlanta how to protect themselves. And then a bunch of Hollywood stars came out to do a concert, for God's sake. Everything becomes bizarre."

"Only when it gets too big to handle on a rational level," Devereaux said. "It's the human mechanism that allows the spring to unwind quickly without snapping. Otherwise, we would all go crazy."

"Yes," she said. "That's it exactly. And now you tell me Foley was taking LSD."

"No. I didn't say that."

She waited.

He picked up his cup of black coffee and sipped it. He put it down and the waitress came over and filled it to the brim again. He fingered the handle of the heavy cup and stared at the saucer. What he would say now would be difficult; he would have to be on guard.

"He was from the Vatican," Devereaux began. "He came here for some reason. Probably to oversee Tunney, to question him. Tunney had already been questioned by the CIA."

"What are you saying?"

"Foley had LSD in him. It didn't mean he took it."

"You think that that cook, Mrs. Jones, in the rectory, gave it to him in his cookies?"

Devereaux said nothing.

"This is fantastic," she said. "Like a spy novel. I read in Gordon Liddy's book that the CIA types were into dosing people with drugs to make them do crazy things—"

Devereaux looked up, sharply. "Why does it have to be the CIA?"

"What do you mean?"

Dangerous ground, he cautioned himself. He backed away from it. "Drug dealers do it all the time. And pimps dose their girls with drugs, to control them sometimes, to kill them other times."

She stared at him and saw no sense of horror in him at what he had just said. For the first time, he frightened her and she felt chilled.

"What does the coroner's report conclude?"

"Nothing. Except that there was LSD in the body. And that he died by drowning." He opened a sheet of paper and passed it to her.

"How did you get it?"

"It wasn't so difficult."

She glanced at it. "You're saying someone killed Foley?"

"It's possible."

"Why?"

"Because he knew too much."

"What?"

"Or because he was the wrong man."

She stared at him.

"Do you see, Rita?" His voice had resumed a low quality, a surging flatness that made the words drift along without individual emphasis on them. "Tunney comes out of Asia. That is bizarre to begin with. The CIA locks him up. Another oddity. He is released here and a man from Rome comes to shut him up or find out what he knows, or something. Third oddity in the chain. And then the real wild card—a woman claims to have been the recipient of a miraculous touch from our missionary. Finally, the man from Rome is killed. Now, are all the oddities connected? If you assume they are, then you have to start looking at all that's happened not as a bizarre series of strange and singular random events but as parts of a pattern."

"The reasoning behind all conspiracy theories," Rita said.

"Yes. But just because so many of them are wrong, don't think conspiracies don't exist."

She was silent for a moment. "You gave me this story. This is a good story. Why?"

"You mean, why don't I steal it?"

"Yes. Something like that."

"You said it yourself. I'm an old-fashioned type."

"That could make you a bad reporter."

"No. Only a tired one." His voice reflected a weariness that was not a lie or part of his disguise to her. He was tired, he realized, not because he had awakened again at three in the morning but because of the lies and the truths he had given her. The truths exhausted him; lies and truths were becoming mixed in his mind.

Like Denisov's lies to him. Denisov was his mirror; he saw Denisov and saw himself; heard him and heard himself.

"Maybe it's more than being tired," she said, touching his hand again. "Maybe it is just the honorable thing."

"A man of honor," Devereaux said, mocking himself.

"Yes."

"Not honor," he said. "Part of my line, like plying you with food." Truths in the lies again, he realized.

"When this is done." She hesitated. "We're going to see each other again, aren't we?"

"You mean in Washington? When you go back to Kaiser? You're going back to work for him?"

"No. I'm may go back to D.C. but not to Kaiser. I can't do that."

"Why not?" he asked.

"Because that's finished," she said, her words final and hard. "We split. He let me go and it was bad, the way it happened between us."

"But you've done stories for him here—"

"Free-lance. I work for myself now. I'll free-lance for the devil and that's different, that's not working for someone. Besides, I have to get the story out, I need an outlet. But I couldn't work for him again."

"You say it like someone ending a friendship. Or a love affair." Spoken softly.

She glanced up at him and shook her head. "We were friends is all. Yes. We were friends. I liked him and I still do maybe, he taught me so many things. But that's all past now. It turns out to be something like trust. When you work for someone, it's part of the trust. If one side betrays the other, then you can't go back and shake hands later and say you didn't mean it."

"How did he betray you?"

"He stopped me. I don't know why but he lied to me, about

this story. I kept feeling that he didn't want me to go on it, not because he thought it was a waste of time—it was because he knew there was something here, something he didn't want me to know. But he wouldn't tell me. It was lying, not telling me. The trust breaks and you can't put it back together again."

The words wounded him.

Rita looked at his face and took his hand. She saw a mark of pain in his gray eyes and imagined it was pity for her.

"Don't worry," Rita said. "I'll get by all right. Especially after all this down here. This is a hell of a story. And when I get the journal—"

The gray eyes changed; they were cold again, unfathomable, the Arctic Ocean stretching to infinity. "You're going to get it."

"Sure. I know it."

"The confidence of youth."

"Watch me."

"I'll watch you, Rita."

"It must be something. Something in that journal, something worth having, something worth all this."

"You mean Foley's murder."

"You say it's murder."

"Yes. Just what I say," Devereaux said.

"Dev." She held his hand tightly across the tabletop. "I trust you. There are things I can tell you I wouldn't—well, I would have told Kaiser. Before. But I can tell you."

He waited, nearly motionless.

It was what he wanted, after all; trust me.

There was something like pity in her eyes, he saw, and then realized it was not pity at all. It was something else, more heartbreaking. He did not want to look at her but he would not break the chain of the moment.

"I know I'm going to get the journal," she said.

He felt tension grab him.

"I talked to Tunney yesterday. In the church, when he was there alone."

Good, he thought. She was really very good. "How did you do it?" He made his voice calm.

"I never left the church," Rita said. She paused for effect.

"Foley has been dead for two days. They had Mass yesterday morning. Father McGillicuddy said Mass. Afterward, he locked the public doors of the chapel. I had brought along some sandwiches and a thermos, I didn't know how long it would take."

"You broke in," he said.

"No. I never left." She smiled. "I went inside the confessional during Mass. I waited is all. Tunney is a priest, I figured sometime he would come to the chapel from the rectory and pray. Alone."

"That's very good, Rita," he said, and realized it was and that it had not occurred to him at all.

"Yes. And it worked which is better." She let go of his hand and took her cup of coffee and sipped it. The waitress came and removed the breakfast dishes. "Father Tunney came in the middle of the afternoon, I must have been in that box for six hours. About two o'clock, I think. It was a little tricky, I didn't want to scare him, he's such an old-looking man. I'm afraid he was startled though, he stared at me as though I were a ghost. And then I saw he remembered me. From Watergate, from the times I've tried to get to him."

"And he talked to you."

"Yes. I haven't done anything with it yet, I want to wait for the right moment. I know Kaiser would kill me if he thought I was sitting on a story. The two of us talked in the chapel, in the middle of the day. What do you think of that?"

He didn't speak.

"He said that everything he saw would be in the journal. Everything. He kept talking about it and then he started talking about Father Foley. Do you know what he told me about Foley? It fits in with everything you said—"

That Foley was a spy, Devereaux thought. But he waited for her without speaking.

"He was a spy for the Vatican, that's what Tunney told me. He said he had become so tired. He said death was after him, that death followed and killed those around him." She stared at Devereaux. "He said he wanted an end to everything and that when the journal was finished, he would give it to me. He said the world would know what he knew and then it would be over."

There, Devereaux thought. It would be easy. She trusted him and she would make it easy for him.

She was looking down again, at her hand on his, at the cups of coffee sitting on the white Formica tabletop. "I started to tell you once. About my brother. Tommy. It all had to do with why I had to find Tunney, find out what he knew."

Devereaux remembered photographs in her bedroom. Family pictures in frames on a dresser. A fresh-faced young man in a high school sweater.

"Tommy went to Asia, you see," she began, her voice becoming distracted as though too many thoughts were intervening. "To Laos finally and Father Tunney must have known him, you see. . . . I knew that from the first, there weren't so many of them in Laos then, because of the civil war. . . ."

He waited for the fragments of sentences to come together in her mind.

"Do you remember several years ago after Watergate? All the investigations going on, about how the CIA routinely used some missionaries in parts of the world as spies? Do you remember that?"

Her voice broke off suddenly and Devereaux was surprised by tears in her eyes. He had not expected tears.

Devereaux reacted silently.

He turned over the bill on the table and took out money and counted it and left it. Without a word, they left the bright morning restaurant together. He held her arm gently, and steered her down the little street of shops filling with people. At the news shop, the vendor was already hanging out copies of that day's *New York Times* and *Chicago Tribune* and *Toronto Star* for the tourists.

After all the rain, it would be a nice day, clear and bright without a trace of pollution in the sky.

They walked to the beach and down to the hard-packed sand at the edge of the water. She took off her shoes and carried them and walked barefoot on the sand and in the water. Morning joggers chugged relentlessly down the beach while elderly gray-haired lovers in leisure suits strolled arm in arm. Devereaux and Rita Macklin were apart, waiting in the silence of the morning for what she had to tell him.

"Tommy was a priest," she began quietly, staring at her feet as she traced her toes in the wet sand.

"A missionary," she continued. Her voice had become very quiet and private. Had she ever told Kaiser such secrets? he wondered.

"You should have seen him. Good-looking, really a handsome kid."

Devereaux saw again the boy in the photograph on Rita's dresser.

"Even if I wasn't his little sister and in love with him, everyone said he was handsome. And more than that. Kind in the way some people are kind without being soft or mushy or stupid about it. Like my father was. Sometime, when we meet again—"

She looked up at him as though he might have gone away. "Sometime I'll show you the family album, all the pictures I've kept. Dad's dead now. And Tommy . . ."

She looked out at the wide Gulf before them.

Devereaux gazed up the beach at the sand where they walked. The wet sand was full of thousands of shells washed up during the night, sparkling now in the sunlight. The water lapped meekly at the shoreline.

"Dad was such a patriot. I told you that. He was second secretary in China in the forties, with Stilwell and that bunch, he worked for the State Department and when McCarthy started witch-hunting about pinkos and commies in the State Department—you remember, they were saying that the pinkos and leftists lost China to the communists—he was sort of forced to resign. I mean, he wasn't a big fish to them but he had been a member of one of the front organizations in college in the thirties, maybe. . . ." She stopped, suddenly, stubbornly. "Oh, damn them all."

Devereaux took her arm and led her along the beach and after a while she began to speak again.

"I'm telling you all this because I have to. Maybe I would have told Kaiser. I don't know. I didn't dwell on it all those years, I'm not crazy. But it all came back to me when Father Tunney returned, when he came out of Thailand. Had he been a spy for the CIA and why had they hidden him? I kept thinking about Tommy and my dad. My dad was so faithful to the country, you know. And they kicked him in the teeth and he still loved it so, he was a patriot. I keep saying that and the word has all these awful connotations but that isn't what he was. I mean, he wasn't a right-wing nut or anything. He was so gentle.

"And Tommy was like him. And religious. He became a priest. And you know what Dad told him, when he was going over to Asia? Don't betray it, he told him. Don't betray the priesthood, he told him. I didn't even know what he was talking about. Not for a long time. And then I realized he meant spying. He knew about spies, about how the government used people like Tommy."

She stopped, turned to him, her face was hard yet she was crying. "I asked him, I asked Father Tunney, did he know Tommy? You see, I had to know someone who knew him. I had to find someone to tell me that Tommy wasn't a spy."

"Why did it matter?"

"It mattered," she said. "Don't you see that?"

"No."

"Because of Tommy and what he was. I loved him, he was the best person I ever knew. Dad loved him, Dad warned him because Dad knew all the dirty tricks. He knew that they would try to use someone like Tommy, especially since his father had been. . . . a civil servant." The last words were spoken bitterly.

"Some people were moved by patriotism. Even priests," Devereaux said.

"But it would have been a betrayal for Tommy. Don't you understand? Some people don't care that much if their wife or husband cheats on them. Even if they find out. They might be hurt but they get over it. And some other people—they can't stand it, they never can get over it. It mattered that much to me and to Tommy, I know it did. And it mattered to Dad. It didn't mean anything to me that Tunney was a priest and he was a spy. I didn't feel good or bad about him. But for Tommy—"

"Why would you have thought Tommy was a spy at all?"

"Don't you know that now?"

And he did, in that moment, staring at her and at the tears.

"Because your brother died," Devereaux said.

"Yes. They said he had a fever. He was very strong, but we got a letter that said he must have been sick for a long time and no one knew it and one morning he died. No one even knew where his grave was. They looked for it for a while and then the villagers said they had buried him in the jungle. The villagers said he had just died of fever."

"And you never knew if that was true," Devereaux said.

"Yes. I never knew. I could accept that he was dead but I had to know the truth about him. I even contacted the Bishop years after but no one could tell me anything. Or they didn't want to tell me anything. I couldn't prove a negative, that Tommy was not a spy. And then Father Tunney. He had been in Laos at the same time—"

"And that's what was more important than the story."

"Yes."

"What you couldn't tell Kaiser."

"Yes."

There was nothing he could do. She cried now. openly, turning her face to the water, away from the strollers and joggers, away from him. He touched her and held her but let her cry and did not speak. He understood tears.

Finally, when she could speak again, she wiped her eyes with the sleeve of her blouse. "He knew him."

"Tunney told you that."

"Yes. I asked him. I told him about Tommy. He said he knew him. He said that Tommy was not in the CIA."

A comforting lie, Devereaux thought. He would not have believed it.

"How did he know? For sure?" Rita had not believed it either. "He said that after he was captured by the Pathet Lao, after he confessed, he was given a list of agents. His name was on the list. The names of others he knew were agents. But Tommy's name was not on the list."

"Was it enough?"

The question was hard, harder than it had to be. She did not look at him but felt his arm around her, holding her, comforting her.

"Yes," she said. "It was enough for me. My father always worried about it, he made his own inquiries, but he died before he was ever sure. I'm sure. It's over for me, that part of it. I know now. I mean, I came here for this story and I'll get it. But I had to know about my brother and how he died."

Devereaux did not speak. He felt no pangs of family loyalty, had never felt them. He accepted her anguish but did not understand it. He only felt pity for her.

"I could tell you, you see," she said, turning to him, letting him still hold her in his arms. "I could trust you."

Yes, he thought. Trust me.

"Do you understand it?" she said.

"Yes," he lied.

"God, there's so much I have to tell you sometime," she said and kissed him then.

He felt her yield herself to him; felt the softness of her body, smelled her breath like a baby's breath; he kissed her even as he thought he was betraying her.

"Rita," he said, then paused. There was nothing more to say because nothing seemed to matter.

She held him suddenly so tightly that he knew his guise was complete, that she would trust him with her secrets and her life. Hanley would be pleased, he thought bitterly.

He took her back to her hotel room where the bed had been made and her clothes were all hung neatly in the closet. On her dresser was a box of crackers and a knife and a jar of peanut butter. He thought the room looked as lonely as his own.

He lost himself in the smell of her, holding her behind the closed door, falling with her to the newly made bed, caressing the long, gentle curve of her back beneath the blouse.

In that moment, he thought he was not betraying her; he refused to let himself think of it, what would have to come at last.

He did not say he loved her.

He kissed her. She let him open her blouse. She let him touch her. She let him cover her with his naked body. She held him, she reached for him with her lips. They did not speak because all the words had been spoken.

They made love for a long time, lingering in the stillness of morning, letting all the secrets that she had opened to him be enclosed in silent caresses.

He told her no secrets.

And, because he did not speak except to make love to her with the eloquence of his body, he did not lie to her.

21
Hanley

The message light on the white telephone in his room was flashing when Devereaux returned to the hotel. He had left Rita sleeping in her bed. For a long time after they had finished lovemaking, long after Rita fell into a soft, childlike sleep, he had lain awake and watched her and traced the soft lines of her face and body with his eyes.

A message to call Hanley, sent in the usual code.

He took his time: He took a long, hot shower and changed his shirt and underclothes and went down to the lobby and dialed the number in Washington from the pay telephone.

Hanley began in his usual abrupt way, without greeting: "There was a meeting this morning."

Devereaux tried to block the image of Rita from his mind and to concentrate on the flat midwestern voice. He pictured Hanley sitting in the cold, bare room in the depths of the massive Department of Agriculture building, holding a black telephone in his hand, connected to a double-scrambler box.

"Not an official meeting," Hanley continued carefully, picking through the words as though they were mines in a poppy field. "Just me. And the A.D. from the Agency. We sat and talked for a while out of earshot on a bench in Lafayette Park." Devereaux winced at the slang; "out of earshot" was current jargon for being in a place safe from bugging.

"I'm glad," Devereaux said. "Were you planning the next espionage ball?"

"Sarcasm," Hanley said. "The matter concerned you."

"Am I being traded to the Competition?"

He realized he was angry, with himself and the control officer at the other end of the secured line. It was all Rita's fault, he thought, and then realized it was his own. He had permitted the intimacy because he had wanted her that moment on the beach, as she stood

183

vulnerable and naked in her need, and now guilt was overwhelming him like a hangover. This is your world, Devereaux now told himself, this gray, these shadows, a world of lies without pain or sorrow or tears, nothing to be proud of and nothing to feel shame about. Only the voice of this dull man on a phone line, telling you secrets.

"No. It didn't concern you specifically," Hanley said, annoyance twanging the Nebraska accent.

Devereaux waited; he couldn't trust his voice. He closed his eyes to the morning light streaming through the lobby and tried to concentrate only on the voice and the words he was receiving.

"Contact between the agencies is only at the official level. In usual times," Hanley continued. The voice was so odd, so strained. Devereaux tried to read the hint of emotion in it. What was wrong with Hanley?

"These are not usual times," Hanley continued. "I told you this was a matter of some delicacy."

"How did he know we were here?"

"Presumably Rice is in as much contact with his control as you are with me. Or more. Rice saw you."

"We didn't see each other," Devereaux said. "I told you, that was the game. We agreed that neither of us was here."

"If there was a time for levity, it has passed. The gist of the talk is this: We're called off."

Devereaux waited. He thought of Denisov and of the "proofs" still hidden in his room. And of Rita. He was close to the journal now, he had betrayed one spy and betrayed one friendship. What was Hanley saying?

"Called off," Hanley reported because there had been no answer. "Come home."

Devereaux opened his eyes and stared at the telephone receiver. "What was the authorization? Do we take the A.D's word for it?"

"We don't take orders from the Central Intelligence Agency," Hanley said sharply, trying to muster indignation for the first time. "The National Security Adviser passed along the word." Hanley rarely used full titles and nomenclature. Was this part of his indignation?

"So we leave the field to the Agency?"

"No. Both of us. We're both called off. Section and Langley."

"Why?"

Again, an uncharacteristic hesitation. Devereaux waited to read the voice.

"The Adviser. He passed the word. He doesn't want to have our agencies muddied by the press, he says that this business with the alleged miracle . . . well, he says that Tunney is not that important, that he's reviewed the whole file on the matter."

"He was important enough two weeks ago."

"Yes. I brought that up. I didn't talk to the Adviser directly, you understand. The Adviser told the A.D. that the Langley Firm overreacted in boxing Tunney in the first place."

"How perceptive of him."

"Yes."

"Do you believe him?"

"The A.D.? That the Adviser passed the order? Yes, I checked it back through channels."

"Do you believe the Adviser?"

Hanley paused. The long-distance line clicked and hummed. Their voices echoed strangely as they passed through the electronic scrambler filter.

"No, Devereaux. Not at all."

"Another element of the bizarre," Devereaux said.

"Yes. I agree." Hanley's voice was flat and defeated now.

"The Adviser isn't concerned about the press," Devereaux said.

"No. That's such an obvious lie. I wonder why he offered it."

"What about the A.D.?"

"What about him?"

"You saw him. What was his reaction?"

"The A.D. isn't a man to show his emotions."

"Neither are you."

"Yes. I know what you mean. The A.D. seemed flat telling me. He seemed knocked out. Just knocked out."

"What the hell is going on?"

"I don't know. I can't remember anything like this happening before. I don't know."

"This is bullshit, Hanley." The voice came low and hard, like a knife thrust into the soft fabric of the conversation.

"I don't want to fight with you, Devereaux." Hanley hesitated.

"I don't understand, I haven't understood from the beginning. If we're called off, why didn't it come down through channels? From the National Security Council, right through the Old Man to us? Why from the A.D. to me to you? On a park bench, for Christ's sake." Because he rarely swore, the mild phrase gave weight to Hanley's frustration.

"Devereaux," Hanley said after a minute. "Do you know what is going on here? In the Section, I mean?"

Devereaux waited.

"This Administration. Pushing, pushing, pushing. All the time. The Old Man has been before the budget council of the Cabinet three times in the past month. The Adviser keeps talking about further centralization of the intelligence effort, he says there is too much wastage—"

"I'm not interested in politics," Devereaux said.

"You should be," Hanley said. His voice was bitter. "This time, you should be. They're putting together a reorganization plan for the next fiscal year. I don't see a place for the Section in it. They want to tie up the loose ends, that's what they call us. There will be two super agencies left, one at Langley, one under the State Department. One for operations, one for intelligence and analysis."

"The Section has a congressional charter."

"Congress is frightened, everyone is frightened."

"So why did you risk me on this? To get the Adviser pissed off?"

He knew Hanley would wince at the crudity of the language. "It was our mission."

"It was never our mission."

"Something was going on—"

"You wanted to make them have to accept R Section. To leave it alone."

"To leave us alone. A calculated risk."

"It was all just politics, interagency bickering."

"Not all of it."

Devereaux thought of the dead priest. And of Rita Macklin whom he would betray at the right moment. He thought it all didn't matter to Hanley, except to save the Section from a budget cut. Goddam them, he thought.

And then he thought of Denisov.

It was not a game.

"Hanley."

No sound from the other end but he knew Control was waiting.

"A Soviet is here."

Still no sound, only the faint humming on the long-distance lines.

Then: "Who is it?"

"Do you remember our friend from Liverpool? In the Hastings matter?"

"Here? In Florida?"

"Yes."

"On this? Are you sure?"

"Of course. He told me so."

"He told you? He told you?" Hanley's voice was rising. He knew the little man would be getting out of his chair now, tightly holding the receiver, walking around the big gray government-issue desk with agitated steps and spastic nervous jerks of his hands. "How did he tell you? When? What are you going to do?"

"You told me to come home."

"Yes."

They waited. Devereaux didn't mention the proof that Denisov had given him. He didn't know why he held back. It was his instinct to do so.

"A conversation with a fucking Soviet agent, Hanley."

"Yes."

Carefully, Hanley spoke now: "When was this?"

"Four days ago."

"Why didn't you tell me then? We could have used it today, to call off the Adviser's order—"

"And have him give it to the Agency to handle."

"You're showing loyalty to the Section, Devereaux. That is uncharacteristic."

"No. Not the Section. Something doesn't smell right, not from the Adviser, not from the Agency itself."

"You should have given it to me."

"There didn't seem any point in it then."

"You always hold back."

Devereaux did not admit it.

"This presents a different problem, doesn't it? I mean, does the Competition have any awareness of the KGB here?"

"I don't know. But it doesn't sound like it, does it? Wouldn't the A.D. have put up a fight not to be called off?"

"Yes. The problem is, so would we."

"Would it have made any difference?"

"Telling us when you should have? Why—"

"Would it have made any difference to the Adviser?"

"I see." Hanley, in his dull, insulated sense of the bureaucracy, was not stupid or unaware of nuance. He understood. "That might be the question after all."

"What is going on?" Not for the first time in his eighteen years in the Section, Devereaux felt a sudden sense of isolation from the corridors of power. He felt alone, without maps or bench marks.

"I don't know," Hanley said. "If we had been called off in any other way . . ."

"It was as though the Adviser wanted the thing done without raising any inquiries in the Administration."

"And over at State. The Secretary at State is all over the place, he wants to run every pie."

"A mixed metaphor."

"But true."

"What should I do, Hanley?"

The bottom-line question. Devereaux would not dangle alone.

"Yes. I wish I had managed to reach you in time today," Hanley said finally. "I suppose you're spoiling to get some sun."

So Hanley was game for a little while, to leave Devereaux in place on the mission while Hanley probed subtly back and forth across the lines of the bureaucracy, trying to track down the reason for calling off the assignment of Leo Tunney.

"This is delicate," Hanley cautioned again.

Devereaux did not answer.

"And Foley's death," Hanley said. "Did you find the information useful?"

"Yes."

"Is your plan working?"

"Yes."

"Is this going to turn out to be worthwhile?"

"I can't judge," Devereaux said. "Except it has been good enough to get the Agency to break their charter and operate on American territory again. And to get the Soviets to send an agent here. And the Vatican."

"Yes. It might be worthwhile."

"It might be more than a little bureaucratic game."

"The survival of the Section," Hanley said. His loyalty to the Section was without parallel.

Devereaux thought of Rita then, of her touch, of her warmth and the openness of her body to him; thought of her words as she trusted him.

"To hell with the Section," Devereaux said quietly.

22
McGillicuddy

Cyrus McGillicuddy had seen death in his time, of course. In Morocco, in those years before the sedentary life of the motherhouse claimed him, he had been in the thick of it, as he never failed to tell anyone who would listen.

But that had been, in a sense, a time of abstract deaths. Even though he was able to muster charity in his heart for the suffering, it was an impersonal sort of empathy, an empathy of his faith and his own expectations of his feelings: He did not actually suffer a sense of loss when children in the desert died of starvation or when the civil war in neighboring Algeria spread to his outpost and innocents were casually slaughtered. He wept, true, and he said his prayers for their souls, but they were not of him. Still, the deaths had been real enough—death by starvation, death by mutilation (an obscure religious ritual was involved), and simple murder, murder by bloodlust. All that he had seen.

Yet Foley's death on the causeway had affected him more than all the deaths all those years in Morocco.

Not only the sight of the body, bloated, white and wet on its wooden slab in the morgue. It was not only that or the fact that he had broken bread with Foley, given him the shelter of his own house . . . no. Something more.

McGillicuddy felt guilt. Guilt for the opportunity he saw in Foley's death. He had seen it from the first moment he was called to the morgue to identify the priest, and it saddened him. He was fifty-nine years old and he did not want to believe that in all the struggle of his religious life, he had managed to save up so little charity in his heart.

But the opportunity was there.

As he had told Foley—God rest his soul—Rome did not pay the electric bill for the Order. It had been his most heated moment in their argument when Foley forbade Father Tunney to say Mass in public. McGillicuddy saw the opportunity that Leo Tunney presented the Order in terms of both new fame—spreading the word of our good works, he had said—and ready cash. The ready cash had become an increasing problem over the years: Small donations were down because fewer and fewer found their way to Sunday Mass anymore, to be moved there by appeals for charity from the pulpit; large donations from wealthy benefactors were also greatly reduced as the benefactors found newer causes to invest their wealth in. As he had once told a fellow sympathizer, the Order just wasn't sexy anymore.

And now Foley was dead.

And Rome was silent.

What should he do? After all, he was superior of the Order. It fell on his shoulders to weigh all the elements of the situation and come up with a correct solution. Yes, that was it; it fell to him.

On Friday morning, three days after the death of Martin Foley, Leo Tunney offered Mass for the repose of the soul of the dead man. In public. In the chapel that once again opened its doors to a large crowd.

Poor Tunney, Cyrus thought. He seemed dazed by it all, confused by the crowds, by Foley's death (and was he even aware that Foley was dead and not merely gone?) and by the world he lived in now.

Tunney wore the black vestments of the traditional Requiem Mass. He sang the bare ritual, rich with mournful chants:

> *Dies irae, dies ila* . . .
> Day of Judgment, day of wrath.

Lu Ann Carter was there, dressed with far more care than on the previous Sunday. She sat straight and prim in a pew up front and followed the ritual with wide, suspicious eyes. The fame of her cure had been widely heralded but it had caused no last-minute conversion to the Catholic faith. As she had said on one of the innumerable talk programs, "God made me a Baptist but I allow He works in mysterious ways." McGillicuddy had said dryly, after hearing her, that she was being extremely generous.

There was no laying on of hands and no sermon yet the cures continued: A woman who said she had suffered from diabetes for twenty years pronounced herself cured. A man who had had a painful goiter the morning before said the swelling shrank to nothing within minutes of entering the church. The fact that these claims were as shadowy and uncertifiable as Lu Ann Carter's claim was beside the point.

And so it began again, with an enormous, groaning crowd at the Saturday morning Mass, filling pews and aisles, streaming into the streets around the motherhouse complex. Again, the police were called and reporters from a half-dozen Florida newspapers were on hand to record the event.

This was for the good of the Church and the Order, Cyrus argued with himself when a devil of a suggestion in his conscience pointed out that he was avoiding the clear rules of the liturgy performed at Vatican Council.

Ends do not justify means; the conscience pricked.

But these are good means as well. The Mass.

The Tridentine Mass is forbidden.

But it is still the Mass, Cyrus argued with himself, finally overcoming.

At 3 P.M. on Saturday, Cyrus opened the doors of the church for the weekly confessions. Father Tunney, who had spent all morning and afternoon on his journal—he had continued to fill page after page in it at a redoubled pace since Foley's death—entered the church from the side door. He wore a purple stole, another symbolic vestment of the Church, signifying his role as intermediary between God and man in the act of penance. He had volunteered to hear confessions and now opened the door of the central confession box and sat down.

The penitents stood in long lines, waiting for him.

Do you see, Cyrus told his devil, how many come on a normal Saturday? A few old women. But here are dozens and dozens, come to reconcile themselves with our Lord.

Conscience did not answer.

In the darkness of the closed confessional box, Tunney sat, listening to the small sins of those who sought absolution. He listened in silence, his eyes closed, the sins recited in humble little litanies, sins of the innocent and the aged, sins of the truly guilty; he listened to them and they seemed to seep into him; he listened, blessed them, he murmured words of comfort and forgiveness.

And then he could stand it no longer.

At four o'clock, with a substantial line of people waiting for him, he opened the door of the confessional and crossed the breadth of the church.

He entered the rectory and walked down the dim hall with the bureau blocking half the way and he entered the middle study where Father McGillicuddy sat at a small teakwood desk, writing in an account book. The week had not been unprofitable, Cyrus had noted with mingled guilt and satisfaction. Poor Martin Foley—God rest his soul—had not understood at all; he had been isolated from the realities of a world of money by the bureaucracy of the Vatican. Money didn't grow on trees, even in Florida where we have very healthy trees, Cyrus would say.

"What is it, Father Tunney?"

"Oh, I feel ill, quite ill." Again, the white-haired man glanced down at the carpet, his hands held before him like a schoolboy called to the principal's office. "I couldn't stand being in that confessional box one moment more . . . the darkness, it reminded me . . ." He let his voice die. And then: "Father, I wonder if you would be so kind as to take my place. I think I want to lie down."

He *is* pale, McGillicuddy noticed, standing up, alarmed.

"Are you sure you don't want anything?"

"No, I—well, I'm all right. I just was reminded of too much. That confessional box. When I was a captive . . . but—" The words failed again, as they so often did; he seemed incapable of explaining anything that had happened to him in the jungle. He had failed at the Mass last Sunday, during the sermon; he had failed several times in conversations with McGillicuddy. Perhaps the journal, because it was a silent and unjudging listener, was the only means by which he could tell what had happened to him.

"No problem," Cyrus said gently, struck by the insight. He understood, in that moment, all the suffering that had burdened Leo Tunney for twenty years; in a moment of excruciating empathy, he finally understood. "No problem," he repeated, patting him on the arm. "I'll take it on for you."

"You are kind," Tunney said, looking up, his clear blue eyes smiling into those of the other man.

"Not kindness. It is our duty," he said in a not atypically pompous voice.

And so, with this act of charity, McGillicuddy ended his days.

The housekeeper, Mrs. Jones, found him.

It was not like him to be late for supper or for any meal. So she had gone into the church. The place was empty, it was late, and the hour for confessions was long past.

She had hesitated, but then, supper was waiting for him. As she said, she hadn't worked all day on it just to have it go cold because he fell asleep in the confessional. That had happened once before. That's what she told the police.

And so McGillicuddy had been found, sitting like a child in his chair in the box, his hands folded on his lap, leaning slightly to one side, a very small neat, bloodless hole in his right temple.

The splinters of wood around the screen on one side suggested even to the newest rookie that one of the people who had been in line for confession had come with another purpose in mind. The bullet that killed Father McGillicuddy had come from a small gun, most likely .22 caliber. When the priest, in the darkness, slid back the door of the screen to hear the confession, he had been shot to death.

23
Rita Macklin

The telephone kept ringing, over and over, and she tried to bury it in her dream but the phone would not stop ringing and she finally awoke.

She was sweating, her forehead was damp and the room felt close.

Dreams? What had she been dreaming?

The phone continued to ring.

Her sleepy voice sounded odd to her; why was she sweating? But she knew it had been the nightmare she could not remember.

"Rita."

Kaiser's voice sounded tired and that surprised her. He never sounded tired, no matter the hour or the day or how long he had been working.

"What time is it?"

"Midnight."

"What's happened? What's going on?"

"Rita. Are you all right?"

"What? What did you say?"

The barrier of sleep, of the night, of the long-distance call seemed to make his words indistinct.

"Rita? Are you awake?"

"Yes."

"Are you all right?"

"Yes. Of course. Why wouldn't I be?" She laughed. "Of course. Except for being awakened in the middle of the night."

"Get out of there."

"What? What did you say?"

"There's danger."

"Kaiser. What's going on? I filed the story, I had dinner, I must have dozed about nine o'clock—what's going on?"

"I don't know. But I just came in. Cassidy took your story."

"Yes?"

"Two deaths," Kaiser said.

"What's going on, what are you talking about?"

"I don't know, Rita. But this is dangerous—"

She tried to make a joke. "You never worried about me before. And now I don't even work for you—"

"—my fault."

"What did you say?"

"Nothing, nothing. Just listen to me, for Christ's sake." He sounded really afraid and he never sounded afraid; he sounded like a man suddenly shown terror in its naked form.

"What is going on?"

"Rita. Get out of there. Right now—"

"Go to hell. I will not get out of here. There's a story here."

"First Foley, now the other priest. I had no idea all this was going to happen."

"Kaiser, what are you talking about?"

"Rita. Trust me. This one time. Get out of there now, tonight, get to the airport any way you can. Don't drive, that would be dangerous. Get a cab, get to the airport, and get back here as fast as you can. I'll take care of you." He seemed to be raving, to be talking to others. "I have my own connections, I got you into this—"

She was frightened then, not by what he was saying but by the horror in his voice, by the edge of fear he was feeding her.

"There's a story here, I'm not going to be scared—"

"Scared? I'm not talking scared to you, Rita, I am talking death. Dying. Final edition. Do you understand me? I did not want to hurt you, ever. That's why I wouldn't let you go down on the story in the first place, I should have known you would go on your own, and now it's all—"

"This is melodrama, Kaiser, stop it, stop it—"

"Rita. Listen. Can you get a cab from the hotel where you are?"

"Yes. I think I can."

"Do it. Call a cab right away. Get to Tampa airport right now. I know it's midnight, you may have to wait until morning for a plane. But maybe not. I don't know what the schedules are but the airport is the safest place for you. Don't stay in your room a minute longer, they must know you're there—"

"Who knows? Who knows?"

195

"Rita, just listen to me and don't ask me any questions."

She had filed the story on the murder of the old priest at eight o'clock. It was a bare account picked up from the police who seemed puzzled by it all and it was embellished by a recounting of the whole history of Leo Tunney from the moment he left the jungle. Death followed him, he had told Rita. But she did not use that line.

There was still the matter of the journal. When she had filed the story, Kaiser was not in; Cassidy took the story. So now Kaiser had read the story and something—some person?—had panicked him into calling her at midnight.

"Will you do it, Rita?"

It was useless to fight him. "Yes. I'll do it. Yes."

The phone connection was broken.

She sat for a moment in the tangle of sheets and felt frightened. And then she flicked on the bedside lamp, got up, and went to the door to check the locks.

She turned on all the lights in the room.

She took a shower with the bathroom door open. From time to time, she peered out from under the running water to make sure.

Sure of what?

She dressed carefully, clothes comfortable for travel. Her jeans, a light sweater, her suede jacket. She pinned her hair back after brushing it vigorously and slipped on her running shoes.

But she wasn't going to run away. It was just that Kaiser had frightened her.

She took her purse and all her money and left everything else.

The hall was quiet except for the humming of the ice machine at the other end. She proceeded down it to the side door that led to the street.

And then she hesitated. What had frightened Kaiser?

She retraced her steps along the green carpet to a middle door that led directly onto the beach. She opened the door and peered out into the clear, warm night. A full moon lit up the beach and even illuminated the sluggish black waters beyond.

It was darker here than along the beachfront between the fishing pier and the first high-rise hotels at the other end. But it was empty and wide and she could see someone—if someone came after her—from a long distance.

Rita considered it and then decided.

She closed the door quietly and listened.

No sounds save for the sounds of water, the sounds of a light breeze, little waves dashing gently against the sandy shore.

Across the thick sand to the waterline where the sand was packed harder and made walking much easier.

She looked back at the hotel.

Nothing. She could see the street beyond the hotel.

A gray car parked under a lamppost at the far end.

The gray car that had followed her one morning.

She began to walk very quickly across the sand.

The door of the gray car. She turned back and, indeed, the door opened. Quickly. A burst of interior light from the car, a form in the darkness outlined by the light, the door closed.

She walked toward the pier.

Don't look back, she thought, and then stopped and turned, frozen for a moment by the sight.

There were two of them, trudging across the loose sand toward her, running.

She turned and cried out, involuntarily, and began to run, too. Not the slow, steady jogging run of the morning but a full-fledged, panic-induced sprint.

They were slowed by the loose sand, but they were running at an angle across the beach and that would cut down on the distance between them.

If only she had gone outside, to the street, she thought. Panic clawed at her throat like an infection; she wanted to scream but she did not have breath for it. She ran and her lungs filled and burned.

They ran very quickly. They were large men in short leather jackets.

She ran into the shadows of the pier, stumbled across a body in a sleeping bag, and fell.

"Hey, what the fuck is going on?" The boy in the sleeping bag shot into sitting position. His companion, in the bag placed next to him followed suit.

"Hey, fuck this shit, what the—"

Rita scrambled up, pushing herself against the sand. The contents of her purse were scattered and she automatically started to scoop them up when she looked again behind her—they were less than thirty feet away.

"Cops are coming!" she said.

She started running again. The kids in the sleeping bags began to stand up, and the two men ran into them, banging their way past.

Now it was better lit and there were even a few people strolling on the far sidewalk, 150 feet from the waterline. But she couldn't run there because of the loose sand—it would slow her and they would catch her.

And would it matter to them anyway?

Who were they?

They had frightened Kaiser, she thought. *Kaiser knew.*

In the parking lot that framed the beach here, kids sat in their vans and watched the three figures running across the sand. They listened to heavy rock music and the air all around them was fetid with the smell of marijuana. It was the usual night beach scene.

One of the kids yelled, "Hey, whatcha chasing that girl for?"

Someone laughed.

Rita heard the laughter. Her lungs were going to burst, her heart was pounding against her rib cage.

Devereaux, she thought. Perhaps she had known that was where she would go.

She ran up the steps of the hotel and turned at the door.

They had stopped, fifty feet behind her.

She could see them clearly in the moonlight. One was very tall, with large hands.

She pushed through the revolving door into the bare, bright lobby. From the bar came the sound of a heavy drumbeat. She went to the clerk at the desk.

The two men pushed through the revolving door behind her.

"Mr. Devereaux," she said.

The young clerk smiled at her, slowly and insolently, as though they had a secret between them. "Are you a guest of the hotel, miss?"

The two men hesitated at the door.

She said, in an urgent half-whisper, "Listen, kid, I'm his wife and I just got in from the airport and I'm tired and I don't have time to talk to you. Just call his room."

The smile faded and turned into a pout. The clerk looked up the name and dialed.

The phone rang.

What if he wasn't in?

The two men at the door stared at her.

If she ran into the bar—but there was no exit from the bar except through the lobby.

"Doesn't seem he's in right—oh, Mr. Devereaux? Sorry to bother you, sir, this is the front desk. Woman here says she's your wife just came in . . . what?"

The two men started at her across the brick floor of the lobby.

"Yes, sir."

"Please—" she began.

He replaced the phone. "Sorry, Mrs. Devereaux, but we have to be strict and—"

"What room?"

"Uh. Fourteen oh three, that's just—"

She pushed away from the desk and ran into the elevator alcove and the two men turned and started after her.

The door whooshed shut before they could get there.

The elevator ascended slowly. She held her finger on the button for the fourteenth floor. Please God she thought; her eyes were wide, her nostrils flaring with the exertion of the run, with the feeling of sick terror gripping her body.

The doors opened and she ran down the hall.

He had opened his door and stood in bare feet and trousers.

"Two men—" she cried as she rushed to him. "Chased me—"

"Inside." His voice was flat and low. He closed the door and locked it and went to the telephone on the nightstand. He dialed the front desk.

"Yes, yes," he said. "They ask for my room number?"

He nodded at the reply and replaced the receiver.

"Dev, I wouldn't want to entangle you—"

"Be quiet, Rita." His voice, still flat and harsh and low, was distracted.

"Kaiser called me and—"

"Tell me later," he said, this time with more gentleness. "Don't be afraid now." He stood at the door and listened, his ear to the door.

They both heard the sound of the elevator bell. Doors opened and closed.

He waited.

Through the thin walls they heard footsteps in the hall.

He glanced at her for a moment as though deciding something. His face was cold, a face for winter, creased with lines around the gray eyes.

He decided.

He reached in the closet for his bag and removed an object from it.

She saw that it was a gun.

Now, standing pressed against the sliding patio doors, she trembled. Who was he? Who had followed her? The entire world had suddenly exploded into betrayal. A sense of madness overcame her. This was what it was to be frightened, she thought, as though she had never been frightened before in her life.

The knob on the door jiggled.

Devereaux put his fingers to his lips. He raised the gun.

"What the hell is going on down here, can't get no goddam sleep or what?"

"Hey, what are those guys doing down there. That guy's got a gun, John, he's got a fucking gun—"

Sounds in the corridor.

Muffled sounds.

Feet running.

Doors were slammed.

"Damned guys had guns—"

Devereaux waited, still, pressed against the wall, gun drawn.

"Burglars," one of the voices, bleary with drink or sleep, said. "Got goddam burglars in the hotel."

"I knew we should have gone to the Holiday Inn, I told you—"

"Burglars, ought to call down to the desk—"

"Right here, I never saw anything like it—"

"Like that movie we saw once, that time, with Cary Grant, remember—"

"He didn't have no gun—"

"What the hell is all that noise—"

"Burglars down there—"

"What? What did you say?"

Devereaux slowly lowered his hand. After a moment of stillness, he turned and replaced the gun in the bag.

The telephone rang.

He picked up the phone and listened and looked at Rita who stood pressed against the glass door that led to the balcony. She was trembling. Her hands were flat against the glass. She stared at him with an expression of horror.

He felt nothing, he thought, but that wasn't true. He felt the coldness in him again, overwhelming him again.

"No. Not here. I think it was down the hall. No. About fourteen fifteen or so. Yes. That's all right. Good night."

He turned and stared at her.

They could not find any words.

Slowly, a humming silence returned—the silence of night in a large hotel. Doors were slammed, shut, water gurgled in the bathroom pipes that connected the rooms, voices were muted and then, finally, stilled.

So he would not have to betray Rita after all, he thought as he stared at her.

Any more than he had.

24
Devereaux

"Who are you?"

Rita stood still against the glass doors, her arms folded defensively in front of her.

Devereaux did not answer. He walked across the thick carpeting and stood in front of her for a moment. He stared into her green eyes that were angry and set against him.

There was nothing to say.

Slowly, he moved past her and slid open the glass door. At this height, the gentle Gulf breeze was cooler and a little stronger. He stepped onto the concrete balcony and looked over the cast-iron railing. No one waited on the well-lit section of beach in front of the hotel; in the parking lot, the last teenagers in the last panel van of the night were being chased away by a Clearwater cop. The van, with rumbling music and rumbling exhaust pipes, slowly pulled onto Gulf View Boulevard and moved away.

"Who are you?" Rita repeated, still standing in the room, staring

"What you suspect."

"Not a reporter."

"No."

"I didn't even check you and you were lying from the first moment."

He waited.

"You're with them. The CIA."

"No."

"I can't believe you." Her voice was flat.

"Not the CIA."

"But you're in the government," she said.

"Yes."

"And you used me. What's your name, even? Your real name?"

"The name is real."

"I was so stupid, I was just like a farm girl, you think I would have smartened up in Washington, you—"

"You weren't stupid. Everything wasn't a lie."

"You had it set up. To use me to get the journal. For God's sake." Her voice caught, she might be on the edge of tears. He did not turn to look at her. He considered the darkness beyond the balcony, the darkness of the infinite water. Gulf led to Caribbean and that led to the ocean and to all the oceans of the world, stretching away from this little moment of hell.

"I told you about that, about the journal. God, I'm sick, I want to throw up. I told you about . . . about Tommy. I even told you that."

He waited for the words like blows.

"I trusted you," she said. "I trusted Kaiser. And Kaiser—" Her voice caught again. "Kaiser knew. Just like you knew."

He turned then and stared at her. "What did Kaiser know?"

"I won't tell you anything."

He waited.

"Damn you. Both of you." She slammed her fist against the jamb of the glass doors. "Damn. He called me tonight and told me to get out. He knew I was in danger."

Kaiser knew, he thought.

"Who were they?" he asked.

"I should ask you. You probably know, you know everything, you set everything up. This is all part of your game, isn't it? None of it meant anything. God. I made love to you."

His eyes were gray, flat, cold; nothing could penetrate him if he stood perfectly still, if he took all that she said and let the blows fall on him.

"Who were they?" he said at last.

"They came from that car, it followed me—"

"A gray car, Ford Fairmont." It was not a question.

"You know them, you set everything up—"

"I don't know them, Rita." His voice was calm and, strangely, it seemed to calm her as well.

For a moment, they stared at each other without speaking.

"Who are they then?"

"I don't know."

"You said you were in the government."

"Yes."

"Not the CIA."

"No."

"Who are you then?"

"I can't say," he said.

"I hate you. I despise you."

"Why did Kaiser know them?"

"He didn't—"

"He called you, he warned you away. Why did Kaiser know them?"

"Kaiser said to get out. He said he didn't want me to get into it. He said . . ." She paused.

"He said," Devereaux continued, "that was the reason he warned you off the story to begin with. To protect you. He knew what was going to happen."

"No. He didn't know—"

"But he didn't take you off the story before, when you were trying to get to Tunney in Washington. At the Watergate. He didn't know it was dangerous then." Devereaux spoke aloud but he was only thinking, the computer of memory and logic spinning new answers onto the screen in his mind.

"You know all this though, don't you?" she said.

"No. None of it. I know this is very dangerous now, Rita, I know that." He paused. They both understood the game had changed; what was in the journal that Father Tunney was keeping? What was worth killing for?

But how would he get the journal now, now that he was blown?

"Why did they want to kill me?" she said.

He considered it calmly but there did not seem to be an answer. Unless.

"When did you tell Kaiser about the journal?"

"I just told you."

"No, Rita. You told Kaiser as well."

"I didn't."

"You had to."

"Why?"

"Because they had to have a reason to kill you."

"Yes," she said, almost in a trance, reaching back into her memory, "I did tell him. I had forgotten."

"Did you tell him that Tunney would give it to you?"

"No. I didn't know yet."

"Are you sure?"

"Yes."

"Then someone is beginning to panic. Everyone is blowing his cover. They waited and waited so patiently. Why blow it now?" He stepped back inside the darkened room but left the glass door open.

"What are you talking about?"

"Miracles. The business with the miracles. This woman, Lu Ann Carter. They've become frightened, something has happened none of them planned on. There's too much attention on Tunney, they'll never be able to keep him quiet. And you've been the most persistent reporter. You were an easy person to get rid of. You weren't even part of a paper or a news agency. And they have Kaiser in their pocket. Kaiser wouldn't say anything. Except that he decided to warn you off, just as he did before, in Washington."

She shivered but he did not see it. He was staring into his own thoughts, trying to make sense of the new pieces of the puzzle.

"Who are they?" Rita said at last.

"I don't know."

"You. 'They' is you. The CIA or whatever you belong to."

"No. I don't think so."

"I trusted you. I told you about my brother, about him dying, and I feel so dirty now. You make it so dirty—"

He turned, looked at her, slapped her with his harsh voice: "Dirty. Yes. All of it. That's the way of it." He glanced at his hands; he was trembling and he did not want to feel what he felt. Not for her, not for anyone. More softly: "As long as you know I'm in the dirty business, I can tell you I ran a check on your brother. Cross-Agency. To see if he had been one of ours."

"No! Don't tell me—"

"Two approaches were made to him. Once here, once in Laos. He turned Uncle down. He was pure as you wanted him to be."

"And he died—"

"It was never clear. It might have been fever. It might have been the Pathet Lao. You see, they were not too exact. If you were white, you might be a spy."

"They killed him?"

"It's not clear. But if he died, he died for the wrong reason." His voice was bitter. "Does that salve your conscience? That he wasn't in this dirty business? That he wasn't like me? Or your father?"

"Yes," she said, "it makes it better. It makes it all right now that you betrayed me. That you used me. I think of your dirty hands on me but that's all right. It's fine because I know that Tommy wasn't one of you. You're scum, all of you."

"Rita."

But it was no use.

I love you, he thought. As soon as he thought it, he realized how foolish he had become. He did not love or hate; it was enough to survive. He had allowed himself a luxury that was not for him anymore.

He opened the closet and pulled out a shirt and buttoned it. He pulled on his corduroy jacket. He reached for the pistol in the case on the shelf.

The pistol was seated in a black leather holster that could be attached to a belt. He removed the pistol, a black Colt Python .357 magnum six-shot revolver.

It was an accurate weapon and reliable. The long, hollow-point bullets could tear a man's belly open.

He set the pistol in the belt of his trousers, behind the corduroy jacket, and buttoned the jacket.

He glanced at her but she stood motionless at the window.

"What are you going to do?" she said.

"Stay here, Rita. It isn't safe to leave now. I'll be back by morning. However long it takes, stay here. They won't come back to the hotel."

"How do you know?"

"I know. If I don't get back by afternoon, call the Tampa office of the FBI—it's in the telephone book. Tell them everything that's happened."

"Fuck you. Fuck the FBI, you can't—"

"Rita." The voice was soft, tinged with sadness. "This is not between us now." But he knew she would only see it that way. He had to keep her out of the way.

He opened his scuffed bag and removed a small green plastic box. He opened it. His pharmacopoeia, the drugs that made him awake after an all-night flight from Tehran, the drugs that put him to sleep when his body could not function anymore without sleep.

He removed a white pill.

"I won't take that, you can't make me—"

"Rita. I want you to sleep."

"You want to kill me."

"Rita." He touched her arm, held her. "It's only a sleeping pill."

"I don't trust you."

"I won't hurt you."

"Let go of my arm." She punched him them, quickly, expertly, in the right side of the belly, below the rib cage. He felt a flare of pain and stepped into it, twisting her arm back and down in one motion.

She fell to the bed and he was on top of her.

She opened her mouth to scream.

He hit her very hard on the side of the head. The blow stunned her for a moment. He pushed her over on her back. She stared at him, her eyes glazed with pain.

He shoved the knuckles of his first two fingers in her mouth and felt her teeth sink against the skin. But because he had doubled his fingers, she could not bite effectively; she only broke the skin.

He dropped the pill down her throat and waited for the reflex to swallow it. She swallowed as she gasped for air.

"You bastard," she said when he removed his hand. He held her down.

"You dirty bastard, you dirty son of a bitch."

He waited.

"Are you going to hold me down like this all night? I'll vomit as soon as I get up—"

He stared at her, straddling her body with his legs and holding down her arms beneath his hands. He was cold again, he was himself—Hanley might say that—he was without emotion. He did not love or hate; his instincts for survival were whole again.

She cursed him again. She said he was hurting her.

He did not move. He pressed her down, scissoring her body with his legs, pushing against her arms.

The clock moved slowly, minute by minute. The room was silent except for her labored breathing.

She yawned.

He stared at her green eyes and did not feel anything; he could not even imagine making love to her that morning.

After more minutes, he felt the body slacken beneath him, the muscles stretching into an involuntary relaxed position. She was sleeping then.

He got off the bed and covered her gently and then closed the doors of the balcony and pulled the drapes across the glass.

Devereaux went to the door of the room, listened at it and then slowly opened it.

The hall was empty and bright. He removed the pistol from his belt and cocked the hammer. Slowly, he walked down the hall.

He paused at the elevator doors and listened but he heard no sound. He walked down to the end of the hall and looked inside the alcove with ice and vending machines.

Empty.

He finally reached the staircase door marked by a large glowing "Exit" sign.

He pushed the door open suddenly and violently and it banged against the stucco wall behind it.

Nothing.

Down the fireproof iron and concrete staircase, slowly.

All the way to the lobby.

He pushed open the door and saw the policeman at the desk. He went out the side door and down the steps.

A police car sat in the parking entrance with its red light slowly rotating.

Answer an alert: burglars in the hotel. She would be safe for a little while in his room.

He waited in the shadows, near some bushes and trees sprouting in a little garden at the curb.

Nothing.

And then he saw it, turning the corner, the same gray car that had followed Rita, the gray car he had been unable to trace.

At the corner, the gray car turned into a side connecting road and waited in the darkness.

For a moment, he stood in the shadow of the hotel and considered the options and the questions.

Why had they—whoever they were—waited patiently so long and then gone on a murderous rampage that claimed two men and nearly claimed a reporter?

And what was his option after all?

The Adviser wanted the Section to call off the game. Hanley had given him a small cover but it would not last very long. How long could he trust Hanley?

And now he was blown. Rita Macklin would not trust him, would seek to expose him. He would not get the journal from her.

The only cards he held were the "proofs" that Denisov had given him, the two photocopied messages that might be true or not and the photograph of Leo Tunney, not much but perhaps enough to ensure his survival in any bureaucratic bloodletting that might follow Rita's exposure. Might, might.

He could kill Rita.

The possibility was there. He thought of it and then let it go. He would not kill her. She was out of the game.

He looked around the corner and saw the two men sitting in the gray car at the cross street.

McGillicuddy was killed in error. He must assume that. The bullet in the confessional was intended for Tunney. First he had a secret that everyone wanted; and now he had a secret that everyone wanted kept secret.

Why? Why kill him now?

He felt frozen by the questions. Perhaps it was time to put them aside. There were two men waiting in a gray car for him, for Rita, for someone.

Devereaux stepped out of the shadows into the lights of the street.

He started down the sidewalk alongside Gulf View, moving slowly and easily to the main road that would eventually lead him to the causeway and the city beyond.

Once, in the light of a shop-window, he saw the gray car turn the corner behind him and move slowly down the street.

They were coming for him; it was time to change the rules of the game.

Devereaux began to walk quickly down Gulf View, swinging his arms.

In the next block, across from the beach, was a building site, announcing shared-time vacation condominiums. A construction site would have to do. He saw that the lot opened on both Gulf View and the parallel street beyond.

Suddenly, Devereaux ducked into the rubble and lost himself in the shadows of the concrete pilings supporting a second deck. Around him was a forest of similar pilings with exposed rods, and stacks of concrete blocks and finishing forms.

The gray car slid slowly past the lot and then sped up.

One in front, one in back, Devereaux thought. A classic trap.

He waited, holding his breath, not moving. He felt the heaviness of the pistol at his belt. He suspected the gray car would stop at the corner and one man would get out and come back down Gulf View to the lot while the second would cut down the cross street to Coronado—the parallel road. Two men, one in the front and one in the back. Men with weapons.

Devereaux waited calmly. He did not feel fear or any other emotion. His hands were still at his sides, his pistol was in his belt.

He could see both streets, both were empty.

A clattering sound, a rock thrown in the lot.

Shadows in the moonlight and a tangle of unfamiliar shapes hiding him.

A second sound, this time a man's step on the rubble.

One man in, he thought.

Time for the pistol.

He reached under the jacket easily and removed the piece with one movement. A game of patience. He had one weapon, they had two; he was one target, they were two, coming from different directions. But in the light, he would see their forms against the streetscape before they could see him.

Sweat broke out in small beads on his face but his eyes were lazy and gray and calm.

"Hey? Hey, you? What the hell y'all doing in there? Y'all come here a minute? This is the police, I'm talking at you."

Devereaux looked to Gulf View. Through the pilings, he saw the police car slide up to the curb.

"Did you hear, come on over here gawdammit, I'm gonna come in and get your ass."

A man emerged from the pilings, not from where Devereaux had expected.

"That's private property in there, son," the cop said. "What the hell were you doing there?"

"Sorry." In contrast, the voice was rough, northern, hard-edged. "Taking a piss. Had too much to drink."

"Gawdam. You all think you come down here and can take a piss in the street? Ain't no gawdam bathroom, ain't they got toilets back up where you come from?"

"Yeah. Listen. I'm sorry."

"Come here and let us look at you. You got some identification on you?"

For a moment, the match was even.

Devereaux pushed away from the piling, his feet scrambling soundlessly over the rubble, moving to the secondary road away from the police car.

The second man would be coming.

Quietly.

Devereaux looked around the corner and saw the gray car stopped at the curb. The door opened with a flash of interior light and a big man got out.

Devereaux pressed himself very hard against the wall of the dry-cleaning shop that formed part of the next building.

If he took him it would be without guns. And it would have to be done quietly, while the first one was momentarily detained by the police patrol on the main road.

The big man stepped cautiously, half-crouching, into the building site.

Not a sound.

Devereaux stretched out and grasped the big man by the right shoulder, swinging him violently around, like the end child on a game of crack-the-whip. The big man careened face first into the red stucco wall. The sound was like that of a sponge thrown against a shower stall.

Dazed, the man went down, blood welling from his broken nose.

The second blow, a hard chop to the shoulder, finished him. He sprawled forward. Devereaux leaned over him and heaved him to his feet. He had decided on a new plan in the moment of action; Tunney would wait a few more hours.

The pair of them staggered into the second street to the empty gray car that waited, idling.

It must be done quickly.

Devereaux spotted the key in the ignition. He pushed the nearly lifeless body against the side of the car while he fished through the window. Keys in hand now, he opened the trunk. He looked around but the street was empty, though at the far end, a car was turning into the drive that led to the causeway.

Devereaux dumped the big man effortlessly into the trunk and stood up, slamming the lid.

He got behind the wheel of the gray car and pushed the lever into drive. The car moved forward slowly. He drove carefully to the toll bridge connecting the island to Sand Key and crossed. He paid at the far end and went on for five more minutes, past small homes and hotels and sprawling residential apartment complexes.

He knew where he was going.

The sign at the side road on the narrow key said a new development was coming in spring; at the moment, the development site on the water's edge consisted of three wooden huts, boarded up, abandoned. They overlooked an old wooden pier that jutted out into the narrow channel that led to the Gulf.

He turned the lights off and drove the gray car into a space between two of the huts.

He had seen the huts on the second day, when he had followed the gray car tracking Rita Macklin on her morning run.

He opened the trunk. The big man was glassy-eyed and bloodstained but conscious.

Devereaux stared at him and the big man crawled painfully out of the trunk. He towered over Devereaux by four inches.

He took a swipe at him suddenly, the hand coming up open and hard.

Devereaux caught the blow on his arm and it numbed him for a moment. He stepped inside the lunge and drove his fingers into the big man's throat. The big man went down hard and Devereaux caught him with a knee to the chin as he fell.

The big man was on his hands and knees, choking.

Devereaux went to the side door of the middle shack and kicked it in. The hinges were rusty; they made a squeak and the dry wood cracked with the force of the blow. The door banged open with a start.

Two rats, in the corner of the empty, dirty room, were startled by the light. One of them hissed; the other ran.

The moonlight was sufficient to distinguish forms in the shadows. An old chair stood by a boarded-up window.

The big man went inside and sat down on the floor.

"I'm bleeding," he said quietly. The voice was hard, as hard as Devereaux's own; he spoke as a surgeon speaks of a tumor, without emotion or pity.

"Who are you?"

"You know I can't tell you."

Devereaux waited.

The two men stared at each other, understanding what roles they would now have to play.

Devereaux felt the coldness envelop him, numb him, protect him. In a moment, he felt nothing and saw nothing but the problem at hand. The patient on the table.

"Who are you?" Devereaux said again, quietly. Sometimes even the professionals, like this one, understood that there was no point to delay, that they had to speak sooner or later, that pain could be so great that loyalty would be betrayed.

Some of them, given the chance, decided it was not worth it.

And others, like this one, had never taken pain before and so they could not understand how it broke all bonds, all loyalties, all secrets.

Devereaux brought the pistol, barrel back, down very hard against the right cheekbone. It broke and blood spurted anew from broken teeth. The head was a bad place to administer pain—there was a danger of killing accidentally but it was a psychological necessity, at the beginning, to let him taste his own blood.

Devereaux stepped on his left hand very hard.

The big man passed out. When he awoke, he retched on the dirty dry wood floor, staining his own clothing.

Devereaux said nothing for a moment.

They considered the silence. And then Devereaux kicked him precisely in the ribs beneath the sternum. The big man fainted again.

When he awoke the second time, Devereaux was still there, the silence was still around them, the pain was still throbbing through him.

The big man considered it again, from the standpoint of pain; pain made loyalty distant, made secrets seem less important: a brutal and direct principle.

But there was a certain strength to the adversary. He fought against the nausea and pain, he tried to fix his thoughts clearly.

"You should have gone away from this. Even now, you could go away from this. Walk away."

Devereaux waited.

"You were warned."

Devereaux stepped on the broken hand again. Pain like a burst of sunlight flooded the big man's vision and then darkness interceded. In a moment—a minute later, an hour later—he awoke and nothing had changed. He understood now, as a professional, that nothing would change: not death, not escape, not an end to the pain.

"My name is Petersen."

Devereaux stared at him impassively, standing away from him, waiting.

"I have responsibilities for global security for a bank."

Devereaux waited still. He considered the voice, which was hard, and he considered the words. What was the truth, what was a lie? But that could be determined later.

The big man stared at him. "That's the truth."

Devereaux's gray eyes were unyielding. "The truth is everything. You haven't said everything."

"This doesn't involve you—"

"It involves me now. Why did you kill the priest?"

"He was a complication."

"Both of them?"

"No. Not both of them."

Devereaux waited, puzzled.

"Not both of them," the big man named Petersen said.

"You killed Foley."

"No. We followed him. I was behind him. And then this other man—came from nowhere. It was unseen." The voice choked a moment and Petersen spit out blood on the dry floor. "Not one of our men. We weren't supposed to kill anyone. It became complicated then."

"You didn't kill Foley."

"No. We were following him."

"Who killed him?"

"A man. We didn't even know what he had done."

"Who was it?"

Petersen shook his head and grimaced with pain. "A big man, too. He wore glasses. He had an umbrella, he bumped into—"

"Glasses?"

"You know, the kind without any rims. Old-fashioned glasses."

"And blue eyes."

"I didn't see his fucking eyes, for Christ's sake. I was a hundred feet behind him. It was raining."

Denisov.

"Who are you?"

"I told you."

"A bank, you said."

"Yes."

"What bank."

"Look, you don't want to be involved—"

Devereaux made a small movement.

Petersen's voice broke. "Don't hit me."

"What bank?"

"InterComBank in New York."

"Why? What did you have to do with Leo Tunney?"

"Everything is connected," Petersen said. "You don't want to examine this. You weren't supposed to be here."

"What?"

"Nothing."

"What did you say?"

"The second priest was a mistake. It should have ended with that."

"You wanted to kill Tunney. You thought Tunney was in the confessional. You killed the wrong man."

Suddenly, the pain welled up in Petersen and his eyes glazed. He reeled as though he would faint. He closed his eyes and blood foamed at his lips. He opened his eyes and hell remained: Devereaux; the room; silence.

"Yes. The wrong man," Petersen said.

"Why did you want to kill him now?"

"I don't know. I have orders."

"That's a lie. You said I wasn't supposed to be here."

"Yes."

He knew the order from Hanley. Where was the leak? At what level?

"Who are you with?" Devereaux began again, patiently, probing like a dentist.

"InterComBank."

"A cover," Devereaux said. "You know too much about me. Don't play games. Now is not the time." Said patiently, an adult talking to a child.

"I don't know what you mean."

"Why didn't you just kill Rita Macklin? In her room? Shoot her on the beach?"

"We weren't supposed to shoot her," Petersen said. His voice had no tone; it was as flat as a shallow sea in a calm. "She was a reporter, that was more of a problem. We were going to feed her to the fishes." He looked at Devereaux. "You were fucking her this morning. Maybe you would have taken the fall for her; maybe the Agency. It didn't matter."

"Sure, it mattered. Your outfit thought about everything until they panicked. I want to know who you work for."

"I told you. I want to sit down. Can I sit down?"

Devereaux stared at him.

Petersen scrambled to his feet and took the chair and leaned against the back of it. His face was flushed still but the blood on his chin was congealing.

Devereaux stood in front of him, holding the pistol lightly in his hand.

"We didn't even figure the big guy with the umbrella killed Foley until we read the paper the next day about him going crazy on the causeway. Then we figured it out. The big guy did the London Touch."

London Touch. The trick of the trade developed by the Soviets first and most successfully used in London in the mid-1970s. Drugs secreted in a hypodermic needle that can be injected from the point of an umbrella on a London street. It was used to induce fatal heart seizures in various KGB targets in that city, including dissidents who were broadcasting anti-Soviet programs on BBC World Service as well as the CIA's Radio Free Europe.

It always rained in London, Devereaux thought. Thus the umbrella.

And then, one day, it rained in central Florida as well.

"Why begin the murders now?" Devereaux said. "You could have killed Tunney at any time."

"Perhaps we didn't know we would be involved at first."

"Who are you?"

"I told you the truth."

"No. Not all of it."

Petersen pushed forward then and his timing was nearly perfect. Devereaux did not expect the big man to have such resources of strength. His body hurtled like a shell into Devereaux and sent him sprawling on the dusty floor, cracking his head against a corner beam. The rats scurried away to far corners, turned, bared their teeth again and made their crooning sound.

Petersen grasped the fallen pistol and fired. The shot cracked the silence like a sudden thunderclap on a warm summer day.

Devereaux had been moving from the minute he struck the ground. The bullet ripped the wood behind him, sending splinters like fragments of a bomb into his body. He kept twisting away, blood welling on the whiteness of his shirt.

Twisting, twisting.

Petersen raised the heavy gun and fired again. Devereaux leaped up and ran suddenly to a boarded window frame and threw himself against it, splintering dry, rotten wood. He fell out of the cabin, into the sand and wild grass clinging to the key at the edge of the water.

Petersen lunged from the cabin and ran around the corner, the pistol in his hand. The finishing touch.

Devereaux hit him with both hands folded together into a human pile driver. Petersen felt the blow in his belly and fell forward, still holding the pistol.

Devereaux scrambled behind him on the loose sand.

Petersen raised the pistol, tried to turn.

The copper-sheathed wire was out of Devereaux's bracelet and around his neck.

Petersen gasped as he felt the cutting edge against his throat. He dropped the pistol and grasped the wire with his hands.

Slowly, Devereaux pulled, leaning back with all his weight against the wriggling form of the terrified man.

The big man's body jerked up sharply, following the wire encircling his throat, his back arching to the breaking point.

When Devereaux released the wire, Petersen's head slumped forward and the body fell on the blood-soaked sand.

Devereaux stood over the dead man, the wire in his hand. The pain from the wounds was spreading across his belly. He reached down for his pistol and then found himself on his knees.

He felt strange, light-headed. He dabbed at the dampness on his shirt and found it was blood.

Slowly, as though he were falling in a dream, he let himself fall forward to the sand, his face next to the staring, dead face of the man called Petersen. His eyes closed and he lay motionless on the ground, without thoughts or senses.

25
Ludovico

The silence from Rome was easy to explain in retrospect: Cardinal Ludovico was simply not told of the death of Martin Foley until the delicate negotiations in Prague were nearly concluded.

The journey across a quarter of the world had been long, made longer by Ludovico's grief.

When the Pan American jumbo jet from London finally touched down late Saturday afternoon at Miami International, Ludovico was very nearly unable to continue. His collapse was physical as well as mental; grief had sapped his strength as surely as a long illness.

For six days, he had sat in on the concluding portion of the negotiations for the Concordance.

He had cabled Foley once and now regretted the sarcasm and scolding that had turned out to be his last words to Martin.

The entourage in Prague had sought to hold back the news of the death. They reasoned among themselves that if the Cardinal knew, he would be unable to continue the negotiations. They did not know the strength of their master. When he learned of his protégé's death, he went on as before and the Concordance was sealed; he did not falter as he finished the details and made arrangements to fly to America. They were all amazed at Cardinal Ludovico's strength. But it was strength summoned at a great price.

The work of the Congregation and the work of the Church cannot be impeded by considerations of personal sorrow, he told his secretary. And the secretary thought he understood and thought it was a privilege to serve one of the great Princes of the Church.

He had stayed over in London Friday night, busying himself with cables, drafts of cables, telephone calls that reached out like a spider's web to agents throughout the world.

Only later in the London night, with mists shrouding the city lights and fog scratching at the windows of his suite, did Ludovico sit alone in the darkness, in the large leather chair turned to the window, and count his loss. It was the loss of a son to him in every sense except the biological.

Martin had been murdered, of course; there was no doubt of that. When he had been informed at last of the death, he had gone to his opposite number in the negotiations and asked him sharply what had happened. The other side made every effort to assure him that they were not involved. But Ludovico, who knew them so well, could never be certain that he could trust the final word of a Soviet.

Martin.

Tears misted his eyes as the fog misted the great city beyond his window; the tears would have surprised his secretary, who only saw the strength of the Prince.

I am truly alone, he thought at last, as the London dawn gave fitful light at last. He felt naked and frightened at that moment, as though he were an old, old man who had survived every member of the family and all the friends of youth and now waited for the end, wondering what would be revealed on the other side of the curtain.

One needs affection, he thought in pity for himself; one cannot love in the abstract. He had realized it long before he met the young, boyishly hopeful and open cleric from Liverpool; celibacy was a concept and not a reality, ever. It forbade not only sex, which was not so difficult as one grew older, but affection, intimacy, a family, a special sense of weddedness to blood, a wife and children. At the last, a priest was merely a man and a man always had to surrender himself to another; to love a wife or child; to find one person to give a gift of love to.

One of the rumors had it that Ludovico had taken Martin as his lover.

It was a terrible rumor and it was not untypical of the stories that made the rounds of the trattorias in the old quarter of the city or even in the halls of the Vatican bureaucracy. The Church was old; Rome was old; a certain veneer of cynicism covered the dealings of both, like moss on a tomb. All things were possible.

A priest, Ludovico had thought when the rumor came to him, is suspected of everything because he presumes to be beyond the mean spiritual life of others. That is what he explained to Martin when he told him of the rumor. He knew the rumor would shock this open man because he had come to Rome with such naïve expectations.

I love you, Martin.

But he had never said it. The Cardinal was a cold Prince, leonine in presence and dignified in manner; he loved Martin as truly as a father and he sought to show his affection as a father would. He sought Martin's advancement at the expense of others who might have been better qualified; he gave Martin gifts, he showed him finally the narrow way of wisdom that was far different from the easy way of simple faith. Faith, he had once told Martin, sustains us when we cannot explain anymore. But in the Congregation, one always sought to explain.

On the long Atlantic flight, he had thought of Martin, dead. Who had killed him?

He lived in a world of too many lies to see the truth clearly; he must be patient and wait for it.

When he arrived he had gone to see Martin at the morgue. Cold, still, white.

He very nearly cried then but he could not. He had a reserve of dignity beneath the cold demeanor that made grief a private matter.

What could he do now?

But he must confront Tunney first; to learn the terrible secret; to force Tunney to tell him.

At the hotel, after a long bath, he dressed and sat down to write. There were always notes, always cables to be drafted. He had forbidden his secretary to accompany him; if the secretary had been there, grief would not be permitted.

Tears stained the ink on the pages and smeared the writing.

Outside the hotel, he listened to sounds of a resort city, a city without grief or loss or a sense of sorrow. He held the elegant gold pen, then put it down; his mind swayed back and forth restlessly like a circus elephant trapped in chains, swaying and bellowing in his captivity.

Martin Foley, I loved you.

The face was cold, white and unsmiling.

He tried to remember the eager eyes but they were already gone from memory.

I am so old now, I am aged in a day because you are dead.

The knock at the door startled him, not only because he had been thinking so deeply of Martin, but because only the Congregation office in Rome knew he was here, in this hotel.

"What is it?"

"Ludovico," the voice answered.

He rose and closed his portable desk and put it away in a drawer. He looked around him to make certain there were no papers visible. He went to the door and opened it.

"Ludovico?"

"Yes."

"I was sent to you. To help you." The other man smiled, his face open and guileless, the eyes smiling behind the rimless glasses.

"Who are you?"

"From the embassy. I am Denisov."

"The embassy—"

"At Prague. You were at Prague and you requested our help." The smile was fixed, Ludovico realized; it had no mirth to it or warmth. "I am Denisov. Do you understand that name?"

The shoulders of the Cardinal seemed to slump in that instant; he felt all the sick grief come back over him. Of course. The Concordance implied an alliance, a mutual need. Of course. It was a new world and Ludovico was still in it, still a survivor waiting for the parting of the curtain.

"Come in," he said dully.

"Yes," Denisov said.

Ludovico closed the door and the two men stood in the modern, bright room and stared at each other without speaking.

"Martin," Ludovico said finally.

"Yes. We think we can help you. It is all contained in the journal—"

"I don't know what you mean—"

"Did he not tell you that? Please, do not be so to your guard. The journal is everything; it is the source."

"What do you mean?" Ludovico felt himself pressed. Grief waited; he became alert again. He backed away, keeping his eyes on the man with large shoulders and the simple face.

"Leo Tunney," Denisov said gently. "Yes. Of course we know of this. Leo Tunney has kept a journal. It is all in the journal."

"What?"

"Whatever we seek." Denisov smiled again without warmth. "We, Ludovico. The Church and us. We seek the same ends this time. We are not enemies now."

And Ludovico, seized suddenly by a sick despair, realized that everything Denisov said was perfectly true.

III
REVELATIONS

26
Clearwater

All night long, Mrs. Jones had dreamed of him, of his fat face in repose, of the small dirty hole at his temple. She had dreamed of shots and of death and of hell; she had seen a hell of real flames and felt a hell of loss. She knew they were only dreams even as she dreamed them and her dream self said she would not be afraid.

When she awoke, it was just after dawn, the usual hour; she had her duty and she would do it. She was nearly seventy years old, though she had told the priest she was fifty-five to get the job. She was a strong woman and she had been a widow for thirty years and had made her own way in the world when it would give her nothing.

She hurried along the still Sunday morning streets and thought of the lonely old man in the house, surrounded by a police guard, alone and frightened in a strange world he had just come back to.

She felt pity for Leo Tunney and had from the first day, when he sat at her table and could not eat the meat.

She opened the kitchen door with her key and noticed the two policemen sitting across the street in the county police car.

The house was cold and she shivered. She went to the thermostat in the hall and saw that it was set on the daytime reading for when the sun was high; the thermostat was always turned up at night but in the excitement, she had forgotten to do it. And Leo Tunney would not have known.

He was like a child, she thought.

She had never had children, she had not been blessed; but she understood children and rather liked them. She understood their confusion at the world.

She turned on the coffeepot and went to the refrigerator for eggs. He would eat an omelet, she had discovered, and she put a little cheese in it. Sliced American cheese which he did not seem to like but it was easy on him, she said. It would cure his diarrhea, she told him, and he had eaten her food meekly.

Poor old man, she thought. Like a child.

Tunney entered the kitchen as soundlessly as a ghost.

His face was pale, his eyes haunted; his hands were trembling, she saw.

"Father Tunney."

"Mrs. Jones. It's you. I'm sorry. I heard the noise. And I was waiting for you."

"Breakfast'll be on in a bit," she said briskly. When faced with death, with illness, it was best to be brisk, she always thought. People wallowed is such things and it was no good for them. People had to pull themselves up by the bootstraps sometimes, even when it was hard. Life was for the living, she always said.

"I—"

"Now don't tell me you can't eat, because you got to eat, you got to keep up your strength, such as it is. And you got to do the work now, you got to put this place in order—"

"I cannot. There's nothing to be done." He sat down at the table.

That was when she saw the red journal in his hand.

"Mrs. Jones."

"Have you slept at all, you poor man?"

"No. There was no time. This had to be finished. The time is all gone now."

She didn't like talk like that; that was talk that defeated you before you started. She knew that times were bad sometimes but you had to stand up to them. A winner never quits, a quitter never wins.

"I want you to do something for me."

"Just as soon as I put this on."

"No, Mrs. Jones." The voice, still soft and flexible as a reed in the water, commanded her oddly. She sat down.

"Mrs. Jones. This journal. This is what they want, all of them."

"I don't want to know nothing about that, none of it. I don't interfere with you men. Catholics same as a Baptist to me, all God's children."

"Mrs. Jones, you're a good woman." The voice was weak again, as though the temporary moment of command had drained it, made it pale and watery.

"And you're a good man too, Father Tunney."

"No. I am not." The voice was very soft. "I know what I am and who I have been. At least . . . since that morning, when the woman, Lu Ann Carter, showed me . . . faith again. I have faith again and that's enough; at least I have that again."

"Father Tunney, you want to eat."

"No. In a little while, I'll open the church. For Mass."

"Father! You're in no condition, why look at you, your hands are shaking."

"We are priests," he said. "We serve God."

"And you're men, just like any man is, and you can't go staying up to all hours and doing labor without breakfast in you."

"Mrs. Jones. The journal. You have to do this for me. Will you do it?"

"What?"

"In a little while, I know it, they're going to come back—"

"The man who killed Father McGillicuddy?"

"No. But someone. They want this journal. I've hidden it from them because they want it . . . not to learn from it, but to destroy it. I see that now. For a long time, I didn't understand that. When they had me in that room, when they talked to me. I didn't understand why they wanted my secrets; and then, I understood. They don't care what happened . . . in Laos, in . . . they don't care about all the suffering. This is all they want." He struck the table but his soft hand made little sound.

"Father Tunney, this—"

"You must do this. There's no danger to you. Take this book. Please, now. It is all I could do. I stayed up all night to finish it. I know what they want me to say now; they are not so clever." His eyes were wide, a little mad, very full of something like sorrow.

She understood after a moment and got up and put on her sweater and took her bag. He gave her the card that had been given to him. A name and address.

She put the journal at the bottom of her purse.

Quietly, she left by the side door and walked across the garden. It was another fine day. The sun was warm and the breeze blew away the humidity. The sky was cloudless and she felt almost light. Except for all that had happened; but one had to endure.

She crossed to the sidewalk and started down the pleasant, broad street framed with palm trees and a thousand varieties of plants growing in gardens. The police car was parked across the street from the church.

At Gulf-to-Bay Avenue, she waited for a bus because it would be a long trip and her legs weren't what they had been. And because Father Tunney hadn't said anything about taking a cab or given her extra money.

She would have to put this down to her accounts.

She didn't mind doing it for him. He was so confused, he just rambled on and on like the Mister had done in his last days.

She rarely thought of the Mister anymore and was struck by the thought.

The bus stopped at the curb and the doors whooshed open.

She sat down near the front.

She held the purse very close to her.

27
New York City

The National Security Adviser declined the cigar. He was a grim man of fastidious appearance and he had long ago concluded that smoking was too dirty a habit for his taste; that the pleasure he took in his personal appearance, down to the custom-made shirts he changed twice a day, was greater than the pleasure he could ever derive from tobacco. He would explain this, tediously, from time to time to his wife who had endured twenty-five years of such explanations. She despised him and had for quite a long time but she was now too numb to do anything about it except not listen to him.

He had been offered the cigar by a man even more fastidious in his dress who, nonetheless, now lit a cigar of his own.

Sunday afternoon in the city. Sunlight glinted coldly off the towers of Manhattan arrayed beyond the windows. They sat in the library which might have been part of an English country estate except for the spectacular view forty-one floors above the street. The room was oak-paneled and the shelves, which stretched from the floor to the thirteen-foot ceiling, were glass-enclosed. The books were all very old and unread for generations.

The whole room was designed to intimidate the rare visitor. It spoke of power and influence and tradition, all as much a part of the appearance of Henry L. Fraser as the books or the careful dress.

Fraser sat in a comfortable wing chair that was 114 years old and worth several thousand dollars. He might have been a lord in his manor, addressing the foreman of the fields; or a duke, accepting the homage of the lord mayor and his council.

Fraser was a man of handsome dimensions that had not been altered by age. His full head of hair was silver and worn long; his nose was finely chiseled and when he smiled, which he did as often as society demanded it, the smile framed the sturdy handsomeness of his bearing.

"This has been a delightful afternoon," the Security Adviser said.

"Yes. I think it went rather well," Henry Fraser agreed with a slight nod of his head. "And I think we shall not be displeased by the results."

"I'm sure," the Adviser said. He reached for his glass of brandy and tasted it again: It was the finest brandy he had ever tasted, even better than that which he had been served at the White House.

"I was in touch with Ngo Ki this morning, before you arrived." Fraser offered the information as a little surprise, like the sweets after a heavy dinner. "Matters are moving rapidly and all the . . . well, you understand, bureaucratic maneuverings can become tedious—"

"Especially in Oriental countries," the Adviser said.

"Yes. He now expects full agreement on TransAsia by November fifteenth at the latest which, given the circumstances, is rather good timing. Of course, they're hungry for it and they realize we're not such fools as to make the investment begin until the . . . safeguards are in place." Fraser spoke slowly and chose words carefully, just as he chose neckties.

"As I've said," the Adviser repeated in the same voice he used when quoting himself to his wife, "I much appreciate the opportunity—"

"And we have appreciated your cooperation. And the good wishes of the Administration. It was vital in order for TransAsia to work at all."

For a moment, both men sat in silence, appreciating the brandy and the cigar and their shared sense of well-being. After all, it had all gone extremely well.

One analyst, noted for his pessimism on the future state of the economy, had said that TransAsia was the most brilliant new financial scheme since the Marshall Plan helped rebuild devastated Europe after the war and, incidentally, helped to keep the American economy humming in the bargain. TransAsia, the analyst said, was the first implementation of the "new realism" preached by such distinguished think tanks as the Tri-Global Committee. This, however, was not strictly true. In the late 1970s, the United States had begun cautiously to involve itself in the economics of the stable Eastern European countries, hoping to realize investment and market opportunities even as it weaned such nations from a strict dependence on Soviet subsidies. The Soviets, for their part, were happy to stand aside once it became clear that the American marketing strategy would not have any effect on actual Soviet dominance of those countries. One of the nations most prominently involved was Poland; trade had accelerated between the United States and Poland to such a point that, following the remarkable strikes of 1980, the Polish government felt confident enough of the relationship to request a three-billion-dollar economic loan from the United States.

TransAsia was a complex plan of capital investment involving a half-dozen companies and investment firms which would take advantage of the docile and underutilized labor pool in the "controlled countries" of Southeast Asia, starting with Vietnam. Fraser had been the key to the scheme in his three roles as unofficial presidential adviser, chairman of International Commerce Bank of New York (popularly called InterComBank) and vice-chairman of the Tri-Global Committee, the discussion and policy group that brought together key leaders in communications, politics and economics.

"TransAsia is, at the bottom line, a good investment not because it will help a backward country come of age or spread the firm grip of peace in a region of the world that has only known war and starvation; it is a good investment because it will make money," Fraser had said a year ago, and it was going to come true. In five years, Americans would be buying television sets assembled by workers in Hanoi and Hue and Ho Chi Minh City (formerly Saigon). In eight years, production of a cooperative world-class car involving a complex of companies and nations would begin in Cambodia, which was still under Vietnamese dominance. And as Vietnam gained in industrial strength, Fraser had said, investment returns would enable U.S. industries to reform traditional areas of production that had become unprofitable—principally metal manufacturing and automaking.

The National Security Adviser had told the President that only a man like Henry Fraser could have conceived such a scheme and brought in enough people to make it work.

The President had agreed.

This Sunday, the head of InterComBank and the Adviser had spent the early afternoon at a private brunch and then returned to Fraser's suite to discuss further details of the TransAsia scheme.

Both men knew there were elements in the complex fabric of American politics that might have opposed TransAsia if they had been more aware of it. But TransAsia was one of those fringe matters in the consciousness of the nation that did not seem to deserve full attention. Which suited both men very nicely.

The Adviser was one of the men closest to the President. He had been with the "old man" from the first days, years before his first primary. He was part of the cabinet within the Cabinet that had easy and regular access to the private President. He had helped to convince the President on the worth of Henry Fraser's economic plan; he had personally vouched for Fraser's politics and political acumen. He had carried the ball for Fraser, as he repeatedly told his wife, and now he was carrying the ball for both the Administration and the TransAsia plan. The Adviser's wife half-listened to his self-congratulations without comment.

Though the general public knew about TransAsia—a story would crop up every now and then in the *Wall Street Journal* or the *New York Times*—the scheme was a matter of esoteric economics and therefore deemed deadly dull. The public was more concerned with the cost of bacon at the moment.

"Mr. Fraser." The private secretary at the door inclined his head in a gesture obviously drawn from Fraser himself.

"Excuse me a moment," Fraser said. He rose and followed the secretary through a connecting door into a small office which was bare of adornment. This room was not designed to impress visitors; it was a place to work. The curtains were drawn across the single window and the ceilings and walls were soundproofed.

"Mr. Vanderglass," the secretary said.

"I'll take it alone on the green line," Henry Fraser said. The green line was the safe line, considered untappable. And Vanderglass was chief of (special) security operations for InterCom-Bank.

The secretary withdrew and pulled the door shut behind him.

Fraser picked up the receiver. "Yes."

"Completed. At ten-thirty hours this morning. I made the usual double check and fully confirmed."

Fraser permitted himself the luxury of a moment of silence as he contemplated the information. He drew heavily on the sweet, musky taste of the cigar and allowed the smoke to escape slowly through his nostrils.

"Good work. Were there any complications?"

"No, none at all. Not in the operation itself. The only problem as I see it is Petersen. He's disappeared since last night when one of our men was hassled by the police. They were—"

"Is this merely an annoyance or is it more serious?"

"It must be something." Vanderglass's voice sounded puzzled. "Petersen is a professional, one of our best men, we got him out of the Agency in 1977 when Turner threw the place up for grabs. . . . Yet the agencies were supposed to withdraw their men and. . . ."

It was not usual for Vanderglass to speak in fragments. Fraser cleared his throat and spoke harshly. "Are you on top of this situation or not?"

"There are some complications."

"You said there weren't."

"Not with the prime operation. None at all. It went off on schedule this morning at ten-thirty. But there have been peripheral matters. This woman, the reporter, we haven't been able to find her."

"Who?"

"A detail. I don't think it matters one way or another, now that the central problem has been taken care of."

"I don't want details left unresolved," Fraser said. "Can you handle this or not?"

"Sure." Vanderglass's voice returned to its usual confident tone. The confidence infected Fraser; Vanderglass, after all, was an excellent man.

"All right. I have a dinner in Boston tonight and I'll be back at the estate by midnight. You can reach me there."

"Yes, sir."

"No details, Vanderglass."

"I understand, sir."

As he returned to the library, Fraser felt a stain of worry spreading across his feeling of confidence.

"Everything all right?" the Adviser asked. He was standing at the window, looking down on the island city.

"Yes. Everything." Fraser looked at the Adviser's back. "Tell me. Did you manage to take care . . . of that matter? The one I discussed with you earlier in the week?"

"What? Oh. You mean the agencies? I passed along the word to CIA."

"Not through channels, I hope."

The Adviser turned. "No. Not at all. Just perfectly low-key. I had a little chat with the Assistant Director, he was in charge of the project in the first place. He was the one who was so keen on it. The Director wasn't really up on it, not until that . . . unfortunate matter at the Watergate Hotel. Damned reporters."

"You're certain? I mean, that the Agency pulled back its men?"

"Yes. Got a full report. I do my homework, I can tell you, Henry. I was telling Evelyn the other day, the difference between men who succeed and the men who merely fail spectacularly is all in the homework, attending to the details."

Henry Fraser stared at the Adviser without speaking. "And the Agency pulled back?"

"Yes. Well, actually, there was a man from one of the smaller intelligence agencies, down there merely meddling, I wasn't even aware of it until the A.D. informed me."

"What?"

"Well, something to do with interagency rivalries or some such." The Adviser smiled but he was now uncomfortable. Henry Fraser's tone had changed perceptibly in the last moment. "Another agency," the Adviser repeated, his voice rising on a note of good cheer. "It didn't mean anything."

"Did they withdraw?"

"Well, there was a problem. Said they couldn't locate their man at the moment."

"They what?"

"This was yesterday, I haven't heard back—"

"There was another agent down there? For another intelligence agency?"

"R Section. You see, Henry, the intelligence apparatus is not quite as centralized as we would like it; as we're going to make it by the next budget, I can tell you. Too much waste."

"We're not talking about politics at the moment."

"That's precisely the point, Henry." Yes, the Adviser thought,

Henry Fraser's attitude had become distinctly unfriendly in the last minute. "Most people think the CIA is the whole ball of wax. I was telling Evelyn, if she only understood how complicated it all was. There's R Section, and the National Security Agency which is a distinct entity, not to mention the Cointel arm of the FBI and the Defense Intelligence Agency. And the Mole Group. But I'm not supposed to mention them at all."

"Damn," Fraser said. "Have your agents withdrawn from that priest or not?"

"Yes."

"But you said you weren't certain about this other . . . agent. From R Section?"

"Yes. R Section. I didn't say that. I merely said I had not double-checked. I gave explicit instructions in the afternoon. To the Section. Withdraw him immediately. They were expecting contact from him momentarily—"

"But you're not certain."

"I'm ninety-nine percent certain. My God, Henry, what's wrong? Is there a problem?"

Henry Fraser banked his rage. After all, Vanderglass exuded confidence. And if the Adviser was a bit of a fool . . . there was no reason to upset everyone.

"No. Not at all."

The voice was calm and courteous again. "Curiosity only. At this stage, I tend to get a little fussy about details. It wouldn't be good for us—for you and me—or for TransAsia to have any little . . . well . . . embarrassment brought up now. Rehash it all in the popular papers, on the talk shows."

"Of course, Henry, I understand completely," the Adviser said, understanding not at all. "If you mean everything that happened . . . well, a long time ago, with this cleric and his connection with the Agency. I can see your point. We don't want to ruffle anyone's feathers, do we? Either our friends in the Administration or the investors. Or our friends in Vietnam, either."

"Precisely. Don't forget InterComBank was also involved with the Agency, laundering funds out of Asia for them. I mean, it's nothing to be ashamed of, it was our duty, but we don't need to see all this brought up again because of some half-crazy old priest. . . ."

235

"Absolutely, Henry, I couldn't agree with you more. You know how it goes. Conspiracies become so popular in the public mind."

"Exactly."

"Do you know what my theory is?" The Adviser put his hands in his trouser pockets and leaned back on his heels in the manner of a raconteur preparing to offer a favorite story. Evelyn, his long-suffering wife, had seen the gesture a thousand times in her marriage and come to dread it.

"The way I see it, this whole conspiracy-theory concept—as a concept—was pretty well discredited after the Kennedy assassination in 1963. I mean, people who ran around talking about two or three rifle shots and all that, they became identified with the lunatic fringe. And that just about did the conspiracy idea in . . . until Watergate, that is. Watergate just gave it a whole new life because of those two damned reporters for the *Post*. I mean, for more than a year, we were watching one story after another, linking one more name to the conspiracy, implicating more and more people. So now we all have to be on our guard again about this conspiracy stuff. Sinister. Everyone sees it as a sinister matter where I think that most conspiracies are for the good. I mean, the work the bank did in the past channeling Agency money back and forth. What was wrong with that? Damned patriotic, I call it. For my part, I say to hell with the critics and let's give InterComBank an award instead of . . . well, hiding its light under a bushel as it were. But fashions, even in politics, change and I'm sure that the bank's turn will come someday to get a full measure of credit."

What a fool, Henry Fraser thought. "A bank is a corporation. It's a person only in the legal sense. I don't think a bank will care one way or another whether it receives a presidential medal."

The Adviser laughed. It was a rare and grim chuckle but the closest he ever came to mirth.

"Yes, Henry. I see your point."

But Henry Fraser wondered about that.

28
Clearwater

"My dear friends . . ."

It was ten-thirty in the morning. Leo Tunney hesitated and looked around him but, of course, none of them were his friends. He knew no one at all. Again, just for a moment, he thought of Phuong and the boy and a stain of bitterness spread across his sea of thoughts. Phuong. In a little while, he thought, I will be with you.

If there is anything after this.

Doubt cast its shadow. In those years with her, he had doubted so long and so profoundly that he thought at times he could not bear it. Pain and loss could be borne, but not doubt; doubt was too much to live with. So he had thought but he had not died; Phuong, the boy, Van, the others had all died but he had lived until now. Until doubt could be put aside. Not destroyed; doubts never were dispelled once they had life; they lived like secret viruses, feeding quietly on the host until it was time to emerge again.

The little church was bursting with people, some coming for the Mass, some for miracles, some out of curiosity because of all that had happened there in the past week. They jammed the pews and stood along the walls fanning out from both sides of the main door. The air carried the varied smells of their packed bodies and an edge of expectation in the restlessness that rode below the polite silence like a murmur.

"My dear friends in Christ," Tunney began again with more confidence. "This has been a time of sorrow for us here. For me, in this place." Again, he paused and waited for words. "I am a stranger who came to you and you welcomed me." No, he thought, this is wrong, this is not to be a speech; he wanted words from his heart.

For a moment, he felt dizzy and swayed at the pulpit, gripping the rosewood very tightly until his thin fingers were white at the knuckles.

"My dear friends," he began again.

The murmur rose, broke through the surface of silence; they

237

began to nudge each other in the pews, they looked around to con-firm their normalcy to each other.

". . . in a time of sorrow, we look around us to the seasons—" He remembered such words from his youth, a childhood of such memories in the deep, narrow valley in western Pennsylvania where the seasons tumbled after each other down the slopes, coming in waves of green, of colored leaves, of snow and finally, in spring, the raging tide of black mud and bitter rains.

Some rose in the pews; others spoke openly; his distress was communicated to them. The sea of people, feeling the sense of each other—the sense of something wrong—roiled in confused waves, waiting for a storm.

He could not speak. He did not have words left. Phuong, he cried in memory. He held her body, the body of a fallen bird, light and cold in death.

But I was given faith again, he thought.

Where are the words?

"Please sit down," he said suddenly, in a clear, calm tone. The moment of panic had passed.

Some who had risen returned to their seats.

Rustling in the crowd, murmurs, coughs.

It was so clear to him now. "As you may know, I was in the jungle, in Asia, for a long time." It was so clear, why hadn't he seen it before?

"Since I have returned, my Church has sent an examiner to me, to ask me what I saw in the jungle. Also my government—your government—and they have asked me many questions. I did not answer their questions not out of stubbornness but because I could not speak, I could not think to speak. I was frightened as I had been frightened before, many times; and I had learned to deal with my fear, with those who caused it. . . ."

He smiled now, the thin face forming a look that combined humor and sadness. His eyes were shining. "I did not speak. I had more than one secret and they could not even guess what the secrets were."

Again, a smile; peace crossed the sun-dark face. "You see, a man in his journey through this life also journeys through his times of doubt. There are many periods of doubt that frighten most of all;

because it is profound, doubt cannot be dispelled by the morning light. A doubt is a secret and it cannot be shared, even when you speak of it; a doubt is the worst fear of all because to speak only enlarges it, lets it fill in all the corners of the mind." He leaned forward, the eyes earnest and shining. "Do not be afraid of doubt. I can see that now."

Restlessness boiled in the pews. He sensed it but ignored it; he was not speaking to them.

He spoke to Phuong who thought he would lose his soul.

He spoke to his own doubt, his heart. In a clear voice that was not afraid.

"Why did I return?

"Because it was time, because there was no reason not to return. If I told them that—if I told the people in your government that or the Church, those who questioned me would not believe me. They wanted secrets from me because that is what is in their own hearts; they have doubts as well and they were afraid of me."

Yes, he could see that; doubt shrank from him, cowered before him.

"I saw many things. I put them down. I felt many things. I put them down. Some of you will be amazed at the matters I have written of—"

He smiled.

Murmurs broke through again. It seemed inevitable that one woman, finally, bent double by deformity, would rise and cry out: "Please, please! Cure me—"

"I cannot," Leo Tunney said quietly, distracted from his words.

"Please! Cure me!"

"You can only cure yourself." Words faltered again; doubt smiled at him. "It is the power of doubt in your—"

The woman, wart-faced, mean and twisted, her arms knobby sticks poking from the folds of her dress, screamed: "You cured her! You cured her and you won't cure me!"

She shook her hand at Lu Ann Carter.

The woman who said she had been cured turned and looked at the old woman, at the tears of frustration staining the cheeks. Lu Ann Carter rose, stared, her face ashen, her eyes wide and hunted;

she saw them all as they were, murmuring, hating her, rising in the pews—

She turned and Tunney stared at her.

Eyes of peace, she thought again. Holy.

In that moment, she understood as well and reached for his hand over the Communion railing. "Please," she said softly. "Please."

He understood, she thought in terror. He understood and it didn't matter to him.

A fever came over them; hysteria backed against them; they felt flushed and mad.

"Please," Lu Ann began, turning to those in the pews. "This is a good man! Please, this is a holy man and now I see it. And I'm a sinner, daughter of the devil! Daughter of evil and this is a man of God come down to cure me!" The voice rose, the muddy accent could not hold it, it rose like a clear running stream never heard before in the wilderness. "I sinned, and I beg God for my heart, I beg His forgiveness!"

Tunney stared at her amazed.

And he saw Phuong again, as clearly as if he were still there, holding the sparrow body in his own frail arms, feeling life leaving her.

He touched Lu Ann Carter's milk-white arm as he had touched her that first day, when she had risen and cast off her crutches and straightened before him.

"You are a holy man," she said, tears streaking her cheeks. "All this trick of mine, this deceit, and you knew and forgave—"

"Nothing." He stepped back. Even this, he thought, his eyes opening wide. "No." He understood—

"I sinned against—"

No. This cannot be the truth; there had been a miracle! He stepped back, bumped into the step, nearly stumbled and fell.

"No miracles!" Lu Ann cried then, in a rapture, spreading her arms. "Nothing but lies of Satan."

Hysteria broke around them. There were moans and shouts from the pews, sobs and cries.

"Forgive me, Father!" Lu Ann cried. She looked up, she held out her arms.

Tunney did not understand; he began a sign of blessing.

And then he stopped.

"I lied to you," Lu Ann cried. "Forgive me! I was wicked, I am cast down!"

He stared at her.

Slowly, Lu Ann Carter showed him. She began to bend back into the position of a cripple, she began to separate her back and shoulders, to form the horrible hunch that pushed her head forward.

Doubt grinned in Tunney's mind; it loomed over him; doubt showed him its triumph.

"But you gave me faith!" Lu Ann Carter cried.

Miracles.

Then Leo Tunney moaned, a single horrible sound, the moan of the soul; he had uttered it when he felt the lightness of Phuong's body suddenly collapse into the heaviness of death as he held her.

All tricks, all fakes, life without miracles, he thought feverishly. All of it was a trick.

Phuong!

At that moment, six rapid sounds of explosions came sharply one after the other from the back of the church. The booms seemed to shake the building, and the crowd, caught in a panic already fed by hysteria, suddenly surged forward, pushing against the pews, leaping over the backs of the pews; others in the crowd—turned into a mob now—pushed along the walls away from the explosions, down the aisles, surging toward the altar.

Another explosion.

Another and another.

They knocked the old priest backward, sending him stumbling against the altar steps; he felt himself falling before the surge of blind bodies—

Screams and terror in the air.

He cried out but had no voice; doubt choked him. He felt the bodies surging over him, crushing him. He felt pain, felt the feet kicking at him, the breath crushed out of his lungs. A weight fell on his heart.

Death and doubt came in black, grinning waves over his mind, suffocating him. He could not see. The blackness held him, strangling him.

"Father!" he cried out once.

Pain and bodies pressing, falling, legs and arms. Blood and pain.

And Tunney smelled death; he was in the village again hidden in the jungle; he saw the child dead, the life that had come from his loins; he saw the dying all around him; he saw the men who marched through the village, burning and killing; he heard the screams; he saw the bombs falling in their beautiful patterns from the waves of planes glimpsed overhead, falling like a shower of stones flung on the sea.

He saw all of it and saw the beauty in death.

Why did I resist You? he thought.

I didn't understand before.

Of course. It was so simple.

My God—

29
Washington, D.C.

Hanley awoke at the buzz of the red telephone on his desk. For a moment, he did not move. He blinked his eyes in the harsh fluorescent light and then looked down the length of his body sprawled on the black leather couch. He realized he had not even removed his shoes before falling asleep. That annoyed him.

He pushed his body up and reached for the telephone. His watch—a twenty-four-hour Swiss-made chronometer—read: 1816. Quarter past six on a Sunday night.

"Hanley."

The familiar voice at the other end of the line sounded weak.

Hanley had spent the last thirty-seven hours in his office, except for the unplanned meeting yesterday morning with the Assistant Director of the Agency on a park bench. So much had happened in the past day and a half. And now the voice was thin at the other end of the line; something had gone wrong.

"Report," Hanley said.

"I was shot for starters."

"What happened?"

"I underestimated my opponent."

"Levity," Hanley said.

"Not really. I don't feel funny."

"Are you all right?"

"For now. I've got some wounds but they're superficial. The bullet missed me. Wood splinters."

"I don't understand."

"Those are terrible rounds the Section provides. If he had hit me, I'd be finished."

"Who shot you? What's happened? Was it the Agency?"

"I don't know. His name was Petersen. About six feet four, an intelligent type. No identification on him, very professional. Yes. Professional." Again, an ironic note in Devereaux's voice.

"Hanley."

Devereaux paused.

"Petersen said he was with security. For InterComBank. In New York. International Commerce Bank, isn't it?"

"That's ludicrous," Hanley said. "Why would he have been involved with you? What happened?"

"Can you check? If they have a connection with us?"

"They don't."

"And the Agency. If they have a connection there?"

"What's happened?"

Slowly, in his methodical way, Devereaux unfolded the events of that night and day. The visit from Rita Macklin after midnight; the confrontation with Petersen in the deserted cabin on Sand Key; awaking in the middle of the morning to find himself sprawled in the sand next to Petersen's body.

"What did you do?"

"I took care of it. He sleeps with the fishes."

"That's cheap gangster talk."

"It's appropriate," Devereaux said flatly, thinking of Petersen's plans for Rita Macklin.

"Why did you become involved with the reporter?"

"Because Leo Tunney was keeping a journal. It contained a

secret worth having. Worth killing for, at least. And Rita Macklin was going to get it for me."

"Where is it?"

"Tunney," Devereaux said with difficulty. "He's dead. This morning. A panic in the church, he was saying Mass, they think he died of a heart attack. The crowd swears there were explosions—"

"What are you talking about?"

Devereaux began again, leading Hanley from the moment he returned to his room to his discovery that Rita was gone to his discovery that Tunney had been killed in the middle of the morning while he still lay unconscious on a stretch of beach near a deserted cabin.

"Then where is the journal?"

"I don't know."

"This has become too complicated, I can't quite—"

"Yes," Devereaux broke in. "That's it exactly. There are too many elements involved and yet they must all be connected."

"What about this 'miracle' woman?"

"A fraud," Devereaux said. "The police have her but they don't know what to charge her with. I suppose it will be fraud. She took a lot of money from a lot of reporters for interviews."

"How was she involved then? I mean, in the journal, this whole business—"

Devereaux paused. He had thought about it all afternoon as well, as he searched both Rita's empty room and the rooms of the shuttered rectory. What was connected? And what was the connection?

"I don't think she was."

"But she was at the center of the matter—"

"No. She was just a wild card. Like the cop who walks into a bank during a carefully planned robbery and breaks it up and it turns out later he only intended to make a deposit. No. Lu Ann Carter was playing her own game. It's just that she threw everything else off. And she panicked the people who decided to kill Tunney and the other priests."

"Who are they?"

"I know one," Devereaux said. "Yes. I have one for you."

"Devereaux."

"What?"

"This has become very dangerous."

"Are you worried about my safety?"

"This is not a time for joking," Hanley said in his priggish way. "A delicate matter has become more delicate. I received a call early this afternoon. From the Adviser. He was in New York and he wanted to check with me. To make absolutely certain we had . . . ah . . . withdrawn from Florida."

"Just a routine check," Devereaux said.

"I did a dangerous thing."

"You lied."

"Yes."

"It wasn't necessary. There's nothing more to do here. Well. One thing more."

"What are you going to do?"

"First, I want you to get computer scans. I have some names and some guesses I want scenarios played on."

"And probabilities?"

"Yes. Probabilities." Devereaux gave Hanley the names and the hunches. Hanley accepted them without a word; he did not write them down.

"Is that all?"

"No. I'm afraid this is just the beginning."

"You asked me to check with our man in Rome. On the Vatican connector. You may want to know that the chief of the Congregation for the Protection of the Faith has flown to Florida. He was in Prague."

"Do we know where he is?"

Hanley gave him the name of a hotel.

"Do you see?" Devereaux said. "There are too many elements in this. The Vatican sends their director of intelligence. The KGB has a man here. And two other men—they arrange two killings. . . ." Devereaux paused.

"Did the Opposition kill Tunney?"

"I don't know but now I'm beginning to think not. If they didn't . . ."

It was not usual for Devereaux to pause when reporting to Control. But Hanley did not show any impatience.

"Hanley. We have to move now. First to protect ourselves, then to resolve this. It's gotten too dirty the way it is."

"How can we? I mean, cover ourselves?"

"We give them something worth the lie you told, worth my borrowed time here."

"What?" Hanley said.

"Proof," Devereaux replied. "Proof and a body to go with it."

"You were holding out?"

"Yes. Until everyone else played their cards." Devereaux paused and when he spoke again, his voice was hard. "Now it's time to survive."

30
Clearwater Beach

Slowly, gravely, Denisov strolled along the shoreline and stared out at the black sea. It was nearly three in the morning; as usual, he had not slept. He stared into the blackness but it was opaque, the moon hidden behind a cloud. His vision was turned back on itself.

All slept.

Again, he yearned for sleep himself as simply as he had yearned for it in the old apartment in Moscow, as he had yearned for it in Gorki during the difficult time of examination caused by Devereaux's betrayal. In sleep, he could forget Devereaux who haunted his thoughts now.

Gogol had approved giving the "proofs" to Devereaux when Denisov notified his control that Devereaux was investigating the Tunney matter. And yet the documents had been so flimsy that Denisov had complained. "All proofs are flimsy," the control had told him. "If we make them more substantial, Devereaux will suspect them."

And yet Devereaux had not used the pieces of paper that

"proved" the priest was a CIA agent working against the interests of the Soviet government.

And the matter in Florida had not been resolved.

The death of Leo Tunney had shut down the source of embarrassment for the Soviet Union. That is the way Gogol had phrased it in his message to Denisov through the New York control. And yet. There was the matter of this journal.

Where was the journal?

Did it even exist?

And who had it?

So Denisov could not come home until the matter was resolved. He yearned to return as a lover yearns. If he could go back to Moscow, to his music, to his little afternoons alone in the Chess Union, he would find sleep and peace.

"What is in the journal that would embarrass us?" he had asked the control officer in the Soviet Embassy in New York.

"We cannot say."

"Do you even know?"

"We cannot say."

Denisov had carried with him the vague feeling that the matter was now beyond containment or control and that if there was blame, it would be apportioned to him.

But this time, he would not be sent down to Gorki for examination and reeducation.

This time fate would not be so kind to him.

He had made one mistake already in killing the priest from Rome.

The matter should have ended with his death. Instead, they made too many investigations. He had worried about the authorities. He had destroyed the umbrella and its lethal cargo of drugs.

Denisov had killed Foley because he could not trust him.

Foley did not know of the Concordance. Foley did not know he had to act in concert with the Soviets. Perhaps it was planned that way by Cardinal Ludovico: If Ludovico could have gotten the journal first, perhaps Rome would have been able to back out of the Concordance at the last moment. Rome must be kept on a tight leash, Gogol had said. The journal would free them from the leash.

Denisov bent down and picked up a shell, one of thousands on the sand, and studied it. The shell was colored silver and ruby. It was beautiful and insignificant.

Denisov threw the shell in the water and it did not make a sound.

Cardinal Ludovico had told him there was no journal.

Was he lying? Was he stalling?

Denisov folded his hands behind his back and walked along the white sand. There were so many secrets and so much was hidden from him: Gogol said that whatever Tunney knew would not have mattered in six months' time but that his secret must be suppressed now. Tunney was a grave threat to the security of the Soviet Union.

But it was impossible, Denisov argued in his mind. A priest. A single man. What could he know?

On the morning after Denisov discovered that Leo Tunney was keeping a journal for Foley, Denisov killed Foley. It was simply a matter of precaution. What if Foley already knew what was to be in the journal?

And then there was the matter of Tunney.

He had to get the journal, he had to kill the priest. He did not want to kill the old man but Devereaux forced it; Devereaux would not use his "proofs" to discredit the priest.

It had all been so complicated. And then someone else had killed McGillicuddy. And this morning, someone had managed to kill Tunney.

Who was working against him?

"This is not Devereaux's work," he had told the control officer at the Soviet Embassy in New York. "There is another element at work."

But what if he failed this time?

The haunting thought drove away sleep.

Denisov crossed under the pilings of the fishing pier in the middle of the public beach and continued on, down to the darker side of the beach.

And then he paused.

There, faintly outlined in the dim light, was a figure he knew, limping along the shore toward him.

Denisov stopped, hands behind his back, his curious blue eyes staring straight ahead.

He knew this other man.

A cold face, more pale in the dim light; a winter-hard face made of ice, burning with a fierce white calm like the Arctic in midsummer.

"I did not expect this," Denisov said in his mild voice.

"Why? Did you think I was dead?"

"No. You are hurt?"

"Who sent the men in the gray car?"

"I do not know."

"Is that the truth?" The voice was hard, mocking in tone.

"As you say, Devereaux. So I should say: 'Perhaps.' But that is not the truth. I do not know the gray car or the men. I gave you proofs." The voice was slow and chiding. "I gave you proofs you would not use. So now the old priest is dead, murdered by Central Intelligence."

"I thought you killed him."

"I do not kill. I had no reason to kill an old man."

"Why did you give me papers to show he was a spy? To show he was still working for the CIA? Why did you call him an agent provocateur?"

"It was my instructions." The burly man shrugged. "I do as I am told. You do as your master says. But you did not give him the proofs."

"The proofs were lies, Denisov."

"Is that the truth? Do you know that? Do you provoke me to agree with you?"

"The proofs were lies, Denisov," Devereaux said again.

Denisov waited and stared at the other man. So long they had been like this, facing each other, testing and probing, telling lies and truths, temporizing, waiting, pushing the other to a mistake.

They stood four feet apart on the empty, dark beach.

"You killed Foley."

Denisov smiled then and took his rimless glasses from his nose and wiped them against his shirt. He replaced them and spoke: "I do not kill."

"You kill as it is necessary. Foley might have had the secret of the journal."

"I don't know what you mean."

"Denisov." The name was uttered softly. An old enemy, an old friend; perhaps the distinctions blurred with the passing of time.

"Only a Soviet would have been clumsy enough to use the London Touch in Florida. What if it hadn't been raining?"

For the first time, Denisov smiled.

Without a word, the two men fell into step, side by side, along the hard, wet sand. Two men of early middle age, their shoulders slumped by a mutual weariness they wore like oxen yoked in the same team.

"Why were you involved at all?" Devereaux said at last as they walked along. "From the beginning, I didn't understand the Soviet factor."

"I do not know. I was to be a messenger, they trusted me with these proofs to give you. It was a little test to me, after you betrayed me to the English. After they examined me in Gorki."

"You were more involved than that."

"I was a messenger only," Denisov said. "I gave you the proofs. Perhaps there would not have been these deaths, all that has happened, if you did use them."

"Perhaps."

"Yes, Devereaux, make a word that does not mean anything. You say 'perhaps' to say nothing. I tell you the truth. We want this treaty with America, this peace agreement in Denmark. So that we will not make war to each other."

"We are at war all the time."

"No. That is in your head, that is not true. You are a man too much a cynic. You must be faithful too, sometime. Like the *bushkas* in the churches."

"The few you have left open."

"I gave you proofs," Denisov said doggedly.

"Trust you. You wanted me to trust you."

"I am going home in a little while. Tomorrow," Denisov said. "I would not guess to see you again."

"Why didn't you try to kill me? Instead of Foley?"

"I do not kill." Denisov paused on the sand. "My English, I beg pardon. It suffers when I spoke English so well when we were in England. Do you remember?" Again, for the second time, the edge of bitterness broke through the flat, mild voice. "Before I came here, to give you proofs, only that . . . when I was still in Moscow." He stared at the Gulf and saw himself. "In my apartment alone with the recording. The Gilbert and Sullivan. It was a pleasure to hear the English voices. *The Mikado . . .*"

He turned and stared sadly at Devereaux. "When the British expel me from England, when you betray me, I spend ten months in Gorki. Then it is not a good time to use the English, is it? Do you see? It is not wise. So much was suspect of me for a long time."

"Yes. I can see that."

"You do that to me, Devereaux," Denisov said, touching the sleeve of the other's coat. Devereaux shook off the slight contact. "Once, you betray me, and yet I am a soldier and you are a soldier. I gave you the proofs."

"I did not believe them. I do not believe you." The voice of the American agent was cold, without comfort or friendship, without a remembrance of other times or a thought for times to come. "You betray yourself, Denisov; I am not your friend and you are not my friend. We are enemies. You gave me those phony papers as a ploy, to turn me off the game, you killed Foley. And now you're on the beach, going to Rita Macklin's room—"

"I do not know this."

"You are a liar, Denisov. You sent those men in the gray car after her."

"I am alone. You know this is true."

Devereaux suddenly made a guess. "Why did you see Ludovico?"

For a moment, Denisov appeared stunned. And then he turned away. "You think you know much, Devereaux. You do not sleep so well, I think, you must dream this. Why would I kill one priest and go to see another?"

"You know he's here."

"Perhaps."

"Ludovico is here."

"I am not concerned."

"This is a pose, Denisov. You are not a simple man." This time Devereaux stepped in front of him. "But this is not an interrogation. Did they treat you badly in Gorki? Did you tell them everything they wanted to know?"

"They are satisfied with me."

"And now? Will they be satisfied with your failure?"

"You have failed. I gave you the proofs."

"And I have the journal."

Denisov stared at the cold, impassive face.

"Is this so?"

Devereaux did not speak.

"I do not know about a journal which you speak."

"I know the secret."

"There is no secret."

"You have failed, Denisov."

Denisov thought again of that confrontation in the darkened hotel room. Yes, he had wanted to kill Devereaux then but that was not the mission. And then Devereaux had asked him: What if you fail again?

"It is you who fail. I am held in regard in Moscow. You fail because you do not use the proofs and you let your CIA agent kill this priest."

"They will not accept failure again. It will not be a matter of returning to Moscow. Or even questioning in Gorki. Perhaps you will be offered the chance of rehabilitation in Murmansk. You can work on the power project—"

The French-made automatic appeared in his hand as though it were a magic trick.

"A pistol, Denisov? Are you going to kill me?"

"Yes. It is time for that."

Devereaux smiled. "You have failed, haven't you? You know what they will do with you—"

"Where is the journal?"

"There is no journal."

"Then your death will be unnecessary. Except that you will be dead in any case."

"Success or failure depends on survival."

"I will survive."

"Yes," Devereaux said. "That has already been arranged. You have defected. Welcome to America."

Denisov stared at him.

"You are a problem and I have to put you in a box. For a little while. If the whole thing blows up, I have to survive and I need a cover. You are my cover; you are my little prize to turn over to them in case everything else fails. You are insurance."

Denisov began to speak, in Russian, and then stopped.

"Again," Denisov said sadly. "You betray me."

"You are the enemy. You cannot betray those you do not trust."

"You cannot have done this thing."

"It is done all the time. By you, by us. Two cables were sent tonight—"

"My government will not believe—"

"Yes. Of course they will. It is not too difficult to feed the paranoia of an intelligence system. Especially the KGB. Two cables, sent in usual diplomatic code. We made sure your people were listening. Right now the intercepted messages are in the Committee for External Observation and Resolution."

Denisov held the gun at belly level.

"The first says you have made contact with an American agent in Florida. As you had planned. The cable is to our British station, seeking background information. You have defected, the cable states. The second emanates from Cardinal Ludovico right here on the beach. He has informed the operations chief at the Congregation back in the Vatican that you have betrayed your masters, that you have defected to the Americans."

Denisov did not speak.

"And now it will be nothing to me to kill you," Denisov said at last.

"No. You won't kill me."

"You have betrayed me again."

"No. Your knowledge of English is still not precise. We are enemies. I have beaten you."

"For nothing. You beat me for nothing."

"To survive," Devereaux said. "Look over there, at the street. Two men. From the Tampa FBI. They'll take you back to Washington. We will talk again."

"I must not." He stopped, looked around wildly. "I must escape this thing."

Devereaux spoke in a flat voice, without pity. "You were a

professional. You took the chance. You tried to use me and it didn't work. There's no place to run."

"No. This would be without hope for you. You could have taken me. You could hold me, capture me. At least there would be exchange for me, for one of yours. It is worthless to have me not to exchange."

"No. That was suggested, but no. Your exit is blocked, it has to be. If everything fails, I will use you to extricate myself. And now the cables have been sent."

Denisov looked down at the gun in his hand. "I could kill you," he said tonelessly.

"The life of a defector is not unpleasant," Devereaux said. "The life of a murderer is spent in our prison system. Our jails are very unpleasant places."

"I could kill myself."

For a moment, Devereaux's face softened. "No, Dmitri Ilyich. That would be an act of despair. That would not be forgiven."

The music came to him in that moment, the last song on the record before he had followed Luriey out the door of the little apartment in Moscow.

My object all sublime
I shall achieve in time,
To let the punishment fit the crime . . .

"I will not see them again, my family," Denisov said.

Devereaux waited.

"This is the cruel thing you have done."

"It is not death, Denisov. You are not obliterated. You survive."

"And you. You survive for nothing. You are still adrift, you are still left outside."

"Yes."

"What will you do to me?"

"Keep you. You know we won't harm you."

"My family will suffer."

"Perhaps."

"Would this be easy for you? To be taken away?"

Devereaux said nothing.

The moon came from behind the cloud; in the sudden stream of white light, Devereaux could clearly see the eyes of the Soviet agent.

They were shining with tears.

And then, slowly, Denisov let the pistol leave his fingertips and fall onto the sand without a sound.

31
Washington, D.C.

Vanderglass studied the building directory in the lobby of the National Press Building for several seconds before going to the elevator bank. He rode up alone; it was shortly after ten on Monday morning, nearly a day after Leo Tunney had been killed. Official Washington was already at work. When the doors opened on the ninth floor, the corridors were empty. It was too late for stragglers going to work and too early for the first coffee break of the day.

He found the offices of World Information Syndicate. With his usual, cool attention to detail, Vanderglass noticed that the "S" was missing from the title on the glass door. Vanderglass noticed everything, remembered everything; it was part of his usefulness as operations director for international security at InterComBank.

This job, he had decided that morning on the plane up from Florida, was important enough to handle himself.

Kaiser was at his desk in the inner office, talking to a young man seated on the leather couch. Vanderglass had never been in the office. He had only spoken twice to Kaiser, both times on the phone.

The offices were incredibly dirty, he thought. The walls were streaked with dirt and the remains of posters, old clippings, pages torn from newspapers. One yellowed page from the *Washington Post* announced that President Nixon had resigned.

A woman sat behind a typewriter in the outer office. She was unkempt and her eyes were large. She had sallow skin and she typed very rapidly on the old Olympia manual office machine.

Vanderglass did not speak to her.

He walked directly into Kaiser's room and stood at the littered desk, careful to keep his trousers away from the grimy edge.

Kaiser looked up at him.

"Kaiser," Vanderglass said in a voice he knew would be remembered by the older man.

Kaiser stared at him and then glanced at the young man on the couch. "Cassidy. Get your ass in gear, get out of here." The voice was harsh, gravelly. "I got business to talk with this guy."

Kaiser lit another cigarette. Cassidy got up, looked at Vanderglass, and then edged his way out of the door of the crowded room. Vanderglass kicked the door closed behind him.

"What the hell are you doing here?" Kaiser said.

Vanderglass stared at him.

"What the hell do you want here?" Kaiser said.

"You must know the answer to that."

"Get out of here."

"I want your girl."

Kaiser gaped at him, the cigarette smoldering in one of his ham fists. "I haven't heard from her. You mean Rita."

"I mean Rita," he said.

"She isn't around."

"You know where she is."

"The hell I do."

"We never found the journal."

"Maybe there isn't a journal."

"One of our men, he talked to the housekeeper at that rectory in Florida. She was a little suspicious of him but she talked to him. Yes. She talked to him at last." Vanderglass spoke in a soft, smoky voice, nearly without inflection, as though he were the mildest of men. "She told us, finally. The housekeeper. The old priest gave her a red-bound book. To give to your girl. Rita Macklin. She has it now and we want it, but you know that, don't you?"

Kaiser's eyes widened. He seemed genuinely surprised. Vanderglass noticed it but did not make a gesture of acknowledgment.

"She got the journal? She got it?" He sounded almost exuberant. "Lovely, Rita. Lovely. She didn't call me, she didn't get in touch—"

"Shut up, fat man," Vanderglass said. His face was as dark as a cobra; his hair was dark, close to the head, his eyes were hooded and his mouth revealed thin, sharp teeth.

"Look, you, you don't come in here with—"

"Shut up, I said." The voice was final. "Where would she go to ground? I mean, if she didn't trust coming back to see you?"

"What did you do to her? I called her—"

"You're the one gave her a warning? You're in trouble, fat man. Very bad trouble. Your son's in trouble too."

"What did you do to her?"

"We can do more. But all we want is that journal. It doesn't matter about her."

"You're going to hurt her."

"We're not going to hurt anyone. No one was supposed to get hurt."

"You killed three men. Three priests. You—"

"We didn't kill anyone," Vanderglass said. His voice was as mild as the truth. "The old priest died by accident, this Lu Ann Carter person got hysterical—"

"Crap," said Kaiser, his voice rising. "Some kind of device down there. There was a story in the *Post* this morning. . . ."

"You don't want to concern yourself with these things," Vanderglass said.

Kaiser felt afraid again.

"You should have told us, Kaiser, when you let your little girl go after Leo Tunney in the first place. It would have saved a lot of problems."

"It was different then. I didn't know InterComBank was involved."

"Who told you that? Did we even mention the bank? I don't

257

want you to become careless, Kaiser. I don't want to hear the name of that bank again."

"But you're involved now—"

"We're all involved, fat man. You and me. And your little girl reporter. Where is she now?"

"She was in Florida."

"I was in Florida."

Rita was on the run, Kaiser thought. She got out in time. The warning had meant something after all. And she had the journal.

For a moment, he thought of her and he was overwhelmed by despair. It was hopeless now; he had ruined everything for her, for himself.

And he knew they wouldn't be able to stop now until they killed her. He understood that clearly. They would have to kill her; it was the only way.

"I don't know where she is."

"Home. Where's her home at?"

"I don't know. You know where she lives in Bethesda—"

"I don't want to waste my time, Mr. Kaiser. She worked for you, remember? She came from someplace, didn't she?"

"I won't tell you."

"You have to tell us. You know that. Don't be unreasonable about it."

"No. You want to kill her. I won't help you kill her."

"No one is going to get killed."

"Liar," Kaiser hissed. "You dirty bastard, you fucking liar. Get out of here, you fucking bastard."

"Did you forget your son? In New York? Did you forget the matter of embezzlement from my employer? He has a life, he has children. Those little daughters of his. Did you forget them?"

"You would remind me."

"He could go away for ten years. Yes. Ten years in a federal prison. Mr. Fraser is a powerful man, I assure you. An example would be made of him."

"But that was my son, that was me. It wasn't Rita." For a moment, his voice broke; he felt the despair like a web closing over his soul.

"Rita," he said.

Vanderglass did not understand. "Yes, Rita Macklin. That's who we're talking about."

"I won't let you kill her."

"Self-interest, fat man. Decent self-interest. On the one hand, you have a reporter you have known for two years. An employee. On the other, you have your son, your kith and kin. Your only kin. You have your daughter-in-law. Can you picture her in your mind? And the two little girls . . . what were their names again? I would have to say for myself it was no contest, wouldn't you say so?"

"But you will kill her," Kaiser said.

Vanderglass stared at him solemnly.

"No," Vanderglass said. "I swear to you before God that we will not harm her. I promise you that on my solemn word of honor. I promise you."

Kaiser stared back at him and yearned to believe him; and yet, he saw the lie. And yet. He had to believe.

"Yes," Kaiser said dully. "You make a promise."

He looked down at his dirty ink-stained hands resting on the littered desk. Reporter and editor, that was all it had meant.

He thought of Rita the first day, frightened and nervous, yet with a certain sense of bearing, a sort of sense of herself and what she would do.

She had gotten the journal just as she said she would.

And now they would have to kill her.

Kaiser did not speak. He realized that he had cared about her and never told her. And now he would have to betray her.

"Please," he said to Vanderglass as though there would be a reprieve, as though the nightmare really had an end to it.

But the dark man waited without a word.

32
Clearwater

Dawn. Monday morning. Red filled the eastern sky, the buildings were colored purple in the shade.

Devereaux turned off the ignition of the rental car and waited in the stillness for a moment. Across the street was the entrance of the white hotel at the end of the beach.

He glanced at the battered bag on the seat next to him. He had checked out of his own hotel two hours before, after making sure that Denisov was delivered by the FBI agents to the airport. About now, he would be on the dawn flight to Washington. It was all over for the Soviet agent; but, as Denisov had said, Devereaux was still outside.

He removed his pistol from his belt and opened the chambers. Six bullets seated in six cylinders.

Would he kill this last man?

That was the only question, he realized; he had to solve the puzzle, he had to understand the third element that had muddied the operation from the beginning. He felt like a scavenger, pulling back pieces and pieces of rotting garbage, seeking the treasure that might be buried beneath the filth.

A dirty business. So he had described it to Hanley. He realized only much later that he had used the term because Rita had thrown it at him in her anger and hatred in his hotel room.

Yes. A dirty business in the end. It always was.

And where would she find safety now? he wondered. She must have the journal, everyone thought she had the journal. What would she do with it?

Would they kill her before she found a safe place?

He thought of Rita smiling at him on the beach that morning. He thought of her, naked beneath his hands, making love to him. He thought of her words, by turns naïve and telling; he thought of the simple sound of her voice in his ear, next to him, wrapped in intimacy with him.

He pushed the pistol into his belt and opened the car door. The interior light winked on. He stood up and slammed the door; it echoed down the empty, dawn street. He buttoned his corduroy jacket over the bulge of the pistol and began to limp across the street. In his hotel room, before checking out, he had taken two pills for the pain and a tumbler of vodka. He had rebandaged the small wounds in the flesh of his belly and side and thrown away the bloodstained remnants of the old bandages. When he had left the room at 4 A.M.— the bed still made and unslept in, the shower stall damp, a single used towel hanging over the shower curtain rod—he realized again that he had occupied the room like a faintly palpable ghost, leaving the barest traces that he had been there at all.

Through the side entrance of the hotel and up the back stairwell to the second floor. Along the quiet hallways to the room.

Dawn was the time for unplanned contacts and hard interrogation. The body was too tired for effective resistance; the spirit was at a low ebb. It was one of a hundred lessons he had absorbed long ago at the special school hidden in the Maryland mountains, the school where he had learned the arts of war and the science of death and the tricks of spies.

The door was simple. He slipped hard plastic between jamb and frame and pushed. The door swung open without a sound.

Cardinal Ludovico, fully dressed, sat in a chair at the window.

For a moment, Devereaux did not move from the doorway.

Ludovico, dressed in a black suit with a clerical collar, turned and stared at him.

Neither man spoke. Devereaux realized that neither had slept last night. Their pale faces reflected each other; the lines around their eyes and the drawn lines around their mouths were too similar not to suggest similiar sleepless nights.

"Yes?" The Cardinal's voice was calm when it came, the gentle Roman accent rubbing the single word as one would rub a cat's body.

Devereaux stepped into the bare hotel room and let the door close behind him.

"Why do you come to me like this? Like a thief?"

"The element of surprise," Devereaux said. "I didn't know if it was necessary."

"As you see," Cardinal Ludovico said softly. He gestured to his garments. "I am waiting for morning. I do not sleep."

"We have a problem," Devereaux said.

"Who are you?"

"November," Devereaux said. "You had sent a cable of inquiry about me. After you met with the Soviet agent here."

"Are you certain?" Ludovico said it in the same, soft voice without concern. Yet Devereaux knew he was already guarded against his questions.

"We have Denisov. Our side."

Ludovico did not move.

"Our man in Rome was able to . . . see your cable. You see, we are not without resources."

"Yes." The voice was tired but the edge of caution remained. "I see perfectly." He made a gesture of dismissal with one elegant hand. "And you have arrested this Soviet citizen?"

"Agent," Devereaux said. "Of the KGB. He has defected, rather than be arrested. But you are aware of this."

For the first time, Ludovico raised his eyebrows. "I do not know what you are saying—"

"Signals were made yesterday," Devereaux continued. "You expressed your awareness to the Congregation that Denisov had defected to our side. And now your people in Rome have been contacted by Moscow. The situation is not satisfactory for you. Or for Moscow. Or for whatever arrangement you have made between you."

Ludovico sighed slowly, the elegant sigh of a tired prince weary of the world's burdens.

"Should I be annoyed at the interference in the affairs of the Church by your agency? Or should I be flattered?"

"I don't care."

"November," Ludovico said softly, caressing the word. He glanced out through the window blinds at the gathering light. "This place is so pleasant, so clean. I think of the whited sepulcher containing corruption inside." The streets were empty; silence flooded the streets with the morning light. "You see what I am: a Prince of the Church of Christ. And yet I am come to this place as a common gravedigger, to bury the dead as my act of mercy. Three dead."

"More than three," said Devereaux. "And there will be more still."

"It is a sad matter," Ludovico said.

"Too sad for polite talk," Devereaux replied.

"Poor Leo Tunney. To know so much worth killing for and to know so little in the end. I think he returned out of the jungle to a world more savage than any he had left there. He was too innocent to be permitted to live."

"What did he know?"

Ludovico went on, ignoring the question: "And in the moment of his death, his one work which would restore him to his faith is revealed to be a fraud. There was no miracle."

"There are no miracles."

Ludovico smiled. "Do you lack faith as well?"

"What did Tunney know?"

Ludovico shrugged. "Do you mean the secret? What he kept in his journal? I do not know, I do not even know if it was worth these deaths."

"Denisov was willing to kill for it."

"Ah. Your Soviet citizen. Your defector. Perhaps whatever was in the journal, perhaps this Denisov knew and sought to stop others from knowing."

"Is that what he told you?"

"You insist that we contacted—"

"Please. No lies, no poses. I know everything."

"Then you do not need to ask questions anymore?" The voice was irritating in its calm measure. "Yes. We met. He presumed that I might be useful to him. That I might serve him. Do you know, it is a curious similiarity between you and the Soviets. The Soviets play the servants who become the owners of the estate in the end. They scrape and bow and play the fool for the pleasure of the civilized world as they edge close to us with their poisoned plates, waiting for our moment of drunken weakness, our indiscretion that will be fatal to us."

Devereaux stood at the door and waited.

Cardinal Ludovico considered his hand in his lap as though it were a small work of art. "And you Americans. With your open arms and your promises of good fellowship and friendship based on equality. You overwhelm the world with your love for it and you do not understand why love cannot be a commodity, bought and sold. And besides, what a fragile base of friendship is love: It is not the strongest bond; it is the weakest, the more precious for its fragility."

Devereaux's voice was not altered. It was plain and flat and hard. "What did Tunney know? Why did you deal with the Soviets?"

"You are a relentless man, November. I cannot offer you honey in my words." Ludovico smiled.

"What did Denisov, the KGB, what did they have over you?"

"Me?" The laughter was musical. "I am beyond reproach, I can assure you. In the name of the church, I have faithfully done the work of the Pontiff."

"What work?"

"You must seek the answer elsewhere. From Denisov who has defected."

"There is no time left."

"Why?"

"Martin Foley informed you of everything. He told you about Rita Macklin, the reporter who found Tunney."

"Ah. The newswoman. In that hotel with the name of your country's most infamous moment, is it not true? Was she very involved in all this? Perhaps it would have been better—for her and for us, even for poor Leo Tunney—if your CIA had kept him a while longer."

"She has the journal."

Ludovico did not move for a moment. And then he turned slightly in his straight chair and stared at Devereaux. Very slowly, he said: "How do you know this?"

"Because it is the only possibility left."

"Where is she?"

"I don't know."

"She will be in danger, I think."

"Yes."

"And does that affect you, November?"

Devereaux stared at him patiently. His eyes were ice, his manner pitiless.

"Why was the Church making a deal on this with the Soviets?"

Ludovico made a tent of his fingers and glanced at them. "I cannot say."

"Yes. You can say."

Ludovico was silent.

Devereaux said, "The Church has made an agreement with the Soviet Union."

"Do you guess this?"

"It is the only possibility."

"You are a man of logic. You rely too much on it."

"We are not talking now of miracles."

"No." Ludovico paused and twisted the ring of his office on his finger. "In six weeks. Before Christmas, there will be an announcement. A certain reconciliation between great powers, one temporal, one spiritual. It will be a good thing—a positive thing, a gesture toward peace—for millions of people in the world."

"By whose judgment will it be a good thing?"

"The judgment of all concerned. This is a complex, very complex matter. There has been a shift in the world, in the axis of the earth. Even in an unreasonable age, a few men must act in a reasonable way. Do you understand me?"

"What is reasonable?"

"Martin Foley is dead. Martin is dead." The words fell like notes in a dirge. "Leo Tunney died and he did not even understand why. And Father McGillicuddy. There was so much death that did not need to happen." Ludovico stared at his white hands. "I do not think I can tell you more than I have."

Devereaux said, "You were in Prague. You were making a deal with the Soviet Union."

"Deal? It is such a common word."

"Deals are common things. You made an agreement to respect the status quo. To share power with the Soviets."

Ludovico smiled. "You have made a guess."

"But it's not far wrong. In the past eighteen months, there has been unrest in Poland and it is spreading. The Church has cautioned moderation, has worked with the existing Polish government to temper the demands of the Solidarity movement."

"So that the few gains it has made will not be crushed."

"Perhaps," said Devereaux.

"The Soviets have become practical. In Afghanistan, in Poland, they have begun to see, as you Americans have, that they have limits to their power. Ideology can wait for tomorrow. Perhaps they have come to see the need for a reasonable new alliance."

"And the Church was willing."

Ludovico looked up, annoyed for the first time. "And did your President Nixon make détente with the Soviets because it suited America? Did your President Carter reject his friends—the great friends of America in Taiwan—and embrace China as a check to the Soviets in the East? All men work in their self-interest. That is a reasonable assumption of the way of the world and you are a reasonable man. Our own interest may impel our actions."

"The Church has agreed to share power in the Eastern Bloc. To reinforce the Soviets."

"I cannot say this," Ludovico said. He paused and stared out the window. "We live in a cynical age. But all ages pass; all times are cynical in their turn. Must the Church of Christ reject the embrace of the Presidium more than it rejected the embrace of a King of another age? Constantine gave us the world to save and we accepted the world from his bloody hands and we took it and civilized it. We must accept the compromises of the world to survive in it. There are few absolutes in this life."

"What is the agreement, Cardinal?"

"To recognize the reality of things. To realize and define the spheres of our mutual influence."

"And what did all this have to do with a half-crazy old priest from Asia?"

"Asia is not our sphere. It never was."

"What was Tunney doing there in the first place then?" His voice was savage. "What did any of this have to do with Leo Tunney?"

"Perhaps I do not have the answer."

"No. Perhaps not," Devereaux said. "Perhaps you did the bidding of Denisov and the KGB because they assured you that the agreement with the Church in Prague would be endangered by this priest. By his secret."

"Yes. You understand. It is their secret that they wanted to protect, not ours."

"And you sent Foley here to get it out of Tunney, to use it as a lever against the Soviets."

"I cannot say."

"And Denisov killed Martin Foley."

Ludovico's face registered shock and then a calm veneer replaced it. "Do you know this is true?"

"Denisov killed Foley. It must be the reason for it."

"Damn him."

The face was still calm, the voice was still soft, but the words carried a passion that seemed to shake the old man to his heart. "Do you suppose this pleases me?" Ludovico said. "Have you asked me my politics? I have lived a long time and I have seen the world torn and torn again. By fascism, by communism, by your greedy capitalism. What is more dangerous? The Black Shirts strutting through Italy or the vices of luxury in America? A man will lose his soul to both. But I am as you are. I am a servant to my cause and we must both obey our masters."

Who had said the same thing? Denisov? But was it always true?

Devereaux had disobeyed his masters and was now stranded alone in a game rapidly closing around him.

Devereaux's voice was still hard, still without pity: "My master did not ask me to kill three men or try to kill a woman. My master did not ask me to embrace the Soviets."

"Not yet. Not this time and not in this place."

"I don't want to talk corrupt philosophy with you. I want to know the details of the agreement you've made with the Soviets."

"Why? Will it help you to find this woman you will look for? Or to find the journal?"

"The agreement," he said.

"I must not tell you."

"Yes. You must tell me."

Silence.

Tricks and deceits came to this in the end; the edge of naked fear and blinding pain must be shown. No one will bend or compromise or go back on his words until brute force and pain permit betrayal of any cause.

Devereaux removed the pistol from his belt. It was a casual act.

"A threat? You would kill me?"

Devereaux did not speak. He cocked the hammer. The black gun waited to give death.

"Why?"

"Because it is necessary. You have made it necessary."

"But there is no need." For the first time, there was just a trace of panic at the edge of the calm voice. But Devereaux was not bluffing; if the threat is made, they had taught as the first rule at that school in Maryland, be prepared to carry it out.

"If you kill me, it profits nothing."

"The matter is simple, Cardinal. I want information from you. If you give it to me, you live because you are no longer a threat to me. Or to my side. If you don't give it to me, you die because it is the only threat I can make to you and I must be prepared to carry it out."

Cardinal Ludovico sighed.

The sigh was a wind breathing its last before moving on with the passing storm. In the moment of dead calm, they both heard the loud ticking of the small clock on the nightstand next to the untouched bed.

"You would do this, I believe," Ludovico said. "And if you have penetrated my belief, then I must think it is so, that you would kill me for your reasons. Do I value my life too highly then? I have lived a long time." He paused. "Let God judge me."

Devereaux waited.

"I place too high a price upon my survival then," Ludovico continued. When he resumed speaking, his voice was detached, coming from a great distance.

"It is to be called the Prague Corcordance. The matter is quite simple. The Soviet Union and the nations of the Warsaw Pact—the Eastern Bloc, as you say—will agree in writing and in constitution to recognize the freedom of the Church in their countries. Freedom of the churches to be open, freedom to worship, freedom again to open our schools and to educate our young and to ordain priests."

Devereaux stood perfectly still.

"And what will the Church do? We will recognize mere reality, what already is. We will recognize the political supremacy of the Communist Party as the ruling organ of the state. We will not take a side against it and we will not give comfort to the enemies of the state. And we will recognize that the Soviet Union has a legitimate sphere of influence in the world, especially in Southeast Asia."

Devereaux made a sound then. Ludovico did not seem to notice it.

"The Soviet Union has a legitimate interest in Asia. And the Church, well, we have very little there. Do you see? We get much and give little. We only accept the reality of the political situation."

"And the other religions? The Jews? The Orthodox Church?"

"This is only a first step. One step at a time. A dialogue will be opened."

"It's called covering your ass and to hell with the rest." Any trace of civility was stripped from Devereaux's last sentence. The tone startled Ludovico. But only for a moment.

"Christian charity is founded upon reality too. The Church is to survive and that is important. What will communism be in a hundred years and what will the ideologies so important now matter then?

"Merely another system, another 'ism' that has been modified and changed, replaced, altered. Just as capitalism is now in its death throes, as it fades in the final light of its era. As socialism has become weakened by democracy, diluted, acceptable to neither the left nor the right because it is nothing. All things fade; all passes as the age of kings has passed and the age of the emperors. All must change and die, in the seasons of the world. The Church only remains and its mission: to save souls."

"No matter what price."

"To pay the price of survival. We render unto Caesar, as we have always done."

Devereaux replaced the pistol. "Yes. The last refuge of the righteous for doing the expeditious thing. Find the appropriate place in the Bible to justify it."

Silence again, as purposeful as a shouting argument.

"And now that you know all this, November, does it solve the puzzle of the journal for you any more than it did for me?"

"No," Devereaux said, staring at the Cardinal. "Nothing is made clear without the journal. Not even this."

33
New York City

Vanderglass held the computer printout in his right hand and stood at something like attention before the big rosewood desk in the corner office on the forty-first floor. Outside, gloomy morning greeted the millions pushing to work in Manhattan. Gray, leaden clouds swirled wetly around the ornate towers of the Empire State and Chrysler buildings; hard winds smacked down the cross streets and hats sailed into the air, stolen by the sudden gusts; umbrellas were whipped open and abandoned by their owners. Winter was coming; street life was buttoning up; delis that had open sidewalk windows a week ago were now shuttered tight against the winds.

"You've found her," Henry L. Fraser said, his voice small and clear in the vast quiet of the office.

"Approximately," said Vanderglass. "She went to ground in Green Bay, Wisconsin."

Fraser made a tent of his fingers, stared at it, broke it. "Does she live there?"

"Worked there once, that was three years ago. Reporter for the *Press-Gazette*. We're afraid she might make contact with the paper."

"I see. You're certain she's there?"

"Yes, sir. We tapped into the computer at the credit-card reporting center in Roanoke, Virginia. She made a charge Sunday, one hundred fifty-six dollars one way American Airlines from Tampa to Chicago O'Hare. Last commuter flight to Green Bay was gone so she rented a car at the Avis counter in the airport; we double-checked the form, she wanted to drop the car in Green Bay and listed that as her destination. That gives us reasonable certainty to that point."

"Go on."

"We got this report from Roanoke, overnight. She must be low on money because she's charging right and left. At the Ramada Inn on the west side of the city near Lambeau Field, she charged twelve sixty-seven for breakfast, including tip."

"She was staying at the Ramada?"

"Negative, sir. We checked that right away. But they have no open billing or registration for her."

"And the other—"

"Yes, sir. Every motel and hotel in Green Bay and for a distance of forty miles around. Little more difficult checking in Door County, that's the peninsula northeast of the city. Some of the motels don't have credit card facilities. We have five men on the peninsula and two at the two main roads leading down from it. She couldn't get by us on a bet."

"She's done well enough so far," said Henry Fraser.

"Sir." Vanderglass took the implied reprimand without a change in his dark expression. "On the peninsula—it's called Door County, as I said—the season is past and most of the hotels are closed. The check won't take much longer. Sir, I want to say: The high level of cooperation with key Agency people has helped us."

"It's a national security matter," Fraser said, as though rehearsing a defense. "If it hadn't been for the cooperation of the National Security Adviser and the Agency, I don't think we would have known about the journal until it was too late."

"Very low key" is the way the Adviser had termed the cooperation of the CIA through the office of the Assistant Director. From the beginning, the Agency had given the private corporation access to its information and to certain "need to know" documents that were turned over to Vanderglass at InterComBank security. The bank and the intelligence agency had a long, easy history of cooperation throughout the world—as Fraser had pointed out to the Adviser. And so InterComBank, through Rice's reports back to Agency headquarters in Langley, had learned of the existence of a journal and of the Vatican's keen interest in it. The information had pushed a panic button inside bank security and Vanderglass had decided to get rid of Leo Tunney by "overt" action. First, his men had tried to kill him in a confessional—and killed the wrong man. Finally, they had arranged the so-called "amp bombs" in the church on Sunday to create a panic.

Fraser rose from his desk and went to the shuttered window and pulled open the drapes. He stared down at the ants moving among the side streets of the city, then he turned away.

271

"And Kaiser. What did Kaiser say?"

"Sir?"

"Well? Did you make it clear to him we were prepared to act on the matter of his son?"

"Sir." Vanderglass retreated into cop jargon. "Sir, we used maximum suasion on him and I took charge of the operation myself and I made assurances to him about the safety of the woman and—"

"And?" Fraser felt a strange, sick premonition.

Vanderglass looked down uncomfortably at his polished wing-tip shoes. "Sir, I'm sorry to have to report this but I believe we have minimalized any damage to us. But he killed himself, sir."

Fraser's voice was calm. "When?"

"Shortly after eight o'clock, sir. Last night. In his office. It was a point forty-five caliber automatic, Army issue, apparently some sort of a war souvenir."

"And what about us? Was there . . . any trace . . . providing a link with us?"

"No, sir. We swept the office right away. We cleared it. Had a man in the building, sir, we were waiting for him to leave for the day because we were going to do a bag job on the place, to get the files on Miss Macklin."

"And did you get them?"

"Negative, sir. He must have dumped them during the day, after I visited him. Nothing at all on Rita Macklin—employment record, W-two filing forms, possible whereabouts. The Agency had arranged a tap for us under the National Security charter but there was nothing, no telephonic contact at all."

Fraser winced at the continued jargon. He realized that Vanderglass was nervous.

"One of our people swept her apartment, we found letters to a woman in Eau Claire, Wisconsin, that's on the other side of the state from Green Bay. Examination and analysis conclude the letters were correspondence with Miss Macklin's mother, this is Mrs. Thomas Macklin, a widow. Also on that, sir, this Thomas Macklin, deceased, was a member of the State Department from 1945 through 1951, part of the China crowd. Very interesting stuff on—"

"I don't care a damn about Thomas Macklin," Fraser said.

"Yes, sir. We put a tap on Mrs. Macklin's phone last night but again, still no evidence of telephonic contact with the daughter, sir.

We scanned appropriate records at the telephone company in Eau Claire as well, through the Agency connection—"

"Yes, yes."

"Sir. We have three men right now in downtown Green Bay around the offices of the newspaper. The *Press-Gazette*. She worked there before her Washington job and I'm going on the theory that she might try to leak the journal to this—"

"My God, Vanderglass. This is a mess, this is a total mess—"

"Sir, I think we have contained the problem, it's now a matter of waiting."

"Yes. Everything has been done, everything is buttoned up, every exit is blocked but somehow this woman is still out there and she's got that goddam journal. Do you understand? She's a loose cargo in the hold and we're in a storm."

"Sir."

"Rita Macklin is out of control," Fraser said. "Out of control."

"Sir, perhaps she doesn't have the journal—"

"Goddam it, Vanderglass. That's just wishful thinking. Why has she gone underground if she doesn't have the journal?"

"Sir. You're right, sir."

"At least Florida is cleaned up. Is it?"

"Sir, we got our men out. Except for Petersen. They found him this morning in the ship channel near Sand Key. He had been garroted."

"God."

"Sir, it has to be this man. The one they never located. Devereaux. From R Section. When the Adviser called off the operation, he was unreachable."

"Code name November."

"Yes, sir."

"Damn it. Vanderglass, I want you in Green Bay now. I want the operation personally overseen by you. And I think you should fashion a signal to the A.D. at the Agency. This is a purely legal matter now. There's been a murder in Florida, one of our men, and both this Devereaux and this woman, this Macklin woman, are involved in it and they've fled the state to avoid inquiries. Let's get this right through official channels, from the Agency to the state authorities in Wisconsin—"

Vanderglass permitted a smile to lighten the cobra features of his face. "Yes, sir. Good. I think this will be very, very good. And we can step in at the point of arrest of the Macklin suspect and retrieve the documentation—"

"The journal," Fraser said. "We have to be certain, we have to have the journal. Without it, TransAsia—well, a lot of matters—can be threatened."

"Yes, sir."

"I want her taken care of. Is that clear?" Fraser's voice had dropped its burden of politeness. "I wanted this goddam woman taken care of and this . . . this agent, Devereaux. Both of them. Taken care of once and for all. Do you understand me?"

"Yes, sir."

"Today. Now. Tonight. I want no more guesses. I want you to be absolutely certain."

"Sir." Vanderglass stood very straight. "We've got everything now. Full authorization. The resources of the bank. Resources of the government. We'll go right down to the local police level on this."

When Vanderglass left the office, Fraser sat behind his large, empty desk and stared for a moment at the Picasso on the far wall. It was a line drawing in a simple chrome frame, a portrait of a woman surrounded by her children.

The portrait jogged his memory.

He pushed a button on the intercom. In a moment, his secretary was at the door.

"I want to see Wilson. Mr. Vanderglass has just reported to me on the theft of some moneys and securities from our commercial loans division. It involves one of our younger men. I want him to take care of it with the proper law enforcement agents."

"Yes, sir," the secretary said. He closed the door behind him.

Fraser leaned back in his chair. Kaiser no longer existed, he thought. Therefore, the reason for blackmail no longer existed; and the need to overlook the crime of Kaiser's son no longer existed either.

The account would be settled by young Kaiser.

And the other accounts as well. All of them.

34
Washington, D.C.

"Perhaps I should have been informed earlier."

Hanley waited for the rebuke to subside in the silence. Neither man spoke for a moment.

Beyond the windows of the cold office tucked into the recesses of the Department of Agriculture building, the lights of Pennsylvania Avenue marched in empty, orange parade to the Capitol.

Nearly ten o'clock and the snug little city was already buttoned up for the night.

For the fifth time in the past hour, the Old Man lit his pipe. It was one of his props, along with the half-glasses he used to read memos and the old-fashioned pocket watch on the gold chain that he wore in his vest. Rear Admiral P. G. Galloway (USN Retired) had long ago learned the importance of appearances in the corridors of Washington power. It was part of the key to his success there and his survival as head of R Section.

It had been another bad day for Hanley who was not accustomed to being the man in the middle. He had been shielding Devereaux from the moment Devereaux had revealed the existence of a Soviet agent in Florida. He had lied to both Galloway and the National Security Adviser.

The Adviser had talked to Hanley two hours before. The Adviser had been informed by the CIA that one of the agents of R Section had remained in Florida after being ordered to withdraw from the Tunney matter. The Adviser had been further informed that the R Section agent—code named November—was now wanted in connection with a murder inquiry in Florida.

"You know our charter," the Adviser had huffed on the phone. "We are not permitted to operate in the United States."

Yes, Hanley agreed. And he lied again. He did not know where Devereaux was, except that he had been withdrawn from Florida. When the Adviser pressed him, Hanley said that Devereaux had been given a leave of absence.

So many lies to keep straight, Hanley had thought; for the first time in his life, he felt a certain oneness with a field agent. He knew what it was to be alone, to have to hold back information for his own survival. He still had not told the Adviser about Denisov; or about the false cables filed; or about the last, indelicate probe of Cardinal Ludovico by Devereaux.

Devereaux.

The agent had become a gambler in the past few hours as he moved around the country, always within a telephone's distance of Hanley. He was bent on using all the frail, remaining resources of the Section in this last, desperate scheme. It might all come down around Hanley's ears tonight—the Section, his government career. Both agent and control officer knew that disaster was waiting for them if they did not succeed.

Now, finally, as the clocks in Washington pushed toward midnight, he began to tell Galloway the truth.

It was too late for Galloway to countermand anything Hanley had done.

Galloway listened quietly, puffing on his pipe, seeming to make no judgment. In fact, in the past few months, Galloway himself had become more and more distant from the Section. He had privately acknowledged more than once that the Section was finished and would be written out of next year's budget, absorbed by the CIA. Galloway was a team player and he had gone along with the Administration in this matter; after all, there was a strong hint that the Agency might be looking for a new Deputy Director for Plans and Operations in the next fiscal year.

When Hanley finished, the Old Man sat silently, puffing at his pipe and filling the cold room with sweet-smelling smoke.

"Well," Galloway began at last. "I suppose the A.D. over at the Agency must be as happy as a pig in slops. This is like the old days for him. Getting involved in a real 'strike' operation with full authorization and an open contract. Have they got the girl yet?"

"I don't know. I don't think so."

"Now, goddammit, Hanley. Stop lying to me. I wonder what the hell this is all about anyway? This journal business, sounds like someone's been reading too many thrillers under the covers." He lit the pipe again and threw the match on the desk top. Hanley made a face and removed it. "You shouldn't have let Devereaux stay down in Florida—"

"Sir—"

"Dammit, Hanley, why didn't you put me in the picture in the first place? Didn't trust me?"

The embarrassed silence admitted it.

"You know, I've been worried about Devereaux for a long time. Even before that British business—involved the same fellow, this Denisov, didn't it?"

"Devereaux is our best man," Hanley said.

"Well, where is he now?"

Conscience rattled Hanley but he didn't speak. "I don't know. Not at this moment." It was close to the truth.

"The Adviser is going to chew you a new asshole on this." Galloway rarely indulged in salty talk; his naval career had been largely spent in the Pentagon, cultivating politenesses. But he felt the need to humiliate Hanley and he knew Hanley had a priggish distaste for scatological language.

"I don't think the Adviser has been forthcoming," Hanley said with mild stubbornness.

"Damn your eyes, Hanley. He explained it well enough to me. This all has to do with InterComBank, they worked as a laundry for our side in the fifties and the bank just didn't want something to come up to upset the old applecart on this TransAsia matter. And I can tell you, the Administration is behind TransAsia one hundred and ten percent."

"Why were people from InterComBank in Florida? Why did they attack Devereaux?"

"That's what Devereaux says," Galloway said.

Hanley was shocked. "Admiral. Devereaux is our man. Our man doesn't lie to us."

"You lied to me. You lied to the Adviser."

Hanley did not speak.

"Goddammit, Hanley, this is a matter of national security as well as the survival of the Section."

"The Section won't survive, sir," Hanley said.

"Who told you that?"

"You know that as well as I do. In the last few days it has become clear to me." His voice was sad and calm.

"All right, let's talk reality, you want to talk reality. R section is finished as of now. Next year, you had a choice of retiring or coming over to the Agency. You're not so old, Hanley, you've got years left in the Agency. And a promotion in grade at Langley, if you played your cards right."

"I had decided about that," Hanley said quietly.

"You had? Is that right? You decided, did you?"

"Yes, sir. I'll take retirement when the Section closes down."

"Hanley."

"It was all that was important," Hanley said. "The Section. It was what counted with me."

The Old Man smiled. Not for the first time, Galloway was amused by this dull little man with his open, flat eyes. A clerk. A goddam bureaucrat who probably curled up and read spy novels at night. Goddam little clerk. Everyone had a joke about Hanley. He kept his office so damned cold to save energy it could freeze a polar bear. He took lunch at the same old place, day after day, year after year, a goddamn little greasy spoon down Fourteenth Street. The secretaries in the Section even joked about it—about Hanley's lunch which was always the same with a single straight-up martini and a well-done cheeseburger. Dull, predictable Hanley, pretending to play spy games.

Everyone knew Hanley.

The Old Man relit the pipe and puffed smoke into the room.

"Devereaux. You know where he is now. I know you do."

Hanley said nothing.

"You let him go after her, didn't you?"

"Yes," Hanley said.

"Dammit to hell, Hanley, dammit to hell."

"But I don't know where he is."

"All right, I'm going to tell you what's going to happen. They're going to get her, Hanley, they got every cop in the world right now up there in that trap in Green Bay. This is a criminal matter and if Devereaux wants to walk into it, he's going to have to dangle out there in the wind alone."

"A criminal matter," Hanley agreed with an ambiguous tone.

Annoyance scratched at the Old Man again. "Devereaux went beyond all authorization this time and I don't want your ass out there with him. It can't be handled quietly now, I would have handled it quietly."

"The big bang. At the end of the world. Or the Section."

"Why on earth did you let us get involved? This man is a killer, Hanley. He's out of control."

"It doesn't matter, does it? The Section is finished."

"Where is he now, Hanley?"

Each waited for the other to speak; the silence of the huge old building was deep and profound; Washington dozed in the darkness.

"I don't know," Hanley said at last.

"All right. Is that the absolute truth?"

Hanley looked at him directly.

"Yes," he said.

They both knew it was a lie.

35
Green Bay, Wisconsin

The red journal was stuffed under a sweater at the bottom of the green-and-gold canvas tote bag that said "Back the Pack" on it.

Rita Macklin was almost there.

She swung the bag on her shoulder and started across Walnut Street against the lights. Traffic was light downtown; it was mid-week suppertime in the old city. Across the way, City Hall squatted on the corner; the wide lawn was brown and the flowers that had decorated the building all summer were long dead, cut and gone.

Rita had been in Green Bay for thirty hours.

For most of that time, she had waited in the little east side apartment on Smith Street that belonged to Ruth.

Ruth and Rita had gone to school together a long time ago and then, after a few years, found each other again in Green Bay. She had gone to Ruth because she trusted her and because Ruth had no link to her present life.

Ruth had been generous without asking questions. Her apartment was on the second floor of a white frame private house; the separate entrance was at the back of the building, at the top of a stairway in an enclosed hall.

Rita had parked her car on the street but Ruth reminded her of the city's overnight parking ban and Rita moved it then into the driveway. She didn't want a parking ticket now, to attract the attention of the city police; Rita had a queer sense that she was moving beyond the law.

After tea and talk of other things, Rita had slept her first deep and drugless sleep in three days. She had dreamed of Kaiser and Devereaux.

Ruth did not want to know the truth; Rita did not tell her.

"I've had some difficulties. I'll tell you about it later," Rita had said. Ruth smiled. Rita had always been a wild one. They talked of college days and double dates long ago. Ruth was settled in the city as a schoolteacher and she seemed very set to Rita now, a part of life already fading into memory.

Ruth had a date tonight. It would be a good time for Rita to slip away. Perhaps when she returned, everything would be all right and Rita would be able to extricate herself from Ruth's life without ruining anything for her. She had had the thought all the way from Florida, on the plane, in the car on the long drive along the lake to Green Bay, that something could go wrong at any moment.

During the day, when Ruth was at work, Rita had sat alone in the little apartment, at the kitchen table, drinking endless cups of tea, reading the red journal.

"I'm supposed to give you this," Mrs. Jones, the housekeeper, had said after marching into Rita's room at the motel. It was just two hours after Rita had managed to stagger there, half-drugged. "This is from the old priest," Mrs. Jones said. "He gave me your name and address." She held up a small card; Rita saw that it was one of her own, the card she had left in the sacristy when she had encountered Tunney there on her third day in Clearwater. Father Tunney had surrendered to her at last: He had given up the journal and its secrets.

Get it out; tell it all. The words merged in her mind: Sometimes it was Tunney. Sometimes it was Kaiser.

Rita became very frightened as she read, from the first sad, profound pages through to the hurried handwriting in the last thirty pages, covered with line after line of quick, crabbed scratchings, the words cold and precise. Words that gave exact locations and meanings; the eyes of a watcher, she thought. The eyes of a spy:

"I had intended to speak of none of this. What is it to me or to my soul? Or to the memory of my beloved, Phuong, whom I will not repent loving?"

So it began.

From time to time, the handwriting would stop, something would be scratched out, and when it resumed, it would be with a new clarity, as though the words had pursued difficult thoughts through a maze and, finding no way out at the first turning, were trying another path.

"They are evil who wish this journal only to examine it as they have examined me; to see what secrets I can tell them that they already know. They wish to suppress this and its secrets; to suppress me; or to use this for leverage against those who are still not finished in their attempt to inflict suffering on my people." The words stopped; when they resumed, the handwriting was different. "My people are in Asia. . . ."

She knew, after a day of reading, how much the secrets were worth. They were worth murders to them; even more.

She had called her old friend at the *Press-Gazette* and they were expecting her.

She swung down Walnut Street and paused for a moment. Two hundred feet away was the old cream-colored brick building that housed the *Green Bay Press-Gazette*. But something was not right. There in the entranceway, between the double set of glass doors, across the faded lawn, were two men. Standing like soldiers. Watching her.

"That's her."

The two men pushed through the glass doors. Rita turned. Two more men were behind her, standing in the shadow of City Hall. They started for her. They were running.

No. Not now. Not when she was this close.

She turned and saw them and saw the police car at the end of the street. She couldn't speak or scream; she dashed suddenly into the traffic. A bus shot out in front of her and the driver slammed its brakes and twisted the wheel; the bus skidded on the pavement and smashed into a parked car, careened into a second, and struck one of the men running from City Hall. He flew into the side of the building and his body broke through an office window with a tinkling crash.

Cries and shouts rose on every side of her in the early evening darkness.

She ran past a row of little shops. At the corner, a tavern's lights beckoned. She ran inside.

Men wearing parkas or flannel shirts stood in groups along the bar; the television set in the corner was blaring and the jukebox was pounding out a country song. The bar smelled of peanuts and stale beer, all layered with smoke from a dozen cigarettes.

She pushed through the crowd at the bar, along the gauntlet to the back of the narrow room.

"Hey, there, looky what come in—"

At the back were three doors marked "Kings," "Queens," and "Private." She pushed through "Private" and found she was in what resembled a living room. A woman sat in an easy chair watching television. She didn't look up.

"You got the wrong door, honey—"

Past her, into a kitchen, past the kitchen through the back door. Garbage cans on a concrete step. Down into the alley, along a row of fences separating yards. Across a lawn and another; she could hear shouts in the distance behind her. She turned into a gangway between two buildings; the way led to a service alley.

Dead end.

The shouts were closer. A police car, flashing lights with menace, snarled into the alley.

No way out except over a locked gate. A nail protruding from the gate ripped her jeans, scratched her leg. She slid down into a second gangway. Through to the next street, residential now, across a yard and into a driveway. Through the wooden gate into a small backyard.

She didn't see the dog until it came galloping toward her.

The shepherd was big. She raised the tote bag and it stopped for a moment, confronting her. She held the bag in front of her as she edged slowly along the fence. The dog barked ferociously.

Rita continued to back her way down the fence.

The dog followed her on stiff legs, its angry black muzzle flecked with foam. She saw the red in its eyes, the teeth yellow and long.

"Go. Go. Go on, go away," she commanded sharply but the dog snapped at her, made a lunge. She swung the bag against its head. The dog backed off a step and watched her. She couldn't turn her back on it; slowly, losing precious seconds, she backed away.

She felt behind her for the catch on the gate.

The dog kept barking and other dogs in other yards took up the sound.

"Schatzi, Schatzi," a German-accented voice called from the rear porch of the frame house. "Who is dot? Vot is it, Schatzi?"

At the sound of the voice, the dog turned and pricked up its ears.

Rita felt the catch at the back gate and shoved it open with a creak. The dog turned back. She slipped through and slammed it shut as the shepherd hurled itself at the wooden gate, gnashing its teeth, barking betrayal.

No alley this time, only a second yard leading to a new street.

Forms appeared at the side gate behind her. The dog ran to greet them barking.

Rita heard a shot; the barking stopped.

She felt the breath tearing from her lungs, felt the weight of the tote bag. They couldn't get it now. After all that—

She ran along the darkened side street flanked by stately white frame houses and wide gravel driveways. The sky was black, without moon or stars; there was a smell of snow in the air.

Two more backyards, into a grassy alley full of garages and garbage cans. Rita was circling back now, around the residential area clinging to the old downtown section. She had parked three blocks from the newspaper building.

At the corner, under a streetlamp, she paused for a moment. In the distance, she heard sirens but they did not seem to be coming any closer.

Dogs barked far away.

The tiny streetlamps strung like pearls on the dark avenue made little stabs into the night. She hurried along. Porch lights were turned on; lamp lights in the windows; canned laughter roared from television sets.

Her car was at the end of the block under a streetlamp. As she ran along the sidewalk, she fumbled in her pocket for the key.

"Miss Macklin."

The voice was dead calm. Rita felt utter terror.

She turned and felt the arm on her shoulder, the fingers clamp into an unbreakable grip. It was he, the man who had chased her on the beach.

She hit him as hard as she could with her doubled fist. He seemed startled by the blow. Blood began to flow from a nostril. He wiped at his face with his free hand and saw the blood; annoyance crept over his dark features.

"We should have killed you in the first place," he said and shoved the gun into her side. "You can give me the book now."

She pushed against him and he slammed the gun very hard into her side. It knocked her breath away; for a moment she thought she would be sick.

Neither of them saw the second man.

Her assailant went down quietly on both knees as though he suddenly thought to pray. He stared at Rita with surprised eyes, his face gone white, his arms down at his sides. Then he keeled forward. Devereaux drew up, glanced down at the man he had just killed. Karras. The man from InterComBank.

Devereaux. . . . He shoved her ahead of him, back into the darkness where he had come from.

They moved softly down the alley. Sirens blared from the street they had just left.

His hand was as hard and cold as ice.

He pushed Rita into a white car on the next street.

"What the hell are you—"

"Just for once," he said quietly, "listen. Get down on the floor of the car and pull that blanket over you. Stay on the floor. This is a net you swam into. And you're the fish."

"That man back there was the man from the beach. One of the men who chased me—"

"And the other is dead," Devereaux said. He started the car and pulled slowly into the middle of the side street. For a moment, she heard nothing and then there were sirens again in the distance. She hugged the bag close to her under the blanket and closed her eyes.

"Shit," Devereaux said.

She didn't understand.

Red and blue Mars lights painted the interior of the car. Devereaux slowed, stopped.

"Yeah, okay," the cop's dull voice said. "You ain't got no girls in that trunk, do ya?"

"Not tonight," he said.

The cop laughed.

Devereaux accelerated, then drove slowly, made a turn, and then another.

"Do you know how to get out of here?" she asked from beneath the blanket.

"It was easier to get in."

"My car is back there," Rita said. "It doesn't belong to me."

"Yes. Rental car. Chevette. Illinois plates AV four five nine eight."

"Oh," was all she said.

Silence for more moments. "It's hot under here," she said. "When can I get up?"

"When we get out of the trap." His voice was calm, nearly flat; she had dreamed of that voice.

"What if we don't?"

Silence.

"We should go to the police—"

"The police want you. The Agency wants you. And InterComBank."

"What's that? I don't— We should surrender—"

"Never give up, Rita," Devereaux said. "Even when it seems the best thing."

"How did you find me?"

"How could anyone miss you? You left a trail as wide as an interstate. Never go into espionage."

"What did I do?"

"Everything wrong."

"I mean, why are these people after me?"

"You took Tunney's journal, from Mrs. Jones. And now you know what he knew."

"Yes."

"What was in the book?"

"Go to hell."

Devereaux smiled. "That's right, Rita. Don't give up. Even when it seems like the best thing."

"How did you know that man was killed? The other man?"

"Because I killed him."

Again silence, but now it was horrible; she felt chilled just hearing his voice, though the heater blasted directly on her from beneath the dash. The car was large and powerful; she listened to the tires humming along the highway. He was picking up speed but when she peeked from beneath the blanket, she saw streetlamps. Too close to the city still; to the trap.

"You can sit up now—"

She climbed into the seat beside him. The highway traffic was light. Big semitrailer trucks whooshed by, heading north, rocking the car on blasts of wind.

He said slowly, "Kaiser is dead."

She stared into the darkness. Lights loomed, fell away; the big car was moving very fast now. The green lights of the instrument panel filled the interior with a strange glow. She looked at his face; it was pale, motionless, eyes fixed on the roadway.

"What happened?"

"He killed himself."

She swallowed it in. She tried to consider it, chew on it in her mind, but the thought was larger than what her imagination could accept. She spoke instead: "When?"

"Monday night," he said in the same flat voice. "They leaned on him; his son was arrested this afternoon. The son worked for InterComBank. He's up for grand theft. The bank blackmailed Kaiser and that was why he warned you off the story. To protect you.

He couldn't tell you the truth, and he didn't want you to get involved with them. I tell you this because you said you couldn't trust Kaiser anymore; I didn't want all your thoughts of him to be bad ones." The edge of sarcasm cut her and she felt the wound.

She could not think of Kaiser as dead. The big man with the fat body and ink-stained fingers, enveloped in the perpetual wreath of cigarette smoke. She could not think of it. Her green eyes stared into the headlights coming up the two-lane highway that wound below Green Bay. The lights gave a pale quality to her face and framed her soft red hair; then the lights fell away and there was only darkness again, silence, the thought of Kaiser dead.

"Why did he kill himself?"

"Stupidity," Devereaux said. The gray eyes did not turn to her. "It was too much for him; or he wanted to give you a chance; or both. To keep them off you. He knew he was their link to you, and he tried to break it. Originally, he destroyed your employment file to keep them away from you. That gave you two extra days. And then it was too much for him, all of it. He told them where he rightly suspected you were, where he himself had told you to go. He thought they were on to you, after you in any case; that they would find you. And he thought that he had killed you."

"How do you know all this? How can you?"

"He explained it all in a letter. He must have mailed it to you in the morning, and then killed himself last night. The letter was delivered to your apartment this morning. It lays out quite a lot that didn't make sense before. Kaiser was a good enough reporter."

"You took my mail."

"It's the least I've done."

"You've got the letter."

"Yes. It's one of the documents I need. You have the other."

"I don't have the journal."

"That's a lie, Rita. The time for lies is over. You were going to the newspaper office. They presumed you had the journal so they were willing to jump you then."

"I've been here for nearly a day and a half."

"Yes. You were staying on Smith Street, but they still had a little time when they found it out. They didn't want to involve your girl friend, nor the people who lived downstairs, if they could help it.

By the time you called the paper, they were tapped into your line. They were ready for you, Rita. They knew you had the book."

Rita stared at him.

It began to snow. The large flakes drove blindly against the windows, lashing them like small white meteors blowing through space.

Devereaux turned on the wipers; through the streaky windshield more lights came up, distorted by the patches of wet and dry glass.

"You're the government," Rita said. "I don't understand this. Why are they after *you?* Why aren't you working with them?"

"Perhaps I am."

"Then why did you hit that man?"

"Because, Rita, it's gone awry this time, all of it."

"I don't understand you—"

"What was in the journal?" Devereaux said.

"Fuck you."

"Yes, Rita. That was well enough when it was still a game. Now the game is over; it's time to quit."

"You bastard. I don't trust you."

"The choices are limited; in fact, they don't exist anymore. You trust me and I trust you, that's the way it has to be now." His voice was hard. "They're sealing off the state above Milwaukee and they know there's just a limited number of ways out of this area. You couldn't have gone to ground in Chicago or Cleveland, could you? You had to pick a dead end."

"I didn't know what to do," Rita said with something like a defensive tone in her voice. "I couldn't go back to Washington, I didn't have an outlet there. I didn't trust Kaiser anymore."

As soon as she said the words, they tore at her. She thought of Kaiser and felt afraid. She hugged the bag to her chest.

"Tell me again. I still don't believe it. Why did Kaiser . . . kill himself? What was all this about his son?"

Devereaux kept his eyes on the road, his hands tightly gripping the steering wheel. He did not speak at first but then his voice was calm. "He had a son who worked for InterComBank in New York. He has a wife and two daughters. He had a lot going for him but he wanted a little more. So he became a thief. When the bank discovered the embezzlements, they decided not to prosecute. Not at first. They decided to use the matter to blackmail Kaiser. Nothing spectacular, but when you're running a big multinational corporation, every little bit helps. They only used Kaiser twice. Nothing important. The first time was when he suppressed a report from one of his steady stringers in Asia. That was four months ago. The stringer had an accurate little report about Soviet advisers going into Vietnamese-held Cambodia. Nothing earthshaking but apparently it was important to the bank. The stringer's name, by the way, was Dang Lau Ky. He was a missionary's son who worked out of Bangkok. He had good sources."

"I know who you mean. He did work for us, I used to edit his copy. He was terrible at English. He also did work for one of the networks."

"Yes. Dang Lau Ky." The voice was hard again. "He was killed, you know. Three months ago, right after he sent that report to Kaiser. The one that Kaiser suppressed. Maybe it wasn't enough for Kaiser to keep the report buried; maybe they had to make certain that his stringer didn't tell any more stories. Or maybe there was no connection between the two events."

"Who would have done something like that to Kaiser?"

"Not a monster. It was strictly business. The chairman of the bank is Henry L. Fraser, you must have heard of him. Friend of the wealthy but with a social conscience. He organized the big relief drive last year for the Cambodian refugees and the Vietnamese boat people. He's a big man with a big heart." Each word was flat, without inflection, but in sum all the words were laced with bitterness. "He has friends in high places, Henry L. Fraser. He went to college with the man who is National Security Adviser. I bet you didn't know that."

"Oh, Kaiser," she said suddenly, letting grief leap out of her. "Kaiser." She began to cry and then stopped abruptly. She pushed the tears out of her eyes with the back of her hand. "Kaiser," she said, her voice turning dull. "I didn't trust him. I thought he had betrayed me."

Devereaux said, "He did betray you. Everyone is guilty in the end; we all betray each other. Sometimes, we don't live to regret the betrayals."

"You betrayed me," she said. "I told you things . . . my secrets. And you were . . . one of them."

"You're getting too old to see the world in such black-and-white terms, Rita." His voice was now gentle and distant.

"Henry Fraser."

Devereaux did not speak.

Rita said, "Henry Fraser. he was behind all this. he killed Kaiser as much as anyone. And all those deaths in Florida. How can a man live with that kind of conscience?"

"Men do it all the time."

"But he killed those men," she said.

He realized she would not understand; he kept his eyes on the road unwinding in front of them.

"And you saved me."

"You're not home free yet."

"But you helped me get out—"

"They were going to kill you, Rita."

"You could have just taken the journal."

Yes, he thought.

It was perfectly true and they both considered it in silence. At an unmarked intersection Devereaux turned to the left, off the main highway, and headed east. This road was not as good. The car bucked and lurched over the potholes. Snow pelted the windshield in a temperamental burst of fury.

Over a rise and then, below, they saw a string of lights at the edge of the great frigid body of Lake Michigan.

"What's in the journal?"

"What you wanted to know," she said dully, the fight gone from her. She realized that she would have been killed had he not been there; he had betrayed her, but he had saved her life.

"Yes. That was the only thing that worried me," he said.

"What?"

"That it might be nothing at all," he said. "That what they all thought he knew did not exist; that they had the secrets and we would be left in the dark."

"He knew you were all after him. All of you," she said with sudden rage.

"I didn't kill him."

"But he died. He had to die. You all knew that he had to die."

They reached the row of lights. Bluffs on the shore tumbled down to the level of the lake. The vast body of water roiled and bubbled; freezing waves smashed at the wooden pier that jutted bravely into the icy wetness. A white boat bobbed in the water, restrained fore and aft by lines lashed to its pilings.

"Didn't think you were coming down," the middle-aged man called out as Devereaux stopped the car. He had a red beard and wore a watch cap over his ears. His eyes were blue and good-natured and his nose and cheeks were red. When he opened the car door for Rita, she could smell brandy on his breath.

Devereaux got out on the other side. Rita followed him in the darkness. It was very cold and the wind went through her like a knife. It was at least twenty degrees colder here than it had been on the street in downtown Green Bay, an hour before.

"You ain't overdressed, are you?" the man with the red beard said, giving her arm a squeeze. She pulled away from him and he laughed.

"Got blankets down in the hold," he continued. "You still game for this?"

"Can we make it?" Devereaux finally spoke.

"That's up to God and the *Susy* but I suppose. What the hell. It'll be coasting, which can be more dangerous. But I'd rather hug the coast on a night like this than try to cross the lake." The high-pitched nasal voice was typical of Wisconsin folk with mixed German and Scandinavian heritage. "All depends on the storm. I was in the shack, listening to the weather radar up at Neenah. She's fierce but Marseilles radar says the storm is north of the border."

"All right," Devereaux said. He removed a roll of bills.

"Are we going to get on that boat?" Rita said.

"Only one here, honey, lest you want to wait for another." The bearded man chuckled. He was already heading for the boat.

They followed him down the narrow white-planked dock.

"Grab hold on the ropes or you'll blow right off and then you're done," the man called cheerfully. "Damned if I know why I'd go out on a night like this except for the money."

They climbed down into the cabin and closed the hatch, cutting the wind. The little boat was damp and cramped; heat came from a catalytic heater. The man with the red beard turned up the gas jets on the stove; the burners flared.

"This is for you," he said, slinging two Army blankets at Rita. "And this." He reached up on a shelf and brought down a bottle of Christian Brothers brandy and opened it. He took a long swallow. "All right, people. Last chance to chicken out."

In a few minutes, the little ship was under way. From the first, it bucked and plunged into the waves; it shook from side to side and the engine drove on, rolling in a steady thump-thump-thump.

"Who is he?" Rita asked at last. The blanket was around her, the bag on her lap. She folded her hands around the mug of coffee Devereaux had just prepared.

"Put some of this in." He poured a little brandy in the coffee. Both of them sipped at it and their faces began to glow. She felt the brandy warm her.

They faced each other across the table.

"Who is he?" Rita repeated.

"One of ours. One who got out of the game." He stared at her as though remembering something. "We hold on to all the names. I needed him when we found out you had come here. He was happy to do the favor. The money helped, of course."

"My God," Rita said. A wave had slammed the side of the boat; now the two of them went sprawling toward the far bulkhead. "Are we going to sink?" she asked anxiously, righting herself.

"I don't know. It's possible. I don't know anything about boats. Red worked the lakes for a long time, before he entered our operation. He knows what he's doing."

"This is madness."

"If I had tried to use a plane, we would have had to land somewhere. Too risky. A car would have been the most obvious of all. I took a chance on the boat; I hope they won't expect it."

"Where are we going?"

"What was in the journal?"

They stared at each other across the table. Rita looked away. "How can I trust you?" she whispered.

"Rita." He spoke quietly, with gentle patience. "I won't tell you any lies to get the journal. This is beyond trust now. If I have to take it, I will. This is my life now and yours and that is the game. It was the game from the minute those two men chased you on the beach in Florida."

"Were they going to kill me?"

"Yes."

"Who were they?"

"They were from InterComBank. Fraser had sent them."

"Are you sure?"

"Yes. One tried to grab you now in Green Bay. The other is dead."

She didn't speak. Slowly, she released her white-knuckled grip on the tote bag in her lap. She took out her sweater and put it on the table. And then she removed the red-bound journal from the bottom of the bag.

"I've been afraid," she said. "From the beginning, when those men broke into my apartment. This has been like a bad dream. It seems to go on and on. They never give up, do they? Like those men following me into the lobby of your hotel. They would have killed me there. Even if I had given them the journal, even if I had surrendered, it wouldn't have been enough. But why am I telling you this? You know it, don't you? You play that game too, don't you?"

Devereaux waited.

In the blackness of the huge lake surging around them, they could hear a ship's foghorn stabbing at the dark.

She held the book in her hand and looked at him. "Do you think this book was worth all those deaths?"

He didn't speak.

"Fraser," she said. "Someone named Henry Fraser who is willing to kill me and blackmail men and drive them to kill themselves. I would kill him now if I could. You see, I'm like you now. Everything is dirty and confused. I can talk about killing someone because I hate him so much."

Devereaux sipped from his cup of coffee and brandy but did not make a sound.

Rita opened the journal.

" 'I had intended to speak about none of these things,' " she read.

" 'What is it to me or to my soul? Or to the memory of my beloved, Phuong, whom I will not repent loving? Or to my son, Ky, who is now dead? No, I will not repent loving any of these people who became my flesh and my blood, even to save my soul. I had lost my soul before I met them, long before; it was they, in their love for me, who returned it to me. My trust belongs to them; and so does my love.' "

Rita paused and glanced at Devereaux but he sat silent and brooding, his cold gray eyes fixed on her face.

She sipped gratefully from the mug. Then she began to read again. " 'But those who want this journal do not want my soul; the worth of a man's soul has no meaning to them, not even to Martin Foley, who is a priest; nor Rice nor Maurice nor the Agency men who kept me hidden and who, I think, conspired among themselves to decide if they should kill me. Is it because I seem such a fool that poor old McGillicuddy thinks I don't know he spies on me for the Agency? None of them wants to know of my torment, though, nor of the death of children, nor of the death of Phuong, whom I held in my arms at the very end. They do not want to know of wars past, nor be reminded of the village destroyed, nor the children murdered, nor men reduced to the state of animals. Do they want to know that we drowned a newborn child in the river because we were dying ourselves?' "

She looked up. The ship creaked and groaned against the tumult of the lake. Her eyes were shining; she stared at him; did he understand?

Devereaux said nothing.

" 'They are evil who wish to acquire this journal. They want it in order to suppress its secrets. These Americans. I come from this same race, but I have grown to detest it. Americans! I detest them, I detest their smug hypocrisy, their stupidity, their selfishness and cruelty, their contempt for all but themselves. Am I a traitor then, to Rice, to the others? What would I be a traitor to? To a cause, or to my nature? All these men are evil. Governments oppress; it is written, it must be so. What does Rice want to know? Are there any men in the world more cruel than the Pathet Lao was to me? Or the Vietnamese soldiers who march along the road with their Russian guns and kill old women in the paddies for sport, even as the Americans did? Or let me tell Rice of the Khmer Rouge coming to power in Cambodia. Of how the highways were lined with thousands of the dead, stinking in the sun, and of the crucifixions in the villages. The pain, the screams, the anguish, the bodies hanging and writhing, begging for death as a favor. No dignity left. That is why the Romans used it; it killed but it did far more. It made a coward of the victim in the last moment of his life, so that he would make a coward of all who could hear his anguish: *Eli, Eli, lama sabachthani.'* "

Again, Rita looked up; she stared at him.

Devereaux gazed back at her for a moment before he spoke: *"My God, my God, why hast thou forsaken me,"* he translated.

Her hands trembled as she read on again, aloud, in the creaking cabin as the boat tumbled into the waves. A record of death and destruction, of starvation seen and felt. Devereaux listened and did not move.

Page after page. She turned them, reading, pausing, looking up. But not another word from the man with gray eyes, seated across from her.

"This is the last part," she began. "He must have finished just before he died. This part was written after McGillicuddy was killed."

Devereaux put his hands on the table. He looked at her so long that she had to look away, but his eyes were still on her.

" 'Phuong died in July but I had been aware of these other matters much earlier. There had been rumors from the other villages. Phuong left me alone, without family or hope, and I could not bear it. I could not survive alone. I did not want to survive alone. And yet some instinct in me moved me; now I must go home; now I must end this life in the jungle. And yet, I could not leave just yet. I had to see these things the villagers talked about. To them, they were simply more guns or more tools of war. But I, I was a watcher, I was trained to understand the difference between guns and missiles. I knew what they were building in the jungles of Cambodia. I knew why there were other white men in the jungle and why they spoke another language. I knew who they were. . . .' "

She stopped.

"So," Devereaux said finally, breaking the spell. "Tunney saw something after all; he had a secret after all."

She read on, slowly, stumbling over some of the words. There were missile sites, twenty in all, and Tunney described them in detail so that there would be no mistake that he saw what he saw. There were Soviet advisers at the sites. The sites were here and there, in this place and that. Tunney numbered them prosaically, the sites he saw and the sites he was told about. The good watcher. The Agency man.

The villagers said the sites would be in operation by March, at the end of the rains. March. Four months from now.

Missile sites. Nuclear missile sites. Placed in a ring and aimed, unmistakably, at China.

Twenty sites in the necklace. Surface-to-air and ground-to-ground missiles. Offensive; defensive.

She closed the red cover of the journal and put it on the table between them.

They did not speak.

Devereaux stared at the book and then reached for the bottle of brandy. He poured a little into the cup. He took a sip, then offered the cup to her.

"The link," he said at last. "Everything makes sense now."

"How?"

"Tunney knew. Tunney knew," he said. "The Soviets were afraid he knew of the missiles. Russian weapons, manned by Vietnamese crews. Just like in Cuba in 1962. The Catholic Church was pushed into a position of using its agents on the Soviets' behalf because they had already agreed to recognize Soviet influence in Asia in exchange for the Concordance."

She gaped at him.

"The Agency was being used. At first, it had wanted Tunney's intelligence. But then it was called off by the National Security Adviser on behalf of InterComBank."

"What are you going to do with all this?"

"Tell you part," he said. "The part you don't know. And keep part of what you have told me."

He did then, as they sat at the table in the cabin of the boat, the sea pounding against the wooden hull. Devereaux told her about InterComBank and its tangled history with the Agency going back to 1954. He told her again about the National Security Adviser and his friendship with the chairman of InterComBank. It was information he had plucked from the Section's computers after asking the right questions.

"Everything goes back to Fraser," she said at one point. "He is death."

"He can't be touched in any of this," Devereaux said. "When you write your stories or whatever you do, you won't be able to touch him."

"But you have proof—"

Proof, he thought. Pieces of paper. "I have no proof. I cannot testify for you or admit anything for you."

"Loyalty."

"I'm a cipher," Devereaux said. "An agent in place and that's all. I draw the rules to survive but in everything else, I follow their rules. When you write whatever you write, I don't even exist. Do you understand?"

"No," she said, her voice hard. "They killed Kaiser."

"They would have come after him in any case. They had to. In the end, he understood the conspiracy better than anyone."

"Kaiser," she said stubbornly. "He cared."

"And betrayed you."

"Yes. I can't understand that."

"It can happen to any of us," Devereaux said.

She stared at him and understood.

Rita took his hand in hers and held it, then looked into the gray eyes to see if she could fathom the truth.

"I gave you my secrets," she said.

"They're still secrets."

The steady chugging of the engine was flatter now; the sea was calmed.

She kissed him.

Secrets, she thought. And then she thought of him on the beach as he had been that morning, holding her.

"No more lies," she said.

He kissed her in return then, held her in his arms as he had before. They huddled against the chill in the wet cabin, beneath the blanket. They held each other for a long time, in the creaking cabin.

Morning streaked a red sky across the lake's vast horizon.

Red came down from the pilothouse, his eyes bleary and watery.

Rita lay asleep in Devereaux's arms, wrapped in blankets.

Devereaux looked up, his own face drawn, reflecting the ashen color of early dawn.

"Getting some squawks from the coast guard on the radio. Real mysterious. Keep talking about patrol boats, calling them in and all. Now, I know the coast guard and they're not about to stir their lazy asses on a morning like this unless there's something up."

"Where are we?" Devereaux said.

"Off Waukegan, about four miles. That'd be about forty-five miles above the Chicago breakwater."

"I suppose we ought to land here."

"They found your car probably." Red glanced at Rita. "She all right?"

"Yes." He shook her gently and she opened her eyes.

"Tell you, I'll go down a little south of downtown, try to find a quiet place."

"Someplace where I can get a car," Devereaux said.

"Legally?"

"Any way I can," he said.

Rita stretched, rubbed at her hair, shivered in the cold cabin. She looked at Devereaux.

"What are we going to do?" she asked.

"Get to the airport," he said.

"What if it's being watched?"

"It's a big airport."

"They'll be watching the Washington flights."

"We'll go to St. Louis first," he said. "Then change for a Washington flight."

The ship chugged toward the shoreline. The lake was empty in every direction. The sun was blood red above the horizon.

"You were there," she said quietly. "In Asia. Was it as Tunney described?"

"Yes," he said.

She reached for the book and picked it up and started to drop it into her bag. And then she looked at him and handed it to him.

He didn't take it. "Hold on to it," he said. "We still have a long way to go."

36
Washington, D.C.

The President did not speak during the entire presentation. The late hour was not agreeing with him; it seemed to age him. His eyelids were puffy and his cheeks were drawn and pale; but the matter at hand was too urgent to wait for morning. And the President was too angry to sleep.

Once, when the National Security Adviser sought to make an objection to the recitation, the President turned on him a withering look that expressed both anger and disgust.

Hanley handled most of the recitation; Galloway provided an introduction and a short wrap-up. In deference to the President, who did not smoke, Galloway's omnipresent pipe was not lit. Galloway fidgeted with it as he spoke; he was still nervous because he realized how close it had been.

They all realized it.

The problem was what to do now.

They were in the Oval Office of the White House and it was nearly midnight on Wednesday, thirty-four days since Leo Tunney had walked out of the jungles of Cambodia along the Thai border to the United States Embassy in Bangkok.

Most presidents used the Oval Office for small chats or infrequent television appearances or ceremonial occasions. The room was actually too small for the number of people summoned to it tonight. But the President preferred it. He sat behind the big desk near the flag stand and listened to the summing up by the director of R Section.

The President's counsel, who sat next to the Chief Executive, leaned over and whispered something to him. The President cupped his ear in a characteristic gesture and then looked at the Adviser.

The Adviser felt compelled to speak. "Sir. TransAsia had the blessing of this Administration. It was not only a patriotic effort but part of our new aggressive thrust around the world and it deserved our full cooperation and support. I did no more than support it."

"The hell you didn't." It was the harsh voice of the Secretary of State who had been the Adviser's mortal enemy from the earliest days of the Administration. "You tampered with national security in the name of national security. You let a private company set foreign policy for this Administration. And you let them betray our new friend in Asia and endangered the entire Chinese connection. What the hell do you think the Thais are going to say about this at this hour?"

The Secretary of Defense, a man of infinite discretion, was no less blunt. "You used the CIA. Used it again just when we were at the point of rehabilitating it, getting this new interagency intelligence bill through Congress. You played right into the hands of the liberals in Congress."

"All right," the President said. "Three hours ago, the Chinese were informed. At this moment, six Chinese divisions are on the Cambodian border and they are going across. I have talked to the Soviet Union on the hot line and I've warned them to stay out of this matter. We've put our SAC on alert and we've stationed six missile cruisers off Cuba. It's going to be tit for tat, we told the Soviets, and we mean it. If those missile sites had been functioning now, there wouldn't have been a damn thing we could do to avoid war. Do you realize that? The Chinese would never have permitted those missiles to stay aimed at them. They would have either capitulated to the reality of the Soviet presence in Asia or gone to war. It would have been their war and our war, gentlemen. The world's war."

"Will the Soviets permit the Chinese to destroy the missile sites?" It was the President's counsel.

Galloway said, "We received a report at eleven P.M. from the Board of National Estimates. They think the chances of a Soviet backdown are sixty to forty for."

"The odds," the President said. "The odds are in our favor."
The words were heavy with irony.

The National Security Adviser was pale; his hands trembled in his lap.

"We were used," said the Director of the Central Intelligence Agency, speaking for the first time. "First the Adviser used us, then InterComBank through the Adviser. I think we're blameless in this matter."

"Do you?" asked the President.

"Leo Tunney had been our agent. We have a charter to gather intelligence abroad. *And to analyze it.* We felt it was well within our charter to investigate Tunney."

"But when the Adviser told you to turn over certain documents to a private concern? And when you actively aided a private security army to threaten the civil liberties of this . . . this newspaper reporter—" The President seemed unable to continue.

"Sir."

It was Hanley; everyone seemed surprised.

"Sir, I think the director of the Central Intelligence Agency is correct."

Even Galloway gasped.

"They had a legitimate concern. But they were misused. An agent follows orders, even an Assistant Director. I think, if I may say this, that the larger matter illustrated here is that expressed by President Kennedy when he helped to charter the Section."

The President stared at him.

"He summed it up this way: 'Who will watch the watchers? Who will spy upon the spies?' If it hadn't been for our own involvement, this matter would not have come to light. If I may say so, sir."

Galloway was stunned to silence. The statement was so obviously self-serving for the Section—so obviously a plea to keep the Section from being disbanded—that they were all shaken by the boldness of a man they privately considered a little clerk.

"That can be discussed later," the Secretary of State said.

"No," said the President. "Perhaps Kennedy understood something better than I did." The President, though a member of the other party, was an admirer of Kennedy. "Perhaps the Section is a useful double check against this kind of abuse ever happening again."

The Adviser then said he would resign for the good of the Administration and to save the President any embarrassment.

"No," said the President. "You were fired three hours ago. The press corps is assembled and I intend to talk to them when this is all over. We are not going to have a Watergate again. This stinks of Watergate. Intelligence agencies used for private vendettas, spying on innocent people—"

They all knew "innocent people" meant reporters. There was a long story now in the early edition of the *Washington Post,* which they had all read. The story told the truth but not all of it; the main element missing was Devereaux. That was intended; it was a part of his bargain with Rita.

Shortly after two in the morning, Galloway offered to drive Hanley home.

"I'm sorry," Hanley said. "I have to go back to the office—"

"You're dead on your feet."

"There are some details," Hanley said vaguely.

"At least let me drive you over to the Ag building then. The streets aren't safe at this hour."

And so Hanley sat in the long, black car next to the Old Man as the chauffeur guided it down the winding driveway from the White House onto Pennsylvania Avenue. It was a short trip.

There was a cold feeling to the night air. November, Hanley thought. It was November already.

"Devereaux was wrong in this," Galloway said, lighting his pipe in the dark confines of the rear compartment of the limousine.

"No. I don't think so."

"He didn't have to give all that information to that reporter. It wasn't necessary to make any deal."

"No," Hanley said quietly. "He needed leverage. In case none of this got out and the whole thing was suppressed. Do you think the Administration would have gotten rid of the Adviser if there hadn't been a story in the *Post?*"

"Dammit. He's a goddam agent. He doesn't set policy. He took too much on himself."

"Yes," Hanley said. There was no point in continuing the argument. Galloway was determined from the first not to understand.

And he would have been happier in the Agency anyway, Hanley realized. He had no affection at all for the Section.

Hanley gazed out the window at the great white obelisk of the Washington Monument on the Ellipse. Two red airplane warning lights blinked like the eyes of a ghost from the top of the monument.

"He could have been wrong at the most basic level," Galloway said. The pipe had gone out and he snapped at his lighter for a flame but it was out of fuel. "Damn." He looked at Hanley but Hanley shrugged; he had no matches. "There might have been nothing, Hanley, nothing at all in the journal. All of this could have been for nothing."

"We knew there a journal," Hanley said.

"Yes, yes, but it could have all been that crap about the soul and about Tunney's love life among the natives." Suddenly, Galloway laughed as though he had said something very funny. But Hanley stared at him until the laughter ended.

The limousine stopped at the side entrance of the darkened Agriculture building.

Hanley stared at Galloway for a long moment as though he were about to speak. Galloway watched him uncomfortably. But then Hanley decided to say nothing. He opened the door of the black car and got out without a word.

The silence annoyed the Old Man nearly as much as words.

37
New York City

The war was not long. The silos were destroyed and the Chinese, after an interval of blood, withdrew slowly across the face of Cambodia. There were more refugees, of course, but that was inevitable. They streamed out of the jungle toward the Thai border, and more refugee camps were set up and more international hand-wringing took place in the councils of great powers and in the United Nations; still the refugees came and were settled in camps and waited; and still some died, slowly, wasting from disease and starvation.

The public was frightened by the war. The Administration was criticized; a congressional investigation was ordered and even held; and yet, there was a curious lack of momentum to all the events, as though it was all too complex to keep the attention of the public for long.

Vanderglass, chief of security for InterComBank and an old Agency hand from Vietnam days, was already under arrest on various charges, including conspiracy to commit murder. The New York Stock Exchange had announced after the close of business Wednesday that it was halting trade in shares of InterComBank stock while the Securities and Exchange Commission made an audit.

Other arrests swiftly followed. But no one mentioned the chairman of the bank, Henry Fraser, who had isolated himself in layers of bureaucracy. There might be a question of "overzealousness" on the part of some bank personnel—that is the way one of the investigators would phrase it—but there was no question of connecting Fraser with criminal matters. After all, Fraser was a friend of the National Security Adviser and several other key members of the Administration.

Rita Macklin's stories in the *Washington Post* and in other newspapers would continue for a week, each story detailing a fresh aspect of the Tunney matter, including the Church of Rome's secret treaty with the Soviet Union. The outcry among American Catholics was predictable.

TransAsia was dead, of course, everyone agreed on that. There was a war in Cambodia now as the Chinese moved swiftly to destroy the missile silos. And there was no profit to be made in someone else's war.

Trading in shares of InterComBank was resumed after several days and an SEC investigation that uncovered no financial trickery in the administration of Henry L. Fraser. Indeed, the chairman of the International Commerce Bank of New York found that guilt and embarrassment were temporary mantles and that they slid slowly and painlessly off his shoulders within a few weeks. The bank had not lost money; in fact, the bank was more prosperous than ever. And there were still a few political and financial commentators in the media who thought that Henry L. Fraser had been picked as a convenient whipping boy by liberal elements in the press. Trans-Asia, after all, was a good idea, an attempt to put the war in Vietnam behind us; hadn't we propped up our old enemies of Japan and Germany and Italy after the Second World War? What was the difference between helping them and helping the People's Republic of Vietnam?

For his part, Henry L. Fraser continued his good deeds and was named chairman of a new relief effort mounted to aid the starving refugees from Cambodia. Fraser was vice-chairman of the Tri-Global Committee and he took seriously his role as an international humanitarian.

Vanderglass, the former chief of security with InterComBank, was prepared to stand trial. He would not involve his superior officer in any alleged criminal matters. There was some speculation among those in the prosecuting team that the case against Vanderglass was very weak—because of national security considerations that precluded introduction of some evidence.

The Vatican, surprised by the sharp reaction among American Catholics to the proposed Prague Concordance, decided for the time being to withhold announcement of the treaty. In Poland, new worker unrest provoked a sudden, ugly Soviet response. Tanks from the Warsaw Pact countries intruded briefly on Polish soil. In Rome, the Pope announced that he intended to revisit the United States in the spring to explain his pastoral role to the faithful.

Everything had changed yet everything remained the same. In a small column devoted to bureaucratic listings, *L'Osservatore Romano,* the official newspaper of the Vatican State, announced that a formal move was under way to disband the dwindling Order of the Fathers of the Holy Word.

Denisov was in the camp in the Maryland mountains, still being debriefed by members of R Section. His life was not grueling. The debriefings occupied the mornings, but in the afternoons he had time for private pleasures. Devereaux had seen to it that he had access to a very sophisticated stereo system and all the recordings of the D'Oyly Carte opera company. Once, when he expressed a sense of loneliness to one of the debriefers, they sent him a prostitute from a nearby town. Denisov was quite amazed but not displeased. He heard nothing of his family; in fact, they were sent by midnight car to Gorki and were never seen in official Moscow society again.

And Henry L. Fraser, who had survived many things in his fifty-seven years, survived all that had happened. He did better than survive; he continued to triumph as chairman of InterComBank and a leading spokesman for a certain political point of view. November dissolved into full winter. Other matters occupied the public attention.

Fraser endured. And he who endures, he was fond of saying, became the eventual winner because he was the one who had not only the chance to write the rules of the game but also the last chance to write the history of the game after it is played.

On December 4, it snowed in New York City.

Henry L. Fraser was running behind schedule, as his secretary had reminded him at least four times. It had been a busy and full day, as all of his days were, and now it was to be climaxed by a dinner to be held in his honor at the Patrician Club on East Fiftieth Street. Fraser was to be honored for his strenuous efforts during the past year to "raise the level of international understanding" and "provide succor" for those refugees in Southeast Asia whose hope of survival depended on "relief, generosity and understanding from the private as well as the public sector of American life." So read the award he would be given.

Shortly before eight o'clock, he left the InterComBank offices and descended to the lobby of the massive building on Madison Avenue. To his annoyance, his automobile was not ready at the curb; he ordered the building security chief to call the garage and find out what was wrong.

The chagrined driver reached at the garage said an absurd thing had happened. Someone had stolen the battery in the limousine and it would be a half-hour before another could be found to replace it. It was a kid's trick, the work of a petty street thief.

Fraser decided to walk to the Patrician Club and meet the car there after the dinner. He was late as it was. Perhaps he could hail a cab on the way.

Curiously, the streets were empty. The day had been full for a number of New Yorkers besides Henry L. Fraser. Christmas decorations were in place in the stores. For a moment Henry L. Fraser paused on the street and glanced up at the Pan-Am Building, which squatted over the low-rise splendor of Grand Central Station. He thought that a city is like a civilization, built upon itself, layer by layer, each tower on the ruins of a tower. The past is beneath our feet, thought Henry L. Fraser, and he decided he would utter this profound remark tonight during his speech.

Garbage bags and cans of garbage were already piled at the curbs, waiting for the morning sanitation trucks; taxis sped in yellow rivers down the cross streets; gases rose from vents in the sewers. Henry Fraser saw none of these things; he thought of the past and of the solidity of life and he was filled with an enormous sense of well-being.

In the darkness of the cross street, he did not even see the hand that held the knife. Or hear the voice behind him.

How soothing.

He fell back as the knife slid smoothly between the third and fourth ribs on the left side of his back, pushing easily into the old, tired heart.

Without pain. That was what surprised him at first.

Blood filled the chest cavity in a moment; the hemorrhage spread, choking the lungs with blood. And he was dying.

But without pain, he thought wonderingly.

Death was a curtain parting before him. His eyes were wide open.

Like a play, he thought—it must be a dream. There would be applause in a moment, he thought. All the applause of the years.

But this was absurd, Henry L. Fraser said to himself. He could not actually die, not in this way, on this street. Victim of a common street mugging, a street attack in this city that he knew, had known all his life. Not die on this night, in the falling snow. . . . No. It was not believable.

His body clattered into the row of garbage cans and Devereaux stood still and let it fall, pulling the knife slowly and easily out of the body as it fell, sliding down on the street, into the wet walkway. Henry L. Fraser was dead before his body stopped falling.

38
Front Royal, Virginia

For a very long time he watched the car from the brow of the mountain, behind the house.

Devereaux wore a flannel shirt, which he always wore in the mountains, and he had been chopping at the cord of wood behind the house, splitting the oak and birch. He had worn a jacket at first because it was cold and snow lay on the mountain; but in the past half hour of work, he had removed his jacket and his face was covered with a fine sheen of sweat.

He had watched the car come down the old road from Front Royal, which he could see from the mountain. The car had turned in at the sign posted against trespassers and it was switching back and forth up the cuts of the dirt road up the mountain. There was one point, halfway up the mountain, where a car could stop and turn around and descend, in case the driver had taken the dirt road by mistake. This car did not turn around.

Devereaux reached for the pistol that was in his jacket and he opened the chamber and he saw the bullets waiting in the cylinders. He cocked the hammer and put the gun down carefully on top of the woodpile and he stood in the open and watched the car ascend.

He had been alone in the mountains for two weeks. He had not spoken to another person, except during one trip down to the town of Front Royal where he had purchased groceries. In the evenings, in the house on the mountain, he had sat alone watching the flames in the immense stone fireplace, slowly drinking chilled vodka, not speaking, not listening to music, not reading. He had spent the evenings in utter silence before the flames and felt their warmth. He had slept for long periods of time; slept so much that the dreams began to fade and sometimes he would awake and not remember dreaming at all.

The car made the last turn a hundred yards below the house and came slowly up the dirt road, the tires sliding and spinning in the snow. Even in summer, the road was treacherous, purposely so;

but now, in the early Virginia winter, the road was very dangerous.

The car stopped fifty feet from the house and the woodpile.

Devereaux glanced down at the pistol waiting on the woodpile and then looked at the dirt-streaked automobile. The door opened on the driver's side.

"You don't make it easy," Rita Macklin said.

Devereaux did not speak for a moment and then he reached for the pistol and gently lowered the cocked hammer. He put the pistol back in his jacket hanging from a peg on the side of the house.

"It took a little trouble to find you," she said, still standing by the car.

"You're going to have trouble getting down the mountain. That road isn't designed for a two-wheel-drive car."

"Now you tell me."

Silence between them; snow began to fall, a lazy snow that came quietly down between the trees and settled around them.

"Well," Rita said.

Devereaux did not speak.

"You told me to come to see this place when I first met you, in Clearwater. You weren't kidding, were you?" She smiled then.

"I didn't expect you to come," he said at last. "I didn't think I would see you again."

"Well," she said.

He did not speak. He looked at her for a long time without speaking.

"You can help me. I want to bring some wood inside."

She closed the car door then and came across the pathway to him. She held out her arms and he piled them with logs and he filled his own arms and he led her around the side of the house to the door. He pushed open the door with his foot and they carried the logs into the big room and piled them on the brick shelf next to the fireplace. The fireplace was already crackling with flames and blowers were circulating the heat through the room.

That night, in silence, they ate and drank a bottle of wine and sat for a long time together on the couch in front of the fireplace and watched the flames until they were sleepy and the wine made them see faces and stories in the fire.

They made love without explaining anything to each other.

When Devereaux awoke in the morning, she was already out of bed. The fireplace was lit and she stood naked at the window on the far side of the room, watching more snow fall upon the snow that had fallen all night.

"I can't get down today," she said. "I'll have to stay."

He smiled then and realized, with a sudden, sharp pain, that he had fallen in love with her.

"This is like home in a way," Rita said, putting her hand in his. "The hills along the Mississippi near Eau Claire. The old river and the old towns. Quiet, like this. Maybe you'll see it someday."

She looked into his gray eyes and saw that they were shining.

He placed his finger on her lips.

Do not speak; do not make promises, he thought.

She wondered if he had tears in his eyes.

I love you, Rita, he thought with sadness. But make no promises to me, in truth or in lies.

They cannot be kept.